Caitlin headed down the broad stone steps to the beach.

Halfway to the bottom, she spotted him. She wished she could read his expression, but the moon hung over his left shoulder and shadows obscured his face.

"Caitlin?" Dominic touched her bare arm, and oh dear lord, the sparks weren't just in her head now but in her blood, too. She throbbed with every beat of her heart.

He pulled her into his arms and she put her arms around his waist, wanting him, wanting him more than she'd ever wanted anything in her life. And even though she knew she was tempting fate, she pressed herself against the hard-muscled warmth of his body, aching to be closer still. "Dominic—"

"Shh," he whispered in her ear. "I think I hear a boat motor."

She heard it, too, growing nearer. "Can you see it?" she whispered.

"Yes. I count two heads. Bloody hell, they've spotted us."

"Is it—"

He silenced her by covering her mouth with his. She knew she should be afraid. But with Dominic's lips warm and demanding on hers, she couldn't think at all.

Also by Catherine Mulvany

Run No More

CATHERINE MULVANY

Shadows All Around Her

POCKET STAR BOOKS
New York London Toronto Sydney

An *Original* Publication of POCKET BOOKS

A Pocket Star Book published by
POCKET BOOKS, a division of Simon & Schuster Inc.
1230 Avenue of the Americas, New York, NY 10020

ISBN-13: 978-0-7434-9384-0
ISBN-10: 0-7434-9384-2

First Pocket Books printing September 2005

10 9 8 7 6 5 4 3 2 1

Cover illustration by Craig White

Manufactured in the United States of America

For information regarding special discounts for bulk purchases, please contact Simon & Schuster Special Sales at 1-800-456-6798 or business@simonandschuster.com

The great enemy of the truth is very often not the lie—deliberate, contrived and dishonest—but the myth—persistent, persuasive and unrealistic.

—John F. Kennedy (1917–63)

Prologue

June 1979
Vulcan's Shoulder, Calix

THE BIRD SWOOPED LOW, so close the young prince flinched, though he managed to stifle his cry. *A prince must never show fear.* That's what his father said. Hard advice to follow when you were nine years old and a thorough coward—afraid of the hot, prickly sirocco and of small, dark spaces, of centipedes and jellyfish and vultures.

Especially vultures, because wherever one found carrion eaters, one also found death, and that was yet another of his many fears. *I won't look,* he told himself. *Even if I smell the decay, I won't look.* He kept his gaze fixed upon the rocky path, one foot in front of the other, praying that his tutor hadn't noticed his involuntary cringe.

The bird gave a raucous cry, as if to mock him, and the prince glanced up, startled. Startled but relieved. Not a vulture after all. Just a common magpie.

The magpie landed on a stunted juniper and preened

its feathers, then tilted its head in a droll manner, pinned the prince with a sharp black gaze, and cawed again, as if arguing that magpies were, indeed, quite *un*common. Strong, intelligent, loyal. Princes among birds.

"He's a cocky one, isn't he, Mr. Hawke?" Chuckling as much at his own misplaced fears as at the magpie's antics, he turned to his tutor. But his laughter faded at the stricken expression on the man's face. "What is it, sir? What's wrong?"

"Nothing," Mr. Hawke said, but the prince didn't believe him. His tutor's skin looked sallow, his mouth pinched, his eyes strained.

"If you're ill, sir, we can turn back. We needn't trek all the way to the meadow."

Mr. Hawke's mouth curved in a smile, not quite his usual smile but almost. "Turn back when we're so close? Nonsense. I'll not deprive you of a much anticipated treat just because I was silly enough to come away without a proper breakfast."

"I've a candy bar in my rucksack," the prince said, though it pained him to make the offer. He adored chocolate but wasn't allowed sweets as a rule. However, Cornelia, the redheaded scullery maid, had packed his lunch this morning, and unlike the rest of the kitchen staff, she believed boys deserved a bit of spoiling.

Mr. Hawke dug a water bottle from his own rucksack and drank deeply. "I'm fine," he said. "I do appreciate the offer, though." He tucked the bottle back in his bag and smiled again. "Let's get going, shall we?"

The prince fell in step beside his tutor, surveying the

steepening incline ahead of them. The sun beat down, reflecting off the rocks in a shimmer of heat. An earthy herbal aroma teased at his nostrils. "Do you smell that, sir?"

"I do, indeed. It's the perfume of the maquis, a blend of myrtle and broom, juniper and rosemary."

The prince breathed deeply. "And dust," he said. "You forgot to mention dust."

"So I did." Mr. Hawke grinned. "Dust, spiced with a soupçon of sheep's dung."

Delighted with the phrase "a soupçon of sheep's dung," the boy filed it away for future reference.

They toiled up the hillside in silence, and in all the empty space around them, nothing stirred—not an insect, not a breath of wind. Even the magpie had disappeared.

The prince wiped the sweat from his brow with the back of one hand and struggled to match his stride to his tutor's. Normally Mr. Hawke spent their walks lecturing on the local flora and fauna, but today he seemed more pensive than usual.

"Sir?" the prince said at last. "Why is this hill called Vulcan's Shoulder?"

"It's named for the Roman god of fire, a fitting appellation for the remains of a long-extinct volcano, wouldn't you agree?"

"I suppose so," the prince said, disappointed that it hadn't, as he'd secretly hoped, been named for the Spock character from *Star Trek*. He and his mother—a big fan of the series—spent many a rainy afternoon watching taped episodes. At least they used to. "How much farther to the lake?"

"Two kilometers," Mr. Hawke said. "Perhaps a little less. And it's not just a lake, my boy. It's a caldera, an immensely deep cavity formed when the mountain vomited up the last of its fire and the magma chamber collapsed."

"A caldera with a lake inside," the prince argued. "I've seen pictures. It's beautiful—green as grass."

"Full of water so corrosive, it can eat through metal."

"Like the acid we used to tell calcite crystals from quartz crystals?" the prince asked in surprise.

Mr. Hawke nodded.

"But where does it come from, sir?"

"Gases bubble up out of the earth and combine with the water to create a toxic witch's brew."

"Like acid indigestion." The boy nodded wisely, having heard the servants discuss this very problem.

Mr. Hawke laughed, and his gray-green eyes crinkled up at the corners the same way the boy's father's used to.

King Charles hadn't smiled much lately. Nor had the queen. Not since the evening her husband spilled his claret. The prince remembered the look of horror on his mother's face. One might almost have assumed from the queen's expression that it was blood, not wine, staining the tablecloth crimson. He'd tried to broach the subject later, but his mother had pretended not to remember the incident. As for his father, the prince was much too in awe of the king to ask any question that might be deemed impertinent.

Mr. Hawke, on the other hand, was quite another proposition. The tutor was paid to answer his questions.

Still, it took the prince a while to screw up his courage. They'd nearly reached the crest of the hill before he said, "Sir, is something wrong?"

Mr. Hawke frowned. "How so?"

"Lately my father seems unnaturally grim, and my mother . . . I've heard her crying."

Mr. Hawke drew him to a halt, then knelt so their eyes were on the same level. "The queen is sad," he said. "They both are."

"Over a little spilt wine?" At the tutor's look of confusion, the prince explained.

"The wine isn't the problem," Mr. Hawke told him. "What frightened the queen was the spill itself. Clumsiness is the first symptom of the curse."

"The curse?" The prince's chest felt tight. Black spots swam in front of his eyes. He knew about the Calixian curse, of course. How could he not when it afflicted so many in the kingdom? Still, it seemed impossible that anyone as tall and strong and handsome as the king could be ill.

"Researchers are working on a cure," Mr. Hawke said.

But what if they didn't find one in time?

Mr. Hawke patted the boy's shoulder in an awkward attempt at comfort, then stood and cleared his throat. "Not much farther now."

For a split second, the prince thought he'd said "Not much *father* now." He nearly collapsed in a sniveling heap right there in the rocks and the dust and the soupçon of sheep's dung, but then he remembered what his father said. *A prince must never show fear.* So he held himself together long enough to realize that Mr. Hawke had said "farther," not "father," at which point he decided he just might die of shame. He was not only a coward but an idiot as well.

He'd scarcely reached this conclusion when they crested Vulcan's Shoulder, and all his worries vanished. He gasped, caught unaware by the grandeur of the vista. Directly in front of them but far, far below—perhaps as much as five hundred meters—lay the lake, a sparkling, secretive emerald green. Much closer, the jagged basalt lip of the caldera marked the edge of the drop-off. Grass, shrubs, and a few hardy trees grew right up to the verge. On the opposite side of the lake, the black knob known as Vulcan's Hammer rose up to touch the sky. Pines covered the mountain's lower elevations in a thick blanket of deep forest green, and between the trees and the caldera's edge nestled a heart-shaped swale, lush with grass and wildflowers. Striga Meadow, their destination.

And then he saw the others.

"Someone's beat us to it," he said. A group of white-clad people danced around a man who lay spread-eagled on the grass. The dancers were chanting something, but the boy and his tutor were too far away to hear more than an unintelligible mumble.

"Is it a birthday party?" the prince asked.

"I'm not certain what—"

The man on the grass suddenly stood and shouted something. The circle opened and he stumbled through, still shouting. He moved toward the lip of the caldera at a shambling run, twice losing his balance and falling.

"Is he drunk?" the boy asked.

"I don't . . ."

The man reached the edge, teetered there a moment, then with an eldritch screech launched himself into the emerald green lake.

The prince turned to his tutor in confusion. "I thought you said the lake was full of acid."

"I did." Mr. Hawke threw himself to the ground and pulled the prince down next to him. "It is." Mr. Hawke, who never used profanity, swore fiercely under his breath.

Far below, the diver hit the water. His agonized screams echoed off the steep rock walls.

The prince grabbed his tutor's arm. "We must help him, Mr. Hawke."

"We cannot interfere."

But a man was dying, dying by inches, his skin dissolving, his muscle and sinew being eaten away. Choking back a sob, the boy squeezed his eyes shut against the vivid pictures parading in front of his mind's eye. Tears leaked down his cheeks. His breath came in labored gasps.

Gradually, the hideous screams grew weaker until they faded altogether.

Confused and angry, the prince wiped his eyes and turned to Mr. Hawke. "Why didn't those people stop him? They must have known what would happen. Why didn't they stop him? What's going on?"

"Shh," Mr. Hawke said. "Lower your voice. Sound carries in this terrain."

"But—"

"I'd forgotten what day it is. The summer solstice." Mr. Hawke's voice fell to a whisper. "Those people"—he nodded toward the dancers—"must have been performing a ritual."

"Are they all going to throw themselves in the lake?" the prince asked in alarm.

"No, I don't think so."

"Then why did they let the other man do it? Why didn't they stop him?"

"They're country folk, lad. They follow the old ways. The man who jumped into the lake? I daresay he was a victim of the curse."

"But—"

"These people put little faith in modern medicine. They'd rather visit a *striga*."

"A *striga*?" the boy echoed. "A witch?"

"A *striga*'s more naturopathic healer than witch. I expect the ceremony was an attempt to cleanse the victim of his illness. When it failed . . ." He shrugged. "I've seen men in the terminal stages of the curse, withered husks unable to walk or speak or feed themselves. Who's to say that man was wrong to choose a quicker end?"

Quicker perhaps, but not quick enough. The boy shuddered.

They returned to the palace without stopping for lunch. But the prince didn't care. He didn't feel like eating. Not even chocolate bars.

A prince must never show fear. A prince must never show fear. The boy repeated the words to himself over and over, a silent mantra to keep his tears at bay. Like the man who'd thrown himself into the lake, his father had the curse. Like the man who'd thrown himself into the lake, his father was dying. Cursed. Dying. But a prince must never show fear.

Anxiety simmered within him all the way back down Vulcan's Shoulder, along the rocky shore, then through the pines that forested the slopes of the Aeternus Mountains. As they broke out of the trees, the royal compound came into view. Only then did the boy begin to relax.

Suddenly Mr. Hawke seized him by the arm. "Something's wrong." He pointed toward the flagpole where the Calixian crest and bars flapped at half-mast.

A prince must never show fear.

The guards must have been watching for them; one came running.

"What's happened?" Mr. Hawke asked the question the boy couldn't frame.

The guard frowned and glanced sideways at the prince.

The boy stiffened his back and pressed his lips together to stop their trembling. *A prince must never show fear.* He wanted—oh, how much he wanted—his father to be proud of him. His father . . .

"There's been an accident," the guard said.

No one spoke for an endless moment. The silence seemed to vibrate with all the words not said, all the tears not shed. *A prince must never show fear.*

He gathered the remnants of his courage. "Is it . . . my father?"

The guard's face flamed red, then went pale. "N-no," he stammered, and the boy's heart leapt.

"Then who?" Mr. Hawke demanded.

"The queen, sir. She's dead."

PART ONE

The Lie

The danger already exists that the mathematicians have made a covenant with the devil.

—SAINT AUGUSTINE, *DE GENESI AD LITTERAM*, BOOK II, XVIII, 37

1

ASSISTANT PROFESSOR CAITLIN O'SHAUGHNESSY surveyed the semi-comatose freshmen who'd shown up for her nine o'clock calculus lecture, and seriously considered setting off the sprinklers. She loved mathematics; she loved *teaching* mathematics, even bonehead calculus. She'd prepared a kick-ass lecture on the mean value theorem, including a real-life economic interpretation designed to engage the business majors currently dozing in the back row. Spring had sprung, and hormones were running amok, which made for late nights and groggy mornings.

She glanced down at her new pointy-toed, stiletto-heeled Ferragamos, the same lovely shade of butter yellow as her skinny, narrow-ribbed sweater. A cold shower might wake up her students, but it would almost certainly ruin her shoes. So forget the sprinklers. She'd go with Plan B.

"Take out a piece of paper," she said, "and number from one to three."

A collective groan went up at the promise of a pop quiz. "This totally sucks" seemed to be the consensus. Caitlin wanted to laugh at her students' outraged expressions, but she kept her facial muscles under rigid control. At least the whining proved that, contrary to appearances, the majority of them were still alive.

"We're going to play a word association game. When I say a word, you write down the first thing that comes into your head." She paused. "Any questions?"

The students exchanged bewildered looks as if wondering if they'd somehow been zapped out of Math 20 into Psych 101.

"No questions. Excellent. First word, closed." She gave them a second or two to scribble their answers. "Second word, open." Again she waited for the pencils to stop moving. "Third word, mean."

"Noun or verb?" a lanky blond kid asked.

"Don't think. Just respond," she told him.

He wrote something on his paper.

Caitlin stifled the impulse to grin. "Okay. Responses? Closed circuits? Closed doors? Closed minds? Closed what?"

"Closed windows?" a girl in the front row suggested.

"What else?"

"Closed bars!" yelled some bleary-eyed joker in the back row. Several people laughed.

"Think math, people. Closed what?"

"Closed interval?" the blond boy said.

"Bingo! Okay, second word. Open."

"Open sesame."

"Open door."

"Open-minded."

"Open-and-shut."

"Open up and say 'ah.' "

"Open bars!" the comedian in the back row yelled, but this time no one laughed.

"Open mouth, insert foot," someone muttered, and a few people snickered.

The comedian flushed.

"Come on," she said. "Don't give up now. Look for a math connection."

"Open-ended?" someone ventured.

"Close, but no cigar."

"Open interval!" the comedian yelled suddenly.

"And the synapses fire! We have a winner." Caitlin gave him a standing ovation, then let her gaze drift across the classroom. "All right, my young brainiacs, we're down to the wire." She tapped out a drumroll on the edge of the lectern. "And finally . . . our third and final word. Mean."

"Mean value theorem," half a dozen voices chanted in unison, and the rest of the class applauded.

Hands on hips, head cocked to one side, Caitlin studied them. " 'Fess up now. You practiced that."

Laughter rippled through the classroom.

Amen. She had their attention. "Which brings us to the topic of today's lecture . . ." She paused expectantly, arms extended, palms up.

"The mean value theorem," the class recited on cue.

* * *

Dominic Fortune sat slumped in the driver's seat of a nondescript rental car, his driver's cap pulled low, his face hidden behind a copy of today's *Scotsman.* Across the street a black Lincoln Town Car with diplomatic plates pulled up to the gated—and well-guarded—entrance to the Calixian consulate. The driver lowered his window to display his credentials, and the car was waved through just as it was every Monday, Wednesday, and Friday at this time. Barring bad weather, the diplomatic pouch arrived on the 10 a.m. flight from Tavia to Edinburgh and was then transferred via official car to the consulate.

The problem was, this was Tuesday and Dominic knew for a fact that the consul general and most of his staff were golfing at St. Andrews.

Apparently someone else knew about the planned outing and had taken advantage of the consul general's absence to smuggle something into the country. The question was, what?

Dominic reached for his cell phone and punched in a number. Inside the consulate, Quinton Gilroy answered on the first ring.

"Your hunch was spot on," Dominic told him. "Something definitely came in on the ten o'clock flight. The car just drove through the front gate. I'm not positive—hard to say with the smoked glass—but I think there may have been someone in the back seat. Check it out, would you? That is, if you can bear to drag yourself away from that mail room clerk you've been chatting up. Charlotte, is it?"

Quin muttered a noncommittal syllable that Dominic

took to mean he couldn't talk, most likely because Charlotte and/or the rest of the mail room staff were within earshot.

"And hurry it up. Janus is waiting." Janus, code name for the head of the Calixian Intelligence Service, the agency for which Dominic and Quin did occasional contract work, was not known for his patience.

Dominic rang off and settled down to wait. Most people equated covert operations with James Bond-esque derring-do. Prior to being recruited, he'd thought that himself. The truth was, even in the course of a really dicey job, he spent eighty percent of his time pulling surveillance, fifteen percent waiting for the phone to ring, and a measly five percent on the risky adrenaline-rush bits.

Twenty minutes later Quin came strolling out of the consulate. The big, broad-shouldered redhead crossed the street, walked past Dominic's rental car as if he hadn't seen it, and shoehorned himself into a decrepit Morris Minor that had not been designed to accommodate an eighteen-stone former rugby player.

Dominic's phone trilled. "Yes?"

"No sign of the pouch," Quin said, "but I spotted your mystery passenger. Hector Yuli."

"Yuli? Any relation to Leo and Orson Yuli, the 'fishermen' the Calixian Coast Guard caught running drugs last year?"

"Younger brother," Quin said. "I gather Hector's cut from the same cloth. Rumor has it he nearly beat a man to death in a bar fight a couple months back."

"So what's a thug like that doing in Edinburgh?" Dominic wondered aloud.

Quin grunted. "And how the bloody hell did he secure a seat on the Royal Air Express?"

"Friends in high places?" Dominic said.

Quin grunted again and rang off.

Dominic traded his cell for the satellite phone with its built-in scrambler. Janus, his voice mechanically altered, answered on the second ring.

"Quin guessed right," Dominic said by way of greeting, then filled his superior in on the details.

"Hector Yuli," Janus said thoughtfully. "Interesting."

"Do you want me to follow him?"

"No, you're too high-profile. I'll put someone a little less noticeable on that job. I have something else in mind for you."

"Oh?"

Janus, apparently in no hurry to explain Dominic's new assignment, ignored the prompt. "Did either you or Quin see what was in the pouch?"

"No," Dominic said. "Quin managed to get into the mail room, but the pouch never showed up. Shunted off to some restricted area presumably." He paused. "I thought perhaps you might have an idea what was inside."

Janus sighed. "Specifically, no, although I can tell you that over the past few months items—priceless and irreplaceable artifacts—have been disappearing from both the palace and the royal treasury."

"But the guards, the sensors . . . How can anything get past security?"

Janus laughed, though he sounded more bitter than amused. "Obviously, there's an inside man. Or men."

"Who?"

"That's what I'm trying to find out." He paused. "Whoever the thief is, chances are he's running scared. Have you seen the latest issue of the *Edinburgh Exposé*?"

"I don't read tabloids."

"Make an exception," Janus said. "This week's *Exposé* features a story about a manuscript recently acquired by Erskine Grant, a professor of medieval literature. The professor claims the manuscript—purportedly written by the great magician Merlin—reveals the secret of immortality and speaks of a treasure beyond price."

"Sounds like typical tabloid nonsense to me," Dominic said.

"To be sure," Janus agreed, "but the manuscript itself is real enough, part of the *Calix Chronicles*, a priceless piece of Calix's cultural heritage." He cleared his throat. "Our people have inventoried the palace library; the manuscript's definitely gone missing."

"So if whoever's behind the pilfering saw the *Exposé* article, he'll realize the cat's out of the bag."

"Yes," Janus agreed. "Talk to the professor. Find out where he got the manuscript."

Caitlin and her current boyfriend, Tony DaCosta, had caught a late afternoon flight to Vegas and were checked into a terrace suite at the MGM Grand by 6:00. By 6:02 they were exploring each other's erogenous zones. By 7:30 Tony had hit the shower.

Caitlin lay on the rumpled sheets, basking in the afterglow of multiple orgasms and trying to work up the energy to move. She needed to take a shower, too, and get dressed. They had dinner reservations at Le Cirque for 8:15, which she would have canceled in a heartbeat in favor of room service. But she suspected Tony had planned a surprise for her birthday. Tony was big on surprises.

Self-warming condoms. Who knew?

She stretched and her body gave a residual zing of pleasure. *Happy birthday to me,* she thought.

The phone rang. Grinning like a fool, she rolled onto her side to answer it. "Hello?"

The phone went on ringing.

Not the room phone, she realized. The cell phone Tony'd left on the nightstand. Caitlin hung up and grabbed the cell. "Hello?" she tried again.

"Tony?" the woman on the other end said.

Geez, did she *sound* like Tony? "No, but I can get him for you."

"Shelley? Is that you, you fucking bitch?"

Shelley, no. Fucking bitch? Um, maybe. "Who is this?"

"You know damn well who it is, slut!" The woman burst into noisy sobs. "I knew the bastard was lying to me. I knew it."

And apparently lying to Caitlin as well.

"Said he had to go to Vegas on business. Business, my ass! He's off screwing around while I'm stuck here in San Jose with four sick kids and a goddamn TV that doesn't work." The woman's furious words dwindled to a sputter of incoherence. But it was the choked, hiccuping sob that followed that pricked Caitlin's heart.

"Tony's married." It wasn't a question.

"Damn straight," Tony's wife said.

"I didn't know that. I'm sorry."

"Not as sorry as Tony's going to be. That bastard will wish he'd never been born."

Caitlin suspected the threat was sheer bravado. If Tony had been married long enough to father four children, chances were slim this was the first time he'd cheated. And if his wife hadn't dragged him through divorce court the first umpteen times she'd caught him screwing around, she wasn't going to do it this time, either.

Caitlin, however, wasn't quite so forgiving. Her first impulse was to deliver a swift kick where it would hurt the most, but upon reflection, she realized humiliation trumped physical pain any day of the week. By the time Tony emerged from the bathroom on a nearly visible cloud of aftershave, cologne, and testosterone, she'd worked out the details of her plan.

"Hey, babe," he said. "Why aren't you dressed? I thought you were hungry."

"I am," she said, "just not for food."

"Sweetheart, you just had a three-course meal," Tony protested.

"But I have my heart set on dessert. Al fresco." She nodded toward the private terrace below.

"Yeah, but what about Uncle Sal? He pulled strings to get us that reservation. If we don't show up, he's gonna kill me."

Caitlin wrapped her arms around his neck and dragged his mouth down to hers.

Tony was the first to pull away. He rested his forehead against hers, breathing hard. "Holy Christ, woman."

"So . . . do I get my dessert?" She rubbed herself against his arousal.

"Hell, yes." Tony's expression—sheer, unadulterated lust—turned her stomach, but she couldn't allow her revulsion to show. Not yet.

Forcing herself to smile, she grabbed his hand, led him down the stairs to the main level and then out onto the terrace, where she shoved him roughly onto a lounge chair.

Tony smirked. "I didn't realize you were into domination."

"There's a lot you don't know about me, Tony." She picked up a length of drapery cord she'd liberated from the living room and dangled it in front of him. "Ever tried bondage?"

His eyes danced. "No, but I'm open to new experiences." He joked the whole time she was tying him to the chair.

"How's that?" she asked when she was done. "Too tight? Too loose?"

He gave his bonds an experimental tug. "I'm at your mercy, babe."

"That's right. You are." *Liar. Cheater.* Caitlin studied Tony's face. He had a very sexy smile, which perhaps explained why she'd never before noticed the weakness of his chin or the shiftiness of his eyes.

God, what was wrong with her? Why did she keep picking these losers?

Tony's smirk grew into a full-fledged leer. "Is this the part where you bring out the whips and chains?"

Caitlin frowned. "I liked you, Tony. I really did."

"Liked?" He shot her a wary glance. "Past tense?"

"I thought you were a nice guy."

"I am a nice guy."

"Not according to your wife."

"My . . . ? What the hell?"

"She called a while ago."

A muscle twitched just below his left eye. "Damn it, Caitlin, the marriage has been over for years."

"You just stay together for the kids, right?"

"Oh, shit." The oh-man-I-am-so-screwed expression on his face should have been laughable. So why did Caitlin feel like crying?

She turned blindly toward the sliding glass door.

"Hey! What are you doing? Where are you going?" Tony's voice grew shrill as it dawned on him she was leaving.

Without a word, she stepped inside and locked the door behind her. Fifteen minutes later, she left the suite, dragging Tony's wheeled carry-on along with her own.

Out on the terrace, Tony was still yelling.

On the flight back to San Francisco, Caitlin started worrying that Tony would try to retaliate, and the thing was, she didn't know him that well—obviously, since she hadn't had a clue he was married with children. The bastard could have mob connections. Not that she was paranoid enough to think that everyone with an Italian surname and an Uncle Salvatore belonged to the Mafia, but damn it, Tony *had* taken her to Vegas.

And he knew where she lived.

On the other hand, she had a good head start on him. Unless his shouting alerted someone or he managed to free himself, he was stuck on that patio until the maid came in to clean tomorrow. And even then, he was going to have problems. She'd locked his luggage (including every stitch of clothing he'd brought with him) and his wallet (containing all his cash and credit cards) in the trunk of his rental car, a car she'd abandoned in long-term parking at the Las Vegas airport.

So with any luck, she should have plenty of time to go to her place, pack enough stuff for a week or so, and then move into her stepfather's house for a few days. Her stepfather, Magnus Armstrong, might have asked a few embarrassing questions had he been home, but as it happened, he wasn't, having left last Saturday for two weeks in Scotland. As a professor emeritus in the English department at Stanford, he'd been invited to participate in a symposium on medieval literature sponsored by his alma mater, the University of Edinburgh. He'd even—would wonders never cease?—asked her to accompany him.

Admittedly, Caitlin, whose passion was math history, had little interest in medieval literature, but she'd always longed to visit Edinburgh, to see Holyrood Palace, the Royal Mile, and most especially, Merchiston Castle, ancestral home of sixteenth-century mathematician—and rumored sorcerer—John Napier, the focus of her dissertation.

In retrospect she probably should have accepted Magnus's invitation. She could easily have arranged for someone to cover her classes. But traveling with Magnus meant spending time with Magnus, talking with Magnus, discussing things she refused to think about, let alone analyze. And besides, she'd already agreed to go to Vegas with Tony . . .

Who even now might be plotting her demise. Or at least a serious bitch-slapping.

Her plane touched down a little after midnight; she was fitting the key to the lock on her front door just under a half hour later.

She swung the door wide and flicked on the entry light to find an untidy pile of mail littering the tiles. Looked as if she'd been gone a week instead of a few hours. She dumped her carry-on, shut and locked the door, then gathered up the envelopes—mostly bills and junk mail—and tossed them on the kitchen counter.

The message light on her phone was blinking an urgent SOS, so she kicked off her heels and padded barefoot across the room to see what was so damned important.

"Happy birthday to you," sang her best friend, art gallery owner Sabrina "Bree" Thatcher, the digital recording tinny but recognizable. "Happy birthday to you. Happy birthday, dear Caitlin. Happy birthday to you. Give me a call when you get in."

The machine gave the date and time, then beeped and went directly to the next message, this one a wrong number from someone named Jerry. The third and final message was Bree again. "Look, Caitlin, please call me as soon as you get back. It's important. I heard something today, something about Tony. I'm afraid he's bad news."

Bad news. That could mean "He's married" or "He's a Mafia hit man." Or both. Plus everything in between.

Caitlin glanced at the mail on the counter, decided she didn't have time to read it now, and stuffed it into the side pocket of her overnight bag.

Ten minutes later she let herself into Magnus's shingled Craftsman-style house in Professorville, an exclusive enclave of pricey historic homes within walking distance of both Stanford University and downtown Palo Alto. With her car hidden inside the detached garage, the doors locked, and the security system engaged, she felt safe for the first time in hours.

Safe and hungry.

Unfortunately, all she could scrounge from Magnus's kitchen was a plate of carrots, raisins, and rice cakes spread with peanut butter. She sat down with her meager dinner and began sorting through her mail. Junk mail went in one pile, bills in another. The one oddball was a notice from the post office saying that they'd tried and failed to deliver a package at 2:43 p.m. but that she could pick it up tomorrow during regular business hours or call to arrange for delivery. Birthday present from Magnus, she'd bet. Hard to guess what he'd sent, though. Knowing Magnus, probably not jewelry or clothing. No cairngorm brooches or tartan shawls. A book maybe. Or a piece of antique silver. Magnus was big on antiques.

Crunching thoughtfully on a carrot, she punched in Bree's phone number.

Her friend picked up on the fourth ring. "Professor Armstrong?" She sounded out of breath, as if she'd just run a four-minute mile or was in the middle of some very athletic sex.

"No, it's me. Caitlin. Magnus is in Edinburgh. I didn't interrupt anything important, did I?"

"I was on the treadmill. Didn't hear the phone at first. Then when your stepdad's name came up on caller ID, I thought, oh geez, something's happened. Are you all right, Caitlin? Tell me you're all right."

"I'm fine."

"Then why are you calling from Magnus's house? I thought he was on your shit list."

"He's not on my shit list, as you so eloquently put it. We just have issues, that's all. And anyway, he's out of the country."

"Which still doesn't answer my question. What are you doing in his house?"

"Hiding from Tony DaCosta."

"Oh, Lord. What happened?"

"Believe me, you don't want to know. What's your big revelation? What did you find out about him?"

Bree exhaled noisily. "He lied to you."

No shit.

"He not an executive at HP. He's a waiter at Spago."

"A married waiter," Caitlin said.

"Married?"

"With four kids."

Bree muttered an assortment of colorful pejoratives under her breath. "I'm sorry—sorry Tony turned out to be a schmuck and sorry your birthday ended in disaster."

"You don't know the half of it," Caitlin said. "I'm starving, and Magnus's cupboards are emptier than Old Mother Hubbard's."

"Now *that* I can fix," her friend said. "How does left-over lasagna sound?"

"Like the answer to a prayer."

"I'll be right over."

Caitlin dumped her makeshift meal into the garbage disposal, then fired up her laptop. Might as well check her e-mail while she was waiting for Bree and the lifesaving lasagna.

Lots of junk in her in-box. Viagra ads. Mortgage refinancing. About ten messages from her Yahoo Groups math history Listserv. All of which she deleted. Which left only a memo from her karate instructor reminding her that he was out of town until a week from Thursday.

Nothing from Magnus, which was a little strange. Absentminded as he was about some things, Magnus was very good about remembering her birthday. She'd expected a cheesy e-mail greeting card at the very least. Of course, there was that package waiting for her at the post office—most likely from Magnus—but it still seemed odd that he hadn't e-mailed. He'd begun his trip with regular, twice-a-day updates on the symposium, but now that she thought about it, she hadn't heard anything from him since early yesterday.

Was it merely a case of out of sight, out of mind? Was he too busy pub-hopping with his old University of Edinburgh cronies to keep in touch? Or was something wrong? A trickle of unease ran down her spine. When the doorbell rang, she jumped and nearly knocked her Dasani bottle off the granite countertop.

Damn it. Magnus always said she had too much imagination for her own good. Maybe for once he was right. She closed her laptop and got up to go let Bree in.

July 1617
Near Drumelzier, Scotland

Hamish MacNeill heard the rumbling and thought at first it was his stomach. He and Maggie Gordon—pretty, wanton Maggie who, with one flirtatious flutter of her thick black lashes, could make him weak with need—had spent the afternoon on the banks of the River Tweed in the shade of an ancient oak. They'd been much too busy supping on each other to bother with the food still rolled up in a cloth and tucked away in his saddlebags.

Again he heard it, that low rumble, and this time he opened his eyes to peer up through the tangled branches at the curdled gray sky. A thunderstorm had slipped up on them. One fat raindrop splatted his forehead. "We must go, Maggie."

She raised her head from his chest and gave him the saucy dimpled look that had attracted him from the first.

"Not yet. It's early. Robert won't be home for hours." She raised herself to sit astride his hips, her skirts rucked up 'round her thighs, her bodice undone. Long dark hair tumbled over her shoulders. She lowered her lids halfway and gave him a provocative smile. "Think, Hamish, what we might accomplish in hours."

Her breasts were small and pert with rosy pink nipples that seemed to beg for his touch. He'd just lifted a lazy hand in answer to that silent entreaty when the wind kicked up. Thunder boomed, much louder this time, much closer.

"No," he said. "A storm is coming. It's not safe."

"And since when has safety been your paramount concern? If the need for *safety* governed your actions, you'd have seduced someone else's wife. You know as well as I that if your uncle catches you, he'll cut off your balls and fry them up for his breakfast."

His crotch tingled unpleasantly at the thought. Robert Gordon, his mother's brother, was an ill-tempered brute and a devil with a dirk. Though if the old man ever, God forbid, figured out what Hamish was up to, castration would be the least of his worries. Gordon was much more likely to lop off Hamish's head—nephew be damned—and hang the gory trophy from the bridge at Drumelzier. He'd done as much earlier this spring with the heads of a pair of cattle thieves.

Maggie leaned forward and nipped at his lower lip. "Concentrate, Hamish. I can't do this on my own." Or then again, perhaps she could. She rubbed herself against him with a delicious friction and he felt his cock grow hard again.

"Ah, Maggie," he said on a sigh as she slid down to sheathe him in liquid warmth. A fiery and demanding lover, her passionate nature was wasted on Robert, who cared more for his cattle than for his young wife.

Hamish gave himself up to the pleasure, ignoring the nervous neighing and stamping of the horses, ignoring the rain coming down now in earnest, ignoring the thunder, so close that it sounded like cannon fire. Maggie squealed in delight as he rolled her beneath him. He quickened the pace, thrusting again and again.

His heart raced. His nerves tingled. Every hair on his body stood up. Gasping for breath, he trembled on the verge of a gut-wrenching climax.

And then the earth shattered with an earsplitting crack, exploded into a million fragments, all fierce, blinding light and deafening noise. The pain came next, excruciating and all-encompassing. A massive jolt blasted through his knees, his palms.

His muscles convulsed, jerking and twitching in uncontrollable spasms that seemed to last forever. Then finally, finally, some semblance of normalcy returned. The pounding rain and rumbling thunder impinged once more upon his senses.

He shoved himself up on his elbows. His hands were tender, the skin raw, burnt. Likewise, his knees. "What on earth . . . ?" he asked Maggie, but she didn't answer. He peered more closely at her face—pale, beautiful, and unnaturally still. "Maggie?"

She made no sound. No movement. Her wide blue-green eyes were open. The rain, slackening off already as the storm passed, gathered in fat drops on her lashes, then dripped into her eyes. She didn't blink.

Horrified, he shrank away from her. *Oh, God.* He made a noise, a faint keening wail, quickly swallowed by the wind.

Was this God's punishment for their sins? He stared at Maggie's limp body in disbelief.

And then he saw the tree . . . or what was left of it.

The lightning must have struck the oak dead-on, splitting it down the middle and denuding the gnarled branches of leaves and twigs. Acrid smoke curled in thin wisps from the blasted trunk.

Hamish stood up and fastened his trousers. He ached from head to toe, as if he'd been pummeled senseless in a tavern brawl. But aside from sore muscles and the burns on his knees and his hands, the lightning had done no harm.

To him.

Maggie was another story. She'd absorbed more of the jolt than he. He knelt at her side and pressed an ear to her chest. No heartbeat. Not even the faintest whisper of respiration. Already her skin was growing cold.

He slumped beside her, dazed and sick. How could she be dead?

And then, *oh God,* the realization hit him. He was dead, too. Robert would finish what the lightning bolt had started. Unless . . .

With clumsy fingers, Hamish fastened Maggie's bodice. "I'm sorry," he whispered. Sorry she was dead and sorry for what he must do to protect himself from a similar fate. Bending low, he kissed her cold, wet cheek one last time.

Her pony was tethered nearby. He set it free to make its way home. No need for him to get involved. Robert's servants would find her body soon enough.

The damaged tree glared at him in silent reproach.

"And what would you have me do then?" he demanded. "Carry her home myself? She's dead. There's no saving her now, but I still have a chance. No one saw us together. But if I show up with Maggie's body . . . The old man's no fool. He'd know at once what we'd been up to. Isn't one death enough?"

The tree stood mute and disapproving.

Shock, fear, and guilt roiled his gut, then spilled over as rage. He flailed at the great oak as if it were responsible for his predicament. He pummeled and kicked, inflicting at least as much damage on himself as on the ruined tree.

Exhausted, he dropped to his knees and pressed his palms flat against the oak's trunk. "Damn you," he said softly, not certain whom he cursed. God? The tree? The storm? Perhaps all three. Or perhaps himself. If only he'd insisted they leave when he heard the first faraway roll of thunder.

The rain stopped and the wind died suddenly; the silence was almost palpable.

He felt it then in his fingertips, a faint throbbing that seemed to emanate from the bark of the tree.

Startled, he jerked his hands away and stared at what was left of the great oak. The two halves leaned drunkenly askew.

Vita aeterna.

Hamish didn't really hear the words. No sound had disturbed the hush. And yet somehow those words had insinuated themselves into his consciousness. *Vita aeterna.* Latin for "eternal life."

He trembled. Could it be the voice of God?

But why would God choose to speak to him, a nineteen-year-old sinner, when the world was full of pious men worthier than he?

He stood, swaying unsteadily.

But if not a sign from God, what? Had he gone mad? Had the lightning strike turned his brain?

Vita aeterna.

Once again the words entered his mind unbidden, a silent whisper. He shook uncontrollably and would have fallen had he not braced himself against the oak.

And again he felt the pulsing, as strong and steady as a heartbeat. Only trees didn't have hearts . . .

He pulled away. "You fool," he said aloud. "Are you afraid of a tree?"

He circled the oak, studying it from all angles before he moved closer, close enough to peer inside the great cleft trunk.

For a moment his brain couldn't make sense of what he saw. But gradually, the shifting patterns of light and shadow resolved themselves into a comprehensive reality. Impossible, unbelievable, but nonetheless real. He leaned forward and touched it. Still partially embedded in the splintered heartwood, a human skull stared back at him.

2

BREE THATCHER SAT AT Professor Magnus Armstrong's dining room table watching her friend Caitlin devour lasagna and garlic bread. Even though Bree knew Magnus was thousands of miles away, she still found it difficult to relax, half afraid he'd walk through the archway from the living room any minute now and fix that dark, disapproving gaze on her. She'd been scared to death of Caitlin's stepfather since fourth grade, when she'd made the mistake of trying to sell him Girl Scout cookies.

"Do you have any idea what you're peddling, young lady?" he'd demanded in a voice like thunder as she stood trembling on the front porch, order form in one hand, ballpoint pen in the other.

"Thin Mints and S-Samoas?" she'd stammered.

"Processed sugars, saturated fat, artificial flavors, and preservatives."

Bree wasn't sure what any of that was; all she knew was that Caitlin's stepdad scared the crap out of her.

Caitlin's stepdad *still* scared the crap out of her.

"No birthday cake?" Caitlin's teasing comment pulled her back to the moment.

"Sorry. All I had was butter pecan ice cream."

Caitlin's blue-green eyes lit up. "My favorite."

"Now tell me what Tony DaCosta did to spook you," Bree said as soon as Caitlin had put a dent in her ice cream.

"More like what I did." Caitlin described her revenge. "So then—you know me, world champion worst-case-scenario thinker—I thought, oh my God, what if he follows me? I mean, he knows where I live and the lock on my front door's a joke. So I packed some stuff and hightailed it over here. I figure I'll hang out in Professorville until the danger's past."

Bree shook her head. "Why do you always pick such creeps? What's wrong with a nice, normal guy for a change?"

"Nice, normal guys have certain expectations."

"You think you can't . . . you think you don't . . . Damn it, you've got to give people a chance." Caitlin was still punishing herself for past mistakes, but Bree knew who was really to blame.

Caitlin frowned. "I don't want to talk about it."

But damn it, they needed to talk about it, though tonight probably wasn't the best time. "Then we won't," Bree said. *Not now.*

Not ever. Caitlin met her gaze. The unspoken words seemed to echo in the silence of the room.

Bree was the first to shift her gaze. She stood, making

quite a business of retrieving the lime and fuchsia harlequin-patterned gift bag she'd left just inside the door. With a flourish she set it on the table in front of Caitlin. "Happy birthday!"

Caitlin burrowed through the layers of tissue paper and pulled out her present. "Joss Whedon's *Firefly,*" she said, the sparkle back in her eyes. "The complete series on DVD."

" 'Complete series' is not as impressive as it sounds," Bree said. "The show was canceled partway through the first season. But since you're such a Buffy addict, I figured you'd enjoy another Joss Whedon series."

" 'I can kill you with my brain,' " Caitlin said.

"Excuse me?"

Caitlin's dimple flicked into view for a second. "It's a line from the show."

"So you do like it."

"Love it. Thanks."

In order to avoid subsisting on rice cakes and peanut butter, Caitlin stopped at the grocery store on her way back from the post office the next morning. What with trying to decide between fresh croissants and bran muffins, raspberries and honeydew, she'd worked up quite an appetite by the time she got back to Professorville.

But her curiosity still outweighed her hunger pangs. She set her groceries on the counter, dug a box cutter from the junk drawer next to the sink, and attacked her package, which was, as she'd expected, postmarked Edinburgh and addressed to her in Magnus's distinctive spiky handwriting.

She slit open the Tyvek mailer and turned it on end. Three items fell out: a small, intricately decorated leather box, its flip-top lid fastened by an ornate metal clasp, a rectangular object wrapped in gray silk and secured with two oversized rubber bands—Magnus's version of gift wrap?—and a plain white letter-sized envelope.

The phone rang before she could examine her haul more closely.

"Guess who finally asked me out." Bree didn't believe in wasting time on small talk.

"Who?"

"Jory Freitag. Can you believe it?" Bree's gallery specialized in American primitives, and Jory, who used vivid colors to create slightly twisted barnyard scenes, was one of her best-selling artists. Caitlin found Jory's fanged cows and Uzi-toting roosters as unappealing as their scruffy, long-haired creator, but who was she to criticize?—especially considering her own recent dating disaster.

"Great," she said, trying to inject a little enthusiasm.

"I'm excited. Two years I've been trying to get that man to notice me. Two *years.*" She babbled another few minutes, inserting "Jory says" an average of twice per paragraph. Caitlin wondered if she herself had sounded as giddy when talking about Tony. Probably.

She was so sunk in gloomy reflection that she didn't notice at first when Bree changed the subject. "Magnus," she heard Bree say, but that was it.

"I'm sorry," she said. "What did you say about Magnus?"

"I asked if you'd heard anything from him. How'd he react to the news about Tony and your temporary relocation to Professorville?"

"I e-mailed him, but so far he hasn't responded. He did send me a birthday package, though."

"Something thrilling, I bet. Let me guess. A genuine tartan tea cozy? No, wait. I've got it. A stuffed salmon. The taxidermy kind, not the eating kind."

Caitlin chuckled. "I don't know what it is. I haven't had a chance to look." As she spoke, she unlatched the leather case and dumped the contents onto the counter. "Oh, my God!"

"What?"

"Bones. He sent me a set of bones."

Silence on the other end. Then, "Bones?" Bree said. "What? Like femurs and ribs?"

Caitlin laughed. "No. Napier's bones. Little rods marked with numbers."

"Numbered rods. Be still, my heart."

"No, really. It's a terrific gift," Caitlin said. "John Napier, the mathematician who was the focus of my dissertation, invented the bones as a sort of seventeenth-century precursor to the handheld calculator."

"Oh, just what you need, another math geek gizmo."

"It's not a gizmo, Bree; it's an antique. The rods are made of ivory and beautifully carved."

"Hey, whatever floats your boat."

Shortly after that, Bree hung up to go wait on a customer, and Caitlin resumed her examination of Magnus's birthday package. Setting the rods aside, she reached for the envelope.

"Dear Caitlin," Magnus wrote. "Enclosed is a set of Napier's bones I found in an antiques shop here in Edinburgh. The dealer swore they'd been custom made to order for Napier himself. He said one could tell because the ends of the rods are marked with small black cockerels."

Caitlin recognized the reference. John Napier, eighth laird of Merchiston, had been rumored to keep a black cockerel as a familiar—proof, according to some, that he dabbled in the black arts.

"But squint as I might, I can't see a cockerel in those squiggles."

Neither could Caitlin. To her they looked more like Chinese characters or Egyptian hieroglyphs.

"I suspect," Magnus continued, "they're actually the artisan's mark, but I didn't argue the point. The set is quite old, and the workmanship is first-rate, well worth the asking price. Enjoy your birthday.

"Love, Magnus."

Caitlin set the letter aside, thinking how odd it was that Magnus hadn't said anything about the silk-wrapped rectangle. Was it a second gift? Something he'd added at the last minute?

Well, one way to find out. She removed the rubber bands and unwrapped the silk covering to disclose a book, a manuscript really, handwritten and bound in cracked leather. "What on earth . . . ?" she muttered half under her breath.

The manuscript appeared to be written in English, though between the hen-scratches handwriting and the archaic spelling, it took her almost ten minutes to make that determination. Old, too, if she was to take the text at face value. "In the year of our lord 1617," she read, "I, Hamish MacNeill of Drymen Village, Stirlingshire, Scotland, set forth the chronicle of my life." A diary then, she decided, or maybe a four-hundred-year-old autobiography. She rifled through the pages, searching for a note, but there was nothing. No note. No explanation.

Puzzling, she thought, though not as puzzling as why Magnus hadn't yet responded to her e-mail. True, he was the quintessential absentminded professor. He often overlooked the minutiae of everyday life. But though he might forget to pick up his dry cleaning or to water the houseplants, he never forgot to check his e-mail.

She frowned. No doubt he was busy; he was scheduled to present his own paper on Friday. But surely honing his presentation didn't require all his free time.

Then again, maybe he hadn't gotten her message; maybe it was lost in the vast reaches of cyberspace.

So instead of fretting, she'd try again.

Caitlin opened her laptop and composed a quick e-mail. She assured Magnus her package had arrived safely and thanked him for the bones. Then she added a "Love, Caitlin" and punched Send.

Professor Erskine Grant wasn't registered at any of the usual tourist hotels. Dominic knew this because he'd spent the best part of the morning checking. For the past three hours, he'd been camped out in the foyer outside the symposium lecture hall, clutching a copy of the *Exposé* folded open to a Bambi-in-the-headlamps photo of Grant. Tired and hungry, Dominic had nearly abandoned hope of catching up with the elusive professor.

The officious young woman at the table just inside the entrance had tried to toss him out earlier because he didn't have an official badge. Amazing, he thought, that anyone would think an outsider would *want* to crash a symposium on medieval literature. He could think of few things more boring than a gathering of garrulous academics. He'd had to exert the full force of his not inconsiderable charm on the woman and promise on his mother's grave that he wouldn't try to slip inside the lecture hall; she'd finally relented and let him loiter in the foyer.

A little after four, the big double doors swung open. Symposium participants trickled out in twos and threes, some headed for the loo, others making a beeline for the refreshment table as if their lives depended upon an immediate infusion of weak institutional tea.

Dominic left his seat against the wall and wove his way through the milling crowd, searching for Grant. He'd spent some time concocting a story to explain his presence in case he ran across anyone he knew—"I'm supposed to meet symposium organizer Richard Pitcairn to discuss a possible donation to my pet charity"—a seemingly reasonable excuse since as far as Edinburgh society was concerned, Dominic was three parts playboy to one part philanthropist, a wealthy hedonist who occasionally used his social position to raise funds in support of St.

Giles Institute for Genetic Research. As it happened, though, he didn't have to use his cover story. He spotted no one who looked even vaguely familiar, and that included Erskine Grant.

After two complete circuits of the foyer, he poked his head through the double doors to make sure Grant wasn't hiding out in the lecture hall. He wasn't. Unfortunately, someone else was.

"Dominic?" To his dismay he recognized Jacqueline LeTourneau standing behind the lectern at the far end of the room.

"What are you doing here?" they said in unison.

He laughed. "Ladies first."

Jacqueline, a willowy blonde with classic features and a wealthy husband fifteen years her senior, smiled at him. "Why, giving a lecture, of course."

"You're an expert on medieval literature?"

She uttered a throaty laugh, at odds with her patrician appearance. "Hardly, though I do know a good bit about witchcraft in the Middle Ages. My talk went over well, if I do say so myself." She smiled again. "And you? What brings you here?"

Unfortunately the lie he'd concocted wouldn't work on Jacqueline since she and her husband, Etienne, moved in the same circles as the Pitcairns. . . . "I'm running a little errand for my great-uncle Wallace, trying to locate a relative of his who's here visiting from America. A professor from Stanford."

Jacqueline's beautiful face went blank for a moment.

"Stanford University," he said. "In California."

She nodded. "Of course. Wallace mentioned him. His younger brother's son, I believe. Etienne and I are quite looking forward to meeting him on Thursday."

"Thursday?"

"Yes, Wallace invited us to dinner at Firth House."

"Don't tell me he's planning another séance." Every time Jacqueline, a telepath of some repute, came to dinner, Wallace Armstrong prevailed upon her to contact his dead wife. Yet despite repeated efforts, Mary Armstrong had proved stubbornly uncommunicative.

"He misses her," Jacqueline said.

The telephone woke Caitlin from a sound sleep a little after midnight. *Magnus.* She groped for the receiver without bothering to switch on the lamp first. "Hello?"

No answer. Just someone breathing softly on the other end.

"Tony? Is that you?"

More breathing.

"Damn it, leave me alone or I swear I'll call the cops."

She listened hard but this time all she heard was silence.

"Hello? Hello?"

More silence, and then a click as the connection was broken.

"Damn," Dominic muttered under his breath. He'd wasted the best part of two days trying to run Erskine Grant to earth, and for most of that time, the man had been dead. He glanced up from his perusal of the *Scotsman.* "Wallace?"

His maternal great-uncle, Wallace Armstrong, his mouth full of oatmeal, grunted acknowledgment across the breakfast table.

"Ever heard of a Dr. Erskine Grant from Aberdeen?"

"What about him?"

"Apparently he, like your nephew Magnus, was in Edinburgh for the medieval literature symposium."

"Yes?"

"A maid found him dead in his hotel room yesterday, victim of an apparent suicide."

"Pity," Wallace said. "Though I suppose one shouldn't be too surprised. Those academic types are all a bit barmy."

Dominic raised an eyebrow. "And you base this judgment on . . . ?"

"Experience, my boy. Experience. Take Magnus, for example, buying that girl of his a packet of old sticks for her birthday. Utter foolishness. Anyone with half a brain knows women prefer feminine fripperies—candy, flowers, jewelry."

"I wonder if Magnus knows."

"Not bloody likely," Wallace said. "Otherwise he'd have bought her a necklace or some bonbons."

"No, I mean, I wonder if Magnus knows about Grant's suicide."

"You can ask him tonight. He's coming to dinner. I've invited Etienne and Jacqueline, too, and Mavis Campbell. She's a bit deaf but a good eater, and that always pleases Cook. Feel free to ask that latest girl of yours, what's-her-name, the one who wears the diamond in her left nostril. Jennifer, is it?"

"Janet," Dominic said. "And for the record, we parted company two weeks ago."

"Good," Wallace said. "She had gold digger written all over her."

Dominic raised an eyebrow. "Her father's Edward Conroy."

"Really?" Wallace held a spoonful of cereal suspended halfway to his mouth. "The financier?"

Dominic nodded.

"Never would have guessed from the way she dressed. If the girl has money, why doesn't she buy clothes that fit?"

The corners of Dominic's mouth twitched. "Chalk it up to the vagaries of fashion."

"Humph," Wallace said and stuffed the oatmeal in his mouth.

October 1617
Stirlingshire, Scotland

Hamish MacNeill drew his cloak close against the chill morning mist as he set off on the footpath along the River Endrick. Maggie's death hung heavy on his conscience. He longed to share the burden of guilt but dared tell no one for fear of the story's leaking back to his Uncle Robert. He ached, too, to speak of the miraculous events that had followed, but the only man he'd have trusted to hold his tongue on that subject was John Napier, neighbor and longtime family friend. Unfortunately, Napier had died the previous April.

Hamish stumbled along in a daze, lost in a morass of

troubling thoughts, not least of which was the possibility that none of the things he believed to have happened had actually transpired anywhere beyond the confines of his mind. Perhaps that massive electrical charge had damaged some essential portion of his brain. Perhaps he could no longer trust the evidence of his senses.

Then again, just because an event seemed like magic didn't mean it was. Science had explained away many of the old mysteries. Early man had seen fire as magic, a gift from the gods. Science had shown it to be a chemical reaction. Perhaps his experience with the bones had an equally mundane explanation.

Gradually the rhythmic thumping of the mill at Gartness impinged upon his consciousness. The pounding echoed eerily through the fog like the footsteps of some enormous prehistoric beast. He hadn't meant to travel so far, but habit had drawn him in this direction.

The mist thinned and Gartness Castle, Napier's country home, loomed ahead, stark and bleak. Empty now. The grieving family had been in Edinburgh for the past few months.

He stared at the grim gray castle wall. If only Napier were still alive. If only Hamish could confide in him.

Napier wouldn't have condemned him as a witch, despite the evidence, not when Napier himself had borne the burden of malicious gossip. For years it had been rumored that he'd made a pact with the devil. Utter nonsense, of course. Napier, a staunch Protestant and biblical scholar, had always been deeply religious. Ironic, really, that anyone would suggest he was a warlock. No, more than ironic. Reprehensible. Slanderous whisperings, dangerous in this day and age when good men and women were burned at the stake.

A magpie flew overhead, chattering noisily, and Hamish started. A bad omen, according to his Grandmother MacNeill, who counted magpie augury among her talents. A single magpie foretold misfortune. Yet what, he wondered bitterly, could be worse than that which he'd already endured? He shot one final wistful glance toward the castle, then trudged on.

Beyond Gartness, the fog closed in again, and a fine mist began to fall. Deciding he was more likely to catch a chill than gain any insight into his problems by continuing his walk, Hamish turned for home.

He hadn't met a soul all morning, so when he stumbled across the poachers, a ragtag pair caught red-handed with a freshly killed stag, he was as surprised as they. And even more surprised when the taller of the two uttered a cry of outrage and fell upon him with the bloody knife.

"Unhand me!" He tried to free himself, to fight, but was hampered by the enveloping folds of his cloak.

"Dinna hurt him," the smaller man said, his voice hoarse with panic.

"I have nae choice. It's him or us." The poacher pinned Hamish tight against his chest with one arm while brandishing the knife with the other.

Hamish twisted and squirmed, but his strength was no match for the other man's. "I have money. Free me and it's all yours."

"It's all ours anyway once ye're dead. Pull his head back," the poacher ordered his accomplice.

The smaller man blanched. "I canna do it."

"Ye must. If he goes free, our lives are forfeit. And how will Jenny feed the bairns wi'out ye?"

"Don't listen to him, man. This is murder."

The smaller man glanced down at his bloody hands. "God forgive me."

"No!" Hamish said.

His head was jerked back so far he didn't see the blade coming.

But he felt it. Pain, fierce and shocking, stole his breath. Blood spurted from the gaping wound. Wet and warm, it soaked his chest. He tried to say something—he wasn't sure what, some murmur of protest perhaps—but the only sounds his ruined throat produced were whistles, wheezes, and gurgles.

"Ah, Jesus!" The smaller man fell to his knees and vomited.

The larger man made some small sound of disgust and gave Hamish a shove.

One magpie, he thought, as he toppled forward in a heap.

3

CAITLIN FILLED HER GAS TANK, then went inside to pay. "I'm on pump four," she told the clerk, a young man with tattoos up and down both arms, a stud in his tongue, and an attitude to match.

"That'll be eight fifty." He stared over her shoulder. "Son of a bitch!"

"What?" She spun around.

"Cheapskate bastard."

"Who?"

"Bozo out there in the SUV. Emptied his trash, aired his tires, and been washing his goddamn windows for the past ten minutes, but did he pump one penny's worth of fuel? Hell, no. Stinking freeloader."

A dark blue Ford Explorer was parked at the pump farthest from the mini-mart. A big, bulky man in a black turtleneck was methodically polishing the SUV's spotless windshield.

Caitlin passed the clerk a ten, then glanced out at her own car. Her windshield could do with a little attention.

But not now.

She pocketed her change and headed for the university.

Okay, yes, she probably never would have been hired on at Stanford without her stepfather's recommendation. And contrary to media reports, it wasn't because the math department harbored an anti-white-female bias—or conversely, a pro-Asian-male bias. Nor was it a prejudice against Berkeley, where she'd done her undergraduate work—stellar undergraduate work, by the way, if she did say so herself. No, it was the fact she'd earned her graduate degrees from a no-name southern university that had hurt her. But thanks to Magnus, she'd been given her chance to prove the naysayers—notably one-foot-in-the-grave/one-head-in-the-ass Professor Emeritus Ronald G. Belzer—wrong. Which she had. At the end of this school year, her official title would be associate professor. Not bad for a female in her twenties.

An hour later she emerged from her lecture feeling both drained and exhilarated, having held the class's attention for the entire period, during which time she'd completed her lecture—including a razzmatazz interactive overhead projector proof—without one undergrad asking if any of this was going to be on the exam or complaining that calculus had no relevance in the real world.

Differentiate that, Professor Belzer.

She grabbed a bottle of Dasani from a vending machine and headed for the parking lot, where she spotted the man she'd noticed earlier at the Shell station. He sat behind the wheel of the blue SUV, which was parked illegally two spots down from her Mini Cooper.

She chewed at the inside of her cheek. Talk about weird coincidences. In this city of sixty-plus thousand people, what were the odds?

He glanced up and Caitlin shifted her gaze, embarrassed to have been caught staring, but darn it, how strange to run into the same man twice in a matter of hours.

If it was the same man. The more she thought about it, the less certain she was. The man at the gas station had been wearing sunglasses. This man wasn't. And yes, this SUV was a dark blue Explorer, but not being a car person, she didn't have a clue whether or not it was the same year and model she'd seen earlier.

But okay, say it was the same man, the same SUV, what did that prove?

Nothing.

Unless maybe Tony had put out a contract on her.

She sneaked a quick sideways glance at the man in the SUV, but he wasn't looking her way. One hand tapped out a rhythm on the steering wheel as he spoke into a cell phone.

Question: Would a hit man take his eyes off his target?

Answer: No.

Irritated with herself for overreacting, she climbed in behind the wheel of the Mini Cooper. Damn it, what had she been thinking? Tony DaCosta wasn't some scary underworld figure. Wise guys didn't wait tables at Spago.

"Can't imagine what's got into that nephew of mine." Wallace stared at the hearth in his study, as if he were searching for the answer to Magnus's enigmatic behavior in the dancing flames. "Not like him not to show up for a dinner party. Missed out on a damned fine venison roast."

"Did you ring his hotel?" Dominic asked.

"Twice," Wallace told him. "No answer."

"Perhaps another obligation took precedence."

"If so, surely he'd have let me know. Magnus has always had impeccable manners."

Wallace's concern seemed disproportionate, unless he knew something Dominic didn't. "What's really worrying you?"

"I don't like coincidences," Wallace said.

"Meaning?"

"Magnus and Grant both attended the medieval literature symposium. First Grant turns up dead. And now Magnus has gone missing."

"But Grant committed suicide. Surely you don't think . . . ?"

Wallace frowned. "I'm not sure what to think after reading the account of Grant's death. A drug overdose seems most unlikely to me. Now if he'd hung himself from the chandelier, that I might believe. But drugs? Good lord, the man didn't even take aspirin."

"You knew him?" Dominic asked in surprise.

"Not intimately, of course, but we did share an interest in salmon fishing. I used to run into him every year in Skye."

Dominic had spent a good portion of his day trying to get inside Grant's hotel room to retrieve the so-called Merlin manuscript. By the time he'd managed to finagle his way in, he'd found that the room had already been emptied of Grant's personal possessions. "Shipped to his next of kin, a sister in Aberdeen," the maid had told him. So tomorrow he was off to Aberdeen. At least that was the plan. He studied Wallace's furrowed brow. "Are you suggesting Grant was murdered?"

"It's a possibility, I suppose, and that's why Magnus's unexplained absence concerns me."

Dominic stood up. "Perhaps I should go check on him in person."

"At this time of night?" Wallace said in surprise.

"It's not that late, only a quarter past ten. Besides, if I don't go, you'll lie awake all night worrying."

"I can't help thinking he may be ill or injured," Wallace said.

Or dead. The unspoken possibility hung in the air between them like a noxious odor.

Caitlin was halfway back to Magnus's house when she noticed a blue SUV two cars back. The vehicle was too far away for her to ID the driver, but she was ninety percent sure it was an Explorer, and yes, there were probably dozens, maybe even hundreds of blue Explorers in Palo Alto, but . . .

She timed her approach to the next light so she went through on the yellow. The light turned red, halting the string of cars behind her, including the SUV.

She accelerated to widen her lead, turned left at the next intersection, then right. Five minutes of random zigzagging later, she congratulated herself on losing her tail—if indeed she'd had a tail in the first place. Though just to be safe, as soon as she got to Professorville, she'd call the police.

True, the man in the blue SUV hadn't actually done anything against the law. He hadn't threatened her. He hadn't spoken to her. As far as she could prove, he hadn't even looked at her. She wasn't even a hundred percent certain he'd been following her. But . . .

Magnus's turn-of-the-last-century detached carriage house turned garage wasn't equipped with an automatic garage door opener, so Caitlin pulled into the driveway, shifted her car into park, and climbed out. She'd barely taken two steps when someone grabbed her from behind, pinning her arms to her sides.

Startled, she let out a yelp.

"Quiet!" her captor warned.

"Let me go!" she yelled at the top of her lungs, hoping to attract the neighbors' attention.

Her attacker growled something under his breath and shifted one hand to cover her mouth.

Big mistake on his part. Caitlin captured the fleshy part of his palm between her teeth and bit down hard. At the same time, she kicked backward at his shin, hoping to knock him off balance. The kick had zero effect. Apparently the man's legs were made of concrete and steel. But the bite drew blood. With a muffled oath, her attacker snatched his hand away.

The second he did, she screamed like a banshee.

After trying to call Magnus Armstrong from the lobby and getting no answer, Dominic had resorted to trickery to get inside the suite. He'd loitered outside the door, waiting for a member of the housekeeping staff to wander by. After ten minutes or so, he caught sight of a maid loaded down with a stack of towels and went into his act. Pretending his Visa card was a key card, he repeatedly tried it in the slot, then swore softly when it didn't work. "Bloody key demagnetized itself again," he muttered just loud enough for the maid to hear.

"Trouble, sir?" she asked.

After listening to Dominic's charming prevarication about the impatient wife who was supposedly waiting downstairs for him to retrieve her wrap, the maid opened the door with her passkey.

He tipped her generously, then let himself into Magnus Armstrong's suite. "Anyone home?" He flicked on the lights.

The large, pleasantly furnished sitting room gave no indication that it had been the scene of a violent crime. If, as Wallace seemed to think, something had happened to his nephew, it hadn't happened here. The room was pristine from the knickknacks on the mantelpiece to the well-plumped cushions of the matching sofas that formed a right-angled seating group in front of the fireplace.

But then, the maid had discovered Erskine Grant in bed. . . .

Dominic strode toward the hallway that led, presumably, to the bedrooms.

Suddenly the room was plunged into darkness. Power failure, he thought for a split second, until someone—a very strong someone—tackled him from behind.

Had Magnus heard him enter and assumed he was a burglar?

But no, Dominic's attacker was taller than Magnus. Taller than Dominic, who at six feet two was far from a small man.

The skirmish didn't last long. Dominic hit the wood floor face first and was knocked silly for a few seconds, long enough for his attacker to flip him onto his back and wrap his hands around Dominic's throat.

Dominic ripped at the thick gloved fingers that were doing their best to choke the life out of him. When that had no effect, he twisted to the side, then rolled back quickly to knee the other man, hoping to catch him in a vulnerable area.

His attacker grunted and released him.

Dominic backed out of range, and moving silently, circled the larger man.

His attacker staggered to his feet, panting and cursing under his breath, curses that terminated in a gasp of surprise when Dominic grabbed him from behind. The man twisted like an eel. Dominic lost his purchase on the thick neck but managed to snag the chain that hung around the man's neck. He cinched down, doing his best to choke the bastard. He might have succeeded, too, if the chain hadn't broken.

When the links snapped, Dominic fell backward onto one of the sofas, the chain still clutched in his hand.

The giant drew a sawing breath. Then, before Dominic could right himself, the other man lurched to the door and wrenched it open.

Dominic caught a brief glimpse of the massive form silhouetted against the hall light in the seconds before the door swung shut. Petty thug Hector Yuli, last spotted at the Calixian consulate.

Navigating by touch, Dominic made his way back across the room. He hit the light switch, and only then did he realize what he'd ripped from Yuli's neck—a Calixian protection charm.

Only this wasn't your typical touristy gewgaw. No, this charm was solid silver. And in addition to the usual inscription, *Tutela*, or "Protection," this one had a second inscription on the back, *Fraternitas*. Such charms were reserved for members of a select organization of the same name. Only men descended from the twelfth-century Crusaders who'd built their castle fortress in the Aeternus Mountains were admitted to the brotherhood, which begged the question, how did a lowlife like Hector Yuli get his hands on one?

What the bloody hell was going on?

If, as Janus suspected, artifacts, including the Merlin manuscript, had been smuggled out of Calix and sold on the black market, then why had Dr. Grant been killed? What point was there in eliminating one's customers?

Moreover, why would Yuli have been searching Magnus Armstrong's suite? Because of his tenuous connection with Grant? Dominic frowned. It made no sense.

Caitlin kicked her attacker again. This time he uttered a gratifying grunt of pain, then swore in heavily accented but highly colloquial English.

She made herself go limp, as if she'd fainted. When the man shifted his grip to keep her from overbalancing him, she elbowed him in the gut and screamed again at the top of her lungs.

Her attacker uttered a muffled oath as Magnus's next-door neighbors, Björn and Inga Svensson, burst out their front door. "What's going on out here?" Björn shouted. "Leave her alone! Inga, call nine one one."

Inga disappeared into the house. Without waiting for backup, Björn advanced on her attacker.

The man thrust her aside and took off down the street. Caitlin slammed against the driver's side door hard enough to get the wind knocked out of her. It took her a few seconds to recover her equilibrium, and by then, her attacker was halfway down the block. She couldn't see his face, so she couldn't be certain it was the same man she'd seen at the gas station and then later at the university, but even at that distance she could tell he was tall, bulky, and dressed in black.

"Are you okay?" Björn sounded as shaky as she felt now that her adrenaline was wearing thin.

"Aside from being completely freaked out, you mean?"

He frowned. "Perhaps I should follow him."

"Let's wait for the police." Caitlin's legs felt a little wobbly. Studying self-defense in class was one thing. Applying it in a real-life situation was something else again.

"What did he want, this man?" Björn asked.

"I'm not sure."

"Did he demand money?"

"No," she said, "but then we didn't really have a conversation."

"Women being assaulting in broad daylight," Björn said. "What is this city coming to?"

Fifteen minutes after the cops left, Bree showed up with a stack of DVDs and a bag of banana chips, the Palo Alto version of junk food. "Jory stood me up," she announced. "Apparently his muse paid a visit this evening, and he couldn't bear to leave her. Want to join my pity party?" She frowned as she got her first good look at Caitlin's face. "What's wrong?"

"I had an . . . . adventurous afternoon." Caitlin led her back to the family room.

"Don't tell me Tony tracked you down." Bree dumped her stuff on the coffee table and took a seat on Magnus's big leather recliner.

"No." Curling up on one end of the sofa, Caitlin gave Bree a brief recap of the afternoon's events.

"Adventurous doesn't begin to describe it, Caitlin. Holy shit!" Bree reached across the coffee table to give her arm a squeeze. "You said the guy had an accent. What kind? East Coast? Jersey maybe?"

Caitlin shrugged. "I don't think so. I don't know. It happened so fast." She shot Bree a sharp look. "Why? You think he was a gangster, someone Tony hired?"

"I know it seems far-fetched. Palo Alto? Organized crime? Who else but Tony could have hired the guy, though? Who else had a motive? Unless, of course," she added, "the attack was random."

Caitlin rolled her eyes. "The guy followed me all over town. The really scary part is, he must have known I was staying here, because when I pulled in, he was waiting for me."

"But how *could* he have known?" Bree said. "You haven't told anyone, have you, aside from me?"

"No one here in town," Caitlin said slowly.

"You told someone out of town?"

"Only Magnus," she said. "It is his house, after all."

"So you finally got hold of him?"

"Not exactly," Caitlin admitted. "He never did answer my e-mails, so I left messages for him all over Edinburgh—at his hotel, at the symposium, even at his Uncle Wallace's."

"You spoke to the uncle?"

"No, the only one home was the butler."

"Magnus's uncle has a butler?" Bree's big brown eyes went round in surprise.

"An English butler, no less. Very stiff and formal."

Bree's mouth curved in a smile. "If this were a mystery novel, I'd say the butler did it. Told the bad guy where to find you, I mean."

"Chalmers may be a pompous old fossil," Caitlin said,

"but I doubt he's in league with the devil. He's been with Wallace for half a century. No, there must be another explanation."

"Someone at the symposium?" Bree suggested.

"I doubt it." Caitlin scoured her memory. She hadn't mentioned her temporary change in living arrangements to anyone else, had she? No, she was positive she hadn't. But . . . "I got a call late last night," she said slowly. "Whoever it was didn't say anything, but I could hear him breathing. I assumed at the time it was either a crank call or a wrong number, but what if it wasn't? What if it was someone trying to track me down? Once the caller heard my voice, he'd know where I was staying. Damn it, it has to be Tony."

"Whoever it is," Bree said, "it's not safe for you to stay here anymore."

Not safe. *Not safe.* Caitlin's thoughts spun in circles. Not. Safe.

She jumped when Bree touched her shoulder. "Should I get that?" Bree asked.

"What?" she said, then, "Oh." The phone was ringing and apparently had been for some time because the answering machine—set to pick up after six rings—clicked on.

"Hullo? Ms. O'Shaughnessy?" Caitlin didn't recognize the caller's voice, a rich baritone with an upper class English accent. "This is Dominic Fortune. Though we've not met, we're connections of a sort. Your stepfather's Uncle Wallace married my mother's Aunt Mary." He laughed. "Clear as mud, eh? At any rate, I need to speak with you. It concerns Magnus and is a matter of some urgency."

Caitlin snatched the receiver. "Don't hang up. I'm here. What about Magnus? Is he all right?"

"Ms. O'Shaughnessy?"

"Yes. Tell me what's so urgent. Has something happened to Magnus?"

"I'm not quite sure. Your stepfather was supposed to dine at Firth House this evening."

"Supposed to?"

"He never showed up. Wallace was a bit concerned. He says it's not like Magnus to ignore a social obligation."

"Magnus is polite to a fault," Caitlin said. "If he'd been held up somewhere, he'd have called to let his uncle know. Did you check his hotel?"

"I rang several times. He didn't answer."

"He didn't answer when I called, either," she said. "And he hasn't e-mailed me since Monday."

"Wallace was worried, so I drove to Magnus's hotel, hoping to track him down."

"He wasn't there," she guessed.

"No," he agreed, "but someone else was." He described his encounter. "I searched the suite thoroughly before I left," he added, "but since I don't know what was there to start with, I have no way of knowing if anything was missing."

Besides Magnus. "Do you know if my stepfather attended the symposium today?"

"No, but I can ask, if you'd like."

"Thank you, but that won't be necessary. I'll handle it."

"Are there any other inquiries I might make on your behalf?"

"No," she said, "though I appreciate the offer." Her hands were shaking, but her voice was steady as she thanked him again and hung up.

"What was that all about?" Bree asked.

Caitlin gave her a quick recap of the conversation.

"So Magnus is missing and no one knows where he is."

"Someone knows," Caitlin said.

Bree shot her a startled look. "Who?"

"Whoever kidnapped him."

"Aren't you leaping to conclusions?"

"No, I don't think so. It's the only scenario that makes sense. I haven't heard from Magnus since Monday. If he were dead, his body would have turned up by now. And if he'd gone off of his own volition, he'd have long since contacted me."

"So what are you going to do?" Bree asked.

"Contact the Scottish authorities and report his disappearance, for starters."

"And after that?"

"I'll be on the next flight to Edinburgh."

"Not without me," Bree said.

"I don't need a chaperone."

"No, but how about a friend? All things considered," Bree said, "it's the least I can do."

"Not necessary." Caitlin knew why Bree was being so insistent. She still felt guilty about what happened at Berkeley years ago. But damn it . . . "How many times do I have to tell you it wasn't your fault? Besides, the two situations are hardly analogous."

"I'm going," Bree said. "Deal with it."

October 1617
Stirlingshire, Scotland

Sheer physical discomfort prodded Hamish back to consciousness. He opened his eyes to find himself sprawled across the muddy riverside path, wet through from the mist and chilled to the bone. He shivered. What in God's name was he doing here?

And then he remembered. The poachers. The knife. The blood.

He felt his throat, and his hand came away sticky with gore. But he'd swear the skin was unbroken. No gaping gash. No wound at all.

He shoved himself up on his elbows. The poachers were long gone and the stag with them. He might, in fact, have thought he'd imagined the entire incident were it not for the pile of deer entrails still steaming in the cold October air.

But if he hadn't imagined the poachers, then chances were he hadn't imagined the attack, either—the knife slicing into his neck, the blood gushing from his body in a crimson flood. And how was he to reconcile that reality with his present undamaged, if somewhat uncomfortable, condition? How could a man suffer such a wound, a mortal wound, and yet draw breath?

Vita aeterna.

The words seemed to echo in the stillness of the cocooning fog, and he shivered again.

4

"CAITLIN O'SHAUGHNESSY IS SCHEDULED to arrive in Edinburgh at eleven-oh-six a.m. after a short layover at Heathrow," Janus said.

"Fascinating." Pressing the satellite phone to his ear, Dominic pried his eyelids open far enough to glance at the alarm clock on his bedside table. Bloody hell. A quarter to six? Janus had called him at a quarter to six? He'd been in bed less than four hours. "And exactly how did you come by that bit of information?"

"I have contacts, Fortune. She made hotel reservations, then canceled, saying she planned to stay with relatives."

"But the only relative she has in Edinburgh is—"

"Wallace Armstrong. Precisely. Volunteer to pick her up at the airport."

"Why?"

"I want you to get close to Caitlin O'Shaughnessy."

"When you say 'get close' . . ."

"The young woman may be in danger," Janus said.

"So that was 'close' as in bodyguard close?"

"And she may know something."

"Ah. 'Close' as in spy-on-her close."

"This is hardly a joking matter, Fortune."

"That was hardly a joke. More like mild impudence."

Janus grunted. "Any luck locating her stepfather?"

"None. He's still registered at his hotel, but no one's seen him in days." Dominic stifled a yawn. "Not at the hotel and not at the symposium. He was a no-show for his scheduled lecture yesterday."

"What do you think? Is he working with our smugglers? Against them? Is he an innocent bystander? Or is he perhaps not involved at all? Is his disappearance merely a coincidence?"

"I don't know. My guess—and I emphasize that word—is that he's an innocent who got caught up in events beyond his control," Dominic said slowly. "I spoke with a waiter who saw Armstrong with Grant."

"When?"

"Monday night."

"And Grant's body turned up . . . ?"

"Wednesday, though by the time the maid found his body, he'd been dead for approximately eighteen hours. Apparently he ingested a lethal combination of sleeping pills and whisky. Officially, the police are calling it a drug overdose, but the tabloid press—and many members of the academic community—are talking suicide."

"He left no note?"

"No note and no manuscript," Dominic said. "I don't

think his death was an accident. Nor do I buy into the suicide theory."

"You suspect he was murdered."

"How else do you explain the missing manuscript?"

"But murdered by whom? Our smugglers have no motive."

"No apparent motive."

Janus didn't respond immediately. "Have you considered the possibility that Magnus Armstrong may have killed Erskine Grant?"

"It occurred to me, yes."

"Perhaps the reason no one's seen him is that he's gone into hiding."

"Perhaps," Dominic said.

"You don't sound convinced."

"If I'd just arranged a colleague's 'suicide,' the last thing I'd do is run. His disappearance is suspicious in itself. I don't think the man's that stupid."

"Nor do I," Janus admitted. "I agree. It seems likely someone's kidnapped him. Why? We don't know. What we do know is that there's a probable Calixian connection."

"You're referring to the protection charm I ripped off the thug who attacked me in Magnus's hotel suite. Funny thing about that charm. Did I tell you it was a Fraternitas?"

Janus didn't say anything for a second or two. "Interesting. I'd heard rumors they were . . . extending their membership. Apparently those rumors were true."

"Extending their membership?"

"And their focus."

"Meaning?"

"An informant—a somewhat unreliable informant, admittedly—reported months ago that an outlaw branch of Fraternitas has turned to smuggling." Janus gave him a moment to absorb this new information. "If Yuli was searching Armstrong's suite, it suggests Armstrong has something Fraternitas wants."

"The manuscript?" Dominic said.

"That would be my guess."

"But why? The *Chronicles* have been around since the seventeenth century. Why the sudden interest?"

"Every schoolchild on Calix knows the legend of Brother Hamish, the monkish recluse of the Aeternus Mountains, but how many people have read the actual manuscripts? None. They've been under lock and key for literally hundreds of years. Perhaps they hold the secret—"

"To what? Eternal life?"

"To something of value," Janus finished, unruffled by Dominic's sarcasm.

"Such as?"

"Hidden treasure, perhaps. Didn't Brother Hamish claim he'd seen a ship full of Roman gold lying at the bottom of the sea?"

"It's a legend, Janus. Granted, some people take it literally. Adventurers have been searching for the wreck for hundreds of years. But if the gold truly existed, don't you think someone would have found it by now?"

Janus considered that. "We may never know why the thieves want the manuscript back," he said at last. "Suffice it to say they do want it and badly. Your assignment is threefold. One, find Magnus Armstrong. Two, recover the manuscript. And three, identify whoever's plundering the treasures of Calix."

"Got it. Find Magnus Armstrong, recover the manuscript, and identify whoever's plundering the treasures of Calix. Plus, get close to Ms. O'Shaughnessy, and perhaps while I'm at it, leap a few tall buildings in a single bound."

Silence stretched the length of three heartbeats. "This is a serious matter of national security, Fortune. Your levity is misplaced. I could sack you on the spot for insubordination."

"You could, but you won't. I'm the most daring and resourceful agent you have."

"Daring and resourceful, yes. Also smug and disrespectful."

"Too true, Janus, but then again I'm charming as hell. Ms. O'Shaughnessy doesn't stand a chance."

Though Caitlin and Bree would be stuck at opposite ends of the plane on the short hop from Heathrow to Edinburgh, they'd been lucky enough to secure adjoining seats in first class for the long flight to London.

Unlike Caitlin, who was too wired to do anything but fret, Bree had slept for the first half of the trip and was now engrossed in the in-flight movie, a quirky action-adventure film featuring George Clooney and some blonde Caitlin didn't recognize.

Caitlin had tried to watch the film, and she might have

succeeded in distracting herself if the star had been anyone but Clooney, whose dark eyes and stubborn jaw reminded her of a younger version of her stepfather.

Frustrated, she dug around in her backpack for the thriller she'd purchased at the airport. Instead her fingers latched onto the manuscript she'd slipped into her bag at the last minute, hoping against all reason that it might yet provide a clue to Magnus's disappearance.

Starting at the beginning, she began to read.

A few minutes later, she let out a muffled whoop and grabbed Bree's arm.

Her friend stared at her as if she'd lost her mind. "What is it?"

"Oh, my God! Oh, my God. Oh, my God. Oh. My. God!"

Bree removed her headset. "What?" she repeated.

"The manuscript Magnus sent me."

"What about it?"

"I think I know now why he included it with my bones. It mentions John Napier."

Bree gave her a blank stare.

"John Napier, the mathematician I wrote about for my dissertation. Hamish MacNeill, the author of the manuscript, actually knew Napier. My God, if only I could have gotten my hands on this before I wrote my dissertation. I mean, to read a firsthand account by someone who was well acquainted with the man . . ."

"Quite a coincidence," Bree murmured, readjusting her headset.

"An amazing coincidence," Caitlin said. "See?" She shoved the pages under Bree's nose. "Right there. See?"

Frowning, Bree removed her headset a second time. "See what? Is this supposed to be English?"

"Takes a while to get used to the spelling, and some of the vocabulary's obsolete, but yes, it's English. Check out this page. Hamish mentions Napier, bemoaning the fact that his friend and mentor is dead."

" 'Called out of this transitorie lyfe.' In other words, deceased. I get that. But where does it say John Napier?"

"Right there." Caitlin pointed.

"You weren't kidding about the spelling. Jhone Neper? That's the bones guy, right?"

"Right, though Napier's logarithm tables were his greatest claim to fame. Without logarithms, there'd have been no slide rule. Without slide rules, there'd have been no space program. Napier's logarithms might not have been as life-altering as the discovery of fire or the invention of the wheel, but on a scale of one to ten, they score a solid eight and a half."

"Uh-huh." Bree glanced at the actors on the miniature screen.

"What I've always found most intriguing about Napier, though, are the rumors that he dabbled in sorcery. I mean, talk about contradictions. Here's this brilliant mathematician and inventor—did I tell you about his designs for war machines?—not to mention a theologian of some repute. And yet he's suspected of being in league with the devil."

"Fascinating," Bree said, *fascinating* in this case clearly code for "Hint, hint. You're boring my socks off."

Caitlin shot her an apologetic grin. "Not as fascinating as George Clooney, though, huh?"

"Not even close."

Dominic didn't even try to go back to sleep after his early morning wake-up call. Instead he hit the shower, then dressed quickly and clattered down the back stairs from his third-floor suite to the morning room that overlooked the back garden.

Wallace, his right foot propped up on a stool, was working his way through a plate of bacon and eggs. He glanced up with a look of surprise at Dominic's entrance. "Good heavens, why are you up and about so early?"

Dominic mumbled something noncommittal as he helped himself from the dishes on the sideboard. He nodded at Wallace's foot. "Gout acting up?"

"Yes. Damned foot's giving me fits again. Doctor says it's my diet that causes the flare-ups, but I swear it's this damp weather." He frowned. "Couldn't have happened at a worse time, either, what with Magnus's girl flying in."

Avoiding the gouty foot, Dominic took a seat on Wallace's left. "She's coming to Edinburgh? Why? Does she honestly think she can trace her stepfather more efficiently than the authorities?"

"She's worried." Wallace frowned. "Can't fault her for that. I'm worried myself. Caitlin and her friend arrive later this morning."

"Friend as in friend? Or friend as in lover?"

Wallace looked nonplussed for a moment. "The

friend's female. I suppose young Caitlin might be a lesbian. Can't say I gave the possibility much thought. I'd assumed this Bree Thatcher was just a girlfriend. Not that it matters." He sighed, as if he found modern mores too taxing to contemplate over breakfast. "At any rate, I've invited them to stay here at Firth House. God knows I've plenty of room. Besides, it'll give Chalmers something to do. Let him earn his keep for once. Cook's ecstatic, of course. The woman likes nothing better than feeding a crowd."

"Two extra women is hardly a crowd," Dominic pointed out.

"Oh, but I've arranged a dinner party."

And a séance, no doubt.

"I'd planned to meet their flight, but with this foot . . ." He sighed in exasperation. "Chalmers will just have to go in my stead."

"I'm sure he has enough to do. Why don't I collect them for you, shall I?"

Wallace's face lit up. "I was hoping you'd offer."

Dominic had been cooling his heels for the last forty minutes, waiting for the flight from London. Delayed by fog, according to the airline representative he'd spoken to. But his wait was nearly over; the plane had hit the tarmac ten minutes ago.

The big challenge now was picking Caitlin O'Shaughnessy and her friend out of the crowd. The only picture Wallace had been able to find was of twelve-year-old Caitlin posing in her softball uniform, face shadowed by the brim of her cap, brown hair confined in an untidy plait. Even if Dominic had been able to see her features clearly, the photo probably wouldn't have been much help since she'd no doubt changed a good bit in the intervening years. He couldn't even count on the brown hair, given current trends in creative hair coloring. He might be looking for a blonde, a redhead, or even a blue.

As for the friend, all Wallace knew about Bree Thatcher was that she owned an art gallery and did some painting herself. "A bohemian type, I expect," he'd said. "Draped in scarves and tatty jewelry."

Travelers had been straggling into the terminal for the past few minutes, but so far no one had fit the bill.

Dominic yawned. Damn Janus anyway.

Just then a slender young woman in low-slung jeans and a snug pink sweater sauntered past, backpack slung over one shoulder. *Caitlin?* Dominic wondered, comparing the fashionable young beauty to the faded photograph of the preteen softball player. The hair was the same color, a deep chocolate brown. But if this was Caitlin—*oh, please, God, let this be Caitlin*—where was her friend?

He realized then that the young woman wasn't alone. Accompanying her was a middle-aged couple with graying hair. *Her parents?* he wondered, searching in vain for some family resemblance. In contrast to the frumpy, faded pair, the girl's skin was pale, her bone structure delicate but distinctive. The thick dark hair fell past her shoulders in a silky shimmer. Even at this distance, it was obvious she was a looker.

The trio paused in the middle of the broad corridor. The girl glanced back, as if searching for someone, then leaned toward the couple, smiling at something the woman said. She murmured a few words, then gestured toward the public facilities. The woman nodded, shook the girl's hand—therefore, probably not the girl's parent—and hustled off. The man, burdened by assorted carry-on luggage, followed more slowly.

The young woman stood still, an island of youthful perfection in a crowd of harried businessmen and rumpled, travel-worn tourists, most with the shell-shocked look of people who'd crossed too many time zones in too few hours. Once again she glanced back toward the gate, as if searching for a familiar face.

"Caitlin!"

He jerked his head around to see who'd spoken. A chic brunette gamine with big dark eyes waved an arm above the sea of humanity and shouted again. "Caitlin! Over here!" This was Bree Thatcher, Wallace's "bohemian type"?

"Bree!" someone called, and he turned to see the young woman in the pink sweater—yes, there was a God!—waving back at the brunette.

Suddenly a nondescript man surged through the crowd, coming up fast behind Caitlin.

"Hey!" Dominic shouted a warning just as the man sideswiped her. She fell to one knee, and the man grabbed her backpack.

Dominic leapt to his feet to go to her rescue, a good Samaritan impulse wasted on Ms. O'Shaughnessy, who launched herself at the thief in a flying tackle. The man went down hard but recovered quickly, kicking free and scrambling to his feet.

"Stop! Thief!" Caitlin shoved herself upright and took off in pursuit.

People stared, but few seemed to grasp what was going on. The security people at the checkpoint, some distance away, glanced up to see what all the shouting was about, but no one moved to intercept the thief.

"Stop him! He's got my bag!" Caitlin yelled.

Never let it be said the days of chivalry were over.

Dominic stuck out a foot as the man ran past. The thief tripped and went sprawling again. Dominic hooked the strap of the stolen backpack with the handle of his umbrella and flipped it out of the man's reach just as Caitlin O'Shaughnessy pounded to a halt.

Dominic stood. "Missing something?"

"Oh, thank you. Thank you!" She smiled up at him, and his heart stopped beating for a solid five count.

Belatedly, he realized his mouth was hanging open—a bloody miracle he wasn't drooling—and shut it. But damned if the woman didn't have the most gorgeous eyes he'd ever seen, a clear blue-green, the exact color of the water in the shallow coves along Calix's northern coast-line. And if that weren't distraction enough, factor in a smile that was two parts sweetness to one part mischief.

Taking advantage of Dominic's preoccupation, the thief cut his losses and took off. Dominic let him go.

He lifted the backpack off the end of his umbrella and presented it to her with a flourish. "Yours, I believe."

She slid the strap over her shoulder. "And again, thank you."

"My pleasure." He wished he could think of something more original to say, something that would coax another smile from her.

"No, I mean it. If you hadn't intervened . . . You're a prince," she said and smiled again.

Struck speechless, all he could do was stare.

Bree Thatcher came rushing up and broke the awkward silence. "Are you all right?" she asked her friend.

"Fine," Caitlin said. "And still in possession of my backpack, thanks to this gentleman."

"Dominic Fortune," he told Bree. "At your service."

"Wallace Armstrong's nephew?"

"Great-nephew," he said. "By marriage."

"But what a remarkable coincidence! I'm—"

"Bree Thatcher and"—he smiled at Caitlin—"this is your friend, Caitlin O'Shaughnessy. Frankly, coincidence had nothing to do with it. Wallace sent me. I'm to drive you to Firth House."

A faint furrow appeared between Caitlin's eyebrows. "You recognized us? How?"

"Recognized? No." He showed her the softball picture. "Not from this. I didn't realize who you were until I heard your friend call your name."

"Just before that jerk grabbed my backpack." Her frown deepened. "So maybe he targeted me on purpose."

Bree shot her a sharp look.

"But why?" Dominic asked. "Are you carrying large sums of cash?"

"No." Caitlin frowned.

"Any news of Caitlin's stepfather?" Bree asked.

"None. Wallace spoke to the officer in charge of the case. The authorities are treating his disappearance as a missing person's case, but Wallace got the distinct impression that Inspector Logan thought Magnus had gone off of his own accord, caught up in the throes of a midlife crisis."

"That's bullshit," Caitlin said.

Dominic nodded. "Precisely what Wallace told the man."

Brother Ambrose raised the heavy trapdoor and shone his flashlight into the hole. Air, rank with sweat and human waste, rose in a fetid cloud. Twenty feet below, Magnus Armstrong blinked, accustoming his eyes to the light. He looked more like a homeless transient than a respected English professor. He was unwashed and unkempt; his clothes were stained and filthy. Scruffy salt-and-pepper whiskers covered the lower half of his face, though they couldn't hide the bruise discoloring his left cheekbone or the swelling of his lower lip. But if Magnus's shirt had lost its starch, his backbone hadn't.

"What the bloody hell do you want?" he demanded.

Brother Ambrose regarded the man with reluctant admiration. He was made of much sterner stuff than Erskine Grant, who'd folded completely at the first threat of pain. After four days, all Magnus had given them was a lesson in the inventive use of epithets.

"Ready to talk?"

The flashlight caught the feral gleam of Magnus's eyes. "I've nothing to say." His voice sounded flat, more bored than frightened.

Brother Ambrose stared at him. His silence would have unnerved most men. Not Magnus Armstrong, whose gaze never wavered.

"So," Brother Ambrose said at length, "where is the manuscript?"

"I don't know what you're talking about."

"I grow weary of your lies. Grant gave you the manuscript for safekeeping. He told us as much."

"The so-called Merlin manuscript, you mean? The one that caused such a stir at the medieval literature symposium?"

"Yes, that manuscript."

Magnus laughed. "But it was an obvious fake."

"Dr. Grant didn't think so."

"Erskine Grant is an old fool."

"*Was* an old fool," Brother Ambrose said.

Magnus's face stilled. "Meaning?"

"He overdosed on sleeping pills. The police are treating it as an accident, but I'm told the academic community believes it was suicide."

"You murdered him?"

"We prefer to think of it as a mercy killing. His career had just gone up in flames. What did he have to live for?"

"You coldhearted bastard."

"We had our reasons." He paused. "It's been almost four days now since you've had anything to eat. Would you like a piece of bread, Magnus?"

"In exchange for what?"

"All you have to do is tell me what you did with the manuscript. Was it in the package you sent to your stepdaughter?"

"No, of course not. All I sent her was a birthday gift."

"Really? Did you know she's in Edinburgh, trying to figure out what happened to you?"

Magnus made a strangled noise.

"Don't worry," Brother Ambrose said. "The brothers are keeping an eye on her."

"If you or your *brothers* lay one finger on Caitlin, I swear I'll—"

"What? Tear me limb from limb?" Brother Ambrose sighed. "Tell me, Magnus, does she have the manuscript with her, or did she fly to Edinburgh to collect it?"

"Are you insane? I would never involve her in anything as dangerous as this!"

Brother Ambrose studied Magnus's face for a long moment, then gave a slight shrug. "You almost convinced me. But then I realized you didn't know at the outset how dangerous this business was. So no more nonsense about the girl not being involved. I have your laptop; I've read her e-mails."

"Even if you had the Merlin manuscript, it would do you no good. Don't you get it? Poor old Grant was off his nut. There's no such thing as immortality."

"Don't be so quick to dismiss that which you don't understand. 'There are more things in Heaven and earth, Horatio, than are dreamt of in your philosophy.' A clever man, Shakespeare."

"A clever writer, certainly. But that line you quoted is from *Hamlet.* A play, not a history book."

"The world is a fine, mysterious place full of inexplicable wonders." He paused. "Where's the manuscript?"

"As I have reiterated ad nauseam, I do not know what you are talking about."

"Brother Hector checked the safe. He checked the entire suite. The manuscript wasn't there."

"Because I never had it in the first place."

Brother Ambrose sighed again. "This is getting us nowhere. We'll talk again tomorrow."

"No, wait!" Magnus said.

"Tomorrow," Brother Ambrose repeated, then slammed the trapdoor shut and wedged the bolt across it.

Caitlin lay atop the peach satin bedspread in her room at Firth House. Bree was napping in the next room, but Caitlin couldn't sleep. She mentally reviewed the strange events of the past few days, searching for a common denominator. Strange Event Number One: Magnus, Mr. Reliable, had apparently dropped off the face of the earth. Strange Event Number Two: She was followed all over Palo Alto and then attacked in the driveway of Magnus's Professorville home. Strange Event Number Three: A man tried to swipe her backpack at the airport. There had to be a connection, but damned if she could see it.

Caitlin had been scowling in frustration at the ornate plaster ceiling for several minutes when someone knocked softly on the door.

She rose up on her elbows. "Yes? Who is it?"

"Dominic Fortune. May I speak with you for a moment?"

Caitlin slid off the bed, crossed to the door, and opened it. "Yes?"

She hadn't realized how tall he was, how big and broad and unequivocally male with wicked, laughing eyes and a stubborn jaw, shadowed now with beard stubble. Damn it to hell, she should have taken the time to pull on her boots. She missed the three-inch advantage those heels gave her. Instead, here she stood in her bare feet, feeling small and vulnerable.

A smile teased the corners of his mouth as he gave her a slow once-over. "Perfect match," he said.

"I beg your pardon?" Her voice held a chill, even though her heart was thumping an erratic rhythm.

The smile widened, as if he knew damn well what was going on behind her cool exterior. "Your sweater and your toenail polish," he said. "They're the exact same shade of pink. May I come in?"

"That depends."

He laughed softly. "Relax. I rarely seduce women I've just met and never under my great-uncle's roof."

That was either reassuring or a damned shame. Caitlin wasn't sure which. Who said blue eyes were cold?

Without a word, she moved out of the doorway, and he stepped inside, brushing past without actually touching her with anything but his gaze. Still, a warm, prickly sensation skated across her skin, and her heart beat a little faster. Okay, a lot faster. Two words formed in the chaos of her mind: *holy shit.*

Caitlin pulled her gaze away from Dominic Fortune's

electric blue eyes with an effort. She hadn't flown all this way to play games, damn it, no matter how interesting those games promised to be. "You wanted to talk to me?"

He leaned against the heavy mahogany chiffonier. "Do you know anything about Calix?"

Calix? Where the hell had that come from? She whipped her gaze back to his. "It's an island in the Mediterranean, right? PBS did a special a few years back. European vacation destinations off the beaten track."

"That's Calix in a nutshell," he said. "Has your stepfather ever mentioned it?"

She searched her memory and came up empty. "Never. Why do you ask?"

"Because of this." He handed her a silver pendant with a broken chain. "I ripped it off the man I surprised in Magnus's suite."

Caitlin held the pendant to the light and examined it closely. Roughly an inch wide, an inch and a half long, and shaped like a flattened teardrop, it was engraved with a head, a man's head with two faces, and below that a Latin inscription. "Is that supposed to be Janus?"

"Yes," Dominic said. "Roman god of gateways and, coincidentally, symbol of the island. What you're holding is a Calixian protection charm."

"Protection charm? Didn't work too well for the burglar, did it?" Caitlin stroked the engraved lettering. *Tutela.* Latin for "protection." "Or maybe it's not all-purpose. What specifically do Calixians need protection from?"

His face went still, and for a split second, the expression in his eyes was bleak, almost stricken. Then he smiled again, a gorgeous, sexy smile that put all her nerve endings on red alert, and she decided she must have imagined that momentary distress. "The charm is supposed to protect the wearer from harm," he said. "A bit like a Saint Christopher's medal."

"And you know this because . . . ?"

"I grew up on Calix. My father still lives there."

"Are they rare?"

"The charms? Not particularly, no. Calixian metalsmiths have been producing them for three hundred years, give or take a decade."

"Three hundred years," Caitlin repeated in awe. "Longer than my country's been in existence."

"I didn't mean to imply this particular charm is that old," Dominic said hastily, "just that the design's been around that long. Nowadays, it's not just the natives who wear them. They've become a popular souvenir for tourists."

"So the man you surprised in Magnus's suite wasn't necessarily Calixian."

"If all we had to go on was the charm, I'd agree, but I saw the man's face, recognized him. And he was definitely Calixian, a petty thug named Hector Yuli."

"You've told the police this?"

"Yes," he said, "though I doubt they'll find him. I imagine Yuli's long gone."

"How about the man who tried to steal my backpack? Was he Calixian, too?"

Dominic shrugged. "I didn't recognize him, but then I don't know every person on the island."

"You suspect he may have been, though."

"Yes. Quite aside from Yuli and the charm, there are other indicators that point to Calixian involvement."

"Such as?"

"It's complicated," Dominic said. "Why don't I explain over lunch?" He extended a hand in invitation.

She stared at that hand, large and tanned. *If I touch him, I'm toast.* But damn it, she'd always liked playing with fire. "Just let me pull on my boots," she said. Maybe those three-inch heels would keep her grounded. Or then again, maybe they'd just put her mouth three inches closer to the danger zone.

October 1617
Drymen, Scotland

Hamish waited until his mother was busy with her guests, the Mistresses Logan, two talkative elderly ladies from Killearn, before slipping in the back door and up the back stairs to his bedchamber.

In the privacy of his room, he stripped to the skin and washed the bloodstains from his body, then examined himself in a handheld glass. As he'd suspected, the skin of his throat stretched smooth and unblemished. But how? *How?*

He should be dead. No one could survive such loss of blood, and yet he had. No wound. Not even a scar. "What manner of witchcraft is this?" he whispered.

Unless . . . oh, God . . . unless, he'd dreamed it all.

His tortured gaze fell on the pile of discarded garments, stiff with dried blood. He obviously hadn't dreamed the blood, but perhaps it was deer blood. Of course, the stag.

Vita aeterna.

He spun around, but no one was there. Again he heard it, that faint disembodied voice: *Vita aeterna.*

"No," he said.

The flames mocked him with a sibilant hiss and crackle. Hell's laughter. And he the butt of the joke.

His dagger lay on the washstand where he'd tossed it earlier. He grasped the hilt, a line from Shakespeare's *The Merchant of Venice* echoing in his head: "If you prick us, do we not bleed?"

5

AT A SMALL FAMILY-RUN RESTAURANT just off the Royal Mile, Dominic watched Caitlin O'Shaughnessy dive into her lamb stew with the gusto of a woman who'd eaten nothing but airline food for the past twenty-four hours.

"I didn't think I was hungry," she said when she came up for air. "I was wrong."

"More bread?" He nudged the basket closer.

"Yes, please." She chose another roll, buttered it lavishly, and took a bite. "Delicious."

There was something very earthy and sensuous, Dominic decided, about a woman who ate with such obvious enjoyment. He thought of Janet and her picky appetite, her mincing little bites, her constant worry about calories and carbs. What a contrast, and how ironic that Caitlin, who sat across from him devouring everything in sight, was a good inch taller and twenty pounds lighter than Janet-of-the-Eternal-Diet.

"You promised to tell me about the other indicators

pointing to Calixian involvement in Magnus's disappearance," Caitlin reminded him.

"So I did." He took a sip of tea. "I've nothing that would stand up in court, you understand, nothing to take to the authorities, merely suspicions, but . . ." He paused. "Did Magnus mention Erskine Grant's presentation at the symposium?"

A faint frown wrinkled her brow. "No, but I know that name. Isn't he the one who wrote *Malory's Arthur: Separating Fact from Fiction?*"

"I wouldn't know," Dominic said. "Literature—medieval or otherwise—was not my principal area of study while I was at university."

"Really? What was?"

"Music," he said. "Specifically, British drinking songs."

"Spent a lot of time in pubs, did you?" She shot him an appraising look.

"Yes, I was thoroughly devoted to my studies." So much so, he'd damned near been sent down his first year, probably would have been if Quin Gilroy hadn't knocked some sense into him, forced him to face a few home truths.

"You were going to share some information about Erskine Grant," she reminded him.

"On Monday Grant shocked those attending the symposium by claiming he'd acquired a manuscript written by Merlin."

Caitlin's eyes grew round. "Merlin, the magician?"

"Yes, only it seems the manuscript only dated back to the early part of the seventeenth century, hundreds of years after King Arthur's time."

"A manuscript dating from the seventeenth century?" Caitlin said, a bemused look on her face. "So it was an obvious hoax."

"Obvious to everyone but Grant," Dominic said. "He maintained that the time discrepancy only proved a theory he'd entertained for years, that Merlin was immortal."

Caitlin raised her eyebrows. "But that's absurd, not to mention illogical."

"Quite," Dominic said. "Apparently the attendees laughed Grant off the podium. The tabloids had a field day, too. Reporters hounded the poor man, followed him everywhere."

"And this was when? Monday?"

"Yes. According to the newspaper accounts, Grant arrived at his hotel quite late that night, told the desk clerk he planned to sleep in and didn't wish to be disturbed. Wednesday, when the maid finally went in to change the linens, she found him dead."

"Dead?" Caitlin said.

"Either late Monday or early Tuesday he consumed a lethal cocktail of sleeping pills and whisky."

She made a small sound of distress. "The ridicule must have pushed him over the edge. How tragic!"

Perhaps, he thought, more tragic than she realized.

Caitlin studied his face. "You don't think it was suicide, do you? You think he was murdered."

This woman saw entirely too much.

"I didn't say I thought he'd been murdered. Certainly the police seem satisfied with their findings."

"But you're not."

How much could he tell her without breaching security? Just enough to gain her confidence. "The missing manuscript concerns me."

She blinked, as if he'd startled her. Did she have some insight she wasn't sharing?

"No one seems to know what happened to Grant's Merlin manuscript."

Caitlin said nothing for a moment, just stared fixedly at the remains of her meal. "This manuscript," she said finally. "You say it was written in the early sixteen hundreds?"

"Yes."

"By someone claiming to be Merlin."

"So Grant said, but—"

She met his gaze then, and the fear in her eyes brought all his protective instincts rushing to the fore. "Do you think whoever broke into Magnus's room was looking for the manuscript? Is Magnus dead, too?"

"I don't think so," he said slowly, "though his disappearance is worrisome. Were he and Grant friends? Might Grant have given the manuscript to Magnus for safekeeping?"

Caitlin didn't say anything, just gazed across the table with a troubled expression on her lovely face.

"If so, Magnus may have feared for his own life once Grant turned up dead. Magnus may have gone into hiding."

"No," she said flatly. "If he were frightened, he'd have gone straight to the authorities, and he would definitely have contacted me. No, if he's alive, then someone's abducted him."

She was telling the truth. He was sure of it. But she hadn't told him all she knew. He was sure of that, too. "What do you know that I don't know? Have you received a ransom demand? Is that why you flew to Scotland so precipitously?"

"No." She shook her head. "No ransom demand. No contact at all. At least I don't think so."

"Meaning?"

"Someone called me a couple of days ago, woke me from a sound sleep."

"And?"

"And nothing. He didn't say a word, but . . ."

"You suspect there's a link between the call and your stepfather's disappearance."

"The next day a man attacked me in the driveway of Magnus's house."

"So you think—"

"I don't know what I think." She paused, staring hard at the tablecloth for a moment before shifting that hard stare to his face. "What's the connection?" she demanded.

"I beg your pardon."

"You talked earlier of a Calixian connection. What is it?"

"The manuscript," he said. "I believe it's the first book of the *Calix Chronicles,* a heroic historical saga. The manuscript recently disappeared from the palace library and is believed to have been smuggled out of the country."

Her eyebrows rose. "By Professor Grant?"

He laughed. "No, I can't see him as a master criminal. I daresay he bought the manuscript, quite unaware that it was stolen property."

"But if he wasn't a thief, why was he murdered? Surely you don't suspect the Calixian authorities executed him!"

"Calix is hardly a police state," he said drily. "No, my best guess is, the thieves want the manuscript back."

"But why?"

He shrugged. "I've no idea."

"I wonder where Grant found it in the first place? An auction? A used book store? A private dealer?"

"Where does one purchase stolen merchandise?" Dominic said.

"On eBay?" Caitlin suggested, and he laughed.

"Somehow I can't imagine the good professor shopping online."

"I suppose not." Caitlin's soft pink lips parted. The corners of her mouth tilted up, and his heart rate kicked up a notch. "Maybe I should check out antiques shops."

He stared at her, distracted by the hint of a dimple in her left cheek. Not a true dimple, just a small depression, there and gone so fast he couldn't be certain he hadn't imagined it.

"I could start with the shop where Magnus bought my bones."

That dragged him back to the moment. "I beg your pardon?"

She smiled again, a full-out toothpaste advertisement smile this time. "Napier's bones," she said, as if that explained everything.

"Who's Napier?" he asked. *And why were people going about selling his bones?*

"John Napier? The mathematician?"

"I'm afraid I don't follow."

Caitlin's mouth curved up in a mischievous smile. "How can you live in Edinburgh and not recognize Napier's name?" Her low chuckle triggered a fresh flood of testosterone. Get close to Caitlin O'Shaughnessy, Janus had said. God, how he ached to fulfill *that* assignment.

"Dominic?" she said, and he realized he was staring at her breasts, temptingly outlined by the snug cut of her pink sweater.

"Sorry." With an effort, he dragged his gaze back up to her face. "I'm afraid I was woolgathering."

She cocked an eyebrow. "I said, how can you not recognize John Napier's name?"

He wondered what she'd do if he leaned across the table and kissed her. "One can hardly be expected to know everyone in the city."

She laughed softly. "Particularly not those who've been dead upwards of four hundred years." She laughed again at the look on his face. "John Napier," she recited in a prim, headmistressy voice. "Eighth laird of Merchiston, born fifteen fifty. Died sixteen seventeen. Inventor of logarithms, the decimal point, and a clever handheld calculating device known as Napier's bones. Because they were sometimes made of ivory," she added.

"Of course," he said, more interested in the rise and fall of her breasts than in some antique calculator.

"Magnus sent me a gorgeous set for my birthday. He bought them from a local dealer, possibly someone Wallace recommended."

"Etienne perhaps," Dominic said. "Etienne Le-

Tourneau, a wealthy expatriate Frenchman who divides his time between his shop in Edinburgh and his yacht, harbored at Marseilles. His wife is a great favorite of Wallace's; they share a fascination with the occult."

"The occult?" she said. "Like tea leaves and Ouija boards?"

"Nothing so pedestrian. Jacqueline's done readings for the elite of European society, including several royals. Wallace is always pestering her to hold séances."

"Wallace believes in ghosts?"

"That he does. 'Ghoulies and ghosties and long-leggity beasties and things that go bump in the night.' "

"Whereas Magnus is a born skeptic."

"And you? Are you a skeptic, too?"

"For the most part." She frowned. "Though I do have a very active imagination. Magnus used to tease me about being a worst-case-scenario thinker."

"He doesn't anymore?" Something in her voice, some odd note, caught his attention.

"Not lately. Not since the worst case scenario materialized." Caitlin spoke flatly, without emotion. Then, "Forget I said that," she added. Her face was shuttered, her expression neutral. So why did he have this gut-deep certainty that some bastard of a man had damaged her in ways too dreadful for her to contemplate?

"Caitlin?"

She met his gaze, her turquoise eyes so full of pain that he was seized by a sudden desire to destroy whoever was responsible. "I can't talk about it," she said.

Her choice, after all, but damn it, how could he fix the

problem if he didn't know what the problem was? He was tempted to probe further, but, "Tell me about your friend Bree," he said instead. "What's she doing here? Surely she has no connection to Magnus."

"None. The truth is, she's scared to death of him." Caitlin frowned. "Bree thinks I'm in danger. She came along because she's convinced she owes me something." He thought for a moment she might say more, but she didn't.

"Bree thinks you're in danger because of the attack in Palo Alto?"

She nodded.

"Would you recognize your attacker if you saw him again?"

"I never got a good look at him, but I might know his voice. He spoke with a distinctive accent."

A Calixian accent? Dominic wondered.

After spending an hour with Inspector Logan, the man in charge of Magnus's case, then interviewing the staff at Magnus's hotel, Caitlin was no closer to knowing what had happened to her stepfather than she had been two days ago. Add to that a nagging headache—tension, according to Bree—and she was in no mood for a dinner party. Particularly not one that was "straight out of an Agatha Christie novel."

She didn't realize she'd spoken aloud until Bree broke off her conversation with an elderly woman in lavender lace and pearls and turned to Caitlin with a grin. "No, definitely more *Bridget Jones.* I'm talking the movie.

Never read the book. Remember the party where Bridget first meets Mark Darcy? Like that. Only, of course, it's not Christmas."

Caitlin glanced around the room. "And Colin Firth is conspicuous by his absence." As was Dominic.

She'd hoped to speak with Etienne LeTourneau, the antiques dealer who'd sold Magnus her bones, but she didn't see him, either, though his wife, Jacqueline, a chic blonde wearing black raw silk trousers and an elegant gold V-necked top, stood directly across the room chatting with their host. Wallace's gout seemed much improved this evening. He smiled and nodded at whatever Jacqueline had said, his face flushed with pleasure and postprandial whisky.

Caitlin leaned across Bree to address the woman in lavender lace. "Have you seen Etienne?"

"I believe he's helping Chalmers set up a table in the library," she said. "Wallace has arranged for some after-dinner entertainment. Doesn't that sound jolly?"

"What sort of entertainment?" Caitlin asked, visions of an endless whist tournament dancing in her head.

"A séance," Bree answered.

Gooseflesh rose along Caitlin's arms. She'd once visited a fortune teller on a dare, an uncomfortable experience she never planned to repeat. "Four," the old crone had said. "Four is your unlucky number." Caitlin had looked into the woman's eyes and seen the truth. Just the memory of the moment sent chills down her spine. The woman had known.

Bree touched her shoulder. "Are you all right?"

Bree might not be a mind reader, but she knew Caitlin inside out. They'd been best friends since third grade.

"Headache," Caitlin said, then deliberately changed the subject. "Have you seen Dominic?"

"Oh, I doubt he'll put in an appearance tonight, my dear," the elderly woman said. "Dinner parties are a bit tame for his taste. Nightclubs are much more his thing. He's a wicked, wicked boy, you know. Comes by it honestly. There's a wild streak running through the entire family."

"Really?" Caitlin said. "Wallace doesn't strike me as a wild man."

"Wallace is only related to the Ramseys by marriage. Mary, Wallace's wife, was quite another story." The woman leaned across Bree and lowered her voice to a dramatic whisper. "Oh, my, yes. And as for Dominic's mother, Caroline?" The old lady gave them an arch look.

"What about her?" Bree asked.

"Suffice it to say, she was a typical Ramsey. Oversexed, the lot of them. The scandals don't bear repeating."

"But you can't leave us hanging," Bree protested.

The woman glanced over her shoulder, then leaned in even closer. "Caroline's parents were relieved to marry her off. Unfortunately, marriage didn't put a stop to her shenanigans. They say she cheated on her husband, then committed suicide when she was found out."

"How awful!" Bree said.

"Dominic's father has lived in seclusion ever since, sent the boy off to school and retreated from the world. An opium eater, according to one version of the tale, but you know how people are wont to exaggerate."

"But not you, my dear Miss Campbell."

Caitlin whirled around to see Dominic standing behind them. She wondered a) how much of Miss Campbell's gossip he'd overheard, and b) how much of it was true.

Turning, Miss Campbell simpered up at him. "So pleased to see you made it, dear boy."

"I had intended to be here in time for dinner but was unavoidably detained," Dominic said, then turned to Caitlin. "Might I have a word with you in private? You'll excuse us, ladies?"

Caitlin felt a bit guilty stranding Bree with Miss Campbell, but not guilty enough not to follow Dominic to a secluded alcove at one side of the enormous salon.

"I did a bit of sleuthing today," Dominic said.

"I hope you had better luck than I did."

"I was able to narrow down the probable time of Magnus's disappearance. I spoke to one of the symposium organizers. He told me no one on the committee saw Magnus after he left the symposium at five o'clock Tuesday afternoon. However, it seems one of the other attendees did. A Dr. Bent Hassing from the University of Copenhagen shared a taxi with Magnus for the ride back to his hotel. Hassing asked Magnus to join him in the bar for a drink. Magnus agreed but said he wanted to make a quick stop in his suite to drop off his briefcase."

"Only he never came back downstairs," she guessed.

"Right," Dominic said. "Which means no one saw him after a quarter to six."

A chill ran down Caitlin's spine. No one had seen

Magnus since Tuesday evening. He'd been missing now for four days. A lot could happen to a man in four days.

She wanted to ask Dominic for more detail, but before she had a chance, Wallace strode to the center of the room and clapped his hands to get everyone's attention.

"As many of you know, Jacqueline LeTourneau is a psychic of some repute. She has assisted the police in three countries, solving murders, locating stolen property, and finding missing persons."

Surely Wallace wasn't planning to prevail upon Jacqueline to locate her missing stepfather, to use Magnus's disappearance as the basis for a parlor game to entertain his dinner guests.

"What you may not know," Wallace continued, "is that she is equally adept at communicating with those who have passed over."

Caitlin relaxed. Not Magnus, then. He wasn't dead, just missing.

"Today marks the twentieth anniversary of my dear departed Mary's death. Jacqueline assures me all the signs are propitious. The planets are aligned and we have enough life force among us to generate sufficient energy."

"Sufficient energy for what?" Caitlin asked Dominic.

"To contact Mary," he whispered. "Wallace worries about her."

"If you would follow me into the library . . ."

Caitlin was fine up until that moment, but when people started moving toward the library, her heart began to race. Her mind filled with memories of the gypsy. *Four.* She felt cold and sweaty all at once.

Maybe she shouldn't fight it. Maybe she should retreat to her room. Her being a guest in Wallace's house didn't mean she was obligated to play by his rules, not when the mere thought of a séance made her sick to her stomach. Dominic took her arm to urge her forward, but panic froze her in her tracks.

"What's wrong?" he said.

"It's been a long day. I think I'll have an early night." She tried to avoid his gaze. Those blue eyes of his saw far too much.

He tucked a finger under her chin and tilted her face up so she was forced to look him in the eye. "Something's frightened you."

"I had a bad experience with a fortune teller once." *Four. Four is your unlucky number. They hurt you, didn't they? But don't worry, my pretty. The past is done, and blood will tell. There's greatness in your future.*

"Jacqueline's no storefront gypsy. She's the real deal, a genuine psychic."

Four. They hurt you, didn't they?

"That's the problem," she said. "Some secrets should stay buried."

Dominic's eyes seemed to burn into hers, but he said nothing. Her skin prickled, but this time she wasn't sure what was sparking her reaction. Was it panic or something else entirely?

"Dominic? Caitlin?" Balancing gingerly on his cane, Wallace stood poised at the far end of the room. "Are you coming, then?"

"Caitlin's feeling a bit done up," Dominic said.

"Oh, but Jacqueline tells me we need a minimum of ten to generate sufficient energy. Believe me, if having ten around the table weren't critical, I wouldn't have invited those tedious MacAuleys."

"Perhaps Chalmers could stand in for her."

"Not a good idea," Wallace said. "Chalmers has a very bad aura." Wallace paused. "And damned little energy."

He looked so disconsolate that Caitlin relented. "If you really need me . . ."

"Oh, we do," Wallace assured her.

Dominic gave her a searching look. "Are you sure?"

She wasn't, but she nodded. *Four. Four is your unlucky number.* She headed for the library.

Flickering candlelight created eerie shadows in the high-ceilinged library. Dominic glanced sideways at Caitlin. A faint sheen of perspiration gleamed across her pale cheeks. *This is not a good idea,* he thought, but he pulled back a chair for her anyway, and she took a seat between him and her friend Bree at the big mahogany table.

"Please join hands," Jacqueline said. "Contacting those in the spirit world requires enormous amounts of psychic energy, more than I possess on my own." She smiled. "I know when mediums hold séances in movies or on television, everyone is silent, but that's merely stage dressing. Feel free to chat among yourselves. As long as the circle of energy remains unbroken, I can concentrate on my search for Mary, regardless of what else is going on around me."

"Oh, isn't this thrilling!" Miss Campbell tittered.

No one answered her. In fact, despite Jacqueline's having given permission for people to talk if they wished, no one did. The library was so quiet that Dominic could hear his own heartbeat.

"He's cold," Caitlin said.

The apprehension threading her voice seemed to wrap itself around his heart.

"Who's cold?" Bree asked. "Dominic? Does Dominic's hand feel cold to you?"

"My hand's quite warm, thank you," Dominic said. Though Caitlin's fingers felt icy.

"So cold," Caitlin said. A shiver ran through her.

"I'm not," Dominic told her. "I'm warm as toast."

Caitlin gave no sign she'd heard him; she stared fixedly into the flames of the candle in the center of the table. "He's cold . . . and in pain."

"Oh," Bree said. "She must be talking about Wallace. Wallace, are you chilly?"

"No, my dear, and I'm not in much pain, either. This new medicine the doctor's put me on is a bloody marvel."

"The brother did it," Caitlin said.

"Whose brother?" Bree said, sounding upset. "What are you talking about, Caitlin? Is this your idea of a joke? Because it's not funny. Not one bit."

"His face." Caitlin shuddered violently. "His poor face."

"Whose face?" Dominic asked.

Caitlin didn't answer. Her eyes were squeezed shut now, but she was still shuddering.

"Caitlin?" Bree said, sounding as unnerved as Dominic felt. "What is going on?"

"She's channeling," Jacqueline said.

"Channeling who?" Bree asked.

"Not Mary," Dominic said.

October 1617
Drymen, Scotland

His mother's screams woke him.

Hamish opened his eyes to find himself lying on his side in a pool of blood on the floor of his bedchamber. He wasn't sure how much time had passed, but it was no longer afternoon. The narrow rectangle of sky visible outside the window was black as sin. His sin.

"Calm down, Mother. I'm all right." He shoved himself to a sitting position. His head swam; his stomach heaved. "I must have fainted," he said.

"Dear God in Heaven," his mother said in a shrill, high voice he scarcely recognized. "I saw the blood, the knife. I thought . . . I thought . . . dear God, I thought you'd killed yourself."

"An accident," he said. "I was removing a splinter. The knife slipped." He met her gaze, willing her to believe him.

Her cheeks were chalky, her lips pale and trembling.

"Doubtless it looks much worse than it is," he said.

A muscle twitched in her cheek. "It looks like Armageddon."

"I'm sorry," he said. "Sorry for making a horrible mess and sorrier yet for frightening you."

She patted her meager bosom and heaved a gusty sigh. "Aye. Such a fright you gave me."

"I truly, truly regret that."

"No more than I regret my hysterics." Her mouth curved in a self-deprecating smile. "Your father always said I had no more courage than a wee mousie. But I suppose I'm brave enough to bind the wound for you."

"You needn't trouble yourself. It's a mere scratch."

" 'Twould be no bother."

"Go on now, Mother. My clumsiness caused the mess. The least I can do is clean up after myself."

"If you're certain . . . ?"

He nodded. "I am."

She left, and he sank down on the edge of the bed. He held his gory wrist out in front of him. Though sticky with congealing blood, the skin beneath showed no sign of a wound. No cut. No scar.

And yet he remembered the feel of the blade slicing through skin and tendon, muscle and sinew.

And the blood. All that blood. Where had it come from if not from his veins?

Miracle, he wondered, or sorcery?

Blessing or curse?

6

CAITLIN OPENED HER EYES to find herself lying on a sofa with a crowd of people gathered around her. She had no memory of how she'd gotten there, just one hell of a headache. "What's going on?" she asked Bree, who was watching her with a wary expression, almost as if she expected to see Caitlin explode into a million pieces. The way her head felt, that might happen yet.

"Ah, she's awake," Wallace announced, giving her an avuncular pat on the shoulder. "You frightened us, my dear."

"What happened? Did I collapse or something?"

"Or something," Bree said.

Caitlin struggled to a sitting position, a move that exacerbated the throbbing in her head.

"You made a psychic connection," Jacqueline said. "Has that ever happened before?"

"No." Caitlin pressed her fingertips to her throbbing temples.

"Don't you remember what happened?" Dominic asked.

"I remember taking my seat. Then Jacqueline asked us to hold hands. I was looking at the flame and . . ."

"And what?" Miss Campbell prompted.

"That's it. That's all I remember." Caitlin caught and held Dominic's gaze. "What did I do?"

Bree squeezed her shoulder. "It's not what you did; it's what you said. Something about a brother."

"And being cold," Wallace's golfing partner, Ronald MacAuley, said.

"And in pain," Mrs. MacAuley added.

"Cold and in pain," Miss Campbell said. "That part was very clear."

"But why would I be babbling about a brother? I don't have a brother." Caitlin turned to Wallace. "This is bizarre. I don't suppose your cook could have seasoned the custard with a little LSD."

"LSD?" Wallace looked bewildered. "I'm afraid I don't follow, my dear."

"It's an hallucinogenic drug," Mrs. MacAuley said. "Our Pippa was a teenager in the sixties. We learned these things the hard way."

"Oh, my goodness, no," Wallace said. "Mrs. Chalmers would never spice things up with drugs. Why, she won't even use cloves. Claims they irritate the stomach."

Caitlin took a deep breath, held it a second, and exhaled. It didn't help. She still felt ill. "I apologize, Wallace, for disrupting your party this way."

"Oh, no, my dear. It was quite the highlight of the evening. Damned shame you can't remember it."

"Yes, well . . . whatever happened, it's left me with a horrible headache. If you don't mind, I think I'll go lie down."

Once upstairs in her room, Caitlin kicked off her shoes and lay down on her bed with a grateful sigh. She felt better just being away from the crowd. "You don't need to stay," she told Bree, who had curled up in an overstuffed chair in one corner of the room and was leafing through a copy of *Scotland Magazine.*

"How's your head?"

"Still attached to my neck." Caitlin managed a smile. "Actually, it's not hurting much anymore. The throbbing's died down to a dull ache."

"That was scary, Caitlin." Bree tossed the magazine onto the table beside her chair. "One minute you were sitting there like the rest of us, waiting for Jacqueline to do her thing, and the next you'd zoned out completely, mumbling about the cold and someone's brother."

Caitlin frowned, trying to dredge up memories of those missing minutes. "Do you remember my exact words?"

Bree sat up straight, placing her feet on the floor. "First you said, 'He's cold,' and Dominic thought you meant him. You were holding his hand, so that seemed a logical deduction."

"Only I wasn't talking about Dominic."

"I don't think so. Jacqueline claims you were channeling."

"Which has to be the stupidest thing I ever heard. I'm not psychic."

"Perhaps you are and just never realized it. How else do you explain what happened?"

"Maybe I have a malignant brain tumor."

"Now there's a cheery thought," Bree said. But she didn't seem cheered; she seemed worried.

Well, welcome to the club, Caitlin thought.

Bree jumped to her feet and paced back and forth for a full minute without saying a thing. Then she stopped as abruptly as she'd started and, brow furrowed in concentration, met Caitlin's gaze. "When we were kids, do you remember how nobody ever wanted to play Trivial Pursuit with you?"

"So?"

"Why not? Because you always won. And why did you always win?"

"Because my head is stuffed with trivia. A side effect of growing up around Magnus."

"And?"

"And I'm a good guesser. I was like that in school, too. Even when I thought I didn't know the answer, it would pop into my head."

"Exactly," Bree said. "I rest my case."

"Meaning what?"

"Meaning you obviously have some natural talent. You pick up on other people's thoughts."

"Read minds, you mean? That's insane. I can't see or hear what other people are thinking. It's not like that."

"What is it like then?"

Caitlin sighed. "I don't know . . . just what I said before. Sometimes things pop into my head. I always assumed it was bits of buried knowledge that surfaced unexpectedly, but . . ."

"Maybe it's more than that," Bree said.

And maybe it wasn't, but Caitlin was too tired to get in an argument. "What do you make of Dominic?" she asked in an effort to change the subject.

"He's okay, I guess, if you go for the dark and dangerous type." Bree grinned. "And what red-blooded woman doesn't?"

"Dark and dangerous? Like Tony DaCosta?" Caitlin said. Once burned, twice shy.

"Tony's dark," Bree said, "but more slimy than dangerous. Dominic's different. He has an aura of recklessness—as if he'd race into danger in a heartbeat and to hell with the consequences." She sighed. "And, of course, that smile of his is sinfully sexy."

"Don't get too infatuated," Caitlin warned. "According to Mavis Campbell, he's a 'thorough rogue' and a 'heartless playboy.' "

"Infatuated?" Bree said. "Me? No, Dominic Fortune is totally not my type. I appreciate the man's fine physical attributes purely from the eye-candy standpoint, but I've never been one to throw myself to the sharks. You, on the other hand . . ."

Yes. Oh, yes indeed.

Dominic and Quin sat at the bar in the hotel where Magnus had been staying. Ostensibly their purpose was to speak with the bartender who'd waited on Magnus Armstrong and Erskine Grant Monday night, but Dominic was already on his second drink, and they'd only been there half an hour. Dominic, damn him, was in one of his moods.

Quin flattened his big-knuckled hands on the modern steel-and-glass bar. "I think we've learned all we can from the bartender."

Dominic gave a noncommittal grunt.

"You hungry? I've heard the food here is excellent."

"She knows something," Dominic said.

"Who?"

"Caitlin O'Shaughnessy."

"You think she faked the episode at the séance?"

Dominic was silent for a moment. "Maybe. I didn't see it that way at the time, but now I'm not so sure. All I am sure of is that she knows something she's not telling."

"Something about Magnus's disappearance? Could he have been in touch with her?"

Dominic shrugged and took another swallow of his whisky.

"Or maybe she's received a ransom demand."

"I doubt she'd keep that a secret." He paused. "Bloody hell, I want to believe her, but . . ."

"Another whisky, sir?" The bartender, slight and fair with a narrow face and a big Roman nose, polished away some smudged fingerprints.

Dominic shook his head and Quin breathed a sigh of relief. Like many Calixian natives, Dominic didn't handle his liquor well. Quin didn't fancy breaking up a brawl in such a posh venue or wrestling Dominic for the keys to the Austin.

"You're quite positive you don't remember anything more about the two customers on Monday evening?" Dominic said to the man behind the bar.

"Look, I already gave my statement to the sergeant. Anything you want to know, ask him." The bartender frowned suddenly, eyeing them in undisguised suspicion. "You two *are* policemen, aren't you?"

Quin was digging for his false ID when Dominic suddenly reached up, grabbed the hapless bartender by his collar, and dragged him halfway across the bar. "Keep your voice down, punk," Dominic said. "We're undercover, and we'd like to keep it that way.

"Now, you have a couple of options. Either you answer our questions civilly here and now, or we haul you in and let you cool your heels in an interrogation room for eight or ten hours, after which you still have to answer our questions. Which is it going to be?"

Dirty Harry with an English public school accent. Quin fought down a grin.

"Ask away," the bartender said, and Dominic released his collar.

Bloody miracle the poor sod hadn't soiled himself. Dominic had "bad cop" down to a fine art.

Dominic ran the tip of one finger around the rim of his whisky glass. "You told us earlier the two men left together."

"Yes," the bartender said. "I'm not sure, but I had the impression they went upstairs."

"To one of the guest rooms? You didn't mention that before."

"As I said, I'm not certain they did. That was just my impression."

"All right. What other *impressions* did you pick up?" Dominic said.

The bartender's Adam's apple bopped up and down. "The older man seemed worried about something. He kept glancing over his shoulder and patting his briefcase."

Dominic raised an eyebrow. "Patting his briefcase?"

The bartender nodded. "As if to reassure himself it hadn't gone anywhere. As if there were something valuable inside."

Quin and Dominic exchanged a look. The manuscript.

Caitlin couldn't sleep. Her body ached with fatigue, but her brain had shifted into overdrive. No matter how often she reviewed the events of the last few days, she always came back to the manuscript and the fact that Magnus hadn't mentioned it in his birthday note. Why was that? Because he'd enclosed it at the last minute? Or because he'd stolen it from a crime scene?

Not that she suspected Magnus of murdering Erskine Grant. He wasn't a violent man. But then, he wasn't a thief, either.

Regardless of how it looked, she should tell Inspector Logan about the manuscript. But if she did, she'd have to give it up, and she wasn't ready to do that, not until she'd had a chance to read it from cover to cover. Magnus must have had some reason for sending it to her instead of handing it over to the police. But damned if she knew what that reason was. She kept thinking maybe the book contained some sort of hidden message, a code or cipher, something Magnus had hoped she'd be able to figure out. But that was so hopelessly *The Da Vinci Code.* So *not* real life.

Where the hell are you, Magnus?

Somewhere cold?

God, was Bree right? Did she have latent psychic ability?

Oh, for pity's sake, use your brain, girl. How often over the years had Magnus said that to her?

"I'm trying," she said aloud. The problem was, her brain was as exhausted as the rest of her.

Tired, but too revved up to sleep.

Quin punched Dominic's shoulder as they let themselves into Firth House via the service entrance.

"What did I do to deserve that?"

The big redhead's hazel eyes glinted with humor, and the corners of his mouth turned up. "Warn me the next time you plan to do your Clint Eastwood imitation."

"Mel Gibson," Dominic said. "Mel Gibson as Martin Riggs in *Lethal Weapon.*"

Quin's bushy eyebrows formed an inverted V that bespoke skepticism. "Martin Riggs never called anyone 'punk.' Martin Riggs's epithet of choice was 'asshole.' "

Dominic shrugged off the criticism. "Chalk it up to poetic license. In deference to the brasserie's tony clientele, I was trying to avoid excessively vulgar language."

"Right. Of course you were." Quin shook his head in resignation and headed for his apartment in the servant's quarters. But as he disappeared from view, Dominic heard him mutter, "I'm too old for this shit."

Grinning, Dominic started up the back stairs.

At half past one, Firth House was silent, or as silent as an old building could be. The stairs creaked, the windows rattled in the stiff breeze blowing in off the Firth of Forth, and the antiquated central heating system alternately hummed and groaned. Dominic climbed the narrow staircase, feeling his way in the shadows. A single low wattage bulb, its light nearly swallowed by the darkness of the stairwell, hung suspended from the ceiling three stories up.

Something struck a wrong note. He froze on the first floor landing, listening hard, not sure at first what had alerted him. Then, in among the usual creaks and groans and rattles, it came again, that alien sound, a soft, frenzied tapping it took him a moment to place: fingers flying across a keyboard. Someone was in the library giving Wallace's computer a middle-of-the-night workout.

Carefully he opened the door to the hall, wincing when the old hinges squealed an indignant protest.

"Who's there?" Caitlin O'Shaughnessy, looking insubstantial as a ghost in a pale, silky robe, stood peering out into the hall from the library doorway.

He strode forward into the light. "It's Dominic. Relax." Advice which apparently missed its target.

She tensed instead. The question was why. Because being so close to him made her nervous? Or because she had something to hide?

"What do you want?" she asked.

"I just got home. I was heading upstairs when I heard a noise and came to investigate. Why are you up so late?"

"I couldn't sleep." Her shoulders lifted fractionally in an almost imperceptible shrug, just enough to set her breasts bouncing. He wondered if she realized how clearly the light behind her delineated her curves.

"So you came down to check your e-mail?"

"I was surfing the Web."

"Find anything interesting?"

"Several things." She shivered. "Do you mind if we continue this conversation elsewhere? It's freezing out here." Which had to explain why her nipples were puckered into tight little points that jutted out against the filmy fabric of her robe.

He followed her into the cozy warmth of the library. "Chalmers has orders to turn the thermostat down to fifty-five at night."

"Fifty-five?"

"Wallace *is* a Scot." Dominic wandered over to the computer to find the Web browser open to a myths and legends Web site. "You're researching Merlin?"

She sat in one of the wingchairs that flanked the fireplace, tucking one leg under her. "Professor Grant's Merlin manuscript seems to be at the heart of the mystery. I thought it behooved me to learn what I could."

Seemed more like a waste of time to him. He crossed to the fireplace and leaned against the mantel. "Making any progress?"

"I definitely know more about Merlin than I did before I started."

"For instance?"

"I'd always assumed the legends were pure myth, but apparently they're based on fact. My research suggests there may have been as many as three distinct Merlins—one a Druid involved with the construction of Stonehenge, one a fifth century Welsh prophet, and one a sixth-century bard with the gift of second sight, a member of the court of King Rhydderch of Strathclyde."

"The real Merlin?"

"Take your pick," she said. "All three were regarded as mystics and visionaries—wizards, for lack of a better word. All three reportedly had, among other powers, the ability to predict the future. One scholar even suggested that the three Merlins were incarnations—or reincarnations—of the same man."

Dominic nodded. "Which isn't all that far off from Professor Grant's conviction that Merlin was immortal."

"Do you know the story of Merlin's betrayal by the Lady of the Lake?"

"She seduced him to learn his secrets, then used his own charms to incarcerate him in a glass tower."

"That's one version of the story. In another, he's imprisoned in a cave. In a third, she traps him inside an oak tree."

"Sounds distinctly uncomfortable," Dominic said.

"And to confuse the matter even more, several locations are cited as Merlin's final resting place, among them Merlin's Mound in Wiltshire, Bardsey Island off the coast of Wales, Bryn Myrrdin near Carmarthen, Wales, Le Tombeau de Merlin in Brittany, and Drumelzier here in Scotland."

"Which would seem to support the multiple Merlins school of thought. Rather puts paid to Grant's immortality theory, though, doesn't it?"

"Unless Merlin faked his own death over and over again to keep people from getting suspicious."

Dominic stared at her. "You don't really believe that, do you?"

A mischievous smile lit her face. "No. But I understand now where Grant got his ideas."

He stared at the gas flames. She wasn't lying, but she wasn't telling him all she knew, either. For a split second, he was tempted to seduce her right there in front of the fire on the library rug. Not hard to imagine how she'd look with her eyes slumberous with passion, her lips parted, her curves soft and inviting in the flickering firelight. Not hard to imagine, either, how she'd taste, how she'd feel, coming apart with him buried deep inside her.

Bloody hell. He drew a ragged breath.

And then afterward, once her defenses were down, perhaps he'd finally get the truth from her.

Or then again, maybe the whisky had impaired his judgment. Perhaps all he'd get was a kick in the balls.

Too early to make a move, he decided. He couldn't afford to fuck this up.

"What else did you research?" he asked.

"I'd planned to look up Calix, but I hadn't gotten that far."

"You wouldn't have found what you needed to know online anyway."

She cocked her head to one side. "And what is it that I need to know?"

"There's a group on Calix known as Fraternitas, the brotherhood, all descendants of Crusaders. It started as a social organization, quite harmless, a group of men looking for an excuse to dress up in chain mail or monk's robes and reenact their ancestors' glory days at the old Crusader castle. In the past year, however, a renegade splinter group has added criminal activity to the agenda."

"Kidnapping?" she asked with an edge to her voice.

"Smuggling."

"Smuggling what?"

"The usual—drugs, gemstones, and antiquities, mostly from the Middle East. Though lately they've added a new twist, smuggling stolen Calixian treasures—jewelry, paintings—"

"Manuscripts," she said.

"Yes. Grant's so-called Merlin manuscript is actually Book One of the *Calix Chronicles,* a saga believed to be a mixture of fact and fiction."

"Not written by Merlin, then?"

"No. The *Chronicles* record the adventures of a legendary figure known as Brother Hamish."

"Hamish?" she said sharply. "Isn't that a Scottish name?"

"Brother Hamish was a Scot," Dominic said. "Shipwrecked off the coast of Calix in 1618, he washed ashore two days later. According to the *Chronicles,* he believed God had spared him for a reason and henceforth devoted himself to good works. He wandered the Aeternus

Mountains for the next two hundred years, healing the sick and comforting the dying."

"Two hundred years?"

"As I said, the story's a mixture of fact and fiction."

"Like much of history." A smile flashed across her face, then faded just as quickly. "What I don't understand is why a respected scholar like Erskine Grant would claim the manuscript was written by Merlin."

"Alzheimer's? Dementia? Mental illness?" Dominic shrugged.

"If the manuscript is nothing more than the legend of a Calixian folk hero, then why was Grant murdered? And why has Magnus disappeared?"

"I don't know."

"And who's behind it?"

"I told you. Fraternitas."

"That doesn't make any sense," she said. "They were the ones who smuggled the manuscript out of the country in the first place and, presumably, sold it for a profit. Why would they now be so determined to get it back?"

"Perhaps they didn't realize its true value until Grant gave his presentation."

"So you're suggesting the manuscript *was* written by Merlin," Caitlin said.

"I didn't say that."

"Or perhaps it holds the secret of immortality."

"I didn't say that, either."

"Then what are you saying?"

"Grant spoke of a treasure beyond price."

"I thought he meant immortality."

"Maybe he did. Or maybe he meant a literal treasure." Dominic paused. "According to the legend, when Brother Hamish's ship went down, he spotted another wreck at the bottom of the sea, a Roman trireme filled with gold and silver coins."

Sighing, she stood up, crossed to the computer, and shut it down. "Gold and silver, monks and smugglers, sorcerers and immortality. I need sleep. My brain's too tired to process all this information."

"I'll walk you back to your room," he said.

"That's not necessary."

"I want to," he insisted, and surprised a flicker of something unexpected in her eyes. Interest? Desire? Calculation? Satisfaction? He wasn't sure.

As they climbed the main staircase side by side, he became aware of little details he'd missed before—the silky dark hair that feathered her shoulders with a lover's touch, the delicate little hollow at the base of her throat, the faint exotic scent that rose from her skin, a scent redolent of the tropics, of oranges and ginger and jasmine.

She was barefoot again. He'd never considered a woman's feet particularly sexy, but the sight of Caitlin O'Shaughnessy's little pink-tipped toes did something peculiar to his insides. Good God, he realized. He wanted her. Not on order. Not because Janus had suggested it. Not as a means to an end. But because she appealed to him on a very basic sensual level.

Neither spoke, but the silence between them throbbed with a whole range of possibilities.

Caitlin paused outside the door to her room and turned to face him. "Magnus isn't your problem, but you've gone out of your way to help me"—a twinge of guilt tweaked his conscience—"and I appreciate that." She stretched up on tiptoe and pressed a kiss to his cheek. "Thank you, Dominic."

And oh, that mouth, soft and pink and full. A twinge of guilt, yes, he'd acknowledged it, but damned if he'd forgo this opportunity. Slowly, relentlessly, he backed her against the door. "You're welcome."

Her eyes widened in surprise and . . . anticipation? He wasn't sure, but she didn't push him away. Nor did she struggle when he gathered her into his arms and lowered his mouth to hers.

Dominic had kissed a lot of women, but none who tasted as sweet as Caitlin, as wickedly decadent, none who responded as generously or as greedily. Seconds grew to minutes, but instead of slaking his thirst for her, the endless kiss only made him want more.

Finally, she eased apart, staring up at him, her pupils so enormous, they nearly obscured her irises. She was breathing fast, her breasts rising and falling under the pale silk of her robe. Rising and falling, rising and falling, and oh God, but his fingers itched to touch her there, his lips and tongue to taste her.

But before he could act on his impulse, "Goodnight," she whispered, and let herself into her room.

He didn't remember climbing the staircase to his suite on the third floor. His brain was preoccupied, remembering the fleeting sensations of softness and warmth and the faint scent of jasmine.

Wallace glanced up from his newspaper as Caitlin entered the room. "Good morning, my dear. I trust you slept well."

"Yes, thank you, Mr. Armstrong. And you?"

Wallace did a double take. Not Caitlin, after all, but her friend, Bree Thatcher. "I'm fine," he said, wondering if perhaps he ought to have his eyes checked. The two young women looked nothing alike, aside from their shoulder-length hair, and even then, Bree's was a shade darker. "Help yourself. The food's on the sideboard."

She lifted the lid off one of the serving dishes. "Ooh. Are these kippers? I've always wanted to try kippers." After filling her plate with kippers, eggs, and fried tomatoes, she slipped into a seat next to him.

"How do I go about hiring a taxi?" she asked.

"You want to go somewhere?"

"Yesterday Caitlin mentioned that she planned to visit one of the symposium organizers."

"Never mind a taxi. Chalmers will drive you," he said, then belatedly remembered it was Sunday. Chalmers would be busy escorting Mrs. Chalmers to church. "Or Quin perhaps."

Bree paused with a forkful of kipper poised halfway to her mouth. "Who's Quin?"

The kippers looked tempting, almost as tempting as the sausages, but neither was on his diet. "Dominic's bodyguard, the big redhead. You must have seen him." Wallace scowled at his oatmeal. Damned gout.

"Dominic has a bodyguard?"

"Bodyguard. Valet. Friend. Hard to pigeonhole Quin's role really. He and Dominic grew up together. His parents work for Dominic's father."

"Redhead, you say? The one who looks like a leprechaun on steroids?"

"Who looks like a leprechaun on steroids?" Dominic smirked at them from the doorway. As Quin was standing directly behind him, Wallace didn't feel it would be diplomatic to answer.

Bree, meanwhile, blushed a delicate pink that looked rather fetching with her blue blouse, a circumstance both Dominic and Quin seemed to appreciate.

"Private conversation," Wallace said. "You're up early."

Dominic glanced at his watch. "I have a meeting."

On the golf links, no doubt.

"But Quin will be around. If you or Caitlin need to leave Firth House, he'll escort you," he told Bree.

"My pleasure." Quin sketched a bow. He moved with surprising grace for such a large young man.

Bree's blush deepened.

"Well, I'm off," Dominic said and left.

"I'll be in the kitchen," Quin told them. "Ring if you need me." Then he left, too.

Bree stared at the empty doorway. "Me and my big mouth."

November 1617
Near Drymen, Scotland

Auld Mòrag lived in a tumbledown cottage a mile or so outside the village. She shared her home with a goat, a pig, a half dozen chickens, and a scruffy stub-tailed tabby cat Hamish tripped over in the dark.

The cat let out a hellish squall that raised the short hairs along Hamish's neck and roused the widow. She threw the door open. Firelight illuminated the opening. Auld Mòrag poked her head out as if she thought her eyes could penetrate the darkness. And maybe they could. A witch she was, according to rumor.

"Who's there?" she demanded. The cat sashayed into the quadrangle of light spilling out of the open door, and the old woman bent to stroke his head. "Are ye all right, Fergus?"

"He's fine." Hamish shoved himself to his feet. "I'm the one who fell arse over teakettle. The cursed creature tripped me."

Auld Mòrag looked up sharply at the sound of his voice, but when he moved into the light, she chortled with glee. " 'Tis why I keep the mangy beast. He's a rare watchdog."

"Watchcat," Hamish said, and the old lady cackled again.

"And what brings ye out so late at night, young Hamish MacNeill? Ye'll be wanting a love philter, I'll wager. Found yourself a comely lass, ha'e ye?"

Maggie's face, still and pale, appeared in his mind's eye

for a moment, and he shuddered. "No," he said. "It's not a love philter I need but advice."

"Advice, is it? Well, come in then," she said.

The room reeked of smoke and cat piss and old woman. Trying not to inhale too deeply, Hamish sat on a three-legged stool next to the hearth. The old woman settled on the pallet against the back wall. The cat curled up in her lap.

Auld Mòrag said nothing, just petted her cat and waited patiently for him to get on with it.

"Do you know the legend of Merlin?"

His question must have startled her; her eyes snapped up to his face. "The sorcerer, ye mean? Aye, I do," she said.

"Do you know how he died?"

"Many a tale has been told, though which is the truth"—she shrugged—"I canna say."

"Some say he's buried near Drumelzier."

"I've heard that, aye."

"Other stories claim he died in Wales."

The old woman nodded.

"He can't have died in both places. Which story is true?"

"Both? Neither?" She shrugged again. "It's a legend, young Hamish, the truth distorted by time and many retellings."

"Do you know the tale of Vivien, the Lady of the Lake?"

"She enchanted the sorcerer with her beauty," Auld Mòrag said. "And once she'd learned all his secrets, she used his own spell to entomb him for all eternity within a crystal cave."

"That's one version. In another, she traps him inside an oak tree."

The old woman turned her hands palms up and spread her gnarled fingers. "As I told ye before, the more a tale is told, the further it strays from the truth. What interest ha'e ye in Merlin, Hamish MacNeill? The man—if he was a man, if indeed he ever lived outside of legend—has been dead these many years."

"I think I may have found his bones," he said. "Near Drumelzier."

7

DOMINIC DID NOT SPEND Sunday morning in church as Wallace would have liked. Nor did he spend it on a golf course as Wallace expected. Instead he scoured Edinburgh for someone who could provide a new direction in his search for Magnus Armstrong.

He spoke to Inspector Logan, to various symposium attendees, and to several members of the hotel's housekeeping staff. None of them had anything to add to what he already knew. But then his luck turned. Noticing the queue of taxis lined up outside the hotel, he decided to interview drivers, and that's when he hit the jackpot. One driver, who'd apparently ferried Magnus to the symposium two days in a row, identified him from a photograph. What was even more helpful, he reported having seen two men bundling Magnus into a car on Tuesday night. The taxi driver could provide only a sketchy description of the two men—big and dark—but he'd retained a vivid memory of the car, a black Lincoln Town Car with Calixian diplomatic plates.

Dominic drove straight to the Calixian consulate, where he tried to find someone—anyone—who knew who had ordered the official car dispatched to Magnus's hotel on Tuesday evening. Unfortunately, on weekends the consulate operated with a skeleton staff, at least half of whom appeared to be seriously hung over. No one knew anything. Or if they did, they weren't talking.

Frustrated, he placed a call to Janus.

"You found the manuscript," Janus said.

"Not yet," Dominic told him, "but I do have a lead on the men who abducted Magnus Armstrong."

"I'm listening."

"Calixian," he said. He gave Janus a quick update.

"Calixian and almost certainly Fraternitas," Janus said. "Any leads on your end as to the identity of their inside man?"

"Someone with enough pull to secure a seat for Hector Yuli on the Royal Air Express, which pretty much limits our search to the upper echelon of government."

"And the royal family," Janus added. "The king is much too ill, of course. And I doubt his elderly aunts would involve themselves in anything illegal. But Prince Maximilian is another story. Did you know he introduced a gambling initiative at the most recent legislative session?"

"The king has always been adamantly opposed to turning Calix into another Monte Carlo."

"The king's energy is limited. He seldom troubles himself these days with politics. And Maximilian knows that. The prince would never have dared to do this a year ago."

"Still, introducing a gambling initiative doesn't put Prince Maximilian in the same category with smugglers and/or murderers."

"Fraternitas backs the gambling initiative," Janus said. "In fact, most people do. They view it as a panacea for our ailing economy."

"Again, I fail to see a connection. The prince has no reason to align himself with a criminal organization like Fraternitas."

"What about power?" Janus suggested. "As things stand, he'll never be king, but he can rule his own little underworld kingdom as the head of Fraternitas. An ambitious man like Prince Maximilian might find that an irresistible temptation."

"No, I refuse to believe he's involved."

Janus said nothing, and somehow that was worse than an open accusation. But when he finally spoke again, it was on another topic altogether. "I understand Caitlin O'Shaughnessy filed a police report shortly before she left Palo Alto."

"A man attacked her in broad daylight."

"And yesterday a second man tried to steal her rucksack at the airport in Edinburgh."

"How did you know that?"

"I have my sources. I also heard about your somewhat unorthodox interview technique last night at the hotel bar."

"Quin," Dominic said in disgust.

"You should know better, Fortune. Gilroy would swear black was white if he thought it would keep you out of trouble. He's not about to carry tales."

"Then who did?"

"As I said, I have my sources. But that's beside the point. You're familiar with the saying 'Third time's a charm'?"

"Of course, but what—"

"Stay close to Caitlin O'Shaughnessy, Fortune. We wouldn't want her to go missing, too, would we?"

When Bree went back upstairs, Caitlin's door was open. Dressed in jeans and a pullover, she sat in a chair next to the window, frowning over the manuscript Magnus had included in her birthday package.

"Something wrong?" Bree asked.

Caitlin looked up, still frowning. "Try everything." She hesitated. "Close the door, would you?"

Bree pulled the door shut and made herself comfortable on the end of the bed. "So what specific 'everything' are we talking about?"

"You know the so-called Merlin manuscript we believe got Professor Grant killed?" She held up the shabby little volume she'd been scowling over. "This is it."

"But I thought you said that was the diary of some Scot, a personal friend of your hero, math genius John Whatsit."

"John Napier, and yes, it is."

"So what does it have to do with Merlin?"

"Nothing as far as I can tell, but I'm only twenty pages in. Hamish MacNeill's handwriting makes for slow reading."

"Then how can you be sure it's the same book?"

"Something Dominic said last night clued me in. Besides, it explains a lot."

"Like your stalker in Palo Alto."

"And the would-be thief at the airport."

"Did you tell Dominic you had it?"

Caitlin stared at her as if Bree had lost her mind. "No way! And you're not going to tell him, either. Not him or anyone else. If the police find out, they'll confiscate the manuscript as evidence and reclassify Erskine Grant's death as a homicide, casting Magnus in the role of prime suspect. Not that they could prove anything because, obviously, Magnus is no murderer. But legal ramifications aside, I don't want to give up the manuscript until I figure out why Magnus mailed it to me in the first place."

"So you're going to spend the day deciphering some seventeenth century diary? I thought you'd arranged to speak with one of the symposium organizers."

"Yes, Sarah Lassiter. She had to cancel, but we spoke on the phone. Unfortunately, she had nothing new to add."

"Bummer." Bree had been hoping to get out of the house for a while.

"Are you looking for a job," Caitlin asked, "or an excuse to see the city?"

Bree grinned. "Both. Magnus's uncle has a lovely home, but I've never been to Edinburgh before."

"You could call or visit local antiques dealers to see if you can find out who sold Grant the manuscript. Even if he didn't buy it in Edinburgh, someone may know who sold it to him."

Bree jumped up off the bed. "Will do."

Caitlin eyed her suspiciously. "You seem awfully cheerful for someone who just pulled a shit detail."

"I'd be pleased with any assignment that offered an opportunity to get better acquainted with the steroid-popping leprechaun."

Caitlin's eyebrows rose. "I'm not going to ask."

"Quin," Bree explained. "Dominic's bodyguard."

"Dominic has a bodyguard?"

"That's exactly what I said." Bree grinned again. "Butlers. Bodyguards. Rich people have all the fun."

She closed Caitlin's door behind her, went next door to grab her jacket and purse, then headed down to the kitchen to find Quin.

Bree Thatcher caught Quin in the pantry stuffing his face with leftover apple tart and reading the *Edinburgh Exposé*.

"There you are," she said, then blushed a delicious shade of pink, as if stating the obvious were a worse crime than eating between meals or rotting one's brain with tabloid trash. What a darling she was—even though she obviously knew nothing about leprechauns.

He tossed the paper on the counter and pushed aside the half-eaten tart. "Are you ready, then?"

She nodded, and he escorted her out the rear entrance and back to the garage. Two of the six parking spaces were empty, but both the Daimler and his own beloved Morris were there. He preferred driving the little Morris Minor but figured Bree Thatcher would be more comfortable in the larger, more luxurious Daimler. He opened the passenger door and handed her in, then circled the vehicle and got behind the wheel. "Where to?"

"Antiques shops," she said. "I'm trying to find out where Erskine Grant bought the Merlin manuscript."

Which could take days. Weeks. "Wouldn't it be more efficient to make inquiries via telephone?"

"People's faces are more revealing than their voices," she said.

He wondered what his face revealed? The crow's-feet at the corners of his eyes made him look older than his thirty-five years. The prominent cheekbones and square chin most likely suggested a stubborn nature. And the oft-broken nose probably marked him as a brawler in her eyes. Weren't redheads notorious for their quick tempers?

In reality, he had always had a placid temperament, and the crooked nose was a relic of his rugby years.

"How can I tell if someone's lying if I can't see their eyes?" she said.

He switched on the ignition, then turned to look at her. "I am not now using nor have I ever used steroids," he said quietly. "True or false?"

Her color rose, but her soft brown eyes held his gaze. "True," she said.

He smiled. "My turn."

"I'm sorry I ever made such a stupid remark." Her expression was so sweet, so sincere, it would have melted a harder heart than his.

"Aye," he said. "And I believe you, lass. Dinna fash yourself." At her puzzled look, he added, "That's my clumsy way of asserting my Scottishness. Half Scottishness. My father's Calixian."

"No Irish blood," she said.

"No *leprechaun* blood." He laughed softly at her chagrined expression.

Caitlin's head ached from trying to decipher Hamish MacNeill's wretched handwriting and even worse spelling, but her excitement outweighed any physical discomfort. She knew now why Magnus had sent her the manuscript—and it had nothing to do with Merlin or treasure or even John Napier. No, it was Hamish's mention of Maggie Gordon that had triggered Magnus's interest. The dates and locations matched. Everything matched except . . .

Hamish had got one thing wrong. Maggie Gordon hadn't died on the banks of the River Tweed. She'd lived to the ripe old age of ninety-seven. Though she'd borne but one child, a son, Robert, in April of 1618, she'd seen her family grow to include eight grandchildren, thirty-seven great-grandchildren, and forty-six great-great-grandchildren, one of whom, Thomas Gordon, had emigrated to the United States.

Thomas, or Big Tam, as he was known, proved nearly as long-lived as Maggie herself. He'd survived a stormy sea voyage, seven years of indentured servitude, war, and pestilence to see his own great-great-grandchild, Liberty, born on July 4, 1776.

Liberty, in turn, had married one Michael O'Shaughnessy. And Caitlin knew this because their oldest great-great grandson, John, was her own great-great-grandfather.

Bree's feet hurt. She and Quin had been walking for hours, back and forth, up and down, around, behind, and through the hundreds of booths set up in the Royal Highland Centre, where an antiques and collectors fair was in full swing. Just when she was sure she couldn't walk another step, Quin suggested they have some tea—tea in his case meaning a double serving of fish and chips and in hers, a lemonade. They claimed a small table, recently vacated by an elderly couple in polyester and Nikes—Bree envied those Nikes—and under cover of the table, she eased off her shoes and wiggled her aching toes. Bliss.

"Care for some?" Quin proffered his chips and she snagged a couple.

"Thanks."

His smile crinkled the skin at the outer corners of his eyes. Not true hazel, she realized, nor brown either, but rather a coppery color like his hair.

"My mother swears by Epsom salts," he said.

She stared. "On French fries?"

He laughed. "To soothe aching feet."

She'd thought her guilty secret safely hidden by the table, but apparently she hadn't been as discreet as she'd thought.

She gulped some lemonade, hoping to quench the fires burning in her cheeks. What was it about this man? Why was merely being within six feet of him enough to destroy her normal sangfroid?

But if he noticed her discomfort, he gave no sign of it, placidly devouring fish and chips.

They finished their "tea" in silence. "Where to next?" she asked once she had set her empty paper cup on the table and touched her napkin to her lips.

He glanced up with a distracted expression, as if he'd forgotten she was there. "Perhaps Etienne LeTourneau has returned to his booth." When they'd stopped by earlier, they'd found the Frenchman's booth manned by a teenaged underling who barely knew his own name, much less which dealers specialized in rare books and manuscripts. "Etienne will know who we should contact. And with him to vouch for us, we may even learn something."

Bree slid her feet back into her pumps, wincing as the leather chafed the blisters on her heels.

"I can carry you piggyback, if you'd like," Quin offered, his manner so matter-of-fact she thought he was serious, until she noticed the teasing glint in his eyes.

She laughed. "I have half a mind to take you up on that."

"Or you could walk about in your stocking . . ." His sentence trailed off as something behind her caught his attention. "Etienne!" He stood. "Etienne!"

Bree turned to see the LeTourneaus approaching.

"And so the mountain comes to Mohammed," Quin said softly.

"Quinton Gilroy," Etienne said, his tone expressing equal parts surprise and delight. "What a surprise to see you! Is Dominic here, too?"

Quin invited the couple to sit down. Once the amenities were out of the way, he explained what had brought him and Bree to the antiques fair.

"I wish I had known you were interested in the manuscript," Etienne said. "I could have saved you a great deal of trouble, for you see, it was I who sold it to Erskine Grant. As to his insistence that it was written by Merlin"—the Frenchman shrugged—"I can assure you I made no such claims. We acquired it, that is, Jacqueline acquired it, at an estate sale in Stirling. Isn't that right, *mignonne*?"

Jacqueline nodded.

"Last November, if memory serves."

"And Caitlin's bones," Bree said on impulse, earning a startled glance from Quin. "Do you remember where they came from?"

Etienne smoothed a hand over his thinning gray hair. "Curiously enough, I believe we purchased the bones at the same estate sale. *N'est-ce pas?*" He turned to Jacqueline for confirmation.

"I think so, yes. I'd have to check my records to be sure. Is it important?" she asked Bree.

"Probably not."

A few minutes later, Etienne and Jacqueline excused themselves to go back to work, and Quin turned the full power of his penetrating copper gaze on Bree. "Bones?" he said.

"A set of Napier's bones, a sort of seventeenth-century version of the handheld calculator. Knowing Caitlin is a major John Napier groupie, Magnus sent the bones for her birthday along with—" She caught herself. "Along with a letter." Had those observant eyes noticed her slip?

Firth House was quiet. Too quiet.

Dominic stood just inside the door, listening. The only sounds were the intermittent drip of a leaky faucet in the pantry and the ticking of the clock on the wall above the servants' call box.

Where was everyone? Chalmers was off today, and Wallace was most likely at his club. He and three of his closest cronies—all of them unmarried—regularly lunched together on Sundays. But that didn't account for Quin, Bree, and Caitlin. Could Quin have driven the women somewhere?

Dominic tried to remember which of the cars had been missing from the garage. The Daimler? Not Quin's usual choice, but perhaps he'd taken it in the interest of comfort. Taken it where, though? That was the question. Shopping? Sightseeing? Sleuthing?

Dominic pushed through the baize doors into the main part of the house. More silence greeted him, a hush so profound, the muted ticking of the grandfather clock on the first-floor landing sounded as loud as a metronome.

"Hullo?" he said. "Anyone home?"

No answer.

He mounted the stairs and headed for the library to check his e-mail. The door was closed, which should have warned him someone was inside, but by then he'd come to the conclusion he was alone.

Only he wasn't.

Caitlin sat reading in a leather club chair, her back to the door. She'd gathered her hair into an untidy knot. Wispy tendrils brushed her collar. His first thought was how vulnerable she looked with her slender neck exposed. His second that he must have a little vampire blood somewhere in his background because he was sorely tempted to nibble his way from her earlobe to the base of her throat, then lower still. Vivid memories of last night's endless kiss teased his mind. And his body.

Then it struck him with the force of a physical blow. He wasn't alone in Firth House. He was alone with Caitlin.

"Hullo," he said, quietly, so as not to alarm her, a tactic that failed miserably.

She leapt to her feet with a startled gasp, then spun around to face him, one hand pressed to her chest as if to prevent her heart's slamming its way past her ribs.

"Sorry." He shot her an apologetic smile. "I didn't mean to frighten you."

She released her breath in a heavy sigh. "No, I overreacted. My nerves have come unraveled."

He frowned. "Because of what happened last night?" Could he have misread her reactions so thoroughly?

"Last night?" she echoed, as if she weren't quite sure what he was talking about. Had he made so little impression on her? Then understanding dawned on her face. "Oh, no. Dominic, no. Of course not. That was"—a reminiscent smile tilted the corners of her mouth—"delicious. No, it's—" A sudden bleak look chased her smile away. She frowned, then closed her eyes for a second. When she opened them again, the expression in their depths set off all his internal alarms.

He took a step toward her. "Are you all right?"

Her eyes were glassy with unshed tears. "The kidnapper called."

Christ, and she'd been here all alone. He strode toward her, intending to pull her into his arms, but she backed away, putting the chair between them.

My God, didn't she trust him? He searched her face, but her expression was as guarded as her body language.

"What did he want?"

"A hundred—" Her voice broke. She drew a deep, steadying breath and started again. "A hundred thousand dollars. I've already arranged for my bank to wire it to me."

He frowned. "Money? He demanded money? I thought this was about the manuscript."

"He wants me to deliver that as well."

"Deliver it where?"

"Calix." She paused. "Your native country."

He shot a sharp glance at her. "You don't think I had anything to do with—"

"Someone told the kidnapper where to reach me."

"Caitlin, you've got to believe me. I have no connection with the men who abducted your stepfather. I don't know how they knew where to reach you, but I swear—"

"It doesn't matter." She sighed. "What does matter is that I'm supposed to wangle an invitation to the Independence Day Ball. Someone will contact me there with further instructions."

"Damn it!" he swore in frustration. Fraternitas was behind this, but how was he to prove it? Worse, how was he to learn Caitlin's secrets if she didn't trust him? "Damn it to hell," he said bitterly.

"It's hopeless," she said. "I just spent half an hour on the Internet researching Calixian Independence Day festivities. The regatta and fireworks are open to the public, but attendance at the ball is by invitation only."

"I can get you an invitation to the ball," he said slowly.

He watched as hope flickered to life in the depths of her eyes.

"But these men won't be satisfied with the money. They'll never release Magnus if you don't hand over the manuscript. And you can't hand over the manuscript because you don't know where it is."

"Actually," she said, "I do."

November 1617
Near Drymen, Scotland

"Lightning hit a tree, aye, and split it asunder. I'm wi' ye so far, young Hamish." Auld Mòrag's sharp eyes followed his every move, judged his every word.

He shifted, uncomfortably aware of all he hadn't told her. His sin. His cowardice. Maggie's death. "The bones were embedded in the shattered trunk, a human skeleton."

The old woman shook her head. "Impossible. Your senses deceived ye."

"I saw them, I tell you. Human bones. The skull was cocked at a rakish angle. It seemed to smile at me."

"Ye'd been through an ordeal, lad. Nae doubt the lightning dazzled your eyes."

Hamish leapt to his feet, startling the cat; it hissed and dove for cover under the cupboard. "I know what I saw, old woman!" He shouted the words, his pulses pounding madly at his temples, his chest heaving.

She studied him, her head canted slightly to one side. "Ye scairt my cat." She nodded toward the stool. "Sit ye down and tell me the rest of it."

"I didn't know what to think. I reached out to touch the skull, to assure myself that it was real, but the moment my fingers made contact . . ." He couldn't say it. He couldn't put it into words.

"Yes?" The old hag's eyes glittered in the firelight.

"I felt a powerful surge that trembled on the verge of pain. It knocked me to my knees."

"Another lightning bolt," she said. "Some say it canna strike the same place twice, but that's nae true."

"It wasn't lightning," he said. "It was the bones, their life force transferring itself to my body."

"Aye?" A world of skepticism in a single syllable.

"I dragged myself to my feet and peered into the splintered heartwood. The skull had vanished, as if it had never been."

"I believe that, aye." Sarcasm sharpened Auld Mòrag's voice.

Hamish scowled, sorry now he'd come. "You think the lightning fuddled my brain or that I dreamt the whole thing, but I tell you, woman, it happened. All of it. And not only that, I've reason to believe those bones belonged to the legendary Merlin."

"What reason?" the old woman asked. "Since absorbing the sorcerer's power, ha'e ye been performing miracles, then? Charming the birds from the sky? Changing lead to gold, perhaps?"

Hamish drew his dirk from its sheath, gratified to see the old hag shrink back upon her pallet, eyes wide. "What are ye about?"

He pushed up his cuff, exposing the blue veins on the inside of his wrist.

Mòrag leaned closer, her frown driving deep wrinkles between her eyebrows. "Ye wouldna!"

"You asked for a miracle." With the edge of the dirk, he sliced through his flesh. Blood spurted from the wound.

Auld Mòrag sprang to her feet with the agility of a woman half her age. "Ha'e ye run mad?"

"You wanted proof." He extended his arm so she could see. Already the blood had clotted. As they watched, his body repaired itself. In half a minute the skin stretched unblemished across his wrist. No wound. No scar.

With one hand the old woman fumbled for the cross that hung around her neck. With the other she touched his bloodied wrist. "What trickery is this?" she whispered.

"It's no trick. Here." He pressed the hilt of the knife into her hand. "You try. Cut me."

Her mouth fell open in surprise. "I canna."

"Cut me," he said. "Go on. Do it. Nothing else will convince you of the truth."

"Truth?" Her face twisted in a fearsome grimace.

"Cut me."

She held the bloody dirk to the light, tested the cutting edge with a blunt fingertip, then bobbed her gray head in assent. "As ye wish."

She moved so quickly, Hamish didn't realize what was happening until she'd buried the blade in his heart. At first he felt nothing. Then a huge starburst of agony exploded in his chest.

"Wha—?" Choking on his own blood, he fell face first to the filthy floor.She grabbed his shoulder and heaved him over on his back, then worked the dagger free, triggering shooting pains with each back-and-forth motion of the blade.

"Why?" Blood burbled up his throat, distorting his speech.

"Why?" Her eyes gleamed red in the firelight. "Why?" Her voice rose to a shriek. Because ye're a demon!" Grabbing the dirk's hilt in both hands, she stabbed him again and again, so many times he grew faint from loss of blood. And then he knew no more.

PART TWO

The Myth

Put not your trust in princes.

—PSALMS 146:3

8

"You have the manuscript?" Dominic said. "But how?"

Caitlin watched his face closely, still not sure what had prompted her to tell him the truth. She knew very little about Dominic Fortune aside from the gossip she'd heard at Wallace's dinner party and her own observations. He was big, strong, handsome, wealthy, and charming as the devil himself. Plus, he kissed like the leading man in all her best erotic fantasies. None of which proved he was one of the good guys, of course, but sometimes you just had to go with gut instinct.

"Magnus mailed it to me," she said. "It arrived in the same package as my bones, though the accompanying note made no mention of the book. This book." She picked up the manuscript she'd left lying on the chair and handed it to Dominic.

He leafed through the small leather-bound volume. "How did your stepfather . . . ?"

"I suspect Grant realized he was being followed and

gave Magnus the manuscript for safekeeping. Then when Grant went missing, Magnus got worried and tucked it into the package he'd already planned to send me for my birthday."

"Only somehow the kidnappers found out you had it. That's why you were attacked in Palo Alto and later at the airport here in Edinburgh."

"I think so," she said.

"But how did they know? Would Magnus have told them?"

"Under torture? Who knows?" She shuddered at the thought.

Something in her face must have worried him; she could see the concern in his expression, feel it in his touch as he pulled her into his arms and held her close. "Don't worry. It's going to be all right."

But he didn't know that any more than she did. There were no guarantees she'd get Magnus out of this alive. No guarantees she'd make it through unscathed herself.

"I know how frightened you must be, but try not to fret. It won't do Magnus any good if you make yourself sick."

She knew he was right, but she couldn't stop worrying on command. "Maybe if I could get some sleep . . ."

He rested his chin on the top of her head and ran his hand up and down her back in long, soothing strokes. "You're having trouble sleeping?"

"Nightmares," said. "Every time I fall asleep, I have the most horrible nightmares full of violence and death."

Up and down, up and down he stroked her. "Would it help to talk about them?"

"Maybe if I could remember them. That's the thing with the dreams. They're vivid at the time, but they fade as soon as I wake up. And all I'm left with are shadows." She shuddered again.

"No one's going to hurt you, Caitlin. I promise. I won't let them." He cupped her cheek for an endless moment, then brushed the hair away from her face in a gesture so unexpectedly tender that it stopped her breath.

And suddenly everything changed. She shuddered again, but this time, it wasn't fear that rippled through her. "Dominic?" She slid her hands up his chest and knew by the heavy thud of his heart beneath her fingertips that he'd felt the change, too. "Dominic?" she said again.

He went very still. "This isn't a good idea," he said. "You don't really want this. You're just feeling vulnerable."

"Not vulnerable. Haunted." She looped her arms around his neck, then stretched up on tiptoe to press a kiss to his lips. "All I want . . . all I need is a little help keeping the shadows at bay."

"But Caitlin—"

"Please," she said, and he swore softly under his breath.

But he was tempted. She could tell he was tempted.

"Please," she said again.

She felt his body's response even before she saw the desire in his eyes.

"Bloody hell," he muttered, then led her up the stairs to his room.

She stripped off his sweater. "This is mad," he said.

"Completely insane," she agreed, as he peeled off her jeans.

"Wild and impetuous." He slid his hands beneath her pullover and jerked it off over her head.

"Liberating," she said, as she removed his jeans.

"Uninhibited." Her underwear joined the growing discard pile.

She stripped off his shorts. " 'Thoroughly,' I was going say." She heaved a sigh. "But I think I'll change that to 'hugely.' "

Laughing, he pulled her into his arms and kissed her and kissed her and kissed her until she didn't have a single smart-alecky comment left in her brain. All she had was need, a need for this man.

She moaned a little, and he answered her unspoken plea by lifting her in his arms, carrying her to the bed, and laying her on the sheets. He lay down next to her and ran a hand down the curve of her hip. Up and down, up and down, his touch warm and sure. He wasn't smiling—she'd thought he'd be smiling. Instead he looked intense, as if he were focusing every fiber of his being on the sensation of his fingers brushing up and down across her hip. And, of course, she knew how that touch felt to her, slow and silky and seductive, but the expression on his face, that fierce concentration made her wonder what he was thinking, what he was feeling. And what he would think if she did the same thing to him.

So she did. She slid her hand up and down the curve

of his hip. Up and down, up and down, enjoying the texture of his skin, the firm muscle beneath.

He shifted his position, leaning over her, focusing all the concentration and intensity of his gaze on her face. She thought for a second he was going to kiss her—and oh, God, how she wanted him to kiss her—but he didn't. He just watched her face as he moved his hand to her breast. He circled her nipple with his fingertip, around and around, around and around until she wasn't really thinking anymore, just feeling.

But then as she watched him watching her, she couldn't help wondering what he was feeling and how he would react if she touched him the way he was touching her.

So she did. She brushed her fingers lightly across the fine dark hair on his chest, then circled in on one flat nipple, around and around, around and around, until the little nub in the center grew hard and tight and she knew what he was feeling then because he groaned.

Then he moved his hand between her thighs, which she should have been expecting, but wasn't, so she jerked a little and made a sound, a needy little sound that made the corners of his mouth turn up. And he did kiss her then, just when she wasn't expecting it, a deep, delicious kiss that stole her breath. "Touch me," he said against her mouth, the faintest breath of sound.

So she did. He was warm and slick and hard. So hard. She slid her hand up and down, up and down, her movements mirroring his. And the warmth spread through her body and the need coiled tighter and tighter.

And then he was kissing her again, his tongue thrusting deep. And she knew she was making noise but she couldn't help it. She wanted, she wanted, she wanted. Oh, God, she wanted.

He jerked away so abruptly, she thought for a second she'd done something wrong. "What?" she said.

"Condom," he answered.

And then he was back, all the way back, buried inside her, thrusting and thrusting and thrusting again as his hands and mouth worked their own brand of magic. Tension grew with each long stroke, winding tighter and tighter until she thought she'd die if it continued much longer. Her heart would stop or her lungs would collapse or her brain would explode. Something fierce and catastrophic threatened. She wanted him, needed him, desperately, and maybe it wasn't love, but it wasn't just sex, either. It felt deeper and more intense than anything she'd experienced before. It was special. Dominic was special.

He groaned suddenly and drove deep inside her, gasping as he spent himself. And that was all it took to trigger her release. She came apart at last, at long, long last, shuddering and gasping and crying out his name.

And when the last ripples of pleasure had faded away, Dominic pulled her close. "Incredible," he said, looking as shell-shocked as she felt.

And yes, she planned to echo his sentiment. *Incredible* was the word. Incredible to the nth power. Only first, she had to catch her breath.

* * *

Comfortably ensconced in Mrs. Chalmers's rocker at one end of the kitchen, Caitlin glanced up in surprise when Quin and Bree burst through the door from the pantry, singing at the top of their lungs.

She knew the instant Quin spotted Dominic, stirring a pot at the stove, because he stammered to a stop, as if he'd suddenly forgotten the refrain of "Scotland the Brave." Bree, blissfully oblivious, finished on her own from her perch on Quin's back. "Hey, no fair," she said, administering a good-natured whap with her shoes, which, for some reason, she was carrying rather than wearing. "You faded there at the end, buddy." Then she saw Dominic . . . and Caitlin beyond him. "Well, hi," she said with remarkable aplomb, doubly remarkable when compared to Quin's tongue-tied state. "We're back."

"I see that." Dominic didn't crack a smile, though Caitlin suspected he was as amused by this turn of events as she.

"Quin offered me a ride," Bree said, "on account of my blisters." She tapped Quin's shoulder. "You can set me down now."

He released his death grip on her legs and she slid to the floor.

"How'd you get blisters?" Caitlin asked.

"Traipsing around the antiques fair," Bree said. "We must have walked twenty miles. It was worth it, though, because we found out who sold the manuscript to Erskine Grant." She paused expectantly.

"Who?" Caitlin asked.

"Etienne LeTourneau. Jacqueline picked it up at an estate sale in Stirling, the same estate sale, coincidentally, where she found your bones."

Dominic frowned. "But—"

"But what?" Caitlin said.

"Nothing." He turned back to Bree and Quin. "Are you two hungry? This soup's almost ready."

"*You* cooked?" Quin said.

"He's coddling me," Caitlin said, a little surprised at how much that pleased her.

"She had quite a shock earlier. The kidnapper called with a ransom demand. Money and the manuscript in return for Magnus." He turned to Quin. "I've already alerted the Gulfstream's crew. We leave for Calix at midnight."

"Which will put us there in the middle of the night," Quin said.

Dominic gave his soup a stir. "And that's good because it's precisely what they're not expecting. So, you'd best eat up while you have a chance."

"Your cooking? I think not." Quin turned to Caitlin, a look of concern wrinkling his brow. "Dominic doesn't know the least thing about cookery. If you're foolish enough to try his soup . . ." He heaved an exaggerated sigh. "All I can say is, I trust you have a strong constitution."

"She does," Bree assured him. "Caitlin never catches anything, not even colds."

"It's true," Caitlin told him. "I'm a genetic freak. All the O'Shaughnessys are the same. No colds. No flu. No heart disease. No diabetes. No cancer. We're immune to everything."

Dominic and Quin exchanged a look Caitlin couldn't interpret. Quin said something she didn't catch and Dominic uttered an equally inaudible reply.

Bree settled near Caitlin on the edge of the brick hearth. "How much money did the kidnapper demand?" she asked quietly, all her earlier lightheartedness gone.

"A hundred thousand dollars."

"A hundred *thousand*?" Bree said. "Thousand? Not million? Does he know how much you're worth? How much Magnus is worth?"

"Apparently not," Caitlin said softly. "Or maybe it's not about the money."

"Fortune here," Dominic said as soon as Janus answered. "New development to report."

"You located the manuscript?"

"Yes, but—"

"Yes? Did you say yes?"

"I did."

"Well done." Janus rarely allowed emotion to color his voice, but his relief and satisfaction were obvious. "Your country is in your debt. I want that manuscript immediately. Send it via the next diplomatic pouch. No, cancel that. We can't be certain the pouch is safe, not when we don't know the identity of Fraternitas's inside man. You'll have to bring it to Calix personally."

"It's not that simple," Dominic said.

"Why not?" Janus snapped. "Would a trip to Calix interfere with your social life?"

Dominic's temper flared. Yes, the rest of the world

viewed him as a playboy, but Janus, of all people, knew better. "This has nothing to do with my life," he said, "social or otherwise. It's Magnus Armstrong's life that concerns me."

"Armstrong? You've located him?"

"In a manner of speaking." Dominic filled Janus in on the kidnapper's ransom demands.

"He asked for money?" Janus asked sharply.

"Why?"

"Something smells wrong. This was never about money. It was about that manuscript. Tell me, did the kidnapper let Ms. O'Shaughnessy speak with her stepfather?"

"No."

"Then how can you be certain he's still alive, or if, in fact, this so-called kidnapper even has him?"

"We can't, but what other choice do we have but to go along with his demands?"

"I don't like it," Janus said. "We can't risk the manuscript without some assurance of success."

"That decision's not ours to make," Dominic told him. "It's Caitlin's stepfather who's at risk and it's Caitlin who has the manuscript."

"Caitlin?"

"That's her name."

"It's not her name I'm questioning but the way you say her name. I told you to get close to her, not to fall in love with her."

Dominic counted silently to ten. "If you're questioning my professionalism, Janus, perhaps it's time for me to resign."

"Don't be silly." Janus laughed. "One doesn't resign from the CIS."

Dominic took a deep breath. "This one does."

They'd taken off from Edinburgh Airport a little before midnight in Dominic's private jet, a Gulfstream fitted with every conceivable comfort. Shortly after takeoff, Bree had retired to the bunk room aft of the main cabin. A few minutes ago, Quin had headed for the second bunk room situated just behind the cockpit. Caitlin considered following their example, but decided it would be a wasted effort. She was much too overstimulated to sleep.

She peered down at the lights scattered across the French countryside, wondering if Magnus would be in this predicament if she'd agreed to accompany him to Scotland in the first place.

Probably not.

Almost certainly not.

So in a sense, this was her fault. Just as the other mess had been her fault. Just as this current situation with Dominic was her fault. Damn it, she knew better. She knew this was the absolute wrong time to get involved with a man, especially a man she knew so little about. And the fact that the feelings she'd experienced while making love with him had been more intense than anything she'd ever experienced before didn't excuse her lapse in judgment.

Damn it. She was such a screwed-up mess of a human being. Caitlin leaned her forehead against the window and shut her eyes, remembering . . .

* * *

An hour into the flight, Dominic emerged from the cockpit, expecting to find the main cabin empty. It wasn't. Caitlin sat in a window seat, staring out at the darkness. He was struck by how alone she seemed. Not just physically but emotionally, as if some enormous, unbridgeable gulf separated her from the rest of humanity.

"Caitlin?"

She turned slowly and he saw then what she'd been trying to hide, the glistening tracks of her tears.

"What's all this?" He sat down beside her, shoved the armrest out of his way, and pulled her into his arms.

"Normally I'm not a crier," she said. "I don't know what's wrong with me lately."

"It's the stress," he said. "You're worried about Magnus."

"If only I'd gone with him to the symposium . . ."

"If you had, the kidnapper might be holding both of you for ransom."

Her muscles tensed, as if she were going to argue with him, pull away, or both. Instead she took a deep breath and released it in a gusty sigh. "I . . . we used to be so close."

"Used to be?"

"Things changed when I hit my teens."

"It's a rebellious age."

"And Magnus was without question the world's most demanding parent. 'Only your best is good enough.' He drilled that into me."

"Sounds like my old tutor."

"I tried to explain that education wasn't as important

to me as it was to him, that I wanted—needed—some kind of social life as well, but he wouldn't listen. Every hour of my day was filled with lessons and classes and tutoring and review sessions."

She stopped abruptly, as if she'd run out of steam. He tightened his embrace, resting his chin on the top of her head. Her scent conjured exotic pleasures.

"I'm guessing once you left for university, you went right off the rails."

She glanced at him, eyes wide in surprise. "How did you know?"

He shrugged. "The one thing Magnus never let you learn was how to handle freedom."

She sighed again. "Yes, well, the truth is, it was more my fault than his. I should have had better sense. When disaster struck, as it inevitably did, he took care of everything . . ." Her voice trailed off. Another tear rolled down her cheek. "Things were never the same between us after that. He distanced himself. Maybe he thought I needed some space. Or maybe he was so disappointed in me that he couldn't stand to be in the same room. I don't know."

She didn't say anything for a long time, and Dominic thought perhaps she'd talked herself out, but then she stirred, pulling away from him. "He invited me to go with him to Edinburgh. I shouldn't have turned him down."

Dominic pulled her into his arms again. She resisted at first, but he coaxed her with whispered words and gentle touches until she relinquished her defenses with an almost inaudible sob. "It's going to be all right," he said, hoping he was right.

After a while, she shifted her position and took his free hand in hers. "You're a good man, Dominic Fortune." She shifted again, moving a little apart so she could look him in the eye. The remnants of her tears still sparkled on her lashes, but a smile touched her lips. And his heart.

"I owe you an apology."

"For what?" he asked in surprise.

"I shouldn't have made love with you. It was wrong, and I knew it."

"Wrong?" He raised his eyebrows. "You're telling me the best sex of my life was wrong?"

"It happened for all the wrong reasons. I was upset. I used you, and for that I apologize."

He studied her face. She looked as fragile as a porcelain figurine. "No apology necessary. What happens in Edinburgh stays in Edinburgh."

She took his hand between both of hers and squeezed it tightly. "Thank you."

"But I meant what I said before about not letting anyone hurt you."

She studied him curiously. "But why? Why are you doing this? Why are you going to all this trouble and expense on my behalf? You scarcely know Magnus."

"True," he said, not sure where to start. "Initially, I helped you because that was my assignment."

"Assignment?" She moved so they were no longer touching.

"Yes, I was supposed to keep an eye on you, locate Magnus, and recover the missing manuscript, which, I might remind you, is rightfully the possession of the Calixian government, Book One of the *Calix Chronicles.* I know how bizarre it sounds, but I do—I did—contract work for the CIS. That's the Calixian Intelligence Service."

"You're a spy?" Her voice rose a full octave in patent disbelief.

"A contract agent. It was a part-time position. And as of yesterday, I'm officially off the payroll."

"You quit?"

"Yes."

"Why?"

"I disagreed with my superior."

"He wanted you to confiscate the manuscript and to hell with Magnus."

"Essentially."

"And you weren't willing to do that."

"No," he said.

"Why not?"

He met her gaze. "You know why not."

She was the first to break eye contact. "Dominic, could your CIS contact have been lying to you?"

"About what?"

"The manuscript. How can it be a Calixian artifact? Bree said Jacqueline bought it at an estate sale in Stirling."

"Perhaps Jacqueline lied."

"Why would she?"

"Because she knew the manuscript was stolen. Because she knew it had been smuggled out of Calix. Because she's working hand in glove with the smugglers."

"Where's the proof?"

"I asked Wallace to check out her story. He's driving to Stirling later today."

"You really don't trust her, do you?"

"Trust is earned."

"Do you trust me?"

"You earned my trust when you admitted you had the manuscript."

Her eyes grew round with shock. "You knew?"

"I'd searched your room." He paused. "Do you trust me?"

She studied his face. "You didn't have to admit you were a spy. You didn't have to tell me you'd searched my room. Yes, I trust you."

And yet he still hadn't told her the whole truth. "You should try to get some rest," he said.

She smiled sadly. "I'm too stressed to sleep. Magnus calls me the world's champion worst-case-scenario thinker, and I'm afraid he's right. I keep thinking of all these horrible things they might be doing to him."

"You need a distraction," he said. "What's your favorite movie?"

This time her smile held a little more conviction. "Guess."

"Hmm." He studied her face from between narrowed lids. "*Casablanca?*"

"Not bad. I love *Casablanca* and *Gone with the Wind,* too, but my all-time favorite is *Roman Holiday.* Do you know that one? Gregory Peck and Audrey Hepburn. He's a reporter. She's a princess. And never the twain shall meet. I've probably watched it two dozen times, and it always makes me cry."

"I've seen it," he said, "though personally, I never bought the tearjerker ending. Why should the princess have to sacrifice her happiness for duty, particularly when her duty apparently consisted of nothing more important than an endless round of charity events and public appearances?"

"I never thought of it that way," Caitlin admitted.

"Be honest, if you were Audrey Hepburn and I were Gregory Peck, would you go back to your boring old life in your boring old castle, or would you stay in Rome and share wonderful adventures—and mind-blowing sex—with me?"

"I can't answer that," she said, "because I'm not a princess."

He met her gaze. "And I'm not Gregory Peck."

The Gulfstream landed at a private airstrip on Calix, where a stocky middle-aged man Dominic called Flavio awaited them. He'd bundled them and their luggage into an ancient Land Rover for the drive to Dominic's villa. Caitlin fell into a light doze somewhere along the way. She woke with a start when Bree touched her shoulder. "We're here."

"Mind the step." Dominic handed her down from the dusty Land Rover with the same care an eighteenth-century gentleman would have afforded a powdered and panniered lady. Never mind that she was wearing jeans and a wrinkled linen jacket.

She found herself standing beneath a starry sky in a graveled courtyard, fragrant with the mingled scents of lavender and pine.

"Welcome to Calix," Dominic said. "I only wish you were visiting under happier circumstances."

She murmured some rote politeness, too tired to carry on a real conversation.

Dominic led her and Bree through a wooden gate to a cobblestone-paved inner courtyard. Quin stayed behind, presumably to help Flavio with the luggage.

"This is nice," Bree said.

Colorful Japanese lanterns hung from the trees—one ancient gnarled olive, some squatty palms, and a trio of pink-flowered trees Caitlin thought might be mimosa, though she wouldn't swear to it, botany not being her forte.

But the focal point of the courtyard was the fountain at the end farthest from the villa. Sculpted in the shape of a two-faced man, it spat streams of water from both its mouths.

"Janus," Bree said.

"God of doorways and new beginnings," Dominic added. "You'll see his image all over the island. When my grandparents built the villa after World War II, they commissioned the fountain from a Sicilian sculptor."

"I like him," Bree said. "Your Janus, I mean. He's got character."

Dominic ushered them through a heavy door, dark oak with intricate carving and copper trim. Inside, an airy foyer opened onto a spacious living room. The brilliant white of the rough plastered walls provided a sharp contrast with the dark woodwork. Comfortably furnished with overstuffed chairs and sofas, antique wood pieces, and jewel-toned Persian rugs, the room offered its own welcome to Calix. If Caitlin hadn't been so sleepy, she'd have been tempted to linger for a while.

"This way," Dominic said, indicating a spiral staircase. As they descended, he explained that the villa stair-stepped down the hillside. The upper level rooms had balconies; the bedrooms his housekeeper had prepared for her and Bree opened onto a wide terrace overlooking the sea. "But you'll be able to appreciate the view better in the morning," he said, giving her arm a squeeze. "Right now you're asleep on your feet."

Caitlin's room was as charming as the rest of the villa. The centerpiece was a huge canopied bed hung with airy chiffon draperies in a soft rose that matched the satin duvet as well as the tile in the attached bath. The rest of the furnishings were simple, a comfortable chair upholstered in a cream and rose floral print, a brass floor lamp, a chest of drawers, and an enormous armoire. French doors opened onto the terrace.

"Do you like it?" Dominic asked.

"It's beautiful."

"Bree's right next door," he said.

"And you?"

"On the top level. Two whole floors away." He smiled. "My housekeeper has a strict sense of propriety."

Caitlin yawned. "She needn't have worried. I'm much too exhausted to seduce anyone."

If she hadn't been so sleepy, she'd have laughed at the look on Dominic's face.

He left.

She was standing in the middle of the room, trying to decide if she had enough energy to take a shower or if she should just strip off the top layer of clothes and crawl into bed, when someone knocked softly on her door.

"Are you still up?" Bree's voice.

Caitlin opened the door. "What's wrong?"

"I really want to take a bath, but my bathroom only has a shower." Bree gave her a look that was half apologetic, half pleading. "Do you have a tub in your bathroom?"

Caitlin nodded. "With a Jacuzzi."

"A Jacuzzi." Bree moaned. "Would you mind if I used it?"

Yes, she would mind. She didn't want to wait until Bree was done bathing before she went to bed. She was tired. She was worn out. She was fricking exhausted.

She sighed. She was also Bree's best friend. "Tell you what," she said. "Why don't we just switch rooms? I prefer showers anyway."

"Seriously?" Bree's eyes lit up.

"Seriously."

"Knock-knock." Quin poked his head in the door. "Where shall I put your luggage?"

"Bree's stuff here and mine next door. We're swapping rooms."

In ten minutes, she was climbing into bed in her new room—this one decorated in stark white and cobalt blue with touches of lemon yellow. In twenty minutes, she was dead to the world.

The burglar alarm jolted her awake some time later—the burglar alarm and the shouting, screams, and pounding feet. She pulled on the jeans and T-shirt she'd discarded earlier and inched her door open to see if she could tell what was going on. No one was in the hall. All the excitement seemed to be out on the terrace.

Caitlin moved to the French doors, shoved the draperies aside, and peered out. Bree, barefoot and wrapped in a sheet, stood just outside her room, yelling, "Did you catch him? Where'd he go?"

"Where'd who go?" Caitlin asked just as Dominic came thundering down a set of exterior stairs with Flavio at his heels. Both men carried guns, Dominic a lethal-looking handgun and Flavio an ancient shotgun.

"What happened?" Dominic demanded.

"Someone broke into the villa," Bree said. "He took off that way." She pointed toward the far end of the terrace. "What's down there?" she asked.

"The beach," Dominic said. "He must have come in by boat." He nodded to Flavio. "You stay here. "I'm going—" The unmistakable sound of an outboard motor starting up cut across his words. He took off at a run, swearing under his breath.

"Don't shoot!" someone yelled from below the terrace. "It's me."

"Quin!" Bree shouted.

Abruptly the alarm shut off, and someone—the

housekeeper?—called from above, "The police are on their way. Is everyone all right?"

Flavio yelled something back, in Calixian, presumably, because Caitlin didn't understand a word.

"Did you get a good look at the intruder?" she asked, but Bree didn't seem to hear her.

Clutching her sheet, Bree ran barefooted across the terrace, yelling, "Quin? Are you all right, Quin?"

Dominic's face, a pale smudge in the darkness, swam into view as he climbed up from the beach, followed closely by Quin. The housekeeper gasped, then launched into what sounded like a good tongue-lashing, though Caitlin couldn't be sure because the woman wasn't speaking English. She shouted a few more vituperative syllables, then slammed the window shut with a bang.

"What—" Caitlin started, then shut her mouth as she got a good look at Quin, newborn naked, though considerably larger. Considerably.

Bree launched herself at him, nearly knocking him down in the process. "Are you all right? He didn't hurt you, did he?"

"I'm fine, but our pervy visitor didn't fare so well. I nailed him a dirty one, broke his nose I think. Definitely blacked an eye."

"Why don't we take this inside?" Dominic said. "Flavio, would you go reset the alarm and make sure we're locked up again?"

Flavio nodded agreement and headed up the exterior staircase.

They all trooped back through the open French doors

into Bree's room. By the time Dominic hit the light switch, Quin was wrapped up in the duvet. Pink was not his color.

"What the bloody hell happened here?" Dominic demanded with a glance around at the chaos of the room. The bedside table was tipped on its side, its contents scattered across the carpet. Clothes and towels littered the floor. The bedding was half-on, half-off the four-poster, and the chiffon that had draped the canopy lay in a tangled heap.

"World War Three?" Caitlin suggested. "Massive earthquake?"

"Not funny," he snapped. "Did the intruder do this?"

"Don't look at me," she said. "I wasn't here."

He scowled at her. "It's your room."

"It *was* my room. Bree and I traded."

Dominic looked at Bree, who nodded. He drew a deep breath, released it, glanced over at Quin, then back to Bree. "I see," he said.

Duh.

"So." This time he directed his question to Bree. "Did the intruder do this?"

"No." Her cheeks matched Quin's duvet.

"The alarm sounded when he opened the door," Quin said. "I yelled, and he took off. I must have knocked over the table trying to untangle myself from the bed curtains."

And quite the mental image that evoked.

Dominic nodded. "So we don't know for sure what he was after."

"The manuscript," Caitlin said.

"Or you," he said.

A little shiver ran down her spine, and suddenly nothing seemed the least bit funny. Nothing at all.

November 1617
Near Drymen, Scotland

Hamish woke with a start, not sure at first where he was or how he'd got there. He was warm enough, too warm to have been buried alive, though that's what it felt like, this weight that pressed down upon him like a layer of sod heavy with rain. Didn't smell like good clean earth, though. He drew a cautious breath, filling his nostrils with the foul stench of pig manure and rotting vegetation.

His heart stuttered with fear as he searched his memory for the how and the why of it. Why couldn't he remember?

And then without warning the memories flooded back, overwhelming him. Auld Mòrag and the dirk. Over and over, she'd stabbed him, screaming all the while. *Demon, demon, get ye back to hell.* He remembered each piercing blow—the pain ripping at his flesh, his gut, his chest.

Surely no mortal could survive such an attack. And yet he lived. Perhaps the old witch had it right. Perhaps he was a demon.

A demon buried in a midden heap.

Of course, he thought. She'd had to hide his body, but

the ground was frozen, and she'd already used up most of her strength in that murderous frenzy. But rotting manure made for easy digging.

He had to get out of here, get home before his mother woke and found him gone. But how? He lay on his stomach, his arms pinned in place by the weight of manure and straw above him. How was he to dig himself free when he could barely move his fingers? He scrabbled at the muck, grunting and straining.

His labor fell into a pattern. He'd dig until his strength failed, rest a few minutes, then dig again. It was during one of his increasingly frequent rest periods that he heard something, a furtive rustling followed by a scratching sound. Someone—or something—knew where he was. Someone—or something—was digging him up.

Not Auld Mòrag. She had no reason to rescue him.

But no one else knew where he was. Except . . .

Oh, God. Please, God. No, God. His mind winced away from the possibility. The devil had come to claim his own.

9

DOMINIC STOOD ON THE TERRACE and stared down the shelving rocks to the sea beyond, a deep indigo stretching to the horizon. His heart ached at the beauty of it. He'd missed the island, missed it almost unbearably, but being here was painful, too.

On Calix, he was constantly reminded of all he'd lost the day his mother committed suicide, not only his mother but for all intents and purposes, his father, too. Devastated by the loss of his wife, his father had become a virtual recluse, closing out everything and everyone—even his son. A virtual orphan at the age of nine, Dominic had soon grown a protective skin, and that was perhaps the biggest tragedy of all. In that one day he'd lost both his parents and his childhood. Small wonder he spent so little time here—virtually none beyond his periodic duty visits to his ailing father.

Small wonder, too, that he'd eventually been drawn to the danger of espionage. The excitement of the work made up in part for the emptiness of his personal life and gave him a purpose, a meaningful way to serve his country.

His housekeeper, Portia, had set the table with a crisp white Battenberg lace cloth and the good silver, china, and crystal. She'd even produced a centerpiece of sweet-scented lavender. Quite an effort for breakfast al fresco. Made him wonder about her agenda.

And while he was considering motivation, what the bloody hell was going on with Quin? He'd known Quinton Gilroy all his life, but never had he seen the man act like this over a woman, especially not a giddy little piece of fluff like Bree Thatcher. Peculiar. Almost as peculiar as his own obsession with Caitlin O'Shaughnessy. He couldn't remember ever feeling so attracted to a woman.

Dominic leaned against the balustrade. To the east rose the Aeternus Mountains and beyond them lay the palace compound, less than ten miles as the seagull flew, fifteen tortuous miles as the goat path meandered, and thirty circuitous miles as the road snaked along the coastline.

He'd been on the phone for the past hour, arranging for extra security, inquiring about the status of the police investigation into last night's break-in, speaking to Lord Chamberlain William Weston, the man who'd run the king's household with military precision for over a quarter of a century, about securing last-minute invitations for the ball tomorrow night, and finally checking in on his father, who, according to his nurse, was having a good day and would welcome a visit later.

A visit he dreaded. A month ago, during his last stay

on Calix, his father's haggard appearance had shocked him. His health had gone downhill rapidly since Christmas, despite the radical new treatment his doctor had hoped would give him a new lease on life.

"Dominic?"

He turned. Caitlin stood at his elbow, looking rested and clear-eyed, very different from the fragile young woman he'd glimpsed last night on the plane. Dressed in faded jeans and a fitted lavender cami that bared her shoulders and emphasized her curves, she looked utterly delectable.

"You slept well?"

"Like a rock. I don't think I stirred from the time I went back to bed until Bree came barging into my room half an hour ago jabbering about a hummingbird free-for-all."

"Did you catch any of the show?" he asked. "The birds' antics can be quite entertaining. The way they go after each other in these territorial disputes, you'd think there was a serious flower shortage, which is not at all the case." He waved an arm to indicate the tubs of geraniums lining the terrace, the roses that filled a bed next to the house, the poppies and lavender that grew in wild abandon along either side of the path down to the beach.

"No, they'd patched up their differences by the time Bree dragged me out of bed." Her smile faded, and he suspected her thoughts had turned to Magnus. "They won't hurt him, will they, if I do as they ask?" she said, confirming his suspicion.

"I don't know," he answered truthfully.

Neither of them spoke for a moment. A tiny lizard, no longer than his finger, slipped out of a crack in the low wall that enclosed the terrace, raced along the balustrade for a foot or so, then abruptly changed direction and disappeared over the edge.

"Are you hungry?" he asked. "Bree ate earlier, but I waited for you."

"You didn't have to do that." She planted her elbows on the balustrade next to him and gazed at the sea as if she expected to spot a mermaid frolicking in the shallows.

"I'm never hungry when I first wake up. Waiting for you let me work up enough appetite to do justice to Portia's spinach quiche. If you're ready, I'll let her know."

Caitlin nodded. "Quiche sounds wonderful. Unlike you, I woke up ravenous."

He walked across to the call button, pressed it to signal the housekeeper, then strolled back to Caitlin's side.

"Incredible, isn't it?" She waved an arm to indicate the sweeping view. To the west curved the sandy shoreline. Above the beach, olive trees flowed down the slope in a silvery green flood that narrowed as it approached the nearby village of St. Agnes.

To the east, the mountains reared up from the water like fierce sea monsters turned to stone in the midst of an assault. Atop the highest peak, the old Crusader castle stood guard as it had for centuries, one section of its massive outer curtain wall hewn from the living rock.

And to the north stretched the sea, the deep blue

Mediterranean of Neptune and Aeneas, its surface glittering like a carpet of sapphires in the morning sun.

"Hard to believe evil could exist in a place like this."

"Calix's beauty is undeniable, but scratch the surface and it's no different from any other place on earth. Evil not only exists," he said, "it flourishes."

She turned to him with a searching look, as if his vehemence had surprised her. "You're not talking about Magnus's kidnapping, are you?"

He fixed his gaze on the Crusader castle. "In many ways Calix embodies the fairy-tale kingdom of legend. We have mountains and forests and picturesque villages, even a palace and a king. But in classic fairy-tale tradition, Calix also has a curse."

"What kind of curse?"

"The worst kind. The kind no magic spell can break. The Calixian curse is in our genes. One of every ten males eventually develops symptoms, which can vary, though for most the disease starts with tremors in the hands or weakness in the legs. At first victims just seem a little clumsier than normal. As the disease progresses, however, they develop a lurching gait and may have difficulty speaking. In the later stages, although intellect and mental acuity remain unaffected, the muscles become rigid, and victims are confined to a wheelchair, often unable to talk."

"How horrible!" Caitlin shot him an appalled look. "Trapped inside a husk of a body, unable to move or communicate?" She shuddered. "A curse indeed."

"It's actually an autoimmune disorder."

"Like AIDS?"

"No, AIDS is a deficiency of the immune system caused by a virus. The Calixian curse is just the opposite, a genetic disorder in which the immune system is overactive. Healthy tissues are damaged or destroyed.

"Oddly, not everyone with the gene develops the disease, so genetic screening isn't particularly helpful. Once the disease is triggered, however, doctors can confirm the diagnosis by checking for the presence of a rogue protein in the blood."

"So why don't they just figure out a way to neutralize the rogue protein?"

"Researchers are working on the problem. They have developed drugs that can slow the disease's progress. And the stem cell work they're doing now in Switzerland looks promising. But so far, there's no cure."

"And ten percent of the population is afflicted?"

"Ten percent of the males. Only rarely are females affected. The first symptoms generally manifest themselves when the person is in his twenties, but there have been cases where the disorder didn't appear until the victim was much older. My father, for example, showed no signs of the disease until he was in his early forties."

"Your father? Your father has the disease?"

"Yes."

Her face went blank. "I know you were born in the kingdom, but I thought your family was Scottish. If it's a genetic disorder . . ."

"My mother was a Scot; my father's Calixian."

* * *

"Why are we really going to St. Agnes this morning?" Bree asked Quin as they hurtled along the coast highway in the dusty green Land Rover at an amazing forty-five miles an hour. Amazing to Bree, at any rate. The engine had made some very ominous clunking and clanking noises when Quin first turned the key in the ignition; she'd figured the top end would max out under thirty.

"You heard Portia. She needs someone to collect her grocery order."

Bree eyed the big redhead with skepticism. "Yes, I heard Portia. I also saw you elbow Flavio when he started to volunteer for the job. So again I say, why are we really going to St. Agnes this morning?"

Quin's smile reminded her of those seen so often in Etruscan sculpture—calm, unruffled, and smug. "You do keep your eyes open, don't you?"

"Flattery will get you everywhere, just not at the moment. Answer the question."

"You're a persistent wench."

"Damn straight."

He laughed. "All right, I admit to an ulterior motive or two. First, I have to run an errand for Dominic. While I'm doing that, I thought you might enjoy looking at the shops."

"What kind of errand?"

"Hector Yuli, the thug Dominic surprised in Magnus Armstrong's suite, lives in St. Agnes with his two older brothers and his dear old widowed mum. I'm to see if he's around."

"Dominic thinks Yuli may have been our burglar last night."

Quin nodded.

"What else?"

"I beg your pardon?"

"You said, and I quote, 'an ulterior motive or two.' End quote. So what's your second reason for volunteering to play errand boy?"

"I need to stop by the chemist's, as well."

"Why's that?"

He shot her an inscrutable look. "To pick up some condoms."

"Oh," she said.

Portia, an energetic little dumpling of a woman with thick dark hair, beautiful brown eyes, and a hint of a mustache, bustled about, serving their breakfast. "Will there be anything else, sir?" she asked Dominic.

"No, Portia, this looks lovely, thank you."

The housekeeper bobbed her head and disappeared into the villa.

"I feel like I'm in an old Cary Grant movie," Caitlin said. And it wasn't just because of the glamorous Mediterranean setting, she admitted to herself. Across the table, Dominic raised an eyebrow, shooting her a saturnine glance. With his thick, dark hair and startling blue eyes, he could have been one of Hollywood's leading men. "Breakfast on the terrace," she said a little breathlessly. "I think there's a scene like that in *To Catch a Thief.*"

Dominic's mouth curved in amusement. "You like old movies, don't you?"

"Some," she said, taking a bite of her quiche. "How about you?"

"Some," he agreed.

They compared notes on their favorite movies. She had a special fondness for Cary Grant and Audrey Hepburn, while his tastes ran more to historical epics and action-adventure films.

Portia's quiche tasted even more delectable than it looked, but despite Dominic's efforts to keep things light, Caitlin's worries gradually crept back to the forefront of her mind, stealing her appetite before she'd put much of a dent in her breakfast.

"Something wrong?" Dominic said quietly. "If you'd rather have cereal or bacon and eggs, I'm sure Portia would be happy to—"

"No," she said. "It's not the food."

"What then? The company?"

She gave him a half-hearted smile. "No. It's just . . . damn it, Dominic, I've been over it and over it, and nothing adds up."

"For instance?"

"For instance, why would the kidnapper make a ransom demand and then try to break into my room?"

Dominic shrugged. "Maybe he planned to kidnap you as well."

"And maybe we're dealing with two separate sets of bad guys."

His blue gaze sharpened.

"The same possibility had occurred to you, hadn't it?"

"Yes," he admitted.

"And another thing," she said. "Why did the kidnapper demand such a paltry ransom? A hundred thousand dollars? I'd have paid millions to get Magnus back."

"Which would argue that it's the manuscript they're most interested in."

"Okay, but if it's the manuscript that matters, why ask for money at all?"

Dominic took a sip of his coffee. "Good question."

"And here's another. I've read almost half the manuscript, and yes, I do see how someone as obsessed with the Merlin legend as Professor Grant might have convinced himself that Hamish MacNeill was the sorcerer reincarnated. But why would anyone commit murder over a myth?"

"Hamish MacNeill is something of a legend on Calix. There are many tales of his heroism, but I've never heard anyone claim he and Merlin were one. What exactly is the connection? Or the supposed connection?"

"According to Hamish, he and Maggie Gordon, his uncle's wife, were . . . How can I phrase this delicately?"

"Shagging?" Dominic suggested.

"I don't believe that term was in common use in 1617."

"How about tupping?"

"Technically, that requires livestock," she said.

"Fu—"

"Indulging in carnal pleasure," she said quickly. "Only, at the critical moment, lightning struck the tree they were lying under and split it down the center. Hamish discovered a human skeleton inside the shattered trunk.

When he touched the skull, it disintegrated, but its power entered his body, granting him immortality."

"I thought my tutor had told me all the Brother Hamish stories, but that's a new one. You say Grant bought it? He must have been as barmy as poor Hamish."

"Actually," she said, "parts of Hamish's story correlate with the Merlin legend. One, Hamish's adventure happened near Drumelzier, one of several places supposed to be Merlin's final resting place. And two, the Lady of the Lake did imprison Merlin in an oak tree—at least according to one version of the tale."

"So Grant wasn't certifiable. He accepted the story because it bolstered his own pet theory."

"Right," she said.

"His presentation at the symposium drew media attention, which in turn triggered violence for reasons which, as yet, we don't understand."

"Right again."

"We know someone from Calix is behind it, someone with access to the diplomatic pouch and the Royal Air Express, someone involved with Fraternitas, someone who's using petty thug Hector Yuli to do his dirty work."

"And," Caitlin added, "possibly someone with ties to Jacqueline LeTourneau, who might have lied about where she got the manuscript." She paused. "You're the expert on Calix. Who fits the profile?"

"Offhand, I can think of half a dozen people, but two stand out." A grim expression narrowed his eyes and hardened his features. "Jacqueline's father, Lord Chamberlain William Weston, and Jacqueline's former lover, Prince Maximilian."

"And you don't want it to be either of them," she said.

"I've known and respected both men all my life. I don't want to believe either of them is involved."

She reached across the table to place her hand over his. He glanced up sharply, searching her face, his expression curiously vulnerable. Was he thinking she'd changed her mind about getting involved with him? Gently, she withdrew her hand. "I'd like to meet your two prime suspects."

"Why?"

"This is probably going to sound ridiculous, but Bree thinks I may have some latent psychic ability . . . because of what happened the night of Jacqueline's séance. I thought maybe if I could talk to the men face-to-face, I might be able to tell if one of them is walking on the dark side." She glanced up, expecting to see skepticism, even derision on his face. Instead he looked thoughtful.

The breeze had blown a lock of dark hair across his forehead. What if she were to lean forward and brush it back off his face? What would happen then? Would he capture her hand? Perhaps press his lips to her palm? She had to stop this. She'd told him she wasn't ready for a relationship, right? But . . .

"I'll arrange it," he said.

Arrange what? she wondered, having momentarily lost the thread of the conversation. Then she remembered. The two prime suspects.

"I'd planned to go to the palace this afternoon anyway to visit my father."

His father lives in the palace?

"You can come with me. While I'm busy with Father, Weston can give you the grand tour. Then afterward, I'll take you to meet my uncle."

"Your uncle?" she asked, though she was pretty sure she already knew the answer.

"Prince Maximilian, my father's younger brother."

"Which would make your father . . . ?"

"King Charles."

"And you?"

"Prince Dominic Charles Ramsey Fortunatus."

"Fortunatus? I thought your name was Fortune."

"Fortune's the Anglicized version. People find it easier to pronounce."

She stared at him, her thoughts flitting back and forth between "Holy shit!" and "Oh, my God!" If Dominic was a prince, they had even less in common than she'd thought. And no chance at all at a future. Oh, God, she was so, so screwed.

Quin parked the Land Rover on a side street near the center of town, a ten-minute walk from the Yuli cottage. He and Bree got out.

"How big is St. Agnes?" she asked.

"Eight thousand people, more or less, mostly fishermen, farmers, and shopkeepers."

"What's Proposition Three?" She pointed to one of the election posters that had been plastered all over the village. It read, "A boon to the economy . . . Vote "Yes" on Proposition 3."

"The gambling initiative," he said. "It's supposed to turn Calix into another Monte Carlo, though some people are skeptical. They fear that legalizing gambling will attract organized crime to our little corner of the world."

"What do you think?" she asked.

"Dominic opposes it, as does his father."

She raised her eyebrows so far that they showed above the frames of her oversized sunglasses. "That's not what I asked."

"All right. In my opinion, if correctly implemented, the change would be good for the country. If gambling is restricted to the upscale casino resort they've proposed, I don't foresee any major negative impact on national morality. Plus, the casino and the luxury resort with all its amenities would generate a significant increase in tourism and provide a badly needed boost to the economy." He locked up the Land Rover. "End of lecture. Now, I'm off to check on the Yulis."

"And I'm off to see the town," she said with a jaunty grin.

He checked his watch. "There's a little café called Gina's right on the harbor. Shall we meet there at ten?"

"Ten it is." Bree saluted and headed off toward Harborview Way, St. Agnes's principal thoroughfare. Just before she disappeared around the corner, though, she paused and waved . . . almost as if she'd known Quin would still be watching.

November 1617
Near Drymen, Scotland

The demon uttered a scream of frustration, a bloodcurdling cry that raised the hairs along Hamish's neck. The scrabbling noises grew more fevered. And closer. Hamish felt a stream of cold air wash across his back.

"Fergus!" Auld Mòrag's shrill voice. "Here, kitty, kitty. Where are you, lad? Have ye cornered yourself a wee mousie then?"

The cat yowled again, digging madly at the midden heap. One claw snagged the fabric of Hamish's cloak.

"Fergus!" the old woman screeched. "What are ye doing? Leave that muck alone and come to bed."

She must have grabbed the cat, because he snarled a protest. Scratched her, too, from the sounds of it. She swore savagely under her breath. "Get out of my sight then," she said. "And don't think it'll do ye any good to beg for a sip come milking time, ye wee ungrateful beastie."

Hamish waited until the sounds of her grumbling had faded to silence before renewing his efforts to free himself. Thanks to Fergus's good work, he was able to escape his smelly burial plot within the hour.

No wonder ghosts were so rarely benign, Hamish thought. Rising from the dead was an arduous chore, enough to try the patience of a saint.

10

"WHAT DO YOU MEAN SHE'S DISAPPEARED?" Caitlin heard Dominic say to someone on the telephone. Portia had summoned him to take the call as they were picking their way back up the steep stone steps after a walk along the beach. He'd sprinted ahead; she'd taken her time, arriving at the villa in time to catch only part of the conversation. Portia hadn't mentioned the caller's name or where he was calling from, but somehow Caitlin knew which "she" Dominic was referring to.

She caught his eye across the width of the big room. "Bree?" she mouthed and he nodded.

"You're positive?" Dominic said, and then after a pause, "Bugger that. You had no way of knowing."

"What's happened?" she asked.

"No, don't." He glanced at his watch. "You're at Gina's? Stay there. We'll meet you in ten minutes." Dominic hung up and turned to face her. "Let's go."

"It's Bree, isn't it? Someone's taken her."

"We can't be sure of that," Dominic said. "All Quin knows is that she didn't show at their rendezvous point. He's worried."

"So am I."

Two minutes later they were on their way in a cherry-red vintage Alfa Romeo that would have turned Magnus green with envy. "Magnus, I understand," she said, "but why Bree?"

Dominic shot her a sideways glance. "Because they mistook her for you?"

She felt mildly nauseated as a combination of guilt and regret caught her off guard.

"You all right?" Dominic said. "Am I driving too fast? You look a little green around the gills."

"I'm not carsick; I'm heartsick. It's my fault," she said. "I never should have let her come."

Dominic raised an eyebrow. "And how would you have prevented her? Bree strikes me as a woman with a mind of her own."

True. But Caitlin could have dissuaded her if she'd tried a little harder. Bree's actions were motivated by a misplaced sense of responsibility. She blamed herself for what had happened to Caitlin all those years ago at Berkeley, and for a time, Caitlin had blamed her, too. If Bree hadn't gone off with that guitar player, leaving Caitlin alone at the bar, she wouldn't have been such an easy target for the creep who'd slipped her the Rohypnol.

But the truth was, none of what had happened had been Bree's fault. Caitlin could have left when Bree did.

Better yet, Caitlin could have chosen to spend the evening studying instead of clubbing with a fake ID.

Caitlin hadn't needed Bree's support this time, either. But she hadn't argued very hard against it, because the truth was, she hated going it alone. And because of her cowardice, Bree was missing—possibly kidnapped in Caitlin's stead.

Dominic shifted down as they hit the edge of town. "It's going to be all right. We'll find her. We'll find them both," he said grimly.

"Brother Ambrose? Is that you?" *Orson Yuli, damn his hide.*

Brother Ambrose glanced around to see if anyone was close enough to listen in on his end of the cell phone conversation. This wing of the palace was invariably full of people—servants, guards, ministers, assorted lower-level bureaucrats, and, of course, members of the royal family. For the moment, though, he stood in relative isolation.

"Have you maggots in your brain, man? I've told you before. No contact between the hours of nine and five."

"But I have a surprise for you, Brother Ambrose. Me and Leo nabbed her for you."

A chill of apprehension raised gooseflesh on Brother Ambrose's forearms. "What the bloody hell are you on about?"

"The girl. The O'Shaughnessy girl. I got a good look at her face last night. Recognized her right off when I saw her down at the harbor this morning. Seemed like fate, it did."

"What have you done?"

"I told you. We snatched her. Got her trussed up in the boot of Leo's car for the time being. Called to ask what you wanted us to do with her. Leo's wanting her out of there, you see. He's got a date lined up for tonight. Might be a bit awkward explaining noises coming from the boot."

Brother Ambrose fought his rising temper; he couldn't afford to lose control, particularly not here. "Fuck Leo," was what he wanted to say. "And fuck you, too." Instead he arranged to meet them at the scenic turnout above Striga Meadow.

Caitlin hadn't said much on the short ride to St. Agnes. Nor had she commented as Quin repeated his story in painstaking detail. She'd just sat there at the little table on the boardwalk in front of Gina's, sipping her tea and tossing shortbread crumbs to the gulls.

"I should have had better sense than to let her wander off on her own," Quin lamented for the third time since starting his recital. The big redhead was taking Bree's disappearance hard.

Caitlin suddenly leaned forward, grabbed Quin by the brawny forearms, and gave him a shake. "You did nothing wrong," she said, pronouncing each word with sharp emphasis. "On the contrary, you were trying to protect her. It would have been foolish beyond permission to take her with you to visit the home of known criminals."

"Yes," Quin said miserably, his face sallow under his

tan, "but I left her unprotected. She might as well have been wearing a sign that read 'victim.' "

Caitlin gave him another shake, harder this time. "Damn it, quit feeling sorry for yourself. Dominic would have done the same in your place, and so would I. So would Bree, for that matter. Suck it up, and let's get on with it."

Dominic put a hand on Quin's shoulder. "Caitlin's right, you know."

Quin nodded, but Dominic felt the shudder that passed through the big body. Quin wasn't just feeling responsible, Dominic realized. He was scared out of his mind, terrified that something horrible was going to happen to Bree.

"Okay, then," Caitlin said, shoving her teacup aside. "Which parts of town have you searched already? No point in our duplicating your efforts."

"Just here at Gina's," Quin said. "And in the shops along Harborview. Several people saw her, but everyone said she was by herself. Nothing suspicious."

"All right." Dominic stood. "St. Agnes's two main attractions are the tourist shops and the water. You check the shops along the little side streets that butt onto Harborview. Caitlin and I will canvas the beach and the wharves. If someone grabbed her, chances are someone else saw it happen."

"What about the police?" Caitlin said.

"Already spoke to them," Quin said, "for all the good it did me. The sergeant said not to worry. St. Agnes is safe as houses. Girls go off on their own all the time and no harm done. But I'm to ring him in the morning if she hasn't shown up by then." With a muffled oath, he slammed his fist down on the table, so hard the teacups jumped. Then without another word, he shoved himself to his feet and took off toward the side streets at a lope.

Dominic gazed after him in troubled silence.

"We could cover more ground if we split up," Caitlin said.

Dominic shifted his gaze to her. "Screw that."

"Yeah, you're probably right." She headed for the beach.

He tossed down a few bills and followed. "Probably?"

"Think about it," she said. "If the bad guys did snatch Bree, mistaking her for me, then they aren't very likely to come after me now, are they?"

"No, but I'll feel better if I can keep an eye on you."

Forty-five minutes and three dozen fruitless inquiries later, they finally got lucky. James Calvin, bewhiskered captain of the fishing boat *Melinda C.*, identified Bree immediately from the picture Caitlin pulled from her wallet and reported seeing her heading toward the beach parking lot with Leo and Orson Yuli. "Thought it a bit odd at the time when they left like that," Captain Calvin said, "being as Leo'd just told me they planned to spend the day on the water."

Brother Ambrose arrived at the appointed meeting place well in advance of the Yulis, even though he'd had to take it slow. The rutted dirt road that wound through the mountains was scarcely more than a goat path in places.

The gravel road that led up from St. Agnes, the road the Yulis would be on, was better maintained, though considerably longer.

By noon, he'd begun to fret, worried that the Yulis might have been caught, and if so, what they might have said to implicate him. Involving them in his little foray into smuggling had seemed a brilliant plan at the outset. They had a boat and no scruples, a seemingly perfect combination of assets. Unfortunately, they also had big mouths and no brains.

By twelve fifteen, he'd decided to try calling Orson's cell phone, only to discover he couldn't get a signal.

By twelve thirty, he'd relinquished any hope of their showing, at which point a dust cloud billowed up above the hump of Vulcan's Shoulder to announce the imminent arrival of Leo's battered white Toyota Corolla. It topped the rise going a good ten miles an hour too fast, slid sideways in the loose rock, fishtailed a bit before straightening up, then pulled into the overlook with a flourish, stopping just inches from his own aging but well-kept Saab.

"I'd quite given up on you," he said.

"We had to stop halfway up," Orson said, "so Leo could answer the call of nature. Took him forever, too."

Leo looked acutely embarrassed. "I'll get the girl, shall I?" He reached under the driver's seat for the lever that popped the boot open. Then he circled around and shoved the lid up all the way. His eyes went round and his jaw went slack. "Holy Mother of God," he said. "We're fucked."

"Mind your tongue," Orson scolded. The eldest of the three Yulis, a devout Catholic who'd once studied for the priesthood, frowned on his brothers' use of profanity, particularly flagrant violations of the third commandment.

"Mind your own damn tongue, Orson. She's gone."

"What do you mean?" Orson, followed closely by Brother Ambrose, rushed to the rear end of the Corolla to see for himself.

Aside from a screwdriver and tangled strips of duct tape, the compartment was empty. "You fool," Orson said. "You locked her in there with a screwdriver? What were you thinking?"

"I didn't," Leo said. "There was no screwdriver, I swear. Do you take me for a blithering idiot?"

Brother Ambrose lifted the center section of the carpeting to reveal the space where the spare tire was stowed. "I daresay she found the screwdriver in there."

"Fuck," Leo said.

"Right," Orson said, "but even if she was able to work the tape loose, how did she get out of a locked boot?"

Leo looked uncomfortable. "Did you leave the car at any time," he asked, "while I was . . . occupied?"

Now it was Orson's turn to look uncomfortable. "You were gone a long time."

"So you did leave."

"She was *locked* in the *boot*!"

"Not really," Brother Ambrose said. He pulled the small knobs near the hinge that released the rear seat backs. They flipped down, revealing a large oval escape hatch into the back seat. "I imagine she got out that way, don't you?"

"Shit," Leo said. "Shit, shit, shit."

Orson was too upset to notice. "Now what?" he said. "Now what do we do?"

"Don't worry," Brother Ambrose told him. "I'll take care of everything."

"Bless you, Brother Ambrose," Orson said.

"Yes, thank you," Leo added.

Neither realized he had a gun, not until it was too late. Orson died instantly as the bullet pierced his brain. Leo tried to run. It took three shots to bring him down, two in the back and one in the head.

Even if no one had seen the Yuli brothers with the girl, the girl herself could identify them. And it followed that once the Yulis were in custody, they would name him as an accomplice. Accomplice in theft, smuggling, murder, kidnapping. The charges went on and on. Calix, civilized European nation that it was, no longer had the death penalty. But for some, life in prison was an even worse punishment.

He dragged the Yulis back to the Corolla. Orson he seat-belted in on the passenger's side. Leo he wedged in the back. Then he got into the driver's seat and drove the treacherous switchback track down to Striga Meadow. Once there, he stopped ten yards from the edge of the caldera, put the car in park, dragged Leo out of the back seat, and belted him in under the wheel.

Rigging a weight to the gas pedal took only a few seconds. Then he shifted into drive and jumped clear. The

Toyota bolted forward like a thoroughbred coming out of the gate. It powered down the slight incline and launched itself into space—a proud testament to the excellence of Japanese engineering. He ran forward in time to see the car disappear with a cartoonish *glub* beneath the emerald surface of the acid lake.

Some people were too stupid to live.

Bree was scared to walk on the road for fear the kidnappers would realize she'd escaped, double back, and find her. She was scared *not* to walk on the road for fear of getting lost. Or worse. Stepping on a poisonous snake, for instance, or falling off a cliff. For someone like Bree, who'd grown up in the city, the countryside was a scary place. Her compromise entailed hiking the grassy verge and diving for cover whenever she heard a vehicle approaching.

So far, she'd only had to dive once, for a farmer with a truckload of bleating sheep. Once she'd realized he was harmless, she'd run into the road shouting, trying to wave him down, but he hadn't heard her over the sheep or seen her through the dust stirred up by his passing.

For an island roughly the same size and shape as Sicily, with a population of nearly half a million, Calix seemed pretty damned deserted. As the morning progressed, fear took a back seat to a plodding determination to get herself safely back to civilization.

She trudged along for another forty minutes before she saw a second vehicle, this one a gray sedan. With no sheep to compete against, she was able to catch the driver's attention this time. He pulled to the edge of the road and waited for her to catch up.

As she approached, he rolled down his window. A rather nondescript man in his early forties with brown hair and gray eyes, he was dressed in a pinstriped gray suit with a starched white shirt and a blue tie, a bit overdressed for the boonies, in Bree's opinion. A definite city type, he looked like a government paper-pusher or maybe a substitute anchor on the evening news.

"Hello," she said, tempted to blurt out everything that had happened but wary as well. The man looked harmless, but . . .

"Lost?" His smile transformed him. Wide and endearing, it revealed a slight gap between his front incisors that humanized his face and made him quite attractive. Still, she didn't know him, didn't know if she could trust him. She'd hold her tongue, she decided, until she was safely back among friends.

"Lost?" she said. "Totally. Am I headed in the right direction for St. Agnes?"

"You are," he said, "though it's a bit of a walk. As it happens, I'm headed that way. I could give you a lift."

He didn't look like a serial killer or a rapist, but . . .

"I say! What happened to your arm?"

Bree glanced down to see what he was talking about. The duct tape had left crisscrossing red stripes.

"It's nothing." She forced a smile. "I feel awkward asking, but do you have a cell phone I could use? Rather than have you go out of your way, it might be better if I asked my friends to come get me."

"Certainly. I quite understand." He dug a phone from his pocket and handed it over. "Just flip it open and you're ready to go."

She did as directed, but the little magnifying glass logo on the screen searched in vain for service.

"Nothing?" he said, sounding surprised.

"Nothing."

"Well, that's annoying," he said. "Interference from the mountains, I expect. I could try again, once I get on flatter ground, I suppose, but I'm a bit uncomfortable about leaving you here on your own." He smiled again and offered his hand. "I'm afraid I didn't introduce myself. I'm Emrys Hawke, social secretary to King Charles."

Surely she could trust the king's secretary.

"And you are . . . ?"

Bree smiled, embarrassed by her unintentional rudeness. "Sorry. Bree Thatcher, tourist. I'm staying at a villa on the north shore."

He raised his eyebrows. "The Fortune villa?"

"Yes."

"Thatcher, you say? How odd. I'd heard about Dominic's guests. You know how word gets around in a place this small. But I thought the young lady at the villa was named O'Shaughnessy."

Bree smiled again. More connections. She could definitely cross Mr. Hawke off the list of potential predators. "That would be my friend, Caitlin," she said, and proceeded to fill him in on her morning's misadventure.

November 1617
Near Drymen, Scotland

Hamish ducked beneath the lintel of Auld Mòrag's cottage and tiptoed into the hovel, heavy with shadows now that the fire had burned down to embers. He stood there, unmoving, while his eyes adjusted to the darkness.

The old hag lay flat on her back on the pallet next to the wall. She snored open-mouthed.

Of Fergus, there was no sign. Out hunting rodents, no doubt. Or demons.

Stepping carefully, so as not to disturb the sleeping woman, Hamish searched the miserable room. She'd taken his dirk, a gift from his dead father. He'd not leave without it.

Mòrag snorted and flopped, and he froze. Old people woke easily; he'd do nothing to disturb her dreams. Not if he could help it. As he stood there, immobilized, waiting for the snoring to resume, he spotted his dirk on the mantelpiece.

The woman snorted again, once, twice, then relaxed, her snores once more falling into a steady rhythm. One step, two, and he reached for the dirk.

"You!"

He turned and saw the old hag sitting bolt upright, her shaking hands making the sign of the cross.

"I've come for my knife, that's all," he said.

"Demon!" she screamed.

"Shut your mouth, woman." Auld Mòrag had no near neighbors, but if she continued to raise an uproar like this, they'd be hearing her all the way to Edinburgh. "Hush, now," he said, taking a halting step toward her. " 'Tis naught but a dream."

"Fergus!" she shrieked, spittle spraying. "Fergus!" Her eyes showed white all around the dark irises.

In response to his mistress's summons, the tomcat shot through the half-open door.

"Fergus," she crooned. "Good boy. Good kitty. I knew I could count on ye." She turned toward Hamish, one long bony finger pointing straight at his heart. "Get him!" she screeched.

The cat bared his fangs and growled low in his throat.

"Call him off," Hamish said.

"Get him, I say!"

The cat snarled and yowled up and down the scale, a display that probably scared the holy hell out of every other tom in the district but did nothing to frighten a man who'd already died once that day.

"Get him! Attack, Fergus! Attack!"

The cat sprang at his face, all teeth and claws, and Hamish, acting on instinct, put his hands up for protection. He didn't mean to kill the cat; he'd forgotten he held the dirk. With his leap forward, the cat impaled himself on the blade.

An unearthly scream split the night. Not the cat this time but his owner. Auld Mòrag rushed toward Hamish, her fingers curled like claws. Hamish flung the cat at her, dirk and all, hoping to deflect her, but she kept coming, keening now, a weird eldritch sound that sent shivers down his spine.

Hamish sidestepped, and the old hag tripped and fell into the embers on the hearth. Renewed screaming filled his ears, screams of pain this time, pain and fear as her matted hair caught fire. "No! No!" She beat at the flames with her hands, rolling back and forth, back and forth.

He should have left then, retrieved his dirk from the cat's corpse and run for home. But then he thought, *What if she talks?* Yes, everyone in Drymen knew Auld Mòrag was a crazy old woman who talked to cats and concocted love philters of rose hips, mandrake root, crushed angle-worms, and goat semen. No one would credit her rav-ings.

Would they?

The promise of dawn lit the eastern sky. He'd never make it home now before his mother rose. And even if he did, how would he explain his clothing, slashed full of holes, soaked in blood and smeared with shite?

He had no choice.

11

CAITLIN WASN'T SURE WHAT TO MAKE of Emrys Hawke. Bree seemed quite taken with him, so much so that Quin was looking rather dog-in-the-mangerish. And Dominic was treating him like a hero, when all he'd really done was drive Bree back to the villa once she'd rescued herself.

To Caitlin's mind, if anyone was a hero around here, it was Bree. All alone in the dark, she'd managed to free herself from miles of duct tape and break out of the trunk without her kidnappers' even realizing she was gone. That took way more guts than picking up a hitchhiker.

The police had put out an APB on Leo and Orson Yuli of St. Agnes, last seen driving a white 2000 Toyota Corolla four-door sedan, vanity license plate LEO-9, heading east on a secondary road toward the Aeternus Mountains. They'd also taken statements from Bree, Quin, and Mr. Hawke. Dominic had given them the name of the fisherman who'd witnessed the abduction, and they'd left shortly afterward, presumably to interview James Calvin, captain of the *Melinda C.*

Dominic had invited Hawke, his former tutor, to eat with them. They were gathered now in the big living room, waiting for Portia to announce that luncheon was served. Caitlin sat silent, letting the conversations swirl around her. She was fairly certain she'd never met Mr. Hawke before, but he looked vaguely familiar. Maybe she'd seen his photograph somewhere. Or maybe he reminded her of someone else?

She shut her eyes, trying to concentrate.

Dominic touched her shoulder. "What did you say?"

She stared at him blankly. "Nothing."

"Yes, you did," Bree said. "I heard it, too. Sounded like 'And since when has safety been your paramount concern?' Only your voice was all weird. Like it wasn't really your voice."

"Because she spoke with a Scottish accent," Quin said. "I didn't know you could do that."

"Do what?" Caitlin felt like screaming, but she kept her voice even, her expression composed.

"Speak with a Scottish accent," Bree said. She turned to Quin, frowning. "I don't think *she* can. I think she was channeling again."

Caitlin happened to be looking in Mr. Hawke's direction when Bree said that, so she caught the expression that flashed across his face, there and gone so fast she almost missed it. Fear. After her little channeling episode, he probably thought she was a complete head case.

* * *

Dominic left the Alfa Romeo parked in the stone-paved courtyard in front of the palace, then escorted Caitlin up a flight of shallow stairs to the porticoed entrance. The uniformed guards standing on either side of the big double doors saluted in unison, then as Dominic and Caitlin reached the top of the stairs, swung the doors wide.

They'd left Quin and Bree back at the villa. Dominic smiled to himself at the memory of Quin's explosive response to Bree's announced intention of recuperating from her ordeal on the beach. "Are you mad, woman?" he'd demanded, only calming down when she'd agreed to a game of chess instead.

Just inside the palace, William Weston, the tall, elegant, fair-haired lord chamberlain, awaited them. He greeted them with a smile and a formal bow. "Your Royal Highness. Ms. O'Shaughnessy."

Dominic nodded. "Weston. How nice to see you again. You're looking well."

"Thank you, sir. And you?"

"Never better." Dominic formally introduced Caitlin, then spent a few minutes catching up on recent palace gossip, principally the ins and outs of the ongoing feud between Mr. Hawke, the king's secretary, and Packard, the king's valet. The two men were as zealously protective of their territory as the hummingbirds in the villa garden.

"Though since Mr. Hawke left earlier to take care of some errands for the king," the lord chamberlain said, "things have been a bit calmer. One of the chambermaids actually reported seeing a smile on Packard's face."

"Did you manage to find us invitations to the ball tomorrow night?" Dominic asked.

"To be sure," Weston said. "I put them in the post first thing this morning. They should arrive at the villa tomorrow. But if, by chance, they don't, let me know."

Dominic nodded, his mind only half attending to his conversation with the lord chamberlain. The other half was enjoying the parade of emotions crossing Caitlin's face as she took in every detail of their surroundings.

"Is that a Toulouse-Lautrec?" She squinted at the vivid painting on the opposite wall, a Parisian nightclub scene.

"Yes," Weston answered.

"You're probably thinking it's rather risqué for a public drawing room," Dominic said, "but my mother loved it. Father bought it for her while they were on their honeymoon." He turned to Weston. "And speaking of the king, how is he this afternoon?"

"Not as lively as he was this morning," Weston said. "He tires very easily these days. But he's quite looking forward to your visit. And if you don't mind, miss," Weston said to Caitlin, "the king would very much like to make your acquaintance."

"I'd be honored," she said.

The lord chamberlain knocked at the door that led to the king's private quarters. Packard invited them all in, but the lord chamberlain declined, pleading pressing business elsewhere. He left, promising Caitlin a tour later.

Apparently the chambermaid had known what she was talking about, because Packard was smiling as he ushered them into the anteroom. Short, balding, and elderly, he was dressed in his customary pale blue shirt, gray trousers, and matching vest. "Your Royal Highness. Ms. O'Shaughnessy." The little man bowed so low he nearly lost the reading glasses perched on the end of his nose. Apparently they'd interrupted his reading. A book lay facedown on a nearby table. *Skinwalkers* by Tony Hillerman.

"Good to see you, Packard. Packard's my father's valet," Dominic explained for Caitlin's benefit.

"Since he was a boy." Packard smiled again. "Make yourselves comfortable. I'll just go see if His Majesty is ready to receive you." He bowed himself through another door.

"What did you think of our first suspect?" Dominic asked the moment the valet was gone.

"There's quite a family resemblance, isn't there, between the lord chamberlain and Jacqueline? Same coloring. Same perfect posture."

"Did he strike you as a kidnapper or as the kingpin of a smuggling ring?"

"Frankly, no," she said, sounding disappointed. "In fact—" Whatever she'd been about to say was cut short by Packard's reappearance.

"The king will see you now." Packard led them down a short corridor to the study, a book-lined room with windows looking out on a small, sunny courtyard. "Go on in," he urged, then slipped away. Back to his mystery novel, presumably.

King Charles huddled in a wheelchair in the darkest corner of the room, head bowed. Dominic would have thought him dozing if not for the gnarled hands plucking nervously at the blanket that draped the lower half of his body.

"Father?" Dominic's voice cracked. Caitlin moved a little nearer and slipped her hand into his.

Silver threaded the king's dark hair. Age and illness had taken their toll, but Dominic knew the resemblance between him and his father was still quite remarkable. Both had narrow, high-bridged noses, square jaws, sharp, angular cheekbones, and arching brows. Only their eyes were different. Dominic's were blue like his mother's. The king's eyes were a deep coffee brown, sharp yet with intelligence. "Dom . . . nic," he said with an obvious effort.

Dominic drew Caitlin forward. "Father, this is Caitlin, Caitlin O'Shaughnessy, Magnus Armstrong's stepdaughter."

"Your Majesty." Caitlin swept a curtsy.

"Charmed, my dear," the king said. "Magnus and I . . . were at university together. Did you . . . know that? He's the one . . . who introduced me . . . to Caroline."

She shot Dominic a questioning glance.

"My mother," he said.

"Try not . . . to worry." The king coughed into a silk handkerchief. "Excuse me," he said, when he'd caught his breath.

"No excuses necessary," Dominic said.

Caitlin frowned. "You know about Magnus's disappearance?"

King Charles nodded. "And the . . . ransom demand. Although the CIS has tried to keep . . ." Again harsh coughing interrupted him. He fumbled for the glass of water that stood on the table next to his chair and drank deeply before continuing, ". . . things quiet, Janus . . ."

"Code name for the intelligence director," Dominic explained. "My father's the only one who knows his true identity."

A faint smile teased the corners of his father's mouth. "Janus tells me . . . everything."

"You'll know then, too, that I'm no longer working for the CIS," Dominic said.

The king nodded. "A little bird . . . told me." And once again that fugitive smile touched his lips.

"You're not angry?"

"I'm sure . . . you have . . . your reasons."

Dominic paced back and forth the width of the four-story, marble-floored foyer as he waited for Caitlin to finish her VIP tour of the palace. He'd stayed behind to visit a while longer with his father. A very little while, as it turned out. The king had suffered a third coughing fit, much more protracted than the earlier ones, and Dominic had had to ring for Packard.

"Dominic!" He turned to see Caitlin coming toward him, her lovely aquamarine eyes sparkling with enthusiasm. "Wow!" she said. "And I thought *my* father had a nice house."

Laughing, he ushered her toward the back of the building. "I take it you enjoyed your tour."

"Absolutely, though Bree would have appreciated it even more than I did. Did you know there are two Picassos in the east wing gallery? Two Picassos, a Rembrandt, a

Titian, an El Greco, a whole flock of French Impressionists, a Klee, a Dali, a Winslow Homer, and a really, really ugly Jackson Pollock. Those are just the ones *I* recognized, and compared to Bree, I know zip." She looked thoughtful. "I wonder why the thieves haven't plundered the art."

"Too difficult to fence," he said. "Plus, I suspect they're trying to steal as much as possible without alerting anyone, and stealing a Picasso would definitely set off alarms."

"Literally as well as figuratively," she said. "The security system here is first-rate."

He raised an eyebrow. "Casing the joint?"

She laughed. "Just keeping my eyes and ears open."

"Observing your guide as well, I assume."

"Him, most of all."

Dominic nodded to the guard on duty at the rear garden entrance. The man snapped a smart salute, then held the French doors open for them.

"And what conclusion did you reach?" Dominic asked once they were out of earshot. "Did Weston do anything to alter your positive first impression?"

"No, he was very nice. Charming without being oily, if you know what I mean. I kept dragging Jacqueline into the conversation, thinking if he were involved, he might act wary or change the subject."

"And did he?"

"No, he chattered away like any other proud parent. I did learn one interesting thing, though. It seems Jacqueline and Etienne are planning to be here for the ball."

"Oh, really? Isn't that interesting? I heard back from Wallace this morning. Jacqueline lied. Neither your bones nor the Merlin manuscript came from that estate sale in Stirling."

"So she must be involved, and if she's involved, then maybe I totally misread her father. Maybe he's in it up to his starched white collar." Caitlin stopped suddenly in the middle of the path. "If you don't mind my asking, where are we going?"

"To my uncle's quarters on the other side of the compound so you can check out suspect number two. I must warn you, though, curiosity is his besetting sin. He'll be just as anxious to cross-examine us as we are him. Unlike my father, he has no idea why you're on Calix. And we're not going to tell him, either, not as long as he's a suspect."

"So what's the cover story? What *do* we tell him?" Caitlin asked.

Dominic smiled. "As little as possible. But be prepared for a bit of awkwardness. He no doubt assumes we're a couple. I'm sure half the reason he invited us to tea was to get all the juicy details of our relationship."

"Like where we met," she said, then frowned. "Where did we meet, according to our cover story?"

"What's wrong with the truth? Especially when it's perfectly innocuous and, what's even more important, easy to remember."

"Makes sense," she said. "Anything else I should know?"

"My uncle has a reputation as a devil with the ladies."

"Runs in the family, does it? Well, if he offers me a pomegranate, I'll watch out for the seeds."

Dominic laughed. "I can quite envision Uncle Max as Hades in his chariot, but you'd make a very poor Persephone. Instead of properly bemoaning your fate, I see your taking a more proactive role, i.e., kicking his royal ass."

"Eight years of karate classes shouldn't go to waste." Her eyes sparkled with mischief. And he was tempted, oh so sorely tempted, to kiss her right there in the garden.

Instead he led her through a gate into the walled garden that had been his mother's special retreat. Here plants grew in great profusion, one flower spilling into another in a glorious tangle, a symphony of color and fragrance.

"How gorgeous!" Caitlin said.

"This is one of my favorite places in all the world." Dominic escorted her along the meandering path to the shallow pond in the center of the garden.

"Oh! I saw something. There in the water." She pointed to the spot.

"A crocodile, no doubt."

"You're joking. There aren't any crocodiles in the Mediterranean."

"There are masses of them on the Nile," he said. "But yes, I was joking. What you probably saw was one of the koi my father imported from Japan. See? There's another."

The shimmering orange-gold fish broke the surface, rolled, then disappeared among a cluster of lily pads.

"They're bigger than I'd thought they'd be," she said, taking a step back from the edge.

"But harmless," he told her. "When I was a child, I used to think their scales were made of gold, that if I could only catch one, I'd be rich beyond dreams of avarice. Mr. Hawke laughed when I told him. He netted one to prove to me that the scales were quite ordinary, not gold at all. A terribly disillusioning experience."

She smiled in sympathy. "I used to wish on falling stars until Magnus explained that they were really meteors burning up in the atmosphere. Didn't seem so lucky after that."

"Science has a lot to answer for," Dominic said.

Prince Maximilian's lugubrious manservant, Trimble, led them to the main salon, where he announced them in a mournful monotone. The prince, who stood near the fireplace at the far side of the room, turned to greet them, and Caitlin was immediately struck by the family resemblance. Like Dominic, he was tall and dark with arched eyebrows and a charming smile, though his elegant bones carried a few extra pounds and there were touches of gray at his temples.

"It's been a while, Dominic," the prince said as they drew closer. "I'm glad to see you haven't abandoned your roots entirely." He extended a hand to Caitlin. "Pleased to make your acquaintance, Ms. O'Shaughnessy."

"And I yours, Your Royal Highness," Caitlin said.

"Have a seat. Have a seat." Prince Maximilian indicated a burgundy velvet sofa with claw-feet, part of a seating group near the fireplace. In front of the sofa stood a marble-topped table inlaid with the Calixian crest. Two high-backed chairs, upholstered in cream satin striped with burgundy, made up the rest of the grouping.

Dominic took a seat next to Caitlin, one arm slung casually along the sofa back. His uncle chose one of the satin chairs.

"What brings you to Calix, nephew?"

"Does one need an excuse to come home?"

"Apparently you do. How long has it been? A year?"

"I came for several days at Christmas and then again last month."

"I must have missed you."

"Last month you were in Monte Carlo. And at Christmas, you were skiing in the French Alps, I believe."

"Swiss," he said. "Have you seen your father yet?"

"We just came from visiting him." Dominic frowned.

"Yes, his health has deteriorated rather dramatically in recent weeks. It's good that you're here."

"Do you know if he plans to give the traditional Independence Day address at the ball tomorrow night?"

"Yes, as far as I know. Not that I'll enjoy it," he added drily. "I expect he'll include some choice comments about my proposed casino complex."

"The king's opposed to the proposal?" Caitlin asked in feigned surprise. "Judging by the posters that cover every flat surface in St. Agnes, he's the only one."

Prince Maximilian smiled. "My brother's a reactionary. He opposes anything that might bring this country into the twenty-first century."

"Perhaps he's concerned about turning the kingdom into a den of debauchery," Dominic suggested.

His uncle's smile took on a devilish glint. "Oh, but Dominic, isn't that the point?" He turned quickly to Caitlin. "Have I shocked you, my dear? If so, I apologize. I was only having a bit of fun at my nephew's expense. I've no intention of allowing Calix to degenerate into another Las Vegas. My very upscale casino and resort will cater only to the crème de la crème and carry the same cachet of exclusiveness and elegance as the casino at Monte Carlo. But we mustn't bore Ms. O'Shaughnessy with local politics," he told Dominic, then turned back to Caitlin. "Are you enjoying your stay so far?"

"It's been exciting, to say the least," Caitlin said without thinking of the possible meaning Prince Maximilian might read into her words.

"Oh, really?" The prince shot an arch glance toward his nephew. "Tell me more."

"I'm looking forward to tomorrow. I've never attended a ball."

The prince leaned across the table to press his hand to hers. "You must promise to save me a dance."

"Of course."

"Jacqueline's going to be there. Did you know that?" Dominic said, and Caitlin remembered his earlier mention of the affair between Jacqueline and his uncle.

The prince raised an eyebrow. "Is that your way of asking if we've"—he paused—"kept in touch since she married the Frenchman?"

"One could hardly blame you," Dominic said. "She is a beautiful woman."

"And completely self-centered. I broke off the relationship when I realized she was more interested in the title than the man behind it. A humbling experience, I assure you. I think she quite fancied herself as a princess. And I wouldn't have minded so very much, but then I learned—quite by accident—that she had another lover on the side."

"Etienne?" Dominic sounded surprised. And no wonder, Caitlin thought. The balding Frenchman hardly fell into the hottie category.

"I shouldn't think so." Prince Maximilian seemed appalled at the suggestion. "Though I was surprised when she married him last year. They make such an unlikely couple, don't they?"

A maidservant set a large silver tea tray on the table in front of him. "Thank you, Louisa. That will be all." He turned to Caitlin. "Would you do the honors, Ms. O'Shaughnessy?"

Caitlin leaned forward to pour the aromatic tea into fragile china cups emblazoned with the royal crest. She handed one to Prince Maximilian. He overreached and a few drops landed on the marble table.

"Sorry," he murmured. "Clumsy of me."

Caitlin wouldn't have thought anything of it if she hadn't noticed Dominic's stricken expression. *The curse,* she thought. *He thinks his uncle has the curse.*

"What's the verdict on suspect number two?" Dominic asked as they drove back to the villa.

Caitlin turned to him with a smile. "If Calix is a fairy-tale kingdom, then your uncle is definitely the Big, Bad

Wolf. The man's a shameless flirt, but I didn't sense a villainous vibe. How about you?"

"No, nothing. Which, I admit, is a relief, even if it is frustrating to have eliminated both of our best suspects. I mean, who's left? The captain of the palace guards? The prime minister? The head of the assembly?"

When Caitlin didn't answer right away, he glanced sideways and saw that she was staring, as if mesmerized, at the sea, where the late-afternoon sun sparkled off the water in a silent invitation. Without examining his motives too closely, Dominic took the next fork to the right, a rutted track that wound through trees and heavy undergrowth to a dead end at a small secluded cove. He parked under an ancient olive tree, its arthritic limbs twisted and bent.

"What are we doing?" Caitlin shot him a puzzled look.

He pocketed his keys, walked around to the passenger's side, and extended a hand. "Come along," he said.

"Come along where?" She studied his face for a moment before placing her hand in his.

"It's a surprise," he said.

A smile spread across her face, and his heart launched into an acrobatics act. "I love surprises."

And I love . . . He tugged on her hand, pulling her out of the car. Then he wrapped an arm around her waist and led her across the sand toward Barrier Rock, the pockmarked volcanic promontory that marked the easternmost boundary of the cove. "This is private land, part of the Fortunatus holdings. Mr. Hawke and I used to come down here for picnics when I was small. I loved it because he'd let me explore the cave on the other side of the promontory."

He stopped at the base of Barrier Rock. "This bit's tricky. One misstep and you'll get a soaking, so if you're worried about ruining your shoes, you'd best leave them here."

"Given the choice between wet shoes and climbing rocks in my bare feet, I choose wet shoes."

"I like a woman who lives dangerously." He flashed her one of his devilish smiles.

Caitlin smiled back at him, and for a second the sparks of attraction between them flared into something altogether more dangerous. Then she shifted her gaze to the crescent of sand behind them. "Does this place have a name?"

"Smuggler's Cove." He offered her his hand. "The rocks are slippery. Watch your step."

They sidestepped along an eight-inch-wide ledge at the base of the cliff, a scant six inches above the wash of the waves. Caitlin squealed once and he thought for a second that she'd lost her balance, but that wasn't the case.

She stared at the water beneath them, panic in her voice. "I saw something moving down there."

He peered into the indigo depths. A lone crab scuttled about among the submerged rocks. "Just a crab," he said. "Quite harmless, I assure you."

She didn't look convinced.

They followed a crevice in the cliff face to a second ledge only slightly wider than the lower one.

"So where's the cave?" she asked.

"Directly above us."

Caitlin stared at him as if he'd lost his mind, and one could hardly blame her. The cavern's mouth, a narrow fissure camouflaged by a jutting overhang and a scraggly myrtle bush, was invisible unless one stood within a few feet of the aperture, positioned at just the right angle.

"Trust me. It's there. Straight up six feet or so. It's an easy scramble with all the footholds, almost like climbing a ladder."

She shot him a dubious look.

"I'll go first. Watch where I step." He clambered up, then lay down on the ledge and reached an arm toward her. "You can grab hold of my hand if you want."

"I can handle it," she said and scrambled up unassisted.

He drew her closer to the cliff, turning her round to face the well-hidden opening. "Voilà!" he said. "Welcome to Smuggler's Cave."

She stepped forward to peer inside. "Can we go in? Is it safe?"

He laughed. "Absolutely. In point of fact, I doubt any smugglers ever really used it. Smuggler's Cave is just what Mr. Hawke and I called it. The cavern extends almost fifty feet back into the hillside. Mr. Hawke claims it used to go even farther, but part of the roof collapsed in an earthquake."

"Earthquake?"

"Three or four hundred years ago. We get some seismic activity here, but nothing compared to California. If you'd like to explore, I've a penlight on my key chain."

"Definitely," she said with a grin. "No matter what you say, I'm convinced we'll find treasure."

"I found an empty bird's nest once. I think a storm must have blown it out of the myrtle bush."

"You're no fun."

"Oh, really?" He pulled her into his arms. "Define 'fun.' "

Their eyes met. The teasing laughter faded from her face even as the expression in her eyes intensified. "Dominic," she said, her voice barely audible. Her arms crept up around his neck, and his heart pounded. "Dominic," she said again, pulling his head down toward hers. He heard a rushing in his ears. "Dominic," she whispered, her mouth so close, he could taste his name on her lips.

And then she kissed him.

For a moment, he just stood there, savoring the softness and sweetness and warmth of her lips, tasting, feeling. And then he was kissing her back, not gently as she'd kissed him, but hungrily, and somewhere, in his head or in his heart or maybe both places at once, something went click, and he knew this was it. She was it. *Caitlin.*

"What?" She gazed up at him, a faint frown wrinkling her brow, and he realized he must have said her name aloud.

"Nothing," he said. Everything. And he lowered his mouth to hers again and lost himself in sensation. Heat, devastating heat. Mouth to mouth and tongue to tongue. She was so sweet, sweet and warm and addictive. And God, he wanted more. Needed more. But . . . Reluctantly he broke off the kiss.

"What?" she said breathlessly.

"I . . ." He paused, alerted by the sudden wariness in her eyes. She'd felt it, too, that connection. He knew it. But she still wasn't ready to admit it. He knew that, too. "I like the way you kiss," he said instead of what he'd intended to say.

She smiled, and he felt her relax. "Good. I like the way you kiss, too."

She pressed another kiss to his mouth, then stepped backward out of his embrace.

His hands wanted to cling, but he let her go. Some things couldn't be rushed.

He pulled his keys from his pocket and switched on his penlight. "Shall we search for that smuggler's gold?"

November 1617
Near Drymen, Scotland

He buried them—woman and cat—in the midden heap. Poetic justice.

12

CAITLIN ESTIMATED THE FLOOR OF THE CAVE was a good thirty inches above the wide ledge where they stood. Dominic made it in one giant step, then turned and reached down to help her up. A part of her relished this excuse to touch him again, and another part of her—the sensible part that knew how really, really stupid it would be to allow this attraction or whatever the hell it was to go any further—was saying maybe she could manage without his help. Or then again, maybe she'd miss her footing and ricochet down the cliff to land in the water below. Not a pleasant prospect. So she put her hand in his and damned if it didn't happen again, that weird zinging feeling like an electrical charge. Not good. Or okay, *tell the truth, at least to yourself, O'Shaughnessy,* it was good, really, really, good. But dangerous.

So with his help, she scrambled up and once she had both feet planted firmly on the ground—or in this case, rock—she dropped his hand like the proverbial hot potato.

Dominic looked at her strangely. And it started again, that freaky, weird zinging feeling, and he hadn't even touched her this time . . . except with his gaze.

She tried to breathe normally, in and out, but her lungs didn't want to cooperate. His fault. Dominic had the most incredible eyes, electric blue—maybe that explained the zinging—deep set and fringed with thick dark lashes.

Holy shit, she was in so much trouble.

A tiny smile tilted the corners of Dominic's mouth, as if—oh, God—he could read her mind.

"Do you have any idea how beautiful you are?"

She opened her mouth to say something—God knew what, she certainly didn't—but before she could make a sound, Dominic leaned over and kissed her again. And she told herself, *He's a prince, Stupid. This isn't real.*

But it felt real. His mouth on hers, fierce and punishing, then warm and coaxing. And she wanted to believe. She tried to believe. But she couldn't. She just couldn't. Fairy tales didn't come true, damn it.

But oh, this kiss, this deep, dark, delicious kiss. With a sigh, she gave herself up to the moment, a blissful journey through time and sensation. Her thoughts drifted in lazy circles.

Minutes, later—how many, she couldn't say because she'd lost all track of time—Dominic broke off the kiss. He touched her cheek with his fingertips. "So beautiful."

Her heart seemed to swell in her chest, and for one dreadful moment she thought she was going to burst into tears.

Then he captured her hand, pressed a kiss to her

palm, and folded her fingers over the warmth his lips had left behind.

"Dominic?"

"Yes?"

She opened her mouth to tell him how she felt, that she knew this was going to end badly, but that she didn't care anymore. She wanted him anyway—as much of him as she could have for as long as she could have him. But then at the last moment, she lost her nerve. "Let's go find that treasure," she said instead.

And if a fleeting shadow of disappointment passed across his face, she pretended not to see it.

Dominic flicked on his penlight and led the way. Caitlin followed, so preoccupied with the chaotic thoughts tumbling through her brain that she scarcely noticed her surroundings.

"Here we are," he said at last. "The end of the road." They'd arrived at the collapsed section he'd warned her about.

Only it looked as if someone had been digging in the rubble. The penlight's beam played across assorted tools—shovels, crowbars, picks—and a solid, squared-off shape covered with a tarp. "Looks like you were right about the smugglers," Dominic said. He dropped her hand and ripped the tarpaulin aside to reveal a neat stack of heavy plastic containers.

"Ammo boxes?" she said. "Who leaves ammunition lying around in a cave? Is someone planning a coup?"

"I can't believe this." Dominic flipped the latches on the nearest box and raised the lid. "Bloody hell," he said.

"What is it?" Caitlin moved closer, craning her neck to see past Dominic. The penlight caught the gleam of gold. Not ammunition. Coins. Gold coins.

"Bloody hell," Dominic said again.

The mantel clock struck a quarter after seven. Ignoring it, Quin concentrated all his attention on the chessboard, determined not to let Bree checkmate him again.

"God, I'm starving," she said. "Who knew a couple of games of chess could work up such an appetite?"

There she went, trying to throw him off his game again. She knew as well as he that she hadn't worked up an appetite playing chess. No, she was ravenous because of all the calories she'd burned in the interludes between play, during which time they'd engaged in some very energetic and extremely satisfying sex. And now, damn it, she had him thinking about sex again.

"What do you suppose is keeping Caitlin and Dominic?"

The first diversion hadn't worked, at least not as far as she could tell, so now she was trying another tack. But it wasn't going to work. He was going to win this game.

"Could they be in trouble?"

Unlikely, he thought, but the first niggling worries began their insidious assault on his concentration.

"I mean, I know Caitlin's a big girl and Dominic's a big guy—not as big as you, of course, but then who, outside of professional wrestling, is? Sure, they can take care of themselves. Dominic must have learned all kinds of ways to kill with his bare hands in spy school, right? And

Caitlin holds a brown belt in karate. Did you know that? But what if those slimeball Yulis ambushed them? It's possible, right?"

"I'm sure they're fine," he said, and made his move.

The instant he took his hand off his knight, she was all over him with her queen. "Him" meaning the knight, unfortunately, not Quin.

"Ha! Checkmate!" she said.

He scowled at her across the scene of his defeat. "You are not a gracious winner."

Bree's gloating smile turned sultry. "So teach me a lesson I'll never forget."

With an incoherent cry, he sprang to his feet, grabbed her, and tossed her over his shoulder. "Taunt me, will you?"

"Hey!" she yelled. "What do you think you're doing?"

"Yes," Dominic said from the doorway. "I'd be interested in hearing the answer to that question myself."

"Me, too," Caitlin said.

Quin set Bree back on her feet, wishing to God he counted invisibility among his talents.

"I beat him at chess for the third time," Bree explained. "He was about to exact his revenge when you saved me, darn it."

Dominic raised his eyebrows.

Caitlin developed a sudden fascination with the carpet, though Quin suspected she was working hard not to laugh.

"So," Bree said to Dominic and Caitlin, "how was *your* afternoon?"

* * *

Brother Ambrose's cottage was built on the site of a much older dwelling. Behind the wine racks in the cellar, one could enter a tunnel, one of many that honeycombed the Aeternus Mountains. In ancient times, the tunnels had served as a vast burial ground, much like the catacombs of Rome. In later centuries, the knights who'd built the nearby castle had used the tunnels, too, mainly for storage, though one section—the section Brother Ambrose was approaching—had been designed to detain prisoners.

Hector Yuli didn't even glance up from his video game at the sound of the heavy door creaking open. "It's about time you got here, you lazy sod."

Brother Ambrose paused on the threshold. "I beg your pardon?" he said in his most arrogant voice.

Hector did look up then, his expression a mixture of surprise, embarrassment, and alarm. He shoved the handheld game under his chair and jumped to his feet. "I thought you were Orson, sir. I meant no disrespect."

"I take it then your brother's late for his shift."

Hector nodded.

"He and Leo were supposed to bring the gold round by boat earlier this afternoon. They never showed up. So imagine my surprise when their faces flashed across the screen on the evening news."

"What happened? Did the coast guard intercept them?"

"No," Brother Ambrose told him. "Apparently, the police have issued warrants for their arrest on kidnapping charges."

Hector's gaze flicked to the trapdoor in the floor. "But how did they find out?"

"Not Magnus Armstrong's kidnapping," Brother Ambrose said. "They're accused of abducting a young woman, an American tourist named Sabrina Thatcher."

"Why would they do a daft thing like that?" Hector asked. "It makes no sense."

"I suspect they mistook Ms. Thatcher for her friend, Caitlin O'Shaughnessy."

"Armstrong's stepdaughter?"

Brother Ambrose nodded. "There's a superficial resemblance."

"But why take such a chance?" Hector said. "And where are they now?"

"Hiding from the authorities, presumably."

"Stupid bastards," Hector complained with a marked absence of brotherly concern. "And meanwhile I've been here ten hours straight. How much longer must I wait?" His tone fell halfway between a whine and a grovel, annoying Brother Ambrose so much that he was tempted to shoot the miserable little worm on the spot. But he controlled the impulse, reminding himself he still needed help transporting the gold.

"Go on then."

Hector was all smiles. "Bless you, Brother Ambrose." He collected his game and got ready to bolt.

"How's our prisoner today?"

Hector shrugged. "Same. Bit weaker maybe."

"Maybe if he gets hungry enough, he'll decide to cooperate," Brother Ambrose observed in a dispassionate tone.

"Least he's not singing anymore. Those old Beatles songs were driving me mad. If I'd had to listen to 'Yesterday' one more time . . ." Hector shuddered.

"When you do catch up with your brothers," Brother Ambrose said, "tell them I'd like a word."

"Right." Hector headed down the tunnel at a trot.

"Time for show-and-tell," Caitlin said, her eyes sparkling with suppressed excitement.

Dominic set the heavy green plastic container on the center of the dining room table. Portia had cleared away the remnants of their meal, and she and Flavio had retired to their rooms on the third floor. Dominic, Caitlin, Bree, and Quin were gathered around the table for the unveiling.

"What's that?" Bree asked.

"It's an ammunition box," Quin told her. "Don't tell me Fraternitas is smuggling arms, too."

"Nothing so paltry." Dominic flipped the latch and opened the lid. The chandelier's light reflected off the dull gleam of gold.

Bree leaned closer to get a better view. "Oh, my God!" She drew in a sharp breath.

"What?" Quin exclaimed. "They're smuggling Krugerrands?"

"Not exactly," Caitlin said.

Dominic passed him a coin.

"Bloody hell," Quin said. "This is Roman, isn't it?"

Dominic nodded. "An aureus."

"Like those mentioned in the legend of Brother Hamish?"

Bree frowned. "I'm not following this conversation."

"According to legend, Brother Hamish—" Dominic started.

"The Merlin manuscript guy, right?" Bree reached into the box and extracted a coin. "Pretty crude compared to coins today."

"But worth a good deal more," Dominic told her. "According to legend, Brother Hamish was on his way to Rome—well, Ostia, actually—when a storm came up and the ship he was traveling on went down with all hands. Hamish was the sole survivor. When he washed ashore on Calix, he claimed he'd seen a Roman trireme full of gold lying at the bottom of the sea quite near where his own ship had foundered."

"This gold?" Bree bit down on the aureus and checked for a dent.

"Possibly." Dominic shrugged.

"How much of this did you find?" Quin asked.

"A stack four by five by six," Dominic said. "Which is . . ."

"A hundred twenty ammo boxes," Caitlin supplied. "All of which currently reside in the boot and every other spare cranny of Dominic's car. Just the boxes. Not the gold. It was too heavy to shift, so we buried it under debris in the cave."

"Hoping the smugglers would see their neat stack of boxes missing and assume you'd taken everything," Quin said. "Not a bad plan for the spur of the moment."

November 1617
Drymen, Scotland

Hamish waited until he was certain his mother had gone to bed. Then he slipped into the house and up the back stairs to his room, thankful that it lay at the opposite end of the house from his mother's chamber.

Earlier he'd washed himself in an icy burn, but the smell of the midden clung to his clothes. He stripped now to the skin and washed again with the water in his ewer, then dressed in clean clothing. Dare he light a fire and burn the filthy rags that lay in a heap on the floor? Or should he dig a hole in the manure heap behind the stable and bury them there? Both alternatives held risk.

No, better he wrap them in a bundle and discard them somewhere far away from Drymen, far away from Auld Mòrag and her cat.

He must leave, not just Drymen but Scotland. He didn't belong here anymore.

But where did he belong? Heaven? Hell? The heights of Olympus?

Vita aeterna. The words seemed to echo in his brain.

He pried up the loose floorboard under his bed, pulled a small brown sack from its hiding place, and reached inside. The bones, a handful of ribs, all—besides him—that remained of the great sorcerer Merlin, clicked softly as they slid between his fingers. The touch of them, slick and cool, comforted him.

"Where, bones? Where am I to go? Where shall I fit in?

Vita aeterna.

Life eternal.

Eternal.

An idea percolated through the layers of despair. Wasn't Rome known as the eternal city?

The bones grew warm in his hand. A sign. He was certain of it.

But whether it signified approval or otherwise, he couldn't determine. Only time would tell.

13

HALF PAST TWO AND CAITLIN COULDN'T SLEEP. She finally gave up trying. The villa was dark and silent, but the moon-silvered sea beckoned from beyond the French doors of her bedroom.

Thinking a jog along the beach might calm her jangled nerves, she changed into shorts, a sports bra, and a pair of running shoes. At the last minute, she grabbed a gauze shirt, not much protection against the cool night air but better than nothing.

The terrace was deserted. Even the hummingbirds had gone back to their nests. The night was calm but not still. Wind soughed through the trees on the hill above the house, waves lapped at the beach below, and crickets chirped from the cracks in the stone retaining wall.

Caitlin tiptoed past Bree's room, then headed down the broad stone steps to the beach. Halfway to the bottom, she spotted him. He stood with his back to her. As she watched, he stooped, chose a stone, and heaved it into the water. She didn't see it hit but heard the splash.

"Damn it," he said, and then again with a little more emphasis, "*Damn* it." He stooped to choose another stone.

"Damn what?" she asked, and he straightened abruptly, spinning around to face her.

"I didn't know you were there."

"I couldn't sleep."

"Nor could I."

Caitlin continued down the rustic staircase, and he watched her descend in silence. She wished she could read his expression, but the moon hung over his left shoulder and shadows obscured his face. She reached the beach and he turned slightly to face her. Moonlight illuminated the sharp cheekbones, the square jaw. "I—" she started.

"I—" he began at the same time. Then, "Sorry," he said, and smiled.

And oh, God, he had a wonderful smile. The first spark of pleasure caught her by surprise. A second followed on its heels.

This wasn't good. Okay, it was good, but it wasn't healthy. With an effort, she tore her gaze away from his lips and those intriguing slashes that bracketed his mouth, and concentrated instead on the toes of her shoes.

"Caitlin?" Dominic touched her bare arm, and oh dear lord, the sparks weren't just in her head now but in her blood, too. She throbbed with every beat of her heart.

He pulled her into his arms, and she didn't resist. She

put her arms around his waist, wanting him, wanting him more than she'd ever wanted anything in her life. And even though she knew she was tempting fate, even though she knew this was going to end with a broken heart—hers and maybe his as well—she pressed herself to the hard-muscled warmth of his body, aching to be closer still. "Dominic—"

"Shh," he whispered in her ear. "I think I hear a boat motor."

She heard it, too, growing nearer. Desire took an abrupt backseat to the fear that prickled across her skin like a thousand tiny spiders. "Can you see it?" she whispered.

"Yes. I count two heads. Bloody hell, they've spotted us."

"Is it—"

He covered her mouth with his, not only swallowing her words but also short circuiting her brain. She knew the danger was real. She knew she should be afraid. But with Dominic's lips warm and demanding on hers, she couldn't think at all.

Some time later he pulled away, and she noted with some satisfaction that she wasn't the only one breathing heavily. He leaned his forehead against the top of her head. "They're gone," he said, and she realized the purr of the motor had been steadily decreasing for a while.

"Who was it?"

"The Yulis, I think. I recognized their boat."

"Planning another abduction? Or heading up the coast to collect the gold?"

"Hard to say." He slackened his grip, holding her a little away from him. Desire shivered through her at the expression on his face.

"Dominic?"

"I want you." Slowly, slowly, he stroked one hand up and down her back, up and down, up and down, and she shivered again at his touch. "You said now wasn't the time to get involved, but—"

"I want you, too." Her voice emerged so ragged with emotion she barely recognized it.

"I can't promise you forever," he said. "I would if I could, but—"

"Shh." She pressed a finger to his lips. "I understand. This is our Roman holiday. You're a prince. You have obligations."

Dominic swore under his breath. *Obligations, she said. If only that were the problem.* He took a deep breath. *Bloody hell, how to tell her?*

She studied his face. "Something's wrong, isn't it?"

"We can't do this, Caitlin."

"Oh, but we can. We must."

"Not until you hear what I have to say."

She nibbled at his lower lip, and his heartbeat quickened.

He groaned. "Caitlin, please."

She stepped away. "All right. Talk."

He led her over to the rock staircase, and they took seats on the bottom step. "I've told you about the curse. You met my father, saw his condition."

"And?"

"I carry the gene. I was tested last year."

"But you told me yourself. Not everyone who bears the gene develops full-blown symptoms."

"True, but I tested positive for the protein as well."

"What?" She stared at him, and he wanted to hide from the look on her face—shock, disbelief, pity.

"I fell down the stairs at Wallace's. That was my first warning, but I told myself accidents happen, that I'd slipped. Then a couple of months later, I was walking down the sidewalk and my left leg gave out without warning. I took a header—but still I didn't want to admit what was happening. I'm only in my thirties. My father didn't develop any symptoms until he was in his forties."

She brushed a stray lock of hair back off his forehead, and the tenderness of the gesture nearly proved his undoing. "What finally convinced you to go to the doctor?" she asked.

"Quin. He'd been suspicious ever since my fall down the stairs. Calixians are so accustomed to the curse; we know the signs.

"One day we were jogging, and I fell. Only this time I couldn't lie about it. He was there. He saw it. He knew I hadn't tripped on anything. My leg just quit on me." He took another deep breath. "Long story short, I went to a specialist and he put me on a drug regimen, somewhat similar to what's used on people in the first stages of multiple sclerosis."

"And?"

"So far, so good, but the medication won't work forever."

"I don't care."

"There's no cure."

"I told you, I don't care."

"Ultimately, I'll end up like my father. Maybe sooner, maybe later. With the curse, there are no guarantees."

She cupped his face in her hands and stared him in the eye. "Even without the curse, there are no guarantees. Don't you get that?"

"I know what you mean, but—"

"Hey, you're looking at the world's champion worst-case-scenario thinker. I can come up with possibilities that would curl your hair. For example, what if you're walking down Harborview Way in St. Agnes and a meteor strikes you?"

"The chances of that happening—"

"Hey, that's the thing about a worst-case-scenario thinker. The more unlikely the event, the more we obsess over it."

"That's sick."

"See? You're not the only one. Here's another possibility. What if you sidestep to avoid the meteor and a tour bus backs over you? Or what if the bus stops in time, but when you drop in at Gina's for lunch, you choke on a brussels sprout?"

"Nonsense. I loathe brussels sprouts."

"Okay, how about fish? What if you choke on a fishbone?"

"I get it," he said. "Human beings are fragile creatures. Life is short and doesn't come with a guarantee."

"Very good," she said. "You're a quick study."

"What makes you so wise beyond your years?"

"I've been to hell and back," she said, "and learned a thing or two along the way."

He studied her face in the moonlight. "What's your definition of 'hell'?"

"The opposite of heaven."

That flip tone didn't fool him for a second. He frowned. "Could you be a bit more specific? You said you'd been to hell and back. What do you mean?"

"It's a long, boring story."

"One I'd like to hear," he said softly.

She drew a long breath, released it, then moved away from him and hugged her knees to her chest. "Remember on the flight to Calix, I told you that I'd gotten myself into some trouble in college?"

"I remember."

"Bree and I bought ourselves fake IDs so we could go clubbing on weekends. We weren't into drinking or drugs, just dancing and a little harmless flirtation.

"Only one night Bree ran into a guy she knew from one of her classes, some guitar player she had the major hots for. They hooked up, leaving me at the club on my own."

Dominic swore softly under his breath.

"While I was dancing, someone slipped Rohypnol, the date rape drug, in my drink."

"Bloody hell," he said.

"I don't remember anything after that, not until I woke up alone the next morning, naked in bed in a seedy motel. I was bruised and the sheets were bloodstained." She made a face. "Big visual clue, you know. Hint, hint, Caitlin. You're not a virgin anymore."

He drew a sharp breath. "You called the police, I hope."

She sighed. "I did. The questioning went on for what seemed like hours, not that I could tell them anything helpful. After that, hospital personnel did a physical examination and ran a whole raft of tests."

"Looking for evidence of rape," he said, his voice harsh.

"And testing for HIV and other sexually transmitted diseases."

"Oh, hell." Dominic wrapped an arm around her and pulled her head down on his shoulder. "I'm so sorry," he whispered.

"Me, too," she said. "Unfortunately, that wasn't the end of it."

"They apprehended the bastard who raped you," he guessed.

"Bastards, plural," she said. "The medical tests indicated four different men, none of whom were ever caught. 'Four. Four is your unlucky number,' " she quoted. "That's what a gypsy told me once. Guess she knew what she was talking about."

"I'm sorry." Dominic rocked her back and forth. "I'm so, so sorry. To hell and back, indeed."

"Dominic," she said in a strangled whisper. "I . . ."

"Thank you for telling me." For trusting him. He cupped her face in his hands and kissed her.

The kiss started out sweet—even gentle—but soon escalated into something fevered and desperate. He'd wanted her this afternoon; he wanted her even more now. He slid his hands under her shirt and down her shoulders, and she shrugged out of the gauzy fabric. The night was cool, but her skin felt hot beneath his hands. "A sports bra?" he said, sliding one finger under the strap.

"I'd planned to go running."

"But you're not . . . running." He traced the deep scooped neckline of her bra.

"It's too late." He watched her nipples tighten, poking against the stretchy fabric. A pulse beat wildly in her throat. "And I don't really feel like it anymore. Running, I mean."

He studied her face. "You're certain?"

"Kiss me."

"I don't want you to do anything you'll regret."

"Regret?" She laughed harshly. "I have many regrets, but you"—she touched his cheek—"will never be one of them." She smiled. "Kiss me, Dominic. Love me. Please. I need you."

Desire shuddered through him. He shut his eyes for a second. When he opened them again, she was watching him, and the look on her face told him there was no turning back. He captured her face in his hands and kissed her.

I need you, she'd said. But Dominic knew the emotional web that enveloped them encompassed more than mere need. Yes, he wanted her in a very basic, carnal sense, but this was about more than sex.

I love you. Those were the words that echoed in his head. He didn't say them, and he wasn't sure why. He'd tossed the phrase around often enough in the past. Not that he'd ever meant a word of it . . .

Perhaps that was the problem. Perhaps he couldn't say the words because this time he did mean them.

He studied her in the moonlight—the curve of her cheek, the sweep of her hair, the gooseflesh on her bare shoulders. "You're cold," he said, and berated himself for a selfish bastard.

"I don't feel cold," she said, but she burrowed closer.

"Let's go inside. I want to make love with you properly in a bed anyway."

She laughed softly. "I don't mind the bed so much, but you can forget the 'properly' part. Improperly's much more fun."

He stood up, pulling her along with him. "Define fun."

"Race you to the top."

She took off at a run with Dominic close on her heels. He didn't catch her, though, until she'd reached the terrace. There he grabbed her from behind and lifted her off her feet. She wriggled loose and turned, pressing her body to his. "You lose," she said, and kissed him.

All right, maybe they didn't need a bed. One of the lounge chairs on the terrace would do just as well.

Or maybe not. Not with Bree's room mere feet away.

"What's the problem, Dominic?" Laughter underlay her words. "Feeling a little anxious?"

"Desperately." He pulled her against him so she could feel for herself the extent of that desperation.

"Oh, my God," she said, which made him laugh. Then

she touched him, and he thought he was going to lose it right then and there.

"Christ," he said. "You're killing me."

"It's that worst-case-scenario thing," she said. "If the brussels sprouts don't get you . . ."

"I'll worst-case-scenario you." He wrapped an arm about her shoulders and hustled her to the door. Once inside, he reset the alarm he'd turned off earlier, then steered her along the hall to the small foyer at the far end.

"An elevator?" she said. "I didn't know the villa had an elevator."

"Two of them, actually." He hit the call button, and the door slid open.

"Where are we going?" she asked.

"My suite." He ushered her inside and punched the button for the third floor.

"My room's closer," she pointed out.

"But mine has one overwhelming advantage."

"Better view?" she guessed. "Bigger bed? No one sleeping next door?"

"Yes to all three, but none of those was the advantage I meant."

She shot him a questioning look.

"Condoms," he said.

"Oh." She thought about it for a moment, then smiled sideways at him. "Plural?"

The elevator pinged as the door slid open. "Absolutely."

At the far end of the hall, double doors opened into his suite. He switched on the lights, escorted her inside, then closed and locked the door behind them. "The bedroom's just through here," he said.

She crossed the threshold, then moved slowly toward the center of the room, staring at his bed.

"Something wrong?"

"I've never slept in a bed perched so high off the floor that it came with its own mini staircase."

"But then," he said, "I doubt you'll be doing much sleeping."

Her gaze met his in the mirror above the dresser. She looked startled for a moment. Then gradually her expression relaxed, and before she looked away, he could almost swear he saw a hint of naughtiness in her smile.

Definitely naughtiness and more than a hint, he decided when she kicked off her shoes and pulled down her shorts to reveal a pair of barely there panties. Black.

Bloody hell.

Dominic hadn't thought he could get any harder, but when Caitlin stripped off her bra and he saw her bare breasts, soft and full and perfect, he proved himself wrong.

"Touch me." Her voice shook just the tiniest bit, which turned his insides to mush.

Yes, he thought, *oh my God, yes.*

He touched her.

She was warm and soft under his hands. And beautiful. So beautiful. He turned her around so he could watch her face in the mirror as he teased her nipples with his thumbs. Her head fell back against his shoulder. Her eyelids drifted closed, and she made a sound that was half sigh, half moan, all pleasure.

While he continued to toy with her left breast, he slid his right hand down her ribs to circle her navel before splaying his fingers across the taut muscles of her abdomen. Her skin was so fine, so pale, like silk beneath his fingertips.

"Touch me," she said again, and guided his hand lower still. He cupped the black silk and felt her warmth.

A few flicks and her breathing quickened. A few more and she came apart. He watched her closely, gauging her reactions. Each time she started to float back to earth, he drove her to new heights of pleasure until finally she wriggled loose.

"My turn," she said. And then she was kissing him, torturing him with lips and tongue while her hands were busy . . .

He pulled away. "What are you doing?"

She laughed softly. "Unbuttoning and unzipping." She peeled his jeans down his hips, down his legs. He kicked them aside.

"Now the underwear," she said.

He sucked in his breath when her fingers brushed his erection. His shorts joined his jeans.

Condom, he reminded himself, and dug through the top drawer of his dresser. He finally found the box hiding under a dog-eared paperback and covered himself. By the time he turned around again, Caitlin had divested herself of that last scrap of black silk and climbed into bed. She lounged against the pillows, the dark blue sheets a perfect foil for her pale skin and dark hair.

"You are so incredibly beautiful," he said.

She smiled and patted the empty spot next to her. "And so incredibly lonesome."

Not for long. He climbed into the big bed and reached for her, but she had other ideas.

She rolled on top of him and straddled his hips.

"What's all this?"

"As I told you before, it's my turn now."

"Your turn for what?"

She smiled. "To drive *you* insane with pleasure." She guided him to the damp folds of her opening, and he entered slowly, inch by delicious inch. When he was buried to the hilt, he drew a shaky breath, vibrating with the effort of not spilling himself immediately.

Caitlin rubbed her breasts against his chest and kissed him, softly at first and then more and more deeply. "I want you," she whispered.

He raised his hips and gave an experimental thrust.

She caught her breath in a little gasp.

He thrust again, even deeper this time. *Yes,* he thought. *Yes and yes and yes again.*

"Yes," she said. "Yes and yes and yes again."

Her silken heat set his heart racing, and he wanted her, *wanted her,* but even more, more than his own pleasure, he wanted hers. Deliberately, he slowed the pace.

Caitlin's eyelids fluttered open. "Dominic?"

She had used his name dozens of times, but this time

was different. This time her soft voice elicited a fierce, visceral reaction. Rolling her under him, he pinned her to the bed, touching and teasing her with his hands and mouth as he kept up a steady rhythm. Thrust, retreat, and thrust again. Her warmth enveloped him, stroking him, squeezing him.

The pleasure built quickly and with it his desperation. "Damn," he said, his voice hoarse with the strain of maintaining control.

And then, just when he thought he couldn't hold on a second longer, Caitlin writhed and shuddered and gasped his name.

His control shattered, and he climaxed with a pleasure so intense he felt as if he were disintegrating. He groaned and clutched at her, out of control, out of his mind. And then, slowly, slowly, all the fragmented bits of Dominic coalesced, leaving him with a deep satisfaction and a stinging back where Caitlin had raked him with her nails.

He buried his face in her neck, kissing her throat, then kissing his way up to her earlobe. *I love you,* he thought. But he didn't say it.

March 1618
Mediterranean Sea

There truly were fates worse than death. Hamish clung to the rail of the Dutch flute *de Gouden Tulp* bound for Rome, breathing deeply, trying to accustom himself to the pitching of the deck beneath his feet. Behind the ship, the sky stretched clear and blue all the way to the southern coast of France, but ahead, dark clouds along the eastern horizon warned of worse to come.

A sea voyage, most seasoned travelers agreed, provided a relatively safe alternative to the more perilous overland routes. Hamish supposed that depended upon one's definition of "safe." Perhaps "safe" meant vomiting more frequently in eight days than in all the rest of one's life put together. Better to face a dozen highwaymen, a hundred flea-infested inns, a thousand rugged alps than this constant nausea.

The deck heaved and so did his stomach. He spat its paltry contents over the side to be carried off by the levanter, the cold east wind of the western Mediterranean. Staggering below, weak and exhausted, he fell onto his bunk. He hadn't expected to sleep, but he did, though fitfully to be sure.

Increasing nausea woke him two hours later. As he emerged on deck, the wind blew his hair into his eyes, then caught the hem of his cloak and whipped it over his head. Sails flapped and rigging creaked as the captain snapped orders in Dutch. Hamish grabbed his cloak, jerked it round him, then hailed Jan Dekker, a snaggletoothed old sailor who spoke a bit of English. "What's going on?"

"Big storm coming," Jan said, pointing toward the southwest.

Hamish turned. Billowing blue-black thunderheads lit by flashes of lightning rolled toward them, filling the sky. "Can we outrun it?" he said, knowing the answer even before he asked.

Jan scowled at the approaching clouds. "Not with a hold full of grain, we can't."

Another seaman ran by and shouted something at Jan.

Jan yelled an answer, then slapped Hamish on the back. "Got to get to work now if we're to survive this blow. Hang on to your arse, boy. We're going for a ride. If you plan to stay topside, lash yourself to something sturdy." He handed Hamish a coil of rope, then headed off in response to another shouted order.

Sturdy? Sturdy like the railing? Sturdy like the mast?

Water slapped him in the face, and he thought at first a wave had broken across the bow, but then he realized it was fresh water, not salt—rain slashing horizontally across the ship in apparent defiance of the natural order. It soaked him in seconds.

Lightning lit the sky. Thunder boomed, and the shock waves set his nerves ajitter. Howling with glee, the wind caught his cloak again. It billowed up, momentarily blinding him. Lash himself to something, Jan had said. Good advice, but easier said than done. He could barely see, scarcely stand. His fingers fought for purchase on the rain-slick railing. Twice, thrice, he looped the heavy rope around his torso and then around the railing, knotting the ends tightly as Jan had taught him.

Lightning flashed again, once, twice, thrice, each bolt accompanied by an earsplitting crack of thunder. The mainmast took at least one direct hit. He heard the crack and felt the impact in the deck beneath his feet. The sails went up in a burst of flame, fiery pennants waving in the wind, and the mast toppled, as if in slow motion.

He reached for his dirk, thinking to cut himself free, but the hilt was swathed in layers of clothing and three wraps of the heavy rope. Terrified now, he fought his bonds, scrabbling desperately at the knots with his fingers, but it was too late, had been too late from the moment the lightning struck. The mast hit his shoulder a glancing blow, but even that was enough to dislocate the joint and shatter the bone. The flaming sail wrapped itself around him, searing his lungs and scorching his flesh. Then the huge timber splintered the heavy railing as if it were a twig. One whole section—Hamish's section—peeled away from the ship.

He might have survived his shattered bones. He might have survived his burns. But he never had a chance to find out. The dangling strip of railing ripped free, and the raging Mediterranean swallowed it—and him—in a single gulp.

PART THREE

The Truth

When you have eliminated the impossible,
whatever remains, however improbable,
must be the truth.

—Sir Arthur Conan Doyle (1859–1930)

14

HECTOR SHONE HIS FLASHLIGHT into the cavern. "The gold's been moved," he said.

"I see that." Brother Ambrose felt light-headed with fury. He'd planned every detail so carefully. This shouldn't have happened. The gold was his. *His.* Unbelievable that the Yuli brothers, those brainless buffoons, had bested *him,* double-crossed *him.* How could this have happened?

He should have realized there was a problem when the Yulis had excavated the cave-in on their own initiative and unearthed Hamish MacNeill's secret stash. Without mentioning it to him, they'd included the manuscript and the bones in a shipment to Jacqueline. He hadn't even realized what had happened until Erskine Grant went public with his wild theories. And by then, the damage was done.

He'd told the Yulis where to find the gold, buried below the stones that floored the hidden room. And how had they repaid him? By putting his reputation in jeopardy. By stealing his treasure.

He'd chosen them in the first place because he'd thought them too stupid to think for themselves. Flattered to believe themselves a part of the Fraternitas elite, they'd fallen in with his plans without a single protest. They'd stolen for him, kidnapped for him, killed for him.

And taken his gold.

Brother Ambrose studied Hector in the backwash of light from his flashlight. Was he complicit as well? Did he know what his older brothers had done with the gold?

Hector frowned, as if he still could not believe his eyes. "I thought you said Orson and Leo didn't make the delivery."

"They didn't, and obviously, they didn't sink the boat, since we found it on its mooring." Brother Ambrose pulled the pistol from his waistband and leveled it at the last surviving Yuli brother. "Where's the gold, Hector? What have they done with it?"

"I don't know. Swear to God." Hector's voice shook. If he'd groveled, he might have lived. But he made a fatal error. In a sudden, desperate move, he wielded the flashlight like a club, targeting Brother Ambrose's gun arm.

Forewarned by the leaping shadows, Brother Ambrose stepped out of range, aimed as best he could in the uncertain light, and fired.

Hector screamed and grabbed his shoulder, dropping the flashlight in the process. Not the kill shot Brother Ambrose had tried for, but a hit.

Light from the rolling flashlight danced across the

cave's interior, illuminating the rough walls, the roots trailing from the roof, the abandoned tools.

Hector grabbed for the pick, but Brother Ambrose anticipated him. The second shot caught him dead between the eyes.

An hour later, Brother Ambrose headed out to sea, knowing he had to keep enough fuel in reserve for the return to St. Agnes harbor. Fortunately, he hit the southern current well before reaching the point of no return. There he dumped Hector's body into the water. It sank like a stone.

Brother Ambrose knew that condition was only temporary. In a day or so, when decomposition set in with a vengeance, gases would accumulate, rendering the body buoyant. But barring the unlikely possibility of its being snagged by the crewmen of a passing ship, Hector's corpse wouldn't make landfall until it hit Tunisia, and by then, hungry sea creatures would have rendered it unidentifiable by anything short of a DNA match. And frankly, Brother Ambrose couldn't see the Tunisian government footing the bill on that one.

Dominic must have drowsed off, because he woke suddenly. Caitlin stood at the edge of the bed, shrugging into his terry cloth bathrobe. He snagged one of the belt loops with his forefinger and dragged her closer. "Going somewhere?"

"I left my shirt on the beach."

"I'll get it." He rolled out of bed, retrieved his shorts from the floor, and pulled them on. Caitlin eyed his every move.

"I never realized," she said, "that watching someone dress could be just as erotic as watching them undress."

He tugged on his jeans, zipped and buttoned them, then slowly, deliberately slid the terry cloth robe off her shoulders. It landed in a heap on the floor. "No," he said. "Undressing is definitely better." He kissed her until her startled expression melted into desire. Then he nipped at her lower lip and patted her bottom. "Keep the bed warm. I'll be right back."

Dominic let himself out onto the terrace. A steady breeze blew off the water, chill and damp, and the first harbinger of dawn, a ghostly gray luminescence, lightened the sky to the east. He padded barefoot down the wide steps to the beach, hurrying. The sooner he retrieved Caitlin's shirt, the sooner he'd be back in bed. Back in bed with Caitlin, Caitlin of the innocent face and incredibly responsive body.

At first he thought her shirt wasn't there, that perhaps it had blown away or been carried off by an animal, but then he spotted it, pooled behind a cluster of poppies. He shook the sand from its folds, then held it up to the light. Gossamer thin, nearly transparent, the shirt might have been woven of moonbeams.

And suddenly all he could think of was how best to convince Caitlin to model it for him—the shirt and nothing else. He was halfway to an erection just visualizing the result, which proved what Quin had been telling him for years. He definitely was a twisted bastard.

He was halfway back up to the terrace when he heard

a boat's engine approaching from the east. *Bit early for fishermen,* he thought. Then the boat came around the point and he recognized it. The Yulis' boat, *Marguerite,* headed home again.

Had they planned to move the gold tonight? If so, they must have been surprised to find all those boxes gone.

Or had they realized the trick he and Caitlin had played on them? Had they found the coins buried under the rubble? Certainly they'd been gone long enough to have excavated half of Troy, let alone one small cave on the Calixian coast. And that was worrisome, because if the Yulis got away with the gold, the fault was his.

Damn it, he should never have kept the information to himself. Suspected smuggling fell under Janus's purview, and unlike Dominic, Janus commanded both the means and the manpower to secure the gold. Damn it, damn it, damn it.

Only when the *Marguerite* drew nearer did he notice there was only one man on board.

So what had happened to the second brother? Was he even now guarding the cave and its treasure?

Dominic tapped on Quin's door.

No answer.

He tapped again, louder this time.

And again, no answer.

He tried the knob. Unlocked. He cracked the door an inch or two. "Quin?" he whispered. Portia and Flavio had their quarters in this wing, too, and he didn't want to disturb them. "Quin?" he said again, edging the door open wider.

Quin hadn't answered because Quin wasn't there. His bed was made, the pillows fluffed, an extra blanket folded neatly across the end. So where . . . ?

The answer was glaringly obvious. Bree's room.

Dominic pelted down the stairs and tapped on the door with one knuckle.

"Yes?" Bree's voice.

"It's Dominic. I need to speak with Quin. Have you seen him?"

Dominic heard a few squeaks and scuffles, some whispering, then Quin threw open the door. "Something wrong?"

"Perhaps. I've reason to think the Yuli brothers may have discovered where Caitlin and I hid the gold. I need to check it out. I could use some backup."

Caitlin sat across from Bree at the dining room table. The chessboard lay between them, though neither woman had been able to concentrate on the game. "I wonder what's taking them so long?" Bree said for the third time in ten minutes.

Dominic and Quin, she meant. "I don't know." Caitlin gave the same answer she'd given the first two times. She didn't know, but her overactive imagination was more than happy to fill in the blanks, churning out an endless stream of possible scenarios, each more horrific and less probable than the last. "Maybe the Yulis got the drop on them," she suggested. "Maybe another earthquake sent the roof of the tunnel crashing down on their heads. Maybe they were attacked by cave-dwelling vampire bats. Maybe the ghost of Brother Hamish returned from the dead to claim his treasure. Maybe a portal opened and sucked them into another dimension."

"Maybe," Dominic said from the doorway, "they dug up the gold and hauled it back here for safekeeping."

"Thank God you're safe," Bree said with conviction.

Quin grinned at her over Dominic's shoulder. "Worried about us?"

"Petrified," Bree said. "I couldn't concentrate on chess long enough to whup Caitlin's butt, and she's the worst player in the entire Bay Area."

"I take it the Yulis weren't there?" Caitlin said, ignoring Bree's comment.

Quin sat down next to Bree. Dominic leaned against the sideboard, feet crossed at the ankle, arms folded across his chest. "They'd been and gone," he said, "without finding the gold."

"If the gold was undisturbed, how do you know they'd been and gone?" Bree asked.

"We found a flashlight that wasn't there earlier," Dominic said. "And one of the picks was lying off by itself on the far side of the tunnel."

Quin nodded agreement. "There was a puddle of blood on the floor, too. Looked like there'd been a struggle."

Caitlin's heart gave a sickening lurch. "Magnus's blood?"

Dominic's gaze steadied her. "I doubt they'd have dragged him up there. No, more likely the bloodshed resulted from a falling out among thieves. Remember the two men we spotted earlier in the Yulis' fishing boat?"

She nodded.

"When I went down to the beach later to collect your shirt, the boat was returning to St. Agnes with only one man aboard. I assumed the second man had stayed behind to guard the gold, but apparently, my assumption was incorrect."

"I've been thinking about that cave," Caitlin said.

Dominic shot her a sardonic smile. "So I heard."

"Not the worst-case scenarios. Serious thinking. For example, who knows about its existence? Is it a big secret or common knowledge?"

Dominic frowned. "It's not marked on any map or mentioned in guidebooks, so its location—its existence—is hardly common knowledge. Mr. Hawke and I used to go up there quite often, and I assume my parents knew where he was taking me, but as to who else knows . . . ?" He shrugged. "I suppose other members of the royal family or the palace staff could be aware of the cave's existence."

"Not many, though," Quin said. "I didn't know it was there."

"Boaters and bathers frequent the beach from time to time, No Trespassing signs notwithstanding," Dominic said. "I suppose a few of them might have done some exploring and stumbled across the cave."

"Are the Yuli brothers into rock climbing?" Caitlin lined up her chess pieces.

Quin dismissed that suggestion with a snort. "I've never known any of the three to exert himself unduly. Money's really the only thing that motivates them."

Caitlin knocked her chess pieces over one by one. "So I have to wonder how the Yulis discovered a cave that's so far off the radar screen."

"Sheer luck?" Quin suggested.

"Okay, predicating they did just happen to stumble across the cave, why would they have gone to all the effort of hauling the gold up there? Seems like a lot of work."

"Maybe they didn't have any other safe place to store it," Bree said.

"Okay," Cailin said, "but then how do you explain the tools? If the cave was just a handy storage bin, why did they haul tools up there?"

"Are you suggesting they were excavating the cave-in?" Dominic asked.

"Exactly," she said. "I don't think they hauled the gold up there. I think they found it buried beneath the rubble."

"But if the Yuli brothers weren't the ones who carried the gold to the cave, who did?" Bree asked.

"Brother Hamish?" Dominic said.

Quin looked thoughtful. "The time frame's right. And it fits the legend."

"Let me see if I have this straight," Bree said. "The Yulis—possibly working with other members of a group called Fraternitas—are running a smuggling operation based on Calix. In addition to the traditional drugs, diamonds, and arms, they start pilfering items from the palace as well."

"Yes," Quin said. "And while searching for an out-of-the-way spot to store their merchandise, they stumble across the cave, and are inspired for reasons unknown to dig through the debris at the far end, where they just happen to find a fortune in ancient Roman coins."

"I don't buy it," Bree said. "That's too much of a coincidence."

"I agree," Caitlin said. "I don't think the Yuli brothers stumbled across the cave by accident. I think someone knew the gold was there, and that same someone told them where to dig."

"Who?" Quin asked.

"Prince Maximilian?" she said. "One of the palace staff?"

"How about Jacqueline?" Bree suggested. "Her father's the lord chamberlain, right? She probably knows that part of the island like the back of her hand."

"I vote for Mr. Hawke," Caitlin said, and the other three stared at her as if she'd lost her mind.

"My father's social secretary? My former tutor?" Dominic vetoed that suggestion with a dubious shake of his head.

"You said yourself that he knew the location of the cave."

"Yes, but—" Dominic started.

"And he certainly had access to the palace. He could easily have smuggled out artifacts."

Dominic shook his head. "I hardly think—"

"Besides that," she said, "yesterday when he was supposed to be doing errands for the king, he was driving around in the boonies—"

"Boonies?" Quin asked.

"Boondocks," Bree translated. "The sticks, the hinterland, the wilderness."

He nodded. "We call it the back country."

"Okay," Caitlin said, "so according to what the lord chamberlain said, Mr. Hawke was supposed to be taking care of some business for the king. If that's true, then what was he doing driving around in the back country?"

"Giving me a lift back to civilization," Bree said. "For which I'm eternally grateful. I don't know what you have against the man, Caitlin. He went out of his way to help me."

"But that still doesn't explain what he was doing up there in the first place," Caitlin insisted.

"He lives quite near the spot where he ran into Bree," Dominic said. "He probably just went home to change his clothes."

"Oh." Caitlin frowned. So much for her pet theory.

"Besides," Dominic said with an amused look on his face, "if Hawke were immortal, he'd never grow old, right? Yet I swear he's aged ten years since Christmas."

"The feud with Packard must be getting him down," Quin said.

Bree leaned forward. "I overheard a phone call Orson Yuli placed to a man he called Brother Something-or-Other. Ambrose, I think. Brother Ambrose."

Dominic and Quin exchanged a look. "You're positive Orson Yuli called the man *Brother* Ambrose?" Quin asked.

Bree shrugged. "The Brother part I'm absolutely sure of. The Ambrose part? I'd say ninety percent."

Another look passed between Dominic and Quin. "All the upper-level leaders of Fraternitas use the title *brother* in tribute to the legendary Brother Hamish," Dominic said, "which would seem to corroborate Janus's belief that Fraternitas is involved in the smuggling."

"We should bring him in on this," Quin said. "See if he can identify this Brother Ambrose."

"I agree," Dominic said.

No one asked Caitlin what she thought, which was just as well since they probably wouldn't have believed it anyway.

"I was wondering how long you'd hold out, Fortune." Not even the hollow, echoing quality of Janus's altered voice could disguise his smug satisfaction.

Dominic pressed the phone to his ear and scowled out the window of his third-floor sitting room. Despite her sleepless night, Caitlin sat at the table on the terrace, poring over the manuscript her stepfather had mailed her. She was probably worried she'd be forced to turn it over to Janus before she'd deciphered the last few pages.

"I didn't call to grovel my way back into your good graces," Dominic said.

"Indeed."

"You were right about Fraternitas."

"Oh?"

"And the involvement of the Yuli brothers. They're working for someone who calls himself Brother Ambrose."

"The CIS has done extensive background checks on

everyone involved with Fraternitas. This is the first I've heard of a Brother Ambrose."

"The name's probably a fake. I doubt he'd trust the Yulis with his true identity."

"I'll do some digging, see what turns up," Janus said.

"I assume you heard about Sabrina Thatcher's abduction."

"The head constable at St. Agnes filed a report."

"We think it was a botched attempt to kidnap Caitlin."

"I'd surmised as much. Both young women are slim and dark-haired."

But only a fool would confuse the two. Bree was attractive enough, but Caitlin was something special.

"The Yuli brothers were smuggling more than stolen palace artifacts. Had you surmised that?" Dominic asked.

"More? Such as?"

"Roman gold. Coins dating back to the first century AD."

Janus said nothing for a moment. Dominic smiled, pleased to have surprised the old goat for once.

"Brother Hamish's gold? You saw it?" Janus said finally.

"I have it," Dominic told him.

"*You* have the gold? But how?"

Janus listened in silence as Dominic explained how a fortune in Roman coins had come into his possession. "Good work," Janus said rather grudgingly when Dominic had finished. "I wish you'd have contacted me immediately you located the coins, though. What if the Yulis hadn't been fooled by your subterfuge?"

So much for a pat on the back, Dominic thought. "Fortunately, they were."

Janus hemmed and hawed for a moment or two, then let it go. "Is Ms. O'Shaughnessy still determined to trade the manuscript for her stepfather?"

"Yes," Dominic said.

"The *Calix Chronicles* are a national treasure. You know that, Fortune. I can't allow the Yulis to get their hands on that manuscript again."

"Quin and I are more than a match for those thugs."

"I doubt they're working alone." Janus hesitated. "Let the CIS provide support. As soon as the kidnappers set a rendezvous point, call me and I'll send in a crisis team."

"And get Armstrong killed?"

"You don't seriously think they're going to let him walk free, do you, regardless of whether his stepdaughter pays or not? Armstrong has seen their faces. His testimony can put them behind bars."

Janus was right, and Dominic knew it, but, "We have to try," he said. He owed Caitlin that much. "We could use the backup, though your people would have to agree to follow my orders."

"That's not going to happen," Janus said. "CIS teams do not take orders from civilians."

"Then reinstate me," Dominic said.

Janus laughed. "I thought you'd never ask."

Dominic found Caitlin curled up in an overstuffed chair in the living room, where she'd retreated to escape the heat.

"Still looking for clues in that manuscript, I see," he said.

She glanced up, blinking uncertainly, as if most of her attention were still focused on the seventeenth century.

"Made any startling discoveries?" he asked, meaning it as a joke.

But Caitlin didn't crack a smile. "Brother Hamish is regarded as a Calixian folk hero, right?"

"Finn MacCool, Robin Hood, and Sir Galahad all rolled into one. Why?"

A slight frown wrinkled her forehead. "He doesn't seem all that heroic to me. By his own admission, he killed an old woman. Granted she killed him first, but even so . . ."

"She *killed* him?"

"But being immortal, he didn't stay dead. He woke up in a manure pile."

"Sounds nasty," Dominic said. "I'm not familiar with that part of the legend. The stories I heard about Brother Hamish always emphasized his wisdom and kindness. He was known far and wide as a healer who could cure any ill with his special elixir."

"Anything but the curse."

"I don't think anyone suffered from the curse in the early part of the seventeenth century, though it's mentioned in records dating back to the sixteen fifties and was firmly entrenched by the beginning of the eighteenth century."

"The manuscript does mention the elixir," she said. "Hamish even includes the recipe. After steeping various medicinal herbs in wine, he mixed in a small measure of his own blood."

"Blood?" Dominic raised his eyebrows.

"Hamish was convinced the contact with Merlin's bones had imbued his blood with special healing properties."

"So he shared it far and wide, a panacea for all ills. It's a damn good thing AIDS wasn't an issue in the seventeenth century."

"No kidding." She looked thoughtful. "Blood or no blood, though, the elixir must have been fairly effective, because people were more than willing to pay for it. Brother Hamish earned a very comfortable income as a healer."

"Income?" Dominic said, startled. "I thought he gave away his elixir."

"Not according to what I just read," Caitlin said.

"Strange, isn't it, that the written record differs so much from the tales I heard as a child?"

"I think after a while legends take on a life of their own." Caitlin closed the book and set it aside. "I'm starving. All this squinting over Hamish's lousy handwriting has given me an appetite."

Dominic smiled. "Which reminds me why I came looking for you in the first place. Quin just called from Tavia. We're invited to join him and Bree for lunch at the Imperial Hotel, after which Bree wants you to try on a gown."

"A gown?" Caitlin echoed with a puzzled frown. "Oh, my God. The Independence Day Ball is tonight, isn't it?"

"She knew you were preoccupied, so she took it upon herself to go shopping."

"Bree lives to shop. She doesn't need an excuse."

"And you?"

"If I'm after something specific, I don't mind, but I hate to browse." She scrambled to her feet. "I guess I'll go change. I imagine lunch at the Imperial Hotel requires something a little dressier than shorts."

And that, Dominic thought, was a pity, because Caitlin O'Shaughnessy had truly spectacular legs and it was a bloody damned shame to cover them up.

The moment Caitlin entered the Imperial's elegant turn-of-the-century lobby on Dominic's arm, the hum of conversation died to a whisper. Every eye in the place seemed to be fastened on them, and Caitlin wondered for one panicked moment if her underwear was showing. Then it dawned on her that no one was more than peripherally interested in her. Dominic—Prince Dominic—was the true focus of everyone's attention.

"Your Royal Highness." The hotel's manager, a well-dressed middle-aged man with thick iron-gray hair and a neat mustache, bowed so low, his nose nearly bounced off his knees. "The Imperial is honored by your presence, sir."

"Good to see you again, Mr. Fitzpatrick." Dominic introduced Caitlin and explained that they were meeting Bree and Quin for lunch.

"Ah, yes," the manager said. "Mr. Gilroy made the reservation earlier. If you'll follow me, sir? I believe our maitre d' put you in one of the private rooms overlooking the garden."

Bree and Quin were there already, standing near the

windows that looked out over the garden below. A smile lit Bree's face. "You made it!"

"Sorry we're late," Dominic said. "The traffic was atrocious."

Quin nodded. "To be expected with the holiday. I took the liberty of ordering. I hope that's all right?"

"Good thinking," Dominic said. "Caitlin's starving."

It took a total of six waiters nearly an hour and a half to serve their meal, a bountiful array of Calixian delicacies, all of which Caitlin sampled.

"What's the plan for this afternoon?" Dominic asked as they were finishing their coffee.

"Caitlin has to try on her dress," Bree said. "Wait until you see it; it's to die for."

As long as it wasn't to die *in,* Caitlin would be satisfied.

"And I thought while the ladies were shopping, we might visit Inspector Reynard."

Dominic nodded. "An excellent idea. If anyone has a clue where the Yuli brothers have gone to ground, it's Reynard."

Ambrose had examined the problem from all directions before coming to a reluctant conclusion. He did not consider himself a violent man. Nor did he hold human life cheap. But there were times when the need for self-preservation outweighed all other considerations, his recent disposal of the Yuli brothers being a case in point.

Getting the manuscript back wasn't enough to protect him now. The O'Shaughnessy girl knew too much. Therefore, the O'Shaughnessy girl had to die. And if Prince Dominic got in the way, he'd have to die as well.

Tonight at the ball, he would set the final phase of his plan in motion.

Bree watched the expression on Caitlin's face as she got her first look at herself in the mirrored wall of the designer's showroom. The aquamarine gown was perfect in every way—the color, the style, the fit. Its chic lines and clever cut clung to Caitlin's curves. Its color echoed and enhanced the blue-green of her eyes.

"Well, what do you think?"

"Holy shit," Caitlin said.

"Can I pick 'em or what?"

"It's gorgeous. You're a genius, Bree."

"No, the designer's the genius, but I *am* blessed with an artist's eye. Here." She passed Caitlin a pair of barely-there satin sandals that matched the gown. "And I think you should wear your hair up."

"No, down. I like it down."

Dominic stood just inside the door, staring at Caitlin with such intensity, such emotion, such heat, it was a wonder she didn't melt.

Bree glanced at Caitlin to see how she was reacting and thought, *whoa, mama,* she'd never seen that look on her friend's face. Caitlin's expression reflected the same heat and intensity as Dominic's, but beneath the surface sizzle, Bree glimpsed other emotions—amusement, pleasure, tenderness, and something else too elusive to name.

Bree smiled. *And so,* she thought, *the plot thickens.*

March 1618
Mediterranean Sea

Hamish drowned twice before morning.

The first drowning occurred shortly after he went overboard. The section of railing to which he'd lashed himself bobbed back up to the surface almost immediately after plummeting into the sea. Unfortunately, he was tied to the submerged side. Despite his struggles, he'd been unable to flip the heavy railing or free himself from the ropes.

Terror, darkness, cold, panic.

Air. He needed air, but there was none. Desperate, he gasped and filled his lungs with salt water. Slow suffocation followed, exquisitely painful. His eyes bulged. His limbs twitched. His heart stuttered. His brain guttered out like a candle in the wind, his last coherent thought, how ironic it was to drown within inches of the surface.

He came to his senses an indeterminate amount of time later. Coughing and retching, he bobbed like a cork in the choppy sea. Above him, the storm still raged, but he could see nothing of *de Gouden Tulp*. He coughed and retched, retched and coughed, gagging up what seemed like gallons of seawater.

Where was the ship? Dear God, if only he could reach it, someone could find a way to rescue him.

He yelled, but a rumble of thunder swallowed his voice.

Daylight—such as it was—was fading fast. If he wasn't spotted soon, it would be too late. Already his arms and legs felt heavy, his movements clumsy and ill-coordinated. He couldn't keep himself afloat much longer.

Then a wave tossed him high and he glimpsed the railing that had spelled his doom. It floated a few yards to his left. Four crew members clung to it. Had one of them cut him free?

He shouted again, but if the sailors heard him, they gave no sign. All their attention seemed to be focused on the battle to keep their heads above water.

Above him, the storm continued. Thunder rolled and lightning lit the darkening sky, flickering in horizontal layers within the clouds themselves.

Then a second wave, larger than the first, lifted his body, and this time he spotted the foundering ship twenty feet to his right, half submerged and listing sharply to stern. There would be no help from that quarter.

The crew members had the right idea. He needed to find a bit of wreckage to cling to, then hope the currents would carry him to land before he died of thirst.

A third wave tossed him high. He squinted into the gathering gloom, searching for something—anything—that might keep him afloat—a timber, a barrel. But the only flotsam large enough to support a man was the section of railing that floated to his left, and it was barely able to sustain the four men who hung from it now.

Unfair, Hamish thought. If anyone had a right to that cursed railing, it was he. He groped for the dirk at his waist, half expecting to find it gone, but he was in luck for once. Then gathering the last of his strength, he struck out for the makeshift raft.

15

AMBROSE SURVEYED HIMSELF in the cheval glass in the corner of his dressing room, pleased with what he saw, except for the new gray hairs he spotted at his temples. He'd never been vain about his appearance. He knew he wasn't the most attractive man in the world. On a scale of one to ten, he probably ranked somewhere between a six and a seven. But he had to admit that he cut quite a dashing figure in his tuxedo.

Jacqueline LeTourneau, wearing a sheer robe that left little to the imagination, slipped up behind him and twined her slender arms around his waist. "I've missed you desperately, darling."

"And I you," he said, working to infuse his words with a little enthusiasm. The truth was, although he still found Jacqueline attractive, he'd long since recovered from his initial wild infatuation. Nevertheless, he pulled her into his arms and kissed her thoroughly. "You should dress. Etienne will be wondering where you are."

"Fuck Etienne."

A smile twitched at the corners of his mouth. "He's not my type."

Her eyes narrowed. "Who is? The Beardsley girl?"

"Don't be absurd. She's little better than a peasant."

"Lydia Quintus?"

He sighed heavily. Lately, Jacqueline had grown quite tiresome. If she weren't such a useful contact, he'd be tempted to end their relationship. "You've no reason to be jealous, darling. Ours has never been a monogamous relationship, not even in the beginning." When he'd been sleeping with her mother.

Conflicting emotions warred across Jacqueline's expressive face. Cautious resignation won out over irritation, fear, anger, and hurt. "You're right, of course. I'm being unreasonable. After all, you never question what *I* do when we're apart."

"No, I don't." The corners of his mouth twitched in a reluctant smile. His kitten had claws.

"But one day perhaps . . ." Her voice trailed off.

"Perhaps what, my dear?" Was she dreaming of happily ever after?

"When Etienne is no longer in the picture, perhaps we can see one another openly. I'd like that."

"You know our relationship must remain a secret."

"But after so many years, who would make the connection?"

"The boy? His father? I can't take the risk."

"The risk is minimal, and you know it. Damn it, don't I deserve something for all these years of silence?"

Ambrose stroked her cheek in a lingering caress. "Are you threatening me, my dear?"

The color drained from her face. Against the pallor, her eyes looked fierce and dark. "I love you. You know that. I would never betray you."

He, unfortunately, could not make the same promise. In lieu of verbal reassurance, he lowered his mouth to hers and kissed her long and deep.

Jacqueline's response was gratifying, if somewhat inconvenient. She wrapped her arms around his neck and pressed her lush body to his.

"It's late," he reminded her. "The ball starts in two hours, and I still have some last-minute details to arrange."

"This won't take long," she said, and dropped to her knees just as she had that day so long ago at the Crusader castle. She slanted a wicked smile up at him. "Remember?"

"How could I forget?" Only this time, of course, there was one big difference. This time there was no chance of the queen's catching them at it.

The palace was lit up like a Christmas tree, a fact Caitlin had ample time to appreciate since the line of cars passing through the security checkpoint was proceeding at a snail's pace. Flavio had chauffeured Caitlin and Dominic tonight in a late-model silver gray Rolls Corniche. Bree and Quin were in line behind them in the Alfa Romeo.

"Why did Bree and Quin come in a separate car?" she

asked. "Kind of defeats the purpose, doesn't it, if the bodyguard isn't close enough to guard the body?"

Dominic laughed. "I don't need a bodyguard, Caitlin. I'm perfectly capable of looking out for myself."

"Then why—"

"My father insists. I attract some attention on Calix, but in the outside world . . . ?" He shrugged. "Most people haven't heard of Calix, let alone its royal family."

"Even though the Fortunatus dynasty has been around since Roman times," she said.

"Two thousand years, give or take," he agreed. "You've been reading up on our history?"

She nodded. "Trying to put all the Brother Hamish stories into some historical perspective."

"You finished the manuscript?"

She nodded. She'd finished the manuscript, read up on Calix, and begun to piece together a theory, though she wasn't ready to share it yet, not without a few more facts to back up her wild speculation. "You didn't answer my question," she said. "Why did Quin and Bree come in a separate car?"

"Just in case," he said.

She didn't ask him to elaborate. She knew what "just in case" meant. Just in case everything went to hell.

Flavio let them out at the main entrance, where they had to negotiate yet another security checkpoint, though this time they were waved through without ceremony as soon as the guards recognized Dominic.

They waited a few minutes for Quin and Bree to catch

up, then climbed the broad stairway that swept in a graceful curve up to the second floor. There, liveried footmen opened the double doors into the ballroom.

Caitlin caught her breath in a gasp of sheer delight. The ballroom was banked with flowers—carnations, roses, and baby's breath—that added splashes of color and smelled heavenly. Punctuating the massed blooms were potted trees strung with fairy lights, and overhead three crystal chandeliers gleamed off the gold leaf of the great vaulted ceiling. An orchestra played Strauss from the balcony while elegantly clad dancers swirled across the marble floor.

"Wow!" Bree said, echoing Caitlin's thoughts.

A little stir of excitement rippled through the crowd as they were announced. Heads turned, but the only people Caitlin recognized were the LeTourneaus.

Jacqueline, glamorous in gold lamé—"Giorgio Armani," Bree whispered in Caitlin's ear—air-kissed Caitlin and Bree, ignored Quin, and took Dominic by the arm. "You're late, Your Royal Highness. Your uncle had quite given you up."

"Where is my uncle?"

"Across the room talking with the oh-so-tedious Marsha Garland."

"The prime minister's wife," Etienne explained to Caitlin and Bree. "A nice woman but . . ."

"A bore," Jacqueline said.

"Have you seen my father?" Dominic asked.

Jacqueline, who, Caitlin noticed, still hung on Dominic's arm, glanced toward the empty dais at the far end of the room as if she expected to find the king holding court there.

"He opened the festivities earlier," Etienne said, "but after half an hour he became fatigued and retired to his private quarters. I understand he plans to return later to make a brief speech."

"Oh!" Bree cried suddenly. "Isn't that Mr. Hawke? I must go say hello. If you'll excuse me . . . ?" She slipped away. Quin followed her.

Dominic disentangled himself from Jacqueline and turned to Etienne with a question about how long they planned to stay on Calix. Jacqueline focused her attention on Caitlin. "I didn't realize your friend knew the king's social secretary."

"We ran into him a couple of days ago." Caitlin kept her response deliberately vague. The less Jacqueline knew, the less she could report back to her Fraternitas connection.

"Oh?"

"Yes. You know how it is in a small place."

Jacqueline raised her eyebrows in a conspiratorial look. "Unfortunately, I do. It's why I no longer live in the kingdom."

"I was surprised to learn you're a Calix native. I'd assumed you were French."

Jacqueline gave a very Gallic shrug. "Most people do."

"I met your father, a charming man. He was kind enough to give me a tour of the palace."

"And no doubt talked nonstop about Jacqueline the

entire time." Etienne smiled fondly at his wife. "She's the apple of her papa's eye." He slid an arm around her waist and pressed a kiss to her temple. "And mine as well."

Jacqueline smiled at her husband. "Etienne and I were about to visit the buffet table. Would you two care to join us?"

"Thank you, but no." Dominic smiled to soften his refusal. "We need to go make the rounds."

The LeTourneaus headed for the buffet tables set up in an adjoining room, and Dominic led Caitlin around the room, introducing her to Calixians big and small, old and young. Caitlin noticed more than one speculative look directed her way.

Bree, a vision in carnation pink silk, twirled about the room in Prince Maximilian's arms.

"Your uncle's a good dancer."

"So am I," Dominic said, offering his arm.

They danced, traditional ballroom dancing with Caitlin's left hand on Dominic's shoulder, her right clasped in his left, his right at her waist. The orchestra played a waltz, and it was all very formal and proper. Why then, did Caitlin feel anything but formal and proper?

Maybe part of it was the rich, romantic music swelling above the chatter of the crowd. And maybe another part of it was her gown, cut very low in back so that Dominic's warm hand rested on bare skin. But most of it—nearly all of it—was Dominic himself, his warmth and nearness, his expression. He looked now just as he had in the moment before he'd brought her to climax—eyes slumberous and heavy-lidded, smile seductive and knowing.

And even though the room was warm and heavy with the scent of flowers, Caitlin shivered.

Dominic noticed. Of course, he noticed, and he tightened his grip, smiled, leaned forward and pressed a soft kiss to her forehead. Caitlin's thoughts spun slowly, like feathers spiraling on a lazy air current. *He loves me. He loves me not.*

"Caitlin?" Dominic said.

"Yes?" *He loves me. He loves me not.*

"The music's over." *He loves me.*

"So it is." *He loves me . . .*

"Not that I have any objection to holding you like this for the rest of the evening, but Mr. Hawke has been trying to get my attention for the last minute or so."

She drew a shaky breath. "Of course."

Dominic led her across the room with one hand under her elbow. Still feeling oddly disconnected from her surroundings, she was grateful for the support.

"It's good to see you, Mr. Hawke," Dominic said, shaking the man's hand.

"Your Royal Highness." Hawke bobbed his head, then turned to Caitlin and offered his hand. "Ms. O'Shaughnessy."

She reached out to place her hand in his, but Lord Chamberlain William Weston jostled her. "Sorry," he mumbled, and moved on.

"How very odd." Dominic stared after him, one eyebrow raised. "Too much fine Calixian wine?"

Hawke raised his eyebrows. "No doubt."

Dominic turned to Hawke. "You wanted to speak with me?"

"Actually, it's your father who wants to speak with you. Or so one of the guards just informed me."

Dominic turned to her, indecision on his face. "I hate to abandon you."

"I'm hardly alone. Mr. Hawke's here to keep an eye on me."

"I'll watch her like a hawk," he said.

Dominic groaned. "That's a terrible play on words."

"Go," Caitlin said. "Your father's waiting."

The orchestra struck up another waltz. Hawke bowed. "Would you care to dance, Ms. O'Shaughnessy?"

She swept a curtsy. "I'd love to, Mr. Hawke."

Then he took her hand in his, and for the first time in her life, Caitlin fainted.

Caitlin lay as still as death on the marble floor. In Quin's judgment, of those crowded around her, anxious to help, three faces stood out—Dominic's, Hawke's, and Bree's. All three were pale and drawn, though each face wore a different expression. Dominic looked worried, Hawke looked shocked, and Bree looked scared.

"Did she eat or drink anything? Did anyone touch her?" Dominic demanded.

"No," Hawke said. "No, she didn't ingest a thing. And no one touched her, aside from you, the lord chamberlain, and me, of course. I was just about to lead her onto the dance floor when she collapsed."

"It's warm in here. Maybe she's overheated."

She didn't look overheated. Not in Quin's opinion anyway, though of course, he wasn't a physician.

Dominic pressed the back of his hand to her forehead. "Her skin's cold and clammy." He felt the pulse at her throat. "Her heart's racing."

Caitlin's eyes popped open and all those bending near took an involuntary step back.

Bree was the first to recover. "Are you all right?"

"Eleven," Caitlin said. "Eleven."

Dominic leaned nearer, as if he weren't sure he'd heard correctly. "What did you say?"

"Eleven," Caitlin repeated, and then again, "eleven." Her eyelids closed halfway. "Eleven," she whispered. "Eleven."

Bree knelt on the marble floor and took one of Caitlin's hands in hers. "Wake up, Caitlin." She shot a pleading glance at Quin, as if he possessed the power to put things right.

"Caitlin," he said. "Can you hear me? Bree's worried. Dominic's worried. We all are."

" 'A mighty fortress is our God,' " Caitlin whispered.

"What?" Bree said. "She isn't making any sense."

"Eleven," Caitlin said. "Eleven."

Dominic leaned closer. "What about eleven?"

"The numbers are talking to me."

Dominic took her hands in his. "And what are they saying, Caitlin?"

"Time is running out."

"Is there a doctor here?" Hawke called out across the buzzing crowd. "This young woman needs a doctor."

"No!" Caitlin said, and sat up, blinking her eyes and

looking around as if she weren't quite sure where she was or how she'd gotten there.

"Caitlin?" Bree said.

Caitlin turned toward Bree's voice. "What happened?"

"You fainted."

"You're kidding."

" 'Fraid not," Dominic told her. "Do you remember anything? What happened immediately before you lost consciousness?"

She shook her head, frowning. "Things got noisy, I think. Voices. Thousands of them. Not individual words, but this bizarre cacophony. It's hard to explain." She bit her lip. "And images, thousands and thousands of images, like film clips superimposed one on top of another and all of them running at light speed." She stopped. "I know it sounds crazy."

Dominic pressed a hand to her forehead again. "You aren't running a fever," he said.

"Panic attack," Hawke suggested. "Hard to say what might have triggered it, though."

A slender middle-aged man elbowed his way through the crowd.

"Ah, Dr. Redmond," Hawke said. "Step back, people, so the doctor can examine her."

"Perhaps somewhere with a bit more privacy?" the doctor suggested, so Dominic, ignoring Caitlin's protests, gathered her into his arms.

"Tell my father there's been a slight delay," Dominic told Hawke, then bore Caitlin off to one of the small drawing rooms. Bree, Quin, and the doctor followed.

Dr. Redmond completed a quick exam and pronounced Caitlin fit, though he recommended further tests. "I don't like to alarm you, but sometimes episodes like this are symptomatic of a deeper problem."

"You think I'm crazy," Caitlin said.

"No." The doctor's thin features looked grave. "I'm concerned about a brain tumor."

"Worst-case scenario," Caitlin whispered, and Dominic squeezed her hand.

The doctor left.

"It'll be all right," Dominic said. "You'll see. You don't have a brain tumor."

"And you're not crazy," Bree said. "Tell her, Quin."

"You're not crazy," he told her. "But I think you were channeling again. You said some things while you were out of it." He searched her face. "You don't remember that part, do you?"

"What did I say?"

"You kept repeating the number eleven over and over," Bree said. "You claimed the numbers were talking to you and that time was running out."

"And you quoted a line from a hymn: 'A mighty fortress is our God,' " Dominic added.

Quin looked at Dominic. "Don't you get it? A fortress, eleven eleven?"

"As in eleven eleven AD," Dominic said slowly. "The date chiseled into the stone of the gatehouse at the Crusader castle."

"Right," Quin agreed. "She was channeling Magnus."

"Whose time is running out," Bree said.

"But they can't be keeping him in the castle," Dominic objected. "Tourists go through there in droves every day."

"Tourists only have access to the chapel, the gatehouse, and the keep," Quin pointed out. "Everything else is off limits."

"What are you thinking?" Dominic asked.

"About all those rumors of tunnels honeycombing the rock beneath the castle."

"Tunnels?" Bree echoed faintly.

Brother Ambrose frowned. Dr. Redmond had reentered the ballroom, but as yet, there was no sign of Prince Dominic or Caitlin O'Shaughnessy. Where the hell were they? And what the bloody hell were they up to?

Across the room, Jacqueline danced with her pathetic cipher of a husband. The Frenchman edged his hand down her back an inch at a time until it rested on the upper swell of her backside. *Randy old bastard,* Brother Ambrose thought, then smiled at the irony of the pot calling the kettle black.

Jacqueline murmured something, and Etienne gazed at her with a worshipful expression Ambrose found amusing.

Jacqueline brushed a wisp of Etienne's thinning hair off his forehead in a display of conjugal tenderness, and judging by the sappy look on Etienne's face, he bought her act. Which would seem to suggest he was not the man Brother Ambrose had glimpsed earlier on the hillside above his cottage, spying on him and Jacqueline.

Brother Ambrose glanced around to see if anyone else

was watching the LeTourneaus, but no one was, not even Jacqueline's doting father. Brother Ambrose waited until Jacqueline was facing his way, then caught her attention with a discreet flick of his eyebrows.

She immediately made her excuses to her husband, wove her way through the crowd to Brother Ambrose's side, and shot him a sultry, pouting look that focused his attention on her full red lips, the same full red lips that had pleasured him so thoroughly earlier. "Is there a problem?"

"I hope not. The prince and Ms. O'Shaughnessy have not yet returned to the ballroom."

"And you want me to check on them."

"We can't risk anything going wrong at this juncture."

"You worry too much," she said. "He's probably just dragged her off to some dark corner. The man is thoroughly in lust." A complacent smile curved her lips. "As blinded by desire as my idiot husband." She turned toward Etienne and blew him a kiss across the room.

She was probably right, but Brother Ambrose didn't believe in leaving things to chance. "Just check it out," he said.

Dominic, Caitlin, and Bree waited in the foyer while Quin went to see about having the cars brought round. "The sensible thing to do," Bree said, "would be to go back to the villa, change clothes, and get the Range Rover."

"It'll take too long." Caitlin had pulled her packet of Napier's bones from her evening bag and was rolling them between her fingers like worry beads. "Time is running out."

"There's a shortcut from here through the mountains," Dominic said. "If we leave from the villa, we'll have to go the long way round."

"That decides it then," Caitlin said.

"Problem?" Jacqueline LeTourneau had slipped up on them unawares.

"Caitlin's still feeling under the weather," Bree said. "We've been trying to work out the logistics of the drive back to the villa. We came in two cars, you see." She gave Jacqueline a disingenuous smile, and if Dominic hadn't known she was lying through her teeth, he'd have bought every word.

"I regret having to miss my father's speech—"

"And the fireworks," Bree added. "I love fireworks."

"But I'm sure he'll understand," Dominic finished.

Quin came through the double doors. "The cars are outside, sir." Dominic knew the "sir" was for the benefit of the palace staff.

"I'm sorry you have to leave," Jacqueline said, then added a perfunctory, "Hope you're feeling better soon," directed toward Caitlin.

"Flavio has something to tell you," Quin told Dominic once they were safely out of earshot of the guards.

"Flavio?" Dominic turned to his driver.

Flavio handed over an envelope. "A boy gave me a message for Ms. Caitlin. He said it was urgent."

"What boy was this?" Dominic asked.

"One of the McHenry boys, I think, from Dromedary."

"Like the camel?" Bree asked with a giggle. Dominic suspected she'd indulged in more than one celebratory glass of champagne.

"Precisely," Quin said. "Dromedary's a village in the foothills named for a nearby landmark, a hill called Camel's Hump."

"Sounds nasty," Bree said with a snicker.

Quin shot her a reproving look.

"Well, it does," she said.

"It's actually quite a nice little place," Dominic told her. "There's a Roman bridge nearby and a hot spring. But that's beside the point." He turned back to Flavio. "Did the McHenry boy say who'd given him the message?"

"I asked, but he didn't know the man."

"Doesn't mean a thing," Quin said. "Dromedary's so remote, the people who live up there probably wouldn't recognize the king."

Dominic held the envelope gingerly by one corner.

"Aren't you going to open it?" Caitlin asked.

"Fingerprints," he said.

"But if it's as urgent as the boy said," Caitlin argued, "we don't have time to wait for the forensics experts to make their report."

"She's right," Quin said. "Besides, I'll wager the only prints on that envelope are Flavio's and the boy's."

Dominic slit the envelope open with his pocketknife, fished out a single sheet of cheap white stationery, and passed it to Caitlin.

"One thirty," she read aloud. "Striga Meadow."

Quin swore under his breath. "Nothing incriminating. No mention of the ransom. These Yuli brothers are brighter than I thought."

"My guess is, the mysterious Brother Ambrose wrote it," Caitlin said. "The only thing he didn't count on was my fit cutting short our stay at the ball. Instead of half an hour's warning, we have ninety minutes."

"So what's the plan?" Bree said.

"Divide and conquer, I think." Dominic cocked an eyebrow at Quin, who nodded his agreement.

"Bree and I will go look for Magnus while you and Caitlin head for Striga Meadow. If we find him before your scheduled rendezvous with the kidnappers, we'll call, so you can abort."

"Call how?" Bree said. "Cell phones don't work on that part of the island."

"I've got my satellite phone," Dominic said. "How about you?"

"In the boot of the Alfa," Quin said, "along with a change of clothes." And some heavy-duty firepower, no doubt. Quin never went anywhere unprepared.

"It's settled then," Dominic said.

"Not quite." Caitlin scowled at him. "Magnus is the reason I'm here. I should be the one to look for him."

"The kidnappers aren't going to negotiate with anyone but you."

"We have ninety minutes. You said so yourself. Why can't we go look for Magnus first, then head for Striga Meadow?"

"Striga Meadow is a thirty-minute drive from here. So

is the castle," Dominic explained, "on a different road. We don't have time to go both places. But if we split up . . ."

"I get it," Caitlin said. "I don't like it, but I get it."

March 1618
Mediterranean Sea

Hamish swam toward the makeshift raft with the dirk in his teeth and murder in his heart. One of the seamen saw him coming and shouted some Dutch gibberish, all but inaudible over the storm's racket. Warning him off, no doubt. The weight of one more man would sink them all, and the sailor knew it as well as Hamish. His shouts alerted the other men, and they added their voices to his.

Ignoring them, Hamish swam on. The waves tossed him about as if he were a bit of flotsam. He could scarcely see or breathe, much less move his leaden limbs. But he kept going. One miserable stroke after another.

And then somehow he was there within inches of the half-submerged railing. He closed his fist around the dirk's hilt and prepared to reclaim his rightful property.

One of the sailors raised his head and stared open-mouthed. "Hamish?"

"Jan?"

The old sailor's mouth opened and closed, revealing swollen gums and blackened snags. "You?" he said, his voice as high and shrill as the keening of the wind. "You were dead. Drowned. I cut you free myself."

"Aye?" Hamish smiled at him. "Then I'll return the

favor." He slashed across the exposed throat, then gutted the man in one sure stroke. One of the other sailors saw what he was about and turned his head away, too exhausted or indifferent to stop him.

Jan Dekker's body sank without a trace, and Hamish took his spot along the railing.

16

QUIN PARKED THE ALFA ROMEO a quarter of a mile from the castle. The spot he'd chosen was only a few hundred feet from the road, but a jutting knob of rock and a thick stand of pines provided good cover in case anyone came snooping around.

Bree climbed out on the passenger's side, stumbling on the uneven ground in her spiky-heeled sandals. Her muttered curses—he'd never heard a woman say "cocksucking son of a bitch" before—struck him funny, but he kept his expression sober. No point giving her a new target for her invective.

She glared at the car as if it were to blame, then kicked the back tire for good measure.

Masking his amusement, he popped open the trunk and removed a tote bag. "I took the liberty of bringing along a change of clothing."

"For me?" she said, sounding surprised.

"For both of us."

She studied him a moment in silence. "But when we left the villa, you had no way of knowing we'd end up here."

"No, at that point I thought we'd be providing backup for Caitlin and Dominic's meeting with the kidnappers." He reached into the tote and handed over a T-shirt, jeans, athletic socks, and running shoes. "Best I could do. Portia said you didn't bring any hiking boots."

A slow smile spread across Bree's face. "You really are a very nice man, Quin Gilroy."

Quin's face grew warm—it was hell being a redhead.

When they'd finished changing clothes he tucked a pistol into his waistband at the small of his back, then grabbed his flashlight and bag of tools. "Let's go."

The Rolls, with Dominic behind the wheel and Caitlin next to him, chewed up the miles. They'd left Flavio behind at the palace, his job being to bring the king up to speed. Dominic had already contacted Janus, the head of the CIS, and arranged for a crisis team to meet them at the rendezvous point. Since placing that call, he hadn't said a word. His silence worried Caitlin; her worst-case-scenario production kicked into high gear.

"Tell me about this place we're headed, this Striga Meadow," she said. Maybe if she had some idea what to expect, she could put a few of her wilder fears to rest. "I gather it's a remote location."

"On the far side of the Aeternus Mountains." He shot her a wry sideways glance. "A small meadow perched on the edge of a caldera. There's a lake."

"Like Crater Lake in Oregon," she said. "I've been there. It's beautiful."

"Striga Lake is beautiful, too, but deadly."

"Drownings?"

"I'm not sure anyone's survived long enough to drown."

Caitlin's skin crawled. "Meaning?"

"The lake is so acidic it can completely dissolve a human body in a matter of hours."

"Great," she said. "As soon as we hand over the manuscript and the money, the kidnappers'll toss us in the lake. No incriminating evidence left behind. It's the perfect crime."

"I won't let that happen," he said so firmly she almost believed it. "My father and Janus both know what's going on; we're not alone in this."

Neither were the Yuli brothers.

Caitlin subsided into silence. She dug the bones from her bag, tipped them into her hand, and rolled them back and forth between her thumb and fingers, deriving an obscure comfort from the repetitive movement.

As they climbed higher, pines crowded the edges of the road. Bisecting the forest at intervals were massive rivers of hardened lava that gleamed in the headlights. Dramatic evidence of the island's fiery birth, the flows stretched long black fingers down the mountainsides.

The Aeternus Mountains, Calixians called them, the Eternal Mountains, though according to her research, the island was a mere infant in geologic time. These most recent flows dated back only six thousand years.

The engine growled as the grade steepened. Still fingering the bones, Caitlin leaned back against the headrest and let her mind drift free. Time passed. Seconds. Minutes.

"What did you say?" Dominic asked sharply.

"Nothing." She angled toward him, suddenly unsure. "Did I?"

"Yes. It sounded like *vita aeterna*, Latin for—"

"I know what it means. You're sure that's what I said?"

"You were whispering. I suppose I could have misunderstood."

Or not. "*Vita aeterna* is what Merlin's bones whispered to Hamish. He described it in the manuscript. What if . . . ? No, that's ridiculous. I'm letting the worst-case scenarios get the upper hand." She fell silent again. Dominic didn't press her.

But the possibility—no, the *im*possibility—consumed her thoughts. "Ambrose," she said a while later.

"What about him?"

A small animal, a rabbit perhaps, dashed across the road ahead of them. Dominic jerked the wheel to avoid hitting it and they slid sideways, the rear tires churning through the loose rock at the edge of the road before regaining traction.

"Ambrose is one of the names associated with Merlin. It means 'immortal.' "

He shot a quick sideways glance at her. "What are you suggesting?"

She took a deep breath. If she told him what she suspected, he was going to think she'd lost her mind, and maybe she had, but . . . "We know the manuscript is not entirely a work of fiction. Hamish MacNeill was a real person, his ship did go down off the coast of Calix in 1618, he lived on the island for some years, and he earned a reputation as a healer. Those are verifiable facts."

"Agreed," he said.

"So what if it's all true? Every bit. What if Hamish did absorb Merlin's essence? What if he did become immortal? What if he's still around? What if he never left? What if he just changes his appearance and assumes a new identity every few decades or so?"

"No one lives forever, Caitlin. There's no such thing as immortality."

The hum of the engine filled the silence that stretched between them.

"Do you believe in television?" she said at length.

"Of course, but what does that have to do with—"

"How do you think people four hundred years ago would have reacted to anyone who tried to describe a box that held talking pictures? They'd either commit that person to a lunatic asylum or burn him at the stake."

"Television is a technological advance," Dominic said, "irrelevant to a discussion of immortality and magic bones."

"Atom splitting."

"Again, technology."

"Dragons."

"All right, you lost me. Dragons aren't any more real than immortals. They're creatures of myth and legend."

"Dinosaurs, then. Don't you think it possible—even likely—that dinosaurs gave rise to the dragon stories?"

"Dinosaurs were long gone by the time people evolved," Dominic objected.

"But not their bones," Caitlin said.

"Bones again," he grumbled.

Caitlin searched for a better example. "Magnetism," she said finally. "Two objects drawn together by an invisible force. We know there's a logical scientific explanation behind the phenomenon, but it seems like magic."

Dominic furrowed his brow. "Granted, but—"

"Just keep an open mind. That's all I ask. Maybe Professor Grant was right all along. Maybe Merlin's essence really did enter Hamish MacNeill's body, rendering him immortal."

"And you base this theory on what? The fact our villain calls himself Brother Ambrose?"

"That's part of it, yes," she admitted. "But it's the manuscript itself that convinced me. Why is Brother Ambrose so desperate to get his hands on it? At first, based on Grant's comments to the tabloids, I thought maybe I'd find a treasure map embedded within the pages of the manuscript. But I didn't. So I asked myself what other secrets the book might be hiding. I read it over and over and over again."

"And what did you discover?"

"That Hamish MacNeill was no hero, for one thing."

"And that's a secret worth killing for?"

"If he's trying to protect his reputation, his sense of self."

"Even if we assume the man is still alive, that is not a strong enough motive," Dominic said.

"We know the head of the criminal faction of Fraternitas goes by the name Brother Ambrose. We believe he and the Yuli brothers were responsible for Erskine Grant's murder and Magnus's kidnapping," she said slowly, "presumably because they're desperate to get their hands on the so-called Merlin manuscript." She paused, gripping the bones tightly. "But if they value the manuscript so highly, why did they sell it in the first place?"

"I assume your theory answers that question."

"From what I've heard, the Yuli brothers aren't the cleverest criminals on Calix. Brother Ambrose must have known that. Maybe he even counted on it. Maybe he hooked up with them because they were petty thugs who'd do as he said without asking uncomfortable questions."

"That makes sense," he said.

"Only what if the Yulis turned out to be more enterprising than Brother Ambrose expected? What if they started selling other items besides the artifacts he earmarked?"

"You're suggesting the Yulis put the manuscript up for sale without Brother Ambrose's knowledge."

"Yes," she said. "And all the subsequent actions were intended to rectify that mistake. We speculated before about the possibility of two separate villains. What if Brother Ambrose didn't learn about the ransom demand until after the fact? What if that was simply another instance of the Yulis taking the initiative?"

"That would explain why the ransom was set so low," Dominic admitted. "A hundred thousand dollars probably sounds like a lot of money to three small-time criminals still living with their mother in a backwater like St. Agnes."

"Only somehow Brother Ambrose found out what they'd done," she said.

"We know the Yulis were behind Bree's kidnapping, but what about the abortive break-in at the villa? Are you suggesting that was Brother Ambrose's attempt to short-circuit the Yulis' plan?"

"Quin bloodied the intruder's nose and probably blacked his eye as well," she said, "but none of our Brother Ambrose suspects have any cuts or bruises. So by process of elimination, that must have been the Yulis, too."

"Because they do have cuts and bruises?"

"I don't know whether they do or not," she admitted. "I haven't been close enough, thank God, to tell."

Dominic was silent for a long time. Fast-moving clouds had been scudding across the night sky, hiding the stars. Now they sat piled up in the south, dark, menacing, and rumbling threats. "Even a normal life span seems like a miracle to a Calixian. I can't imagine living forever."

"But—"

"I can, however, imagine men committing all manner of crimes for gain—whether it's ransom money or Roman gold."

He didn't believe her. And who was to blame him? She

wasn't sure she believed herself. The bones, warm now from prolonged contact with her fingers, seemed to vibrate with a barely suppressed energy. Or maybe that was merely another figment of her imagination.

She slid them back into their case.

Bree huddled behind a rock, waiting for Quin to finish reconnoitering. The Crusader castle reared up in front of her, black and sinister, blotting out what little light the growing cloud cover hadn't already extinguished.

Off to the southeast, lightning flashed. She counted the seconds before she heard the echo of distant thunder. Eleven. Not close then. Good. Crawling around the ruins in the middle of the night was bad enough. Add in a thunderstorm, that ultimate in horror movie clichés, and she wasn't sure she could have forced herself to go through with it.

Tunnels, Quin had said. She shuddered. She wasn't a coward about most things, but as an admitted claustrophobic, she avoided small, enclosed spaces—even elevators—whenever possible. Only tonight, it wasn't possible. She gritted her teeth together, shivering in the cool night air. Where the *hell* was Quin?

Bree searched the darkness. No light. No movement. No indication that there was another human being within miles.

And then she heard it, a whisper of sound behind her, a faint rustling. She turned, careful to make no betraying sound herself. Shadows lay thick and dark, almost palpable. Nothing moved, but she knew she hadn't imagined that furtive noise. The wind trailing ghostly fingers through the pines? Or some small animal scurrying through the underbrush?

A hand gripped her arm and she bit back a scream.

"Bree?"

"Damn it, Quin," she said in a furious whisper. "You nearly gave me a heart attack."

The night was too dark to reveal his expression, but Bree got the distinct impression he was laughing at her. His voice sounded perfectly serious, though, as he told her to follow him. "I didn't spot any guards posted outside," he said, "but it's still best we keep our voices down." He headed toward the gatehouse. She followed.

"That's odd, isn't it?" she said, frowning. "I mean, if Magnus is here, surely they wouldn't leave him unguarded. What if he escaped? Where's their ransom then?"

"Maybe he's in no condition to escape," Quin said quietly.

A chill ran down her spine. "Dead, you mean?"

"Or injured."

Dread settled in the pit of her stomach.

A heavy iron-sheathed portcullis and a thick wooden door would once have protected the entrance to the gatehouse, but over the centuries both had disappeared, victims of oxidation and rot—or perhaps pilferage. Quin shone his light at the stone lintel, illuminating the date chiseled into the stone, MCXI. One thousand, one hundred eleven. Eleven eleven.

"What's the purpose of the holes in the ceiling?" she asked. "Ventilation?"

"They're murder holes," Quin said. "The castle's defenders would have used them to drop things down upon the invaders—rocks, boiling water."

"Boiling water? I thought they used boiling oil."

"Unlikely," Quin told her. "Oil was a precious commodity in the Middle Ages, too precious to squander."

"And the holes in the walls?" she asked.

"Arrow slits."

"So even if the invaders made it past the portcullis and through the gate," Bree said, "they weren't out of danger."

"Hardly. The outer walls of the castle are twenty feet thick, the gate entrance three times that long, a very dangerous passage." He led her into a stone-paved courtyard encircled by a second stone wall or curtain. Like the outer wall, it was crenellated and buttressed at intervals by massive round towers. They passed beneath another vaulted entry and emerged into a larger courtyard. "Where are we?" she whispered.

"The ward," Quin said. He flashed his light on a large fortified tower built into the wall. "And that's the keep."

She stared at the massive building surrounding them. "This place is huge. How will we ever find Magnus?"

"Process of elimination," Quin said. "We know he can't be anywhere that's open to tourists, so all we have to do is check the parts that are off limits."

"Like the dungeon," she said.

"Like the storage area under the keep."

Bree followed him inside. "Not exactly a storybook castle, is it?"

"People romanticize the Middle Ages," Quin told her.

"In reality, castles were essentially fortresses, built for strength rather than beauty."

They made their way through twisting passageways, past small, cell-like rooms, down a flight of spiraling newel stairs—designed, according to Quin, to fit inside a tower—past more rooms, these even smaller and less welcoming, then into another tower and down another set of newel stairs. At the bottom a heavy wooden door barred their way. Above it hung a sign: Keep Out! A shiny modern padlock reinforced the message.

"Dead end," she said.

"Or not." Quin drew a set of bolt cutters from his bag of tricks and made short work of the padlock. The door swung open silently on well-oiled hinges. "Interesting. Somebody's been through this way recently."

But not *too* recently, Bree thought. The door had been locked from the outside, which meant the bad guys were outside as well, unless, of course, there was another entrance to the nether regions. Gooseflesh prickled along her arms.

The door opened onto a narrow flight of stone steps. Quin went first. Bree followed. The stairs dead-ended in a low-ceilinged cellar, the walls patchy with mold and mildew, the floor strewn with debris.

"Oh, ick." Bree shuddered.

Quin glanced over his shoulder. "What's wrong?"

"I just stepped on a centipede."

He gave her hand a squeeze. "They thrive in the damp."

She shuddered again.

"No talking above a whisper from here on," he cautioned. "If we've guessed right and Magnus is in the castle, they'll have guards posted."

"How much farther?"

"Not much," he said. "Can you hear that?"

"What?"

A scowl of concentration turned his features into a gargoyle mask in the backwash of the flashlight. "Listen. Sounds like someone's singing."

Singing? Bree shivered. *Singing?* And then she heard it, a raspy voice giving a weird, echoing rendition of "Yesterday."

"Magnus," she whispered.

Quin turned his gargoyle face on her. "Are you certain?"

"He's a huge Beatles fan, and 'Yesterday' is his favorite song. He used to drive Caitlin crazy singing it, humming it, even whistling it, which wouldn't have been bad—she has nothing against the song—except, as you can hear for yourself, Magnus can't carry a tune."

"Any idea where the sound's coming from?"

Bree cocked her head to listen. "That way," she said, pointing toward a corridor that led off to the right.

The ceiling was so low that Quin had to hunch over to avoid hitting his head. "I'm going to switch off my torch," he said. "If there's a guard on duty, no point warning him."

The darkness, musty with mold and centuries-old filth, closed in around her. Bree couldn't see or breathe or even think rationally. In her mind's eye, she envisioned the corridor crawling with centipedes, all of them bent on wriggling into her hair or under her clothes. Something brushed her cheek and she stifled a scream, but it was only a flyaway strand of her own hair, full of static electricity.

"Stay close," Quin whispered.

Like she'd dream of doing anything else. She hooked a finger through one of his belt loops. "I'm right behind you."

The hoarse singing grew louder and louder until it sounded as if it were coming from under their feet. Quin halted so abruptly, she bumped into him. "Easy does it." He put out a hand to steady her. "I don't think they've left a guard. I'm going to use the torch."

The welcome glow bounced off the walls of a small room, surprising Bree, who'd thought they were still in the tunnel. If she hadn't been so deep in panic mode, she'd have realized Quin was no longer walking hunched over and that the air smelled fresher. She glanced around at the walls. No centipedes in sight.

She drew a cautious breath of relief.

"Someone's been here recently," Quin said, nodding at the incongruous sight of a metal folding chair, an empty soda can, and a scattering of cigarette butts lying next to a trapdoor in the floor.

Beneath their feet, Magnus was still singing "Yesterday."

Bree knelt next to the trapdoor. "Magnus? Are you in there?"

Quin dropped to his knees, balanced the flashlight on

the seat of the folding chair, drew the bolt, and raised the heavy door.

"Magnus?" Bree said, leaning as far over the edge as she could without losing her balance. "Magnus?"

Magnus's voice quavered on a high note. Quin grabbed the flashlight and used it to probe the depths of the hole. The empty hole.

Bree sat back on her haunches. "I don't understand."

"There." Quin pointed, but she had to look twice before she realized what he was talking about.

At the bottom of the pit lay a small CD player.

March 1618
Mediterranean Sea

The storm was nearly spent and so was Hamish's strength. He pulled himself up on top of the railing and flopped there, winded, but clear at last of the lapping waves. With only one man to support—he'd rid himself of the poachers one by one—the stout wooden railing floated high in the water.

The sky had already begun to lighten off to the east when he heard the noise. It started as a creak and a rush, then rapidly grew to a fearsome sucking roar. His makeshift raft spun in a lazy circle, slowly at first, then faster and faster.

Half-forgotten tales of ravenous sea creatures leapt to the forefront of his mind. Charybdis. Was it not she who lurked just beneath the surface, ready to drag unwary sailors to their deaths in her bottomless whirlpool?

He rose up on his elbows, peering about, and that was when he spotted her, an ominous dark, hulking figure looming up against the pearly predawn sky. She uttered an agonized groan that raised gooseflesh along his body. Had he survived a shipwreck only to be devoured by a monster?

Debris spun by—a bucket, a spar, a broken mop handle—and he realized what was really happening. It wasn't some mythical beast that threatened him but *de Gouden Tulp*. The fine Dutch flute was breathing her last, creating a huge vortex as she sank.

Dawn broke, unfurling rosy ribbons of light, and with one final outraged shriek, the ship submerged, sucking him down with it. Down and down and down.

17

DOMINIC PULLED INTO THE OVERLOOK above Striga Meadow at twenty-six minutes after midnight. Aside from the Rolls, the crescent of gravel was empty.

"What are you planning to do for the next hour?" Caitlin asked.

"Change out of this tuxedo, for one thing."

"You brought other clothes?"

"I did." He stepped out of the car, circled around the hood, and opened Caitlin's door. "Portia packed some things for you as well."

She smiled up at him, not a flirtatious smile or a provocative smile, just an ordinary, run-of-the-mill Caitlin smile, but his heart kicked up a notch all the same as he helped her out of the car.

"At your request?" she said.

He nodded.

The phantom dimple appeared for a second. "Thanks."

"Don't thank me. Thank Mr. Hawke. 'One should always be prepared.' He used to drill that into me on a daily basis."

"Then thanks to Mr. Hawke. I'd thought of ripping the side seams up to my thigh to give myself room to maneuver, but I'm glad that won't be necessary. This is the most beautiful gown I ever owned. It would be a shame to ruin it."

"A shame," he repeated, not sure what they were talking about, aware only of the softness of Caitlin's hand in his, the faint jasmine and citrus scent of her perfume, and the sweet curve of her mouth. *Kiss her,* his baser instincts urged. But if he kissed her, he knew where it would lead. And this was not the time or place.

Her lips parted.

Hell, man, she wants you to kiss her.

Yes, but . . .

"Kiss me," she said.

Oh, bloody hell.

He kissed her, and he was lost. How could anyone look so sweet, he wondered, and taste so deliciously wicked? His skin tingled, his blood burned, and his heart beat so loud, he couldn't hear what she said when she eased away. He couldn't hear, but he could feel her words as soft warm puffs of air caressing his mouth. He could taste them, their flavor sweet on his tongue. He could see them in the seductive movements of her soft lips.

He kissed her again, and it was like plunging into the turquoise waters of Smuggler's Cove, warm and sensuous, but not without risk. Always there was the chance, however slight, that one might drown.

Caitlin placed her hands on his shoulders and gave him a shake. "Dominic," she said, "listen to me."

"I'd much rather kiss you."

"Yes," she said softly, "and you do it so well, but I'm afraid it's starting to rain."

"Rain?" He tilted his face toward the sky, and two fat drops splatted his face. "You're right. Best take cover till the storm's past." He handed her in on the passenger's side, shut the door, and then went round to the trunk to get their change of clothing and the gym bag that held his weapons.

He clambered into the back seat just as the sprinkle became a full-fledged downpour.

"Good timing," she said.

"No, good timing would have meant the rain held off another hour."

She laughed softly, the low, sexy sound triggering another spike in his heart rate, and for a second or two the blood thrumming in his ears drowned out the rain pounding the Rolls-Royce's roof.

"Here." He handed her the clothes Portia had packed. "I know it's awkward trying to change in the car, but you probably ought to give it a go. God knows how long this rain will last. We need to be ready for Brother Ambrose when he shows up."

Undressing in the dark wasn't too difficult, but dressing proved more of a challenge. On his first attempt he ended up with his shirt on backward and inside out. And then, he somehow lost his second shoe. "How are you doing?" he asked Caitlin, once he'd set himself to rights.

"All safely zipped and buttoned," she said.

Was that a hint, he wondered, that he keep his lips to himself from now on?

"Dominic," she said, "I've been thinking."

Thinking, the ultimate anti-aphrodisiac.

"I might know who Brother Ambrose is."

Her words brought him back to earth with a jarring thump. This wasn't some romantic interlude. They'd come to bargain with a kidnapper. A thief. A murderer. A man they knew only as Brother Ambrose. "Who?"

"Lord Chamberlain William Weston."

Dominic flinched as if she'd swung a bludgeon at his head. "Impossible. Weston's above reproach."

"I heard tonight that he's planning to retire in six months."

"He's due, Caitlin. He's been in charge of my father's household for over a quarter of a century. That's a lot of responsibility."

"But the timing's suggestive, don't you think? Just before he's due to retire, rare artifacts start disappearing. Maybe he's feathering his nest in preparation for retirement."

"Nonsense," Dominic said. "It's a coincidence, nothing more." Wasn't it?

"Okay," she said, "then how do you explain his behavior tonight at the ball?"

"What about it?" He hadn't noticed anything out of the ordinary.

"I spoke to him twice," she said slowly. "The first time, he was so preoccupied with his own thoughts, he didn't even hear me. The second time, his response was brief and perfunctory."

"He had a lot on his mind."

"And later, just before my little channeling episode, he bumped into me, mumbled an apology, and hurried away."

"That was odd," he admitted. "I remember wondering if he'd drunk too much champagne."

"I don't think he'd been drinking at all," she said. "I never once saw him with a glass in his hand."

"Then the worst you can say is, he's either absent-minded or clumsy, and neither makes him a villain."

"But he *is* Jacqueline's father," she pointed out. "And we know for a fact that she's involved."

"William Weston is a man of honor. He is not Brother Ambrose."

"Then who is?"

Who is? The rain drummed the roof of the car. *Who is?* "I don't know," he said, shying away from the most obvious answer.

His uncle, Prince Maximilian, had always been the black sheep of the family, a gambler and womanizer who frequently lived beyond his not-inconsiderable means. Who was to say what he might not be capable of under pressure to pay off his debts? He might even enjoy the risk involved in smuggling expensive artifacts out of the palace under the noses of the guards.

"I kept an eye on your uncle tonight, too," Caitlin said, as if she'd read his mind. "Aside from one rather awkward encounter with Jacqueline LeTourneau, however, he did nothing to raise my suspicions."

Caitlin kept talking, but Dominic didn't hear what she said. He'd caught the faraway gleam of headlights out the rear window. Someone was coming, approaching from the direction of the palace. The crisis team Janus had promised him? Or Brother Ambrose?

He reached automatically for his Glock.

"What is it?" Caitlin said, then, "Oh, my God." She'd spotted the approaching car, too. "So soon? The rendezvous isn't until one thirty; surely it can't be one yet."

He glanced at the luminous face of his watch. "One-oh-five, actually."

"Oh, God."

"Try not to worry. It's probably just the crisis team Janus promised to send along as backup."

"Probably," she repeated, but she didn't sound convinced.

"The rain's slacking off." Though more clouds were moving in. "Do you see the stone posts that hold up the guardrail?"

"Yes."

"I want you to go hide yourself behind one of those posts until I figure out if our visitor is friend or foe."

"Dominic, I . . ." She grabbed his hand and held on tight. "I don't want to leave you."

"You're not leaving me," he said. "You're my backup." He gave her hand a squeeze, then released it. "Go before he gets any closer."

She started to open the door.

"No, wait," he said. He reached into the front and switched off the interior lights. "Okay, now," he said.

She slipped out, closed the door quietly behind her, and melted into the shadows.

"Divide and conquer," Quin muttered. The headlamps cut a swath through the darkness as they raced against time. Even if he pushed the little car to its limits, he'd never make it to Striga Meadow in time.

"That's what Dominic said earlier, isn't it?" Bree said.

"Exactly." He shot her a bitter look. "We thought we were splitting up to cover all the bases. As it turns out, we're the ones who've been divided. We're the ones who're supposed to be conquered." He passed her the satellite phone. "Call Dominic. The least we can do is warn him."

Bree fiddled with the phone, and he drove. The mileposts along the south beach highway flew past in a blur. Please, God, please don't let them be too late.

Bree shook her head. "I don't know what I'm doing wrong, but I can't get it to work."

"Let me try." Quin reached for the phone. Seconds later, he tossed it aside in disgust.

"Did I break it?" Bree asked.

"No," he said, "you didn't do anything wrong. It's been sabotaged. Deliberately."

"By Brother Ambrose?"

"Or someone who's working for him."

"But how and when?"

"The saboteur must have broken into the boot of the Alfa Romeo while we were at the ball."

Bree made an involuntary sound of protest. "Brother

Ambrose isn't going through with the trade, is he? He never planned to play fair. He's going to kill Magnus if he hasn't already, and once he has what he wants, he's going to kill Caitlin and Dominic, too."

"Divide and conquer," Quin said grimly.

Dominic recognized the car as it drew closer, and for a second the enormity of the betrayal stole his breath. By the time the gray Saab sedan crunched to a halt a few feet away, a cold, hard anger had steeled him. He drew his pistol.

Emrys Hawke stepped out. "Surprise, surprise," he said.

The rain had stopped for the moment, but the wind was shifting direction as it so often did in the Mediterranean. They'd caught just the edge of the storm earlier, but now the massive bank of clouds was on a collision course. Dominic counted a three-second delay between the flash of the lightning and the clap of the thunder.

Hawke glanced up at the roiling thunderheads, eerily lit by ripples of sheet lightning, and sighed. "A complication I hadn't bargained for." He smiled at Dominic. "But I daresay we'll manage. Did you bring the ransom?"

"Did you bring Magnus Armstrong?" Dominic countered.

Hawke's face mirrored a series of emotions: confusion, understanding, hurt, annoyance, and finally, amusement. "You think I'm Brother Ambrose?"

"Aren't you?"

"Of course not!"

Dominic narrowed his eyes. "If you're not Brother Ambrose, then why did you say, 'Surprise, surprise'? If you're not Brother Ambrose, then how do you know about Brother Ambrose? That name never appeared in any news reports."

"The CIS doesn't rely on the media for its information."

"The CIS? You're saying you work for the CIS?"

"I *am* the CIS, Fortune." Hawke never called him Fortune, but . . .

"You're Janus?"

Hawke tipped his head in acknowledgment. "As I said, 'Surprise, surprise.' "

"But what are you doing here? You're not a field agent."

"No. However, this operation is so crucial that I decided to oversee the crisis team personally."

"I don't see any crisis team," Dominic said. Suspicion lay as heavy on his heart as the gun in his hand.

"And I don't see Ms. O'Shaughnessy, but I assume she's here. You can make a similar assumption about the team."

" 'Assumptions can get you killed. Trust the evidence.' "

Hawke laughed. "Throwing my own words back in my face? Very good, Fortune. I did teach you a thing or two then, didn't I?" He pulled a walkie-talkie from his pocket and pushed a button. Dominic half expected an explosion, but nothing happened. "Barrister, flash your torch. Fortune here needs evidence that the team's in place."

Light flashed from a small copse of trees on the rocky hillside above them. Excellent position for an observation post. Dominic couldn't have chosen better himself. He'd never worked with Nigel Barrister, but the agent had a solid reputation, apparently well deserved.

"You're Janus," Dominic said. "I can't believe it."

Hawke's smile edged into smirk territory. "The perfect code name, wouldn't you agree? Like Janus, I wear two faces. To most people, I'm the king's social secretary, a self-effacing man. Yet I'm also head of the Calixian Intelligence Service, and as such, one of the most influential people in the kingdom." He paused. "Where's Ms. O'Shaughnessy?"

"Here." Caitlin stepped out from behind the stone post. "Call your father, Dominic."

"Why?" Dominic frowned.

"This could still be an elaborate charade. You told me yourself—the only one who knows Janus's true identity is the king. Call your father."

"Regrettably there's no cell phone service up here," Hawke said.

Caitlin shot him a suspicious look. "Which is why Dominic brought his satellite phone."

Hawke sketched a mocking bow in her direction. "Then by all means, call the king. I'm sure he won't mind being awakened at"—he glanced at his watch—"one sixteen in the morning."

"Call him," Caitlin said. "After Flavio filled him in on our plans, I very much doubt he went to bed."

"Flavio?" Hawke asked.

"My chauffeur." Dominic dialed his father's private number.

The king picked up almost immediately. "Dom . . . nic? Are you . . . all right?"

"So far. No sign of Brother Ambrose yet."

"Has"—a harsh, hacking cough interrupted the king—"Janus's team . . . shown up?"

"They're here," Dominic said. "Who *is* Janus, Father?"

"I thought . . . you said . . . they'd shown up."

"They have, but I need to hear it from you. I need to be sure. Who is Janus?"

"Hawke," his father said.

"My father confirmed his identity," Dominic told Caitlin once he'd ended the call.

Hawke didn't say a word, but his body language screamed, "I told you so."

Caitlin still looked uneasy, as if she suspected they were the victims of a conspiracy, a conspiracy so far-reaching that it included the king. "Call Quin," she said. "He and Bree should have located Magnus by now."

"You have no objection?" he asked Hawke.

Hawke spread his hands, palms up. "None whatsoever if it will put Ms. O'Shaughnessy's mind to rest."

Dominic punched in Quin's number, but all he got was a busy signal. "That's odd," he said.

"What?" Caitlin demanded.

"His phone's busy."

"Perhaps he's trying to call you," Hawke said.

"Perhaps," Dominic agreed.

"Well," Hawke said, "how do you want to work this? I assume you brought the ransom?"

"The money's in the trunk of the Rolls," Caitlin said. "The manuscript's in my backpack."

"Perhaps I should take charge—" Hawke started.

His walkie-talkie suddenly crackled with static. "Car coming," a disembodied voice reported.

Caitlin squinted down the road. "I don't see any headlights."

"Barrister has a better view from up there," Hawke said.

"Brother Ambrose?" Caitlin's voice shook.

"That's my guess." Dominic motioned for her to duck back behind the post, then turned to Hawke. "You should take cover as well."

"I may look like an anemic schoolmaster," Hawke said, "but I know how to handle myself. And this." He pulled a .38 from under his tuxedo jacket.

Dominic studied his former tutor, a smallish, nondescript man, not handsome, not ugly, not fair, not dark, not old, not young. To look at him, one would never suspect he was one of the most powerful men in Calix, the king's most trusted confidant.

Like Caitlin, Dominic's mother had never really warmed to Mr. Hawke. And yet in those dark days after her death, when his father had retreated from the world—and his son—to grieve in private, Mr. Hawke had been the only one to spare a thought for Dominic.

Overhead the storm moved closer. Lightning split the sky. Thunder rumbled.

And on the winding road below the overlook, the lights of the oncoming car pulled into view.

"He's moving fast." Hawke took up position behind the Saab.

Dominic moved behind the Rolls.

The car, a late-model Daimler, roared up the final incline and churned to a sudden stop inches from the Saab's passenger side door. Lord Chamberlain William Weston erupted from the driver's seat.

"Stop right there, Brother Ambrose!" Hawke's voice rang out over the rush of the rising wind, the rolling thunder, but Weston didn't even pause.

He lunged toward the other man. "Damn you!" he shouted. "Damn you to hell!"

"Stop!" Dominic yelled. "Stop!"

For a split second, Weston turned his wild-eyed gaze on Dominic. "You can't stop me. No one can stop me this time." He leveled a pistol at Hawke's chest. "I should have done this long ago."

"No!" A woman's scream shrilled above the keening of the wind.

Caitlin, Dominic thought at first, then realized the sound had come from the wrong direction.

"No!" he said, but it was already too late.

Hawke's and Weston's weapons discharged almost simultaneously. Hawke staggered as his body absorbed the impact, but he managed to remain upright. Weston, on the other hand, dropped in his tracks. Dominic rushed to the lord chamberlain's side, but Weston was already dead, a bullet hole between his eyes.

"Is he—" Caitlin knelt next to him. When had she emerged from hiding?

"Dead," he said and stood up.

Caitlin's gaze met his. "Was he Brother Ambrose?"

"Yes," Hawke said. "I've had him under surveillance for some time, but until tonight I couldn't be certain." He knuckled his breastbone as if it pained him.

"Are you hurt?" Dominic asked sharply.

Hawke gave a weary smile and shook his head. "Nothing permanent. These new Kevlar vests are remarkably effective."

"It's over then," Caitlin said.

"Or almost," Dominic told her. "All we're waiting for now is that call from Quin and Bree saying that they've rescued Magnus."

"Try them again," Caitlin said, so he did—with the same result.

"Line's still busy."

She frowned. "That doesn't make sense."

Hawke circled around the Saab and toed Weston's body. "Unless our friend Brother Ambrose here disabled Gilroy's phone."

"How would he do that?" Caitlin asked. "And why?"

"Because he wanted to keep you in the dark." Jacqueline materialized out of the shadows. Dressed in black from head to toe, she carried an Uzi as if she knew how to handle it.

"What's going on?" Hawke demanded sharply.

"You tell me," she said. "Was it my father on the hill above your cottage?"

"Focus on the big picture, Jacqueline."

"And what picture is that? The picture of you shooting an innocent man in cold blood?" Her voice rose shrilly.

Unstable, Dominic thought. "Stay behind me," he whispered to Caitlin.

"He was the aggressor, not I," Hawke said.

"He thought he was protecting me. He must have seen us together and thought his nightmare was happening all over again. You destroyed his marriage, and now you were doing the same to mine."

Hawke advanced one careful step. "You know that's not true."

"My father thought it was. He knew nothing of our bond."

"Bond?" Caitlin whispered too softly for anyone but Dominic to hear.

"No one knew. No one but the queen, and you took care of her, didn't you, Emrys?"

"Took care of her?" Dominic said. "Why? How? What are you saying?"

Jacqueline raised her eyebrows. "Shall I tell him, Emrys?"

"Why not?" Hawke heaved a weary sigh. "I'd thought to avoid any more bloodshed, but the cat's already halfway out of the bag."

Meaning what? Dominic wondered. *That it didn't matter what she said because he was going to kill them all anyway? Just try it, Brother Ambrose. I dare you.* Dominic had been in enough dangerous situations to recognize—and welcome—the rush of adrenaline flooding his bloodstream.

"Emrys and my mother had been lovers for as long as I

could remember, but when I turned fifteen, he noticed me," Jacqueline said. "I was having trouble with geometry; he offered to tutor me for free." She paused. "He was a very talented tutor." The smile she directed at Hawke raised the small hairs along the back of Dominic's neck. "One day we were up at the Crusader castle—this was before it became a mecca for tourists—and the queen caught us in fellatio delicto, as it were. She called him a child molester and threatened to tell the king."

"And?" Rage, cold and relentless, filled Dominic. Caitlin gave his arm a warning squeeze, but he scarcely noticed the warmth of her touch.

"Emrys sent me home. I didn't see what happened next. But later they found Queen Caroline's broken body lying below the parapet." Jacqueline shrugged.

Dominic's incredulous gaze raked Hawke. "I was your alibi, wasn't I? That was the day we hiked up here to Striga Meadow."

Hawke took an involuntary step backward, as if propelled by the force of Dominic's fury. "It was an accident. I swear."

"You lying bastard." Jacqueline brought the Uzi up to fire, but Hawke anticipated her. He raised his pistol.

And that was the chance Dominic had been waiting for. As Hawke aimed at Jacqueline, Dominic centered him in the crosshairs.

Two shots rang out. Jacqueline collapsed, dead before she hit the ground. Dominic's shot pierced Hawke's left temple—no chance that the body armor would save him this time—and he crumpled in slow motion.

March 1618
Mediterranean Sea

Hamish dreamed of gold, riches beyond imagining, a wealth of Roman coins scattered across the sand at the bottom of the sea near the bones of an ancient trireme. A treasure his for the taking. But how, he wondered, was he to rescue his newfound wealth when he could not even rescue himself? He peered up through the murky depths. Somewhere up there sunlight danced across the surface of the sea. But he was dead, unable to reach the light.

Abruptly, his dream shifted focus. He was still under the water, but the gold was gone. Somehow he knew he'd been adrift in a fast-moving current, but now he was tangled in a jungle of seaweed that billowed in the underwater stream like sails before the wind.

A smiling dolphin swam past, then doubled back. He studied Hamish curiously, then bumped his nose into Hamish's ribs, as if to say, "Come play with me, human."

"I'm caught," he explained.

The words emerged garbled and indistinct, but the dolphin nodded as if he'd understood every syllable. The great beast grabbed a mouthful of seaweed in its jaws and ripped. The long strands floated free. So did Hamish.

Again the dolphin urged him to come play, and it hardly seemed polite to refuse. So Hamish climbed upon the creature's broad, sleek back and rode to the surface where an island arose from the sea, and he thought perhaps he hadn't been dreaming at all.

18

CAITLIN STARED IN SHOCK AT THE CARNAGE.

The past is done, and blood will tell. There's greatness in your future.

Greatness. The irony of the gypsy's prediction sickened her. Here she stood, all alone in the middle of nowhere. All alone with three corpses. All alone. Except for . . .

Dominic? Where was Dominic? She spun in a circle. Had Hawke killed him as well as Jacqueline and her father? But no, he'd been standing right beside her. If he'd fallen, she'd have noticed. If he'd fallen, he'd be on the ground. And he wasn't. He wasn't anywhere. "Dominic?" She yelled to make herself heard over the wind. Her hair blew into her face; she shoved it aside. "Dominic!" Even louder this time.

Lightning tore a jagged rip across the clouds. Thunder boomed, deafeningly loud, and the rain came down suddenly, torrents of it, drenching her to the skin in seconds. "Dominic!" she screamed again.

Something touched her shoulder. She jerked away, stifling a scream.

"Sorry," Dominic said. "I didn't mean to frighten you." He pulled her into his arms and she hugged him tight, afraid to admit even to herself how much he meant to her, how frightened she'd been that she'd lost him.

"Where were you?"

She felt the laughter rumbling in his chest and jerked out of his embrace. "Don't laugh. I was terrified something had happened to you."

"I was laughing at myself, at the big strong hero. Undercover operative. Prince of Calix. I'm forced to shoot a monster, and how do I respond?"

She gazed at him in confusion. "By laughing?"

He shook his head. "By emptying the contents of my stomach over the guardrail. Some hero."

"Oh, Dominic." She pulled him into her arms and held him close. "It's no weakness to be sickened by the taking of a life. I don't think I could feel the way I do about you if you were the sort of man who could kill without remorse."

He pulled a little apart so he could see her face. "And how is it that you feel about me?"

"I love you," she said, surprised at how easy it was to say the words.

The downpour had plastered his hair to his head. Water ran down his face and dripped off the end of his nose, but he had never looked more attractive to Caitlin. "Say it again," he demanded.

"I love you."

"I love you, too," Dominic said softly.

"How very touching."

She turned her head at the sound of Hawke's voice. Dominic went deathly still. She'd have thought him turned to stone if not for the faint rise and fall of his chest beneath her splayed fingertips.

Hawke stood three yards away, the wound in his temple nearly healed. "Very slowly, Dominic, use your left hand to remove the gun that's tucked into the back of your waistband and toss it this way."

Dominic did as he was told. "So it's true," he said. "Hamish MacNeill still lives. Caitlin tried to warn me."

Hawke's eyes bored into hers. "I knew you were trouble from the first moment I saw you."

"Because I look like Maggie," she said.

A muscle twitched below his right eye. "You read the manuscript."

"Your diary, you mean."

"My release," he said.

"She wasn't dead. You rode away and left her there, but she wasn't dead."

The muscle twitched again. "What are you talking about?"

"Maggie. Maggie Gordon, my however-many-greats grandmother. I think a small fragment of Merlin's essence must have entered her, too, because she lived well up into her nineties, quite extraordinary longevity in those days. In fact, all your descendants are long-lived. Genetic anomalies, according to my stepfather. We never get sick. Not even colds."

"What are you talking about, woman? I don't have any descendants. I can't father children, and God knows I've tried."

"Maybe the lightning strike fried all your sperm," she said. "Or maybe sterility is the going price for immortality. But the thing is, Maggie was already pregnant before lightning split that oak tree in two."

"Robert—" he started, the muscle in his cheek twitching madly.

"Was sterile," she said. "He had two wives before Maggie, neither of whom gave him an heir. I suspect he'd had mumps as a young man." She forced herself to smile. "But thanks to you, Maggie produced a strapping young son almost nine months to the day after your tryst on the riverbank, which meant she wasn't required either to break her neck in a tumble down the stairs like Robert's first wife or to drown in the burn like the second."

Caitlin watched his face. She'd rattled him, but not enough. He was still in control, still thinking rationally.

"Why was the manuscript so important to you, Hawke?" Dominic asked.

"I told you," Caitlin said. "It showed him in a less than heroic light, and he couldn't bear to see his legend tarnished." But as soon as she said the words, Hawke's expression told her there was more to it.

"Why, Hawke?" Dominic said. "Why kill so many people? What secret are you trying to protect?"

Caitlin drew a deep breath. "Is that it? Is that your secret—that you've killed so many people? Auld Mòrag,

Jan Dekker, the sailors from *de Gouden Tulp,* and of course, more recently, Erskine Grant."

"I never touched Grant. That was Hector Yuli's doing."

"Speaking of Hector," Dominic said, "whatever happened to him? No one's spotted him or his brothers in days. Tell me, Hawke, how does one disappear on an island this size?"

His eyes betrayed him, flicking to the left for a brief second.

"You killed them," Caitlin said, suddenly certain of it. "You dumped their bodies in the lake."

"They were scum." Hawke's voice quivered in outrage. "They tried to steal from me."

The gold, he meant.

"Still," Caitlin said, "most of those you murdered were innocents."

"Innocents? The old witch stabbed me to death with my own knife, and Dekker was responsible for my drowning."

"I'm not talking about them," Caitlin said. "I'm talking about the curse victims."

Hawke sucked in his breath with a hissing sound. "I only meant to help."

Dominic looked from her to Hawke. "What? How?"

"The elixir," she said.

"My elixir worked!" Hawke protested.

"In the short term," she agreed, "but it had an unfortunate side effect, didn't it? Exposure to your blood caused genetic abnormalities. How many generations did you treat before you suspected what was happening?"

"I never meant any harm," he said. "I became a healer to atone for my sins, not add to them. I've served the people of Calix in one capacity or another for almost four hundred years."

"Served us?" Dominic said softly. "Or served yourself? Jacqueline was a child when you corrupted her."

"Jacqueline was never a child."

"I was a child when you murdered my mother."

"I told you. That was an accident."

"And was it an accident when you stole artifacts from the palace?"

"I never stole anything from the palace. I recruited the Yuli brothers to help me in my smuggling enterprise. We dealt in opium, gemstones, and antiquities from the Middle East. That was it."

"What about the manuscript?" Caitlin protested. "What about the first book of the *Calix Chronicles*?"

Hawke shifted his gaze to her. "One, I didn't sell the manuscript, the Yulis did, and two, it's not the first book of the *Chronicles*."

"That's what you told Dominic."

"Well, what was I supposed to tell him? The truth? That it was a personal journal I'd written in the sixteen hundreds?"

"How did the Yuli brothers get their hands on it?" Dominic asked.

"We'd been using the cave to store our product. One night they got bored, started sifting through the rubble, and discovered the chamber beyond the cave-in, the room where I spent my first years on Calix. That's where they found my journal."

"And the gold," Dominic said.

"Enough talk." Hawke leveled his gun at Caitlin. "Hand over the manuscript."

Dominic squeezed her arm. What was he trying to tell her? To refuse? To play along? To distract Hawke long enough for Dominic to draw a weapon? If she made the wrong choice, did the wrong thing . . .

"I can't."

"Hand it over, or I'll shoot."

"I can't, I tell you."

"I don't make idle threats. Tell her, Fortune."

"He means what he says," Dominic said.

"But if you require further proof . . ." Hawke suddenly shifted his weapon, targeting Dominic.

"No!" The explosion deafened her. Dominic's grip on her arm went slack. He sagged and fell face first in the muddy gravel. "Dominic!" she screamed, and dropped to her knees next to his inert body.

"You're next," Hawke said, "unless you give me the manuscript."

"I don't have it." She slid a hand under Dominic's throat, felt for a pulse, and found one, weak but discernible. She needed to turn him over, locate the wound, and stop the bleeding.

"So I'm supposed to believe you were lying earlier when you said it was in your backpack."

"It is in my backpack, but . . ." She tried to turn Dominic's body, but he weighed too much. She couldn't budge him.

Hawke grabbed a handful of her hair and forced her to look at him. "But what?"

"I don't have the backpack anymore. I pitched it down the hill when you first drove up."

"I don't believe you."

"Check for yourself."

"And leave you alone? I don't think so." Increasing the tension on her scalp, Hawke dragged her to her feet. Caitlin cried out at the pain. Her eyes filled with tears.

Then Hawke released her hair, spun her around, and shoved her toward the stone post where she'd taken refuge earlier. She stumbled and nearly fell, recovering her balance just in time for another rough shove.

Caitlin's brain worked frantically, searching for a way out. But by the time they'd covered the eight or ten yards that separated them from the guardrail post, the best idea she'd come up with was to somehow get Hawke to lean over the guardrail, then give him a shove. Even in theory, this was a lame plan. In practice, it was completely worthless since Hawke wasn't foolish enough to allow himself to be maneuvered into such a vulnerable position.

Instead, she was the one forced to lean over, sandwiched between the metal railing and Hawke's body, her arms and legs completely immobilized. He pressed hard against her, the gun barrel biting into her throat, while he used the flashlight in his left hand to direct a beam of light down the steep, rocky incline. "Where is it?"

"I just gave it a heave. It was too dark for me to see where it landed."

"Are you lying to me?" Hawke captured her earlobe between his teeth and bit down. "My God," he said. "You even taste like her."

Caitlin's heart thudded loud in her ears but not loud enough to drown out the sound of Hawke's ragged breathing. For one endless moment, terror struck her dumb. *He's going to rape me, and there's not a damn thing I can do to stop him.*

But then her brain kicked in. She couldn't do a thing to stop him as long as he had her pinned down. But if she could somehow convince him to let her go . . .

"Yes, I lied," she said, her voice so shaky she scarcely recognized it. "I didn't toss the bag over the edge. It's still in the Rolls. On the floor in the back seat." Another lie. She'd actually stashed the backpack on the other side of the stone post, but there *was* a bag on the floor of the back seat of the Rolls, the bag full of weapons Dominic had packed. If she could get to it first, she'd have a chance. "Dominic booby-trapped it," she said, "but I know how to disarm the device."

"Tell me how, and I'll disarm it."

"If I tell you, you'll kill me."

He pocketed the flashlight, then ran his hand over the curve of her backside. "Oh, I don't think I'm ready to kill you just yet."

The gun went off, the blast shockingly loud, and she thought, *Oh, my God, he's changed his mind. He's decided to shoot me after all.* Only it didn't hurt, and that was weird.

Then it dawned on her that Hawke's pistol was no longer gouging her neck. Hawke's weight was no longer pinning her to the guardrail. She turned to find him lying in an untidy heap, the back half of his head missing.

Next to him lay Dominic, still clutching his Glock.

Quite unexpectedly, her legs gave out on her, and she fell to her knees. "Dominic?" she said, afraid he was dead, afraid he'd spent the last of his strength to save her.

He raised his head an inch or two. "Rope in the boot. Tie up the bastard before he regenerates."

The rain had stopped by the time the Alfa Romeo powered up the last steep incline toward the overlook above Striga Meadow. *Please, God, please don't let us be too late,* Bree prayed silently.

As they topped the rise, their headlights illuminated a crouching figure near the guardrail. *Caitlin.* Bree was already out of the Alfa Romeo and hurrying to her side before Quin had set the emergency brake. Caitlin didn't even glance up. Bree laid a hand on her shoulder. "Are you all right?"

"I'm fine, but Dominic's been shot. Here, hold this against the wound." She pressed a wad of fabric into Bree's hand. "I'm going to check the trunk of Hawke's Saab for a first aid kit." She took off at a run, brushing past Quin as if she hadn't seen him.

"My God." Quin's voice shook. "There are two bodies over by the cars, Jacqueline LeTourneau and William Weston."

"Hawke shot them," Dominic said, startling Bree, who'd thought him unconscious. "Shot me, too."

Hawke, who lay bound and gagged next to the guardrail, writhed back and forth, fighting the ropes that held him and mumbling an unintelligible protest.

"I shot him," Dominic said.

"Who?" Quin asked.

"Hawke. I shot him twice."

"Don't talk," Quin said. "Save your strength. You need medical treatment." He hoisted Dominic into his arms.

"I shot him twice, but he wouldn't die. Caitlin was right. He is immortal."

"He's hallucinating," Quin told Bree. "We've got to get him to the hospital immediately. We'll take the Rolls. It has more room."

Bree ran ahead to open the door.

"Not hallucinating," she heard Dominic say. "I swear."

"God, he's burning up. No wonder." Quin laid Dominic on the back seat, wadded up Dominic's discarded tuxedo and stuffed it under his head as a makeshift pillow. He turned to Bree. "What's Caitlin doing?"

"She said she was going to look for a first aid kit in Hawke's car."

"Damn it, he needs surgery, not a Band-Aid. Go see what's taking her so long."

Caitlin screamed, and Bree's heart lurched. She dashed back toward the Saab, where Caitlin stood, one hand on the trunk lid, one on her throat.

"What is it?" Bree asked. "What's wrong?"

Caitlin's shocked gaze locked on hers. "Magnus," she said. "It's Magnus, and I think he's dead."

Bree circled around the car and peered into the trunk. A very filthy, unkempt Magnus Armstrong lay pretzeled inside. "Not dead," she said. "His chest is moving." She leaned over and shook his arm. "Magnus? Magnus, can you hear me?"

In answer, he snorted and turned onto his other side so that he was facing away from the glare of the trunk light.

"Not dead." Caitlin's voice sounded so faint and faraway that Bree thought she was about to faint. "Asleep."

"Drugged is my guess," Bree said. "We need to get him to the hospital. Him and Dominic both."

Caitlin frowned. "I called for an ambulance and the police. They're on their way."

"We can't wait," Quin said.

Bree jumped at the sound of his voice. She hadn't heard him approach.

"I'll wedge Magnus into the back seat of the Alfa Romeo, and you two can follow me. You drive, Bree. Caitlin's in no condition to get behind the wheel." He gathered Magnus into his arms and Bree went ahead to open the back door of the Alfa Romeo.

"What about Hawke?" Caitlin said as Quin folded Magnus into the Alfa Romeo. "I tied him up, but we can't leave him alone. He might work himself free."

"No chance of that," Quin said drily. "How many meters of rope did you use anyway?"

"All I could find," she said, "but you don't understand.

He's not really Hawke. Or not just Hawke. He's Janus, too, and Brother Ambrose and Hamish MacNeill and maybe even Merlin. If we leave him here for the police, he'll get away, either by escaping his bonds or by talking his way out of trouble."

Quin looked at her as if he thought she was as confused as Dominic.

Her eyes narrowed dangerously. "Damn it, Quin, I'm not making this stuff up. But even if you don't believe me, at least humor me. Toss him in the trunk of the Rolls, okay?"

For the past six hours, Quin, Bree, and a very pale and subdued Caitlin had been camped out in the ICU waiting room of St. Ignatius Hospital in Tavia, hoping for good news. Inside the intensive care unit, Dominic fought for his life.

Quin shot a worried glance at Caitlin. She sat by herself on the far side of the room, poring over the damned manuscript. What was she looking for? What secret did she hope to unravel? With Hawke safely behind bars, what did it matter? If it were up to him, by God, he'd burn the bloody book and toss the ashes to the four winds.

He leaned over to whisper in Bree's ear. "Shouldn't Caitlin try to get some rest?"

"She can't sleep, not until she finds out whether or not Dominic is going to make it."

"How about Magnus?"

"According to the doctor, he's in surprisingly good

shape aside from being half-starved and somewhat dehydrated. Once the sedative Hawke gave him wears off and they get him pumped full of fluid, he should be fine."

Dominic's prognosis was not so promising. He'd lost an enormous amount of blood before and during surgery—so much that the hospital had run out of B negative blood. Without a transfusion from Caitlin, also type B negative, he wouldn't even have made it through the operation.

Dr. Redmond, the king's personal physician, suddenly appeared in the doorway.

Caitlin leaped to her feet. "Dominic? Is he . . . ?"

Redmond nodded, and Quin thought for one dreadful moment that she was going to pass out. The doctor must have feared the same thing because he quickly added, "No, I didn't mean . . . He's fine, in fact, remarkably well, considering. You can see him now if you'd like."

Pale as chalk, Dominic lay in a hospital bed. Tubes and wires connected him to a half dozen machines and monitors. Caitlin thought he was asleep at first, but then he must have heard her, because he opened his eyes. He blinked a couple of times as if he were having trouble focusing. "Caitlin?"

She leaned closer. "Yes?"

"It is you. I thought I was dreaming." He smiled, and a lump lodged itself in her throat.

She gathered his right hand, the one not sporting an

IV, in hers. "I don't know if they told you, but they got the bullet out. It didn't hit anything vital."

"I was lucky," he agreed.

"Lucky? You almost bled to death. If Quin and Bree hadn't shown up when they did . . ." She drew a shaky breath.

"And Hawke?"

"Safely behind bars. He's been charged with two counts of murder and one count of attempted murder, as well as treason against the state and numerous lesser charges related to the smuggling. The authorities plan to drag Striga Lake. If they can find any evidence, they'll charge him with the murders of the Yuli brothers as well."

"Good," he said.

But not good enough. Not nearly good enough. "Even if he's convicted on every count, the harshest sentence he'll receive is life in prison."

"Yes," Dominic agreed. "Life in prison. Locked away for all eternity."

She frowned. Anemic justice for such a cold-blooded, self-serving murderer.

"How's Magnus doing?" he asked in an obvious attempt to distract her.

She met his gaze. "I don't know what drug Hawke gave him, but he's still out of it. The doctors have assured me that he's all right, though. No permanent damage. And that's a relief."

He squeezed her hand. "I was afraid he was dead."

"I suspect Hawke planned to dump all of us into Striga Lake at once—kill us and destroy the evidence of his crime in one fell swoop." She paused. "Maybe he wasn't such a bad person in the beginning, just weak and a little selfish, but . . ."

" 'Power corrupts,' " he quoted.

" 'And absolute power corrupts absolutely.' "

Dominic tightened his grip on her hand. "Promise me something?"

"Anything," she said softly.

"Promise you won't leave Calix while I'm stuck in here."

"I won't leave Calix while you're stuck in here," she said solemnly. "I'll stay for as long as you want me."

"I want you forever"—her breath caught in her throat at the look on his face—"But all I can promise is a lifetime, however long—or short—that proves to be."

She loved him so much it hurt, physically hurt, a sharp pain in her chest. "You don't deserve the curse. No one does."

"So we'll redouble our efforts to find a cure"—his blue eyes softened—"and love each other for as long as we can."

Life didn't come with a guarantee, but it should, damn it. It should.

Magnus floated in and out of consciousness. During his semi-lucid periods, he caught snippets of disconnected conversation that wove themselves into his dreams.

". . . high on painkillers. Won't be coherent for a good while yet. Might as well get some rest."

". . . white as a ghost, and no wonder. The vampire prince nearly sucked her dry."

"They're asking for life imprisonment, but the prosecution's afraid he'll appeal on the grounds that such a term would constitute cruel and unusual punishment."

"John, Paul, George, and Ringo would be proud of him."

He woke to find Caitlin asleep in a chair next to his bed, the bones he'd sent her for her birthday clutched in her hand. As if she'd sensed his gaze, she slowly raised her eyelids. She looked so pale and exhausted that he ached to hold her in his arms and call her his baby girl, the way he used to before they grew apart, before those four faceless bastards raped her body and shattered her ability to trust. But then she smiled—a big, beautiful, incandescent smile—and he knew she wasn't broken anymore.

"Magnus," she said. "You scared me. Don't do that again."

"I won't, baby girl."

And just like that, in the space of a heartbeat, her smile faded and tears sprang to her eyes. "You haven't called me that in a long time."

"My mistake," he said. "I thought you needed space, but maybe all you really needed was a father."

Caitlin caught her breath in a sob. "You have no idea how much I wanted to hear that." Tears filled her eyes, then spilled down her cheeks. With an inarticulate cry, she threw herself into his arms.

Magnus patted her back, stroked her hair, and murmured nonsensical soothing phrases. Though her anguish tied him in knots, he also felt a welcome sense of relief. He'd missed this closeness, this sense of being needed.

At length, Caitlin regained control, released her death grip on the front of his hospital gown, and gave him a watery smile. "I was so afraid I'd lost you. If Hawke had killed you . . ." Her expression darkened.

"Hawke?"

"You probably knew him as Brother Ambrose."

"That sick son of a bitch." He studied her face. "You said 'knew.' Does that mean he's dead?"

"No." She drew a long, shaky breath. "This is going to sound crazy . . ." She launched into her story, and yes, Magnus had to admit, it did sound crazy, but Caitlin was one of the most rational people he'd ever known, and if she believed it . . .

"Who's 'we'?" he asked when she was finished.

A frown knit her forehead.

"You said, '*We* confronted Hawke and he admitted he'd been living on Calix in one guise or another for the last four hundred years.' "

"Dominic and I. Dominic Fortune." And the way she said his name, Magnus knew what was coming even before she put it in words. "I love him." Caitlin met his gaze defiantly, as if she expected him to protest or disapprove.

A knot of tension in his chest, a knot he hadn't even realized was there, suddenly came unraveled. Warmth took its place, spreading and spreading and spreading until he couldn't contain it any longer, and it manifested itself as a smile.

Caitlin's defiance melted into confusion. "You don't mind?"

"Mind? Why would I mind, baby girl?"

"Because I'm not going back to Palo Alto, back to Stanford. I'm staying here. With Dominic."

He smiled. "Teaching's a noble profession, but Stanford's not the only school in the world."

"Bite your tongue," she said.

He laughed. "I'm sure Calix University could use a good math professor, but that's beside the point."

"It is?"

"It is." He sobered. "I thought you'd never be able to trust a man again. To hear you say you've fallen in love? That's music to my ears."

Three days later, Magnus booked a seat on the evening flight to Edinburgh, where he planned to stay with Wallace for a few days to tie up loose ends before flying home. But when Caitlin mentioned that she intended to visit Emrys Hawke, he insisted upon accompanying her. They sat waiting for Hawke now in a glass-walled interrogation room at the Tavia city jail. Caitlin's stomach churned at the thought of facing the monster again. Only a cold, hard core of determination kept her from running away.

Magnus glanced at his watch, compared it to the clock on the wall, and frowned. "Wonder what the holdup is."

"Hard to say." She dug the bones from her purse and

dumped the little ivory rods into the palm of her left hand. They nestled there, warm and comforting.

"Frankly," Magnus said, "I'm surprised the bastard agreed to talk to you."

Caitlin nodded. She was more than a little surprised herself. Hawke's only stipulation, to which both she and the police had agreed, was that the meeting be completely private—no microphones, no recording devices.

Magnus touched her arm. "Showtime."

She glanced up to see two guards ushering Hawke into the room. Dressed in bright orange scrubs with his hands cuffed behind his back and a hobble wound around his ankles, Hawke shouldn't have looked dangerous. But his eyes sparkled with such malice, it took every ounce of her willpower not to cringe. One guard shoved him into a chair across the table from Caitlin and Magnus and fastened his hobble to the bottom rung, while the second used an extra pair of handcuffs to fasten Hawke's wrists to the chair back.

"We'll be right outside," the taller of the two guards said. "Buzz when you're ready to go." They left, closing the door behind them.

"Came to gloat, did you?" Hawke said.

Caitlin didn't answer. She didn't have to. She was the one in charge of this interview, not Emrys Hawke. "I'm curious about something," she said at length. "On the night of the ball, how did you get me to channel Magnus?"

Hawke smirked. "You didn't channel Magnus; you channeled me."

"How could you be sure it would work?"

"I wasn't. Jacqueline suggested we try. If you hadn't reacted, she planned to go into a fake trance and provide the same cryptic information. I had to split them up, you see. I knew I could handle Dominic, but he and Quin both would have been a bit of a challenge."

"You almost killed him."

"Yes, pity my aim was off."

Caitlin wanted to scream at him. She smiled instead. "Did you hear what happened to the gold?"

Hawke narrowed his eyes. "My gold?"

"Yours?" she said. "Nonsense. Anything discovered on the king's property belongs to the king. You'll be pleased, I'm sure, to learn that he's donated it to the endowment supporting the hospice for curse victims."

"The fuck he did!" Hawke said.

"Watch your language, man," Magnus said, clearly outraged.

But Hawke continued to spout obscenities.

Caitlin had been sitting with her hands in her lap. Now she raised her left hand and let the bones spill onto the table with a clatter.

Hawke stopped in mid curse. His eyebrows slammed together in a frown. "What are those?"

"Don't pretend you don't recognize a set of Napier's bones when you see them. After all, you considered Napier a surrogate father."

Hawke didn't say a word, but Caitlin knew she had his attention.

"And these particular bones are special." If she hadn't

been watching him so closely, she might have missed the tightening of his jaw. "At least to me. They were a birthday gift from *my* surrogate father." Hawke's jaw relaxed. "But then, you knew that already, didn't you? You read my e-mail to Magnus."

"I wanted to know if he'd sent you the manuscript."

"Yes," she agreed. "You did. It must have been an unexpected bonus to realize I had your bones as well."

"My bones?" His voice held just the right degree of surprise, but he couldn't disguise the sudden tension in his shoulders.

She held one up so he could see the markings on the end. "Looks like random scribbling at first glance, doesn't it? But then, you never did have very good penmanship. It's your initials, an *H* superimposed over an *M*. An H and an *M* for Hamish MacNeill."

Magnus picked up a bone and studied the markings. "Damn, I think you're right."

Hawke shrugged. "Well, I can't see it. Apparently the two of you have better imaginations than I."

"Maybe so." Caitlin smiled. "I, for example, can almost hear the bones talking to me. '*Vita aeterna*,' they seem to say."

Hawke's face blanched.

"You made them from the ribs you found embedded in the oak tree, didn't you? And it's not too difficult to figure out why. If someone had discovered you were hoarding a bag of human bones, you'd have been in trouble—accused of murder or witchcraft—but a harmless calculating device wouldn't raise an eyebrow."

"Ribs are curved," Magnus objected.

"He straightened them," Caitlin said. "Or"—she studied Hawke's face—"they straightened themselves . . . like magic."

Spots of hectic color stained Hawke's waxen cheeks. "They're no good to you. You don't know how to use them."

"I don't want to use them," she said. "I have no desire to live forever."

"What do you intend to do?" Hawke demanded, though his arrogance seemed forced.

"You're not really immortal, are you?"

"I never claimed—"

"If you were immortal, you'd still look nineteen, not forty-five. You need the bones to maintain yourself. It didn't matter so much when they were buried in the earthquake, because they were close enough to provide some protection. You aged, but at a much slower than normal rate. Only then the Yuli brothers shipped them off to Jacqueline, who sold them to Magnus, who, in turn, sent them to Palo Alto—much too far away to provide any rejuvenating effects. I should have picked up on it sooner. Dominic mentioned how much you've aged lately." She heaved a sigh, then turned to Magnus. "I'm ready." While she gathered the bones and packed them back in their case, he buzzed the guards.

"But what are you going to do?" Hawke asked, his voice ragged, his eyes wide with fear.

"End it," she said. *End you.*

* * *

Caitlin and Magnus left the jail at a little after ten. By noon, they stood at the lip of the caldera above Striga Lake. The sun felt as warm on Caitlin's shoulders as the bones felt in her hands.

"How did you know?" Magnus asked.

"I wouldn't have if you hadn't sent me the manuscript; the clues were all in there."

"An odd quirk of fate," he said.

"That the manuscript mentioned my ancestor, Maggie Gordon, you mean?"

Magnus shot her a puzzled look. "Who?"

Caitlin frowned. "That's not why you sent me the manuscript?"

"I sent it to you to get it out of the country. Didn't you read the note I enclosed with the bones?"

"Your birthday note?"

"No," he said. "The sticky note I shoved into the case just before I mailed your package."

"Inside the case?" She pulled the little leather box from her purse and peered inside. "Oh, my God." Using two fingers, she peeled a square of paper from the bottom of the case. " 'Take care of the manuscript. I think it may be stolen. More later. Magnus,' " she read aloud, then started to laugh. Her laughter rippled out across the lake, echoing eerily off the caldera walls. She sank slowly to her knees.

Magnus knelt beside her. "Caitlin, are you all right?"

"This was all random. Chance," she sputtered between gales of hysterical laughter. "Chaos theory."

Magnus put his hands on her shoulders and turned

her to face him. Her laughter died at the expression on his face. "I don't believe in accidents," he said. "There's a purpose for everything, a reason. Even if we don't always recognize it."

She studied his face, searching for the answers to all the questions plaguing her, but in the end, she only verbalized one. "Am I doing the right thing, Magnus?"

"I think so," he said.

So one by one she tossed the bones into the beautiful green depths of the lake.

Epilogue

Three Months Later
Smuggler's Cove, Calix

DOMINIC SPREAD A BLANKET in the shade of the old olive tree, stretched out full-length, and beckoned for Caitlin to join him.

She dropped her beach bag, lay down beside him, and snuggled close. A smile teased at the corners of her mouth. "I thought we came down here to swim."

"Did you now?" He raised an eyebrow. "We could have swum anywhere along the coast, including the beach below the villa. But privacy"—he slid a finger across the pale skin just above the top edge of her bikini top—"is harder to find."

"And it's only going to get worse," she said. "Once they finish the new casino complex . . ." She seemed to lose her train of thought as he kissed and nibbled his way up her throat.

"I love you," he whispered against her pulse point. "And I very much want to make love with you, but first I have something to say."

Her expression shifted from awakening sensuality to concern.

"Now, don't give me that look," he scolded.

"What look?"

"The worst-case-scenario look. Aliens haven't invaded, nor are we having brussels sprouts for lunch."

"Then . . . ?"

"You know I went in for my quarterly checkup two weeks ago."

"Yes." Her frown grew deeper. "You told me you were fine, that the curse appeared to be in remission."

"Yes, well, I went back in last week for more extensive testing, and the doctor has changed his diagnosis."

She gave a little gasp and pressed both hands flat against his chest. "You're not in remission."

"No," he agreed. "I'm cured."

She stared at him blankly. "But I thought there was no cure for the Calixian curse."

"There wasn't until now."

"I don't understand."

"Neither does Dr. Redmond, but he'd like to do more tests, if you don't mind."

"Why would I mind?"

He shrugged. "He thought perhaps you had an aversion to needles."

"He wants to test *me*?"

"Your blood."

He watched realization dawn. "The transfusion," she said.

"Apparently it saved my life twice over."

" 'Blood will tell,' " she whispered. "That's what the gypsy predicted."

Dominic kissed the end of her nose. "A very perspicacious woman, that gypsy. Dr. Redmond plans to send a sample to St. Giles Institute for Genetic Research in Edinburgh. If they can pinpoint the component that reversed the disease's effects, they may be able to replicate it in the laboratory."

"No more curse," she said. "No more victims."

Tears sprang to her eyes and Dominic kissed them away. She smiled up at him then, her mouth soft, her eyelashes spiky, her eyes warm, and his heart skipped a beat. He loved this woman—his wife, his consort, his soul mate—with all his heart. Capturing her face between his hands, he kissed her long and deep. "Know what I just realized?" He leaned his forehead against hers.

"What?" she whispered, her eyes closed, the pulse in her throat beating wildly.

"If Hawke hadn't shot me, I wouldn't have needed a transfusion, and we'd never have known about your blood's special properties. Too bad he didn't live long enough to appreciate the irony . . ."

"Too bad," Caitlin agreed.

According to the guards, Hawke had aged fifty years in fifteen minutes. Cause of death: extreme old age. "Seems odd, doesn't it, that no one's come up with any rational explanation for his sudden death?" Dominic observed.

A series of emotions flitted across Caitlin's face too quickly to be identified. "Magnus says there's a reason for everything even if we don't always recognize it." She touched the scar just below his left collarbone, then shifted a little so she could meet his gaze. What he saw in her face made his heart thump erratically.

"My dear, dangerous, darling Dominic." She caressed his cheek, a fleeting touch, then pressed her fingertips to his lips.

Emotion blindsided him; tears blurred his vision. Gradually Caitlin's face swam back into focus. "I love you," she said, and kissed him.

The warmth started in his chest and quickly spread throughout his body, an unparalleled sensation of deep satisfaction, and he realized that the fairy tales had it all wrong. Yes, this warmth, this feeling of intense joy, was the essence of happily ever after, but it really wasn't the end at all.

Enjoy the following excerpt from

Catherine Mulvany's

paranormal romantic thriller,

RUN NO MORE

Now available from Pocket Star Books

1

April 2004
Half Moon Bay, California

IAN MACPHERSON sat hunched in his wheelchair with a Colt Python .357 shoved in his mouth. Blowing his brains out would take care of his problems, but leaving Paulinho to deal with the resulting mess hardly seemed sporting. His ex-cellmate barely spoke English.

On the other hand, what did he have to live for besides revenge? A revenge that shimmered like a distant mirage forever beyond his grasp.

The kitchen lay deep in shadow, the only illumination a pale swath of moonlight admitted by the window over the sink and the eerie green glow of the digital clock on the microwave. Two-thirty-seven.

How very appropriate, he thought in sour amusement, dying in the dead of the night. His finger tightened on the trigger.

The creak of the dog door distracted him. Not a particularly alarming noise . . . unless, of course, one didn't own a dog.

He leveled the pistol at the plastic flap.

Thin and agile, a young woman squeezed through the narrow aperture, a penlight clenched between her teeth. He waited until she was all the way in, then said, "Burglary's against the law."

She gasped and dropped the light. It spun across the kitchen tiles, throwing weird, flickering shadows into every corner of the room, briefly illuminating in turn the cupboards, the appliances, the butcher block, and finally Ian with his revolver.

"Don't shoot." She got to her feet, extending her hands in surrender.

"Why not? It's what one does to intruders." He flipped on the overhead light, and she blinked in the sudden glare. With her odd monochrome coloring—skin and hair almost the same shade of pale honey beige—she reminded him of an old sepia print. Portrait of a waif. He wondered if the effect was calculated.

"All I was looking for was something to eat." She met his gaze, and her eyes captured his attention. Unusual eyes, a pale silvery gray ringed in black. Even more unusual, the expression in their depths—neither fright nor defiance, just a sad resignation, a sterile lifelessness.

Abused, he thought. She looked like someone who'd endured so much in the past that she was prepared now to suffer quite stoically whatever new horror presented itself. Even a crazy, gun-toting, gray-bearded cripple.

"Hunger seems an unlikely motive for breaking and entering."

"Are you going to call the police?"

He studied her a moment in silence. "When did you last eat?"

"A truck driver bought me dinner yesterday. I didn't stick around for breakfast." She shifted her gaze to the toes of her ragged sneakers. "I don't have any money, but I can pay you for the food the same way I paid the trucker."

"You'd barter your body for a crust of bread?"

Her soulless eyes locked on his. "And count it a fair trade."

Bitterness welled up, all but choking him. "Your sacrifice won't be necessary." He glanced down at his ruined body. "My injuries preclude it. I have minimal sensation below the waist."

He was used to pitying looks and polite murmurs of, "I'm sorry." But the dead-eyed girl drew a deep breath, then released it in a ragged sigh. "Some people have all the luck."

Tasya huddled naked in the dark. Richard would be coming soon. He saved his nastiest games for the hours between dusk and dawn. Though she had no clock, she knew it was late. Like a threat, darkness pressed against the barred window high up on the cellar wall. The color of midnight.

Every instinct urged her to run, but there was nowhere to go. Nowhere to run and nowhere to hide. If only I could die, *she thought. Just curl up and die, leave her body behind, go to a place where Richard couldn't follow. But he would never permit it. He enjoyed torturing her, but he was careful not to inflict life-threatening injuries. He liked her to fight, to scream, to beg, and dead women did none of those things.*

Suddenly the fluorescents buzzed on overhead, flooding her prison with a harsh glare. He was coming. Oh, God, he was coming.

The lock clicked, and the door at the top of the stairs swung open. She didn't want to look, tried not to, but she couldn't help herself. His gaze met hers. He stared at her for an endless minute, then smiled, his eyes bright with anticipation.

And she knew it was going to be bad.

Tasya awoke with a start, shuddering at the memory of the joyous malevolence in Richard's blue eyes. *He can't hurt me,* she told herself over and over in what had become her own personal mantra. *He can't hurt me anymore.*

Slowly the nightmare faded and her surroundings registered. She lay tangled in the sheets of an antique four-poster, the sort of bed normally found in the pages of glossy magazines.

Oh, God. Another of Richard's games? She shoved herself upright, panicking, her heart beating frantically.

But no. Richard couldn't hurt her anymore. She was alone now. Alone and safe for the moment. Only . . . alone where?

Disjointed memories of the night before teased her mind. She frowned, forcing her brain to sort through her impressions.

She'd thought at first the old man intended to shoot her. Instead, he'd fed her hunks of crusty bread and something he called *feijoada,* a filling dish of garlic-flavored black beans and meat, ladled over rice. She'd eaten one big plateful and half of a second, the only sounds in the room the click of her fork against the blue-and-white stoneware and the soft creaking of the wheelchair as the old man moved about the kitchen.

She'd gobbled her food, afraid he would realize his mistake any minute and call the police. But he hadn't, and when she'd eaten all she could hold, he'd shown her to this sumptuous room, a room she'd been too tired to explore last night. She slipped out of bed to rectify that oversight.

She frowned at the rumpled covers of the four-poster. The old man had claimed sex was out of the question, but he could have been lying. In her experience, that was what men did best.

But she had to admit, she'd done her share of lying. Last night she'd claimed she'd broken in to look for food. In truth she'd planned to rob the old man. Still planned to rob him. She needed cash, and from the looks of this place, he wouldn't miss it.

A smudge on the sheet caught her eye. She'd slept in her clothes, too exhausted the night before to undress. Now she realized with embarrassment that her filthy clothing had soiled the bedding. Surely one of the room's three doors led to a bathroom.

At random she tried the door to the left of the armoire, but it opened into a walk-in closet larger than the living room of the Idaho farmhouse where she'd spent the first fifteen years of her life. The closet was full of clothes, men's clothes. And the lightweight collapsible wheelchair parked against the back wall confirmed her earlier suspicions. This was the old man's room.

A headache throbbed at her temples. Nausea churned her stomach. Had she escaped one exploitative male only to have been captured by another?

Luck was with her on her second try. The door opened into a spacious bathroom equipped with both a whirlpool tub and a tiled shower enclosure. Tasya opted for the shower.

She dropped her soiled clothing in a pile, adjusted the water temperature, and stepped under the pounding spray. She scrubbed herself, then stood there, eyes shut, body relaxed, as the grime sluiced away.

Only after the water grew tepid did she turn off the faucets and step out of the shower. She dried herself on one of the thick blue towels that hung from the heated towel rack, wishing she had a change of clothing. Instead she'd have to dress again in the same dirty clothes she'd filched from the Salvation Army four days ago in Carson City, Nevada.

If she could find her dirty clothes, that was. She wrapped herself in the towel, frowning at the spot where she'd dropped her things. Either they'd evaporated or someone had taken them.

Payback time already? Cynically, she speculated about the old man's intentions. Normal sex was out of the question if what he'd told her was true, but she knew firsthand about the other ways a man could use a woman to pleasure himself.

Angry now, she shoved the bedroom door open, then stopped dead just inside the room. She'd expected to find him waiting for her in bed, but the room was empty.

Someone—presumably the same someone who'd taken her clothes—had been here, though. The bed had been made, the room tidied.

In the doorway behind her, someone cleared his throat.

Startled, she spun around, tightening her grip on the towel. "Who are you?"

An ebony giant examined her, his impassive gaze flicking up and down her body.

"Who are you?" she repeated, but instead of answering, he turned and bellowed something incomprehensible down the hall. Tasya didn't recognize the language. Neither French nor Spanish, though with elements of both.

"Quiet," the old man said from somewhere beyond Tasya's line of sight. "The girl needs her rest."

Another torrent of impassioned speech erupted from the giant.

"No wonder," the old man said, "with you carrying on like a demented idiot." He wheeled his chair into the doorway and nodded at Tasya. "You're up early. Did you sleep well?"

"Well enough, thank you, though I seem to have misplaced my clothes."

"Ah, yes." The old man held a low-voiced consultation with the giant, then turned to her. "Paulinho put your things in the washer. They'll be ready in an hour or so. In the meantime, feel free to borrow something." He gestured toward the closet door, then spoke again to Paulinho. The giant shot a glare in her direction, grunted, then moved off down the hall, grumbling under his breath.

A sardonic smile tilted the corners of the old man's mouth. Though his face was lined, his hair graying, he had the saturnine good looks of a fallen angel. With his piercing dark eyes and devilish black eyebrows, he'd have broken a few hearts in his day. "Join me for breakfast on the deck when you're dressed." He delivered the invitation in a rich baritone, deep and resonant, another reminder of the man he'd once been.

"I'd like that," she said, meaning breakfast. She wasn't so sure about the company.

"Did you see the bruises on her arms and shoulders?" Paulinho said in Portuguese.

"Yes, and the ligature marks on her wrists and ankles," Ian answered in the same language.

"And her neck. Did you notice? Someone tried to throttle her. The girl is trouble." Paulinho tied an apron over his khakis.

"The girl is *in* trouble," Ian said. "I think we both can relate to that."

A muscle twitched in Paulinho's cheek as he stood at the sink, scrubbing his hands. "You know nothing about her, Senhor Ian. She might be a thief, a murderer even."

"A thief like me? A murderer like you?" Ian laughed. "Besides, the bruises were on *her* neck."

"Humph." Paulinho dried his hands on a blue-checked towel and began preparing breakfast.

"She's been abused. I knew that. I saw it in her eyes."

"And did it not occur to you that there are women—whores—who let men do these things to them in exchange for money?" Paulinho slapped a side of bacon on the meat board. Wielding a knife with the élan of a surgeon, he cut paper-thin slices.

"Does she look like anyone's paid her lately?"

"No," Paulinho admitted. He broke eggs into a bowl, poured in some cream, and whisked the mixture to a froth. "But what if she is a runaway? What if the police are after her? If they come looking for her, they may get suspicious, and our papers—"

"Don't worry about our papers. They're the best money can buy. Don't worry about the police, either. I have enough to buy them as well, should it become necessary." He ran his chair over to the window. Redwoods and eucalyptus screened the rooftops of his neighbors down the hill but allowed glimpses of the ocean.

"I, too, noticed her eyes, Senhor Ian, and I am telling you, this one has been touched by Exú."

"Exú?" Ian shot a skeptical glance at his friend.

Paulinho rubbed the gold crucifix that hung around his neck, then crossed himself quickly, oblivious to the irony of using Christian symbols and Catholic rituals to protect himself from a Macumba devil.

Ian turned back to his view of the distant ocean. "I'm sixty-one years old. I have no family, no life beyond the constraints of this damned mechanical contraption." He smacked the arm of his chair. "Last night I came close to blowing my head off. This morning instead of grilling bacon and chopping chives, you could have been scrubbing my brains off the wall and trying to explain to the police in your damned poor excuse for English how you had nothing to do with the senhor's death."

"You thought of killing yourself?" Paulinho sounded shocked. "But suicide's a mortal sin!"

"The strange part is, just as I was about to pull the trigger, the girl squeezed through the dog door I've been threatening to have sealed off for the last six months."

"I will fix the latch after breakfast," Paulinho said.

"You're missing the point. If the flap had fastened properly, she couldn't have shoved her way in. And if she hadn't shoved her way in, I'd have pulled the trigger. The girl saved my life. In fact, I haven't felt quite so alive in years."

Paulinho's spatula clattered on the counter. "So now you want to keep her? This skinny girl someone tried to throttle?"

"Keep her?"

"For your woman." Paulinho grated cheese with a vengeance. Fine shreds of cheddar flew from his grater like confetti.

Ian shook his head. "Are you mad? What good is a woman to me at my age? In my condition?"

"There are many roads to pleasure."

"Not for that child. You saw her poor dead eyes, Paulinho. She needs help. For once in my life, my motives are entirely altruistic. I assure you, I have no designs on her virtue."

"Humph." Paulinho scowled. "You're fooling yourself,

Senhor Ian. She attracts you, with her long limbs and smooth skin, her eyes like silvery mirrors."

"She's interesting looking, yes, even beautiful, but—"

"Only a fool trusts a beautiful woman. Who is she? Where did she come from? What does she want? Do you know the answers? No. I pray to God she will not end up destroying you."

"Impossible. Alex Farrell already did that." Hatred stirred in the depths of his soul like an oily black sludge. "I'm not a religious man like you, my friend, but I believe that girl was sent as an act of divine intervention. It was not destined that I die last night. Why? The only answer I can come up with is, I have something yet to accomplish. I think the girl was sent to help."

Paulinho snorted and dumped the bowl of eggs into an omelet pan. "Help you to an early grave, perhaps."

Sunlight gleamed off the big black man's shaved head. Paulinho didn't like her much, Tasya thought, judging by the sullen look he sent her way as she took her place across from the old man at the table on the deck. She couldn't fault his cooking, though.

She stuffed herself with bacon and omelet, fresh fruit, and hot buttered rolls.

The old man said something to Paulinho she didn't understand, and Paulinho took his scowl into the house.

A sparrow balanced on the deck railing as if waiting for crumbs. She broke off a bit of roll and tossed it to him. "What language is it that you and Paulinho speak?"

"Portuguese," he said. "I lived in Brazil for many

years." He shot her a quick smile, and she caught another glimpse of the charmer he'd been in his youth. "But how rude of me. I never introduced myself last night. I'm Ian MacPherson, also known as Cat." He held out his hand, and they shook across the remains of their breakfast.

"Cat?"

"A nickname." He leaned back, a wry half smile twisting the corner of his mouth. "My turn to ask a question."

"Of course." Wary, but not wanting him to see it, she lowered her gaze to the tablecloth.

"What's *your* name?"

She didn't know how much the police had figured out or what they'd released to the press, and Ian MacPherson was obviously a man who stayed abreast of the news. She couldn't chance the truth. "I-Ivana. Smith."

"How original." Again that cynical twist of the lips.

"My mother was a Russian immigrant, my father American." That part, at least, was true.

"And where are they, your parents?"

"Dead." Her mother and the man she'd called Dad for the first fifteen years of her life had died in a two-car pileup on Highway 55 south of Horseshoe Bend, Idaho. Only after the funeral had she learned that Joe Flynn wasn't her biological father. She knew nothing about the man who'd provided half of her DNA.

"Do you have other family? Friends perhaps?"

"No." The sparrow finished the crumb and took flight. Just as she would . . . once she located her crumb.

"You're on the run, aren't you?"

Speechless, she stared at him.

"From whom? The police?"

"They might be looking for me. I don't know for sure."

"Is that why you lied about your name? Because you think the police are after you?"

"I'm sorry. I can't tell you any more. Thank you again for the food and the bed, but it's time I was on my way." She stood.

His fingers closed around her wrist, his grip surprisingly strong. "Don't go. Not yet." She must have made some involuntary sound of protest, because he released her instantly, his voice softening as he added, "Please."

Please. She couldn't remember the last time she'd heard that word. She sat down.

"I didn't mean to frighten you."

Tasya stared at the remains of her breakfast. "You didn't. I don't like being touched, that's all." She took a deep breath. "You've been very kind, but I can't involve you in my problems."

"Too late. I *am* involved." His gaze captured hers. His eyes were so dark a brown, she couldn't distinguish his pupils from his irises, their expression so intense, she couldn't look away.

"You don't understand. Getting involved in my troubles would be a mistake. A dangerous mistake."

"I've been in and out of trouble all my life." He smiled. "And I rather enjoy danger."

She gazed at him helplessly. How to explain without telling him everything?

He cocked his head to one side. "If you don't let me help you, what will you do? Where will you go?"

"I'm not sure. Maybe L.A."

"Stardom. The American dream." A trace of condescension colored his expression.

Her cheeks grew warm. "I'm not some pathetic starstruck runaway, deluding herself that she's the next Julia Roberts. I plan to try my luck as a stunt double."

His mouth twitched as if he were suppressing a smile. "A profession requiring its own talents."

"Talents I have. I trained in gymnastics for eleven years. I have excellent reflexes. I'm fast, flexible, and well coordinated."

"Ideal attributes for a stunt double." He was humoring her.

Tasya's temper flared. "Watch." She jumped onto the railing and, using it as a balance beam, moved through the elements of an old routine, only slightly hampered by the baggy borrowed sweat pants. She finished with a round-off triple-twist dismount.

"Brava!" The condescension had vanished, replaced by genuine enthusiasm and a hint of something that might have been speculation. "You are, indeed, talented."

She sat down across the table from him. "Why didn't you call the police last night?"

"Let's just say I have a soft spot for thieves."

She studied his face. "That's not the only reason."

"Do you believe in fate, Ms. Smith?"

She frowned. Was he trying to change the subject?

"I do," he said. "I believe you were destined to enter

my life at a critical moment, as I, perhaps, was destined to enter yours." He paused. "Who hurt you?"

The blood drummed in her ears. "I can't tell you that."

He inclined his head. "Fair enough. I dare say there are things I'd not wish to share with a stranger, either."

She studied the harsh lines of his face. "You seem a decent man. You've treated me kindly, but—"

"You're curious about my motivation. Wondering what I expect in return for my 'kindness'?"

She nodded, then looked away, unable to face his dark scrutiny.

"Nothing you're unwilling to give. I promise."

Men always promised. And they always lied. "Then why did you put me in your room last night? In your bed?"

He raised his eyebrows at the accusation underlying her tone. "The guest room beds weren't made up, and you were asleep on your feet."

A simple explanation. Possibly even true. She flicked a glance at him. He seemed to find her amusing.

"Even were I not . . . incapacitated, you'd still be safe with me. I'm not a child molester."

"And I'm not a child." She stared steadily at him. A shadow passed across his face, a flicker of emotion there and gone so fast she couldn't name it.

"Quite so," he said and shifted his gaze to the distant ocean.

"You don't sound American," she said abruptly.

He laughed. "I'm a Scot by birth, originally from a village northwest of Inverness. I emigrated in my teens."

"A Highlander?"

"Aye, lass." His exaggerated accent mocked her. "The MacPhersons belong to Clan Chattan. 'Touch not the cat, but a glove.' Our motto."

"'But a glove'?"

"Archaic language for 'without a glove.' In other words, watch out. We have claws."

"That explains your nickname."

He made no comment but smiled again, a charming smile this time that crinkled the corners of his dark eyes and revealed strong white teeth.

Tasya broke off eye contact. Condescension, she could handle. Mocking irony, she could handle. But charm set off her internal alarms. "So . . . how long were you in Brazil?"

"Thirty years, more or less."

"Thirty years! Doing what?"

He laughed again. "Avoiding gang rape, for the most part. Not that I could have felt anything, you understand, but one doesn't care to be used."

His careless words stirred the murky depths of her memory. Tasya bit the inside of her lip until she tasted blood.

He hadn't noticed her distress. She swallowed hard. "Are men often raped in Brazil?"

He tugged at the corner of his mustache, smoothed his neatly trimmed beard. "Only in prison."

She shuddered. "How did you end up behind bars?"

"I trusted the wrong person." A bitter smile twisted his mouth. "I'd been a thief all my life, so I suppose I deserved incarceration. But I didn't deserve to lose the use of my legs. I didn't deserve this damned wheelchair. Dreams of retribution were all that kept me alive in that pesthole, but I've been free for over six months, and I'm no closer to achieving revenge now than I was the day I got out." He paused. "Then last night fate sent you."

"Me?"

He'd been staring at some point over her head, but now he focused on her. She wanted to look away but found she couldn't. "If I'm not mistaken, you, too, have been betrayed. So you'll understand how I feel."

"Yes," she said, even though it hadn't been a question. He knew. Somehow he knew. "What do you want from me?"

He examined her face, a smile hovering around the corners of his mouth. "I'm a cat burglar confined to a wheelchair. I need an assistant, someone young and agile. All those admirable skills of yours—speed, flexibility, coordination—make you ideally suited for the job."

"I don't mean to insult you, but"—she felt herself flushing again—"I'm not sure I want to make a career of thievery."

He frowned. "You had no such qualms last night."

Oh, God, he knew about that, too. "That was different. I was desperate."

"So was I. I'd decided to kill myself. When you interrupted, I believed it was a sign." He smiled. "And when you demonstrated your gymnastics skills just now, I knew it for another. Fate has smiled on me at last."

"But—"

"Don't worry. I'm not proposing a crime spree. One

caper. That's all you'd be involved in. One payback caper."

"Revenge," she said.

"Yes. I'd get satisfaction, and you'd get money. A million dollars. No strings attached."

A million dollars? "But—"

"Don't say no. Try the training first," he said. "You can back out at any time. No hard feelings. But if you stay the course, you can build a new life with the money you earn."

She considered his proposal. Outrageous, yes. Dangerous, without a doubt. But with a million dollars at her disposal, she could do as she pleased and never have to answer to any man again. "A new life," she said, the words sweet on her tongue. A life without Richard. Without fear. She nodded. "All right, I'll try it."

"Very well, Ivana Smith, shall we—"

"Don't call me that. You were right. I lied about my name. It's Tasya."

"Tasya what?"

She hesitated. "Flynn."

"A good Irish name." Smiling, he reached across the table to seal their bargain with a handshake.

His grip was warm and firm, his expression kind, but Tasya had learned the hard way not to accept anyone at face value. Only time would tell if Ian MacPherson would deliver the salvation he promised . . . or if she'd just made a pact with the devil.